THE COSMIC CLUES

INDIA'S FIRST ASTRO-DETECTIVE

MANJIRI PRABHU

JAICO PUBLISHING HOUSE

Ahmedabad Bangalore Bhopal Bhubaneswar Chennai
Delhi Hyderabad Kolkata Lucknow Mumbai

Published by Jaico Publishing House
A-2 Jash Chambers, 7-A Sir Phirozshah Mehta Road
Fort, Mumbai - 400 001
jaicopub@jaicobooks.com
www.jaicobooks.com

THE COSMIC CLUES
ISBN 978-81-8495-479-1

First Jaico Impression: 2013

Page design and layouts: Special Effects, Mumbai

Printed by
Kaveri Print Process Pvt. Ltd
114, Patparganj Industrial Area, Delhi - 92

To my mother, Shobha Prabhu
—an astrologer par excellence—
for giving the Soul to this book

Acknowledgements

When a novel gets a second lease of life, the sense of gratefulness deepens...

So thank you Kate Miciak, Frances Collin and Scott Eyman.

Heartfelt thanks to Kanishka Gupta for introducing me to the fabulous *Jaico Publishing House.*

Tons of gratitude to the entire editorial team of Jaico Books—Akash Shah, Sandhya Iyer, Lakshmi Krishnan and Nityasya Belapurkar. Also Savita Rao, Nita Satikuwar, Dhaivat Chhaya and Swapnil Sakpal—thank you for treating *The Cosmic Clues* as special.

Eternal gratitude to my sisters Leena, Purnima and Sonia and brother Rajeev. And special thanks to my husband Bipinchandra—I sincerely appreciate the fact that all of you are always there for me.

And finally, all my love to my darling Rambha—my 'official' cat and my muse for this novel—be happy wherever you are...

Contents

CHAPTER 1

The Cat Walks Out

"This is Stellar Investigations and we don't read horoscopes!" Jatin unsuccessfully checked the exasperation in his voice and slammed down the receiver. He thrust a restive hand through his untidy mop of hair and wheeled around to face his boss. Sonia Samarth stood by the table, scanning the newspaper with interest.

"That was the twelfth call demanding if this was an astrology institute!" Jatin exclaimed.

"Natural, isn't it?" Sonia shrugged nonchalantly. "After all, it's common fact that people do get attracted to anyone who can predict the future."

"But we don't predict the future. We are investigators!" he emphasized.

"With a difference," Sonia pointed out gently. "Relax, Jatin, I'll take the next call. You go finish your novel, till I need you."

Sonia settled in her cushioned seat and took up the paper again. The advertisement was small and crisp, as per budget constraints, but, to be absolutely impartial, hardly deserved the misunderstanding it had created.

STELLAR INVESTIGATIONS

Now, a detective agency which combines astrological science with investigations! If you have a problem, contact us at...

All morning the phone had peeled constantly, ringing from all corners of Pune city. Voices—timid, uncertain, overconfident and even incredulous, all requesting appointments. The questions were many—How much did they charge? Did they need the horoscope? Was it possible to predict the date of marriage? Could they predict without a horoscope? Initially Jatin had braved the tide of queries on his own, intelligently masking his inexperience. Gradually, however, his polite, wordy explanations had turned to one-liner wisecracks and finally to downright insolence and refusals.

Sonia bore the misunderstanding with better tolerance and patience. People were basically insecure, bogged down with innumerable worries with a tendency to clutch at hopeful straws. Sonia knew and understood that feeling. She may have just set up her business a few months ago and had barely two cases to her credit, but she had a Masters in criminal psychology. Perhaps it was her understanding of human nature which had further led her to study Vedic astrology—a science she deeply respected and used as a guideline. It had all begun in fun—reading horoscopes for friends, predicting their love affairs and life partners in college. Then finding missing articles at home, first for the family and then for relatives. It was when she successfully tracked down the missing son of a close friend that she realised that she had stumbled on to a rather apocalyptic and pivotal discovery. Her in-depth study of Vedic astrology would prove invaluable in her lifelong ambition to become a detective.

A rented office and two itsy-bitsy cases later, however, the knowledge had dawned on her that people did not look kindly upon her brilliant brainwave. Reading horoscopes for fun was one thing; using it to solve life and death issues was quite another. The result was filling the long office hours with chores like cleaning up or reading books on astrology and listening to music over cups of *chai*—tea with milk—and sandwiches, to avoid boredom! Luckily for Sonia, Jatin was an ardent detective-cum-office assistant, willing to hang on for the big break, however long it may take.

Sonia recalled her parents' reaction on seeing the ad that morning and smiled. They'd just finished a hearty breakfast of *pohey* and coffee. Her mother, petite and dignified in a pure silk peach sari draped around her exquisite figure, was skimming over the paper. Sonia adored her beautiful mother. She was her idea of a perfect mother and woman. Unfortunately, perfection does not always equate with compatibility of thought. Despite being a businessperson and working shoulder-to-shoulder with her husband, Mrs. Samarth had her qualms about Sonia's profession. Her voice was a sigh as she studied the advertisement.

"Need you be so open about your operative methods? You may end up making a fool of yourself! I can't understand why you must make yourself an object of ridicule!"

Mr. Samarth took the newspaper from his wife and spent a thoughtful, leisurely minute over it. He was tall with an athletic body maintained in good form due to a strict tennis routine and a controlled diet. To Sonia's immense relief, he nodded in approval, sealing his role as her lifelong champion. He patted her on the shoulder and smiled that wonderful encouraging smile he'd used on her ever since she was a kid.

"Keep moving, never mind in which direction, but don't sit still!" he remarked with a wink.

It was exactly what she had in mind.

Now as she sat in her office, she realized that her parents, regardless of their initial hesitation, had been supportive. It hadn't been easy to accept that their only daughter had plunged into an unaccountable, crazy fancy, relinquishing all claims on the family business and nipping off the lucrative marriage proposals. However, Sonia's firmness of mind had reassured them to a marginal extent and finally reconciled them to the idea. So, here she was, launched in her sparsely furnished yet comfortable abode of work—with no work at all!

But at least she had been lucky enough to find an office on F.C.Road. It was a prime location of Pune. She had managed to rent one of the two-room offices lying vacant on the ground floor. The box window overlooked the main road and a small garden surrounding the building—an ideal office in the centre of the city. The only problem being the traffic sounds, since F.C.Road was a crazy route at office hours.

For a minute, she glanced out of the window. The May sun beat down, like a sweltering heat wave on the passing vehicles. It had been an unusually hot summer; she only hoped the monsoons would drive away all this heat.

The traffic was at its peak hour this morning. Black and yellow autorickshaws screamed and made their way skillfully between the Maruti vans, Zens and Indicas. And the famous scooters and motorbikes—commonly called the two-wheelers—weaved through the gaps, at breakneck speed! Driving was a necessary evil in the cozy yet fast churning city of Pune. Not for the girls though. Teenagers and women office-goers were wrapped from head to toe in scarves, suncoats and dark glasses to escape the sun. Totally unrecognizable, they enjoyed their anonymous freedom and mobility through the city.

Sonia's attention returned to the newspaper in her hand. Her eye traveled down from the first page, to the next and halted on a write-up of the Rebel Cross gang. Sonia had followed this particular news story with a great deal of interest. The rebel cross was a group of unidentified young people with queer ideas of morality. They wore a cross, stamped like a tattoo on their bare upper arm. They tracked down injustice and passed their own judgment. The spate of recent happenings, thefts, or thrashings in the city was an outcome of their policy.

Sonia shook her head. Strange is the idea of justice for some people!

In the outer room, Jatin switched on his portable Television, and Sonia smiled. Jatin, who was boyishly good-looking and had just stepped into his twenties. He had agreed to work with her on one condition. That his TV set get a permanent position in a corner of thc outer office and that he could watch cricket, whenever his mind pleased. Sonia had instantly agreed. She couldn't dare refuse such a request in a cricket-crazy country like India. Besides, she needed Jatin and at this point, couldn't afford to displease him.

Folk music emerged from the television, followed by a male voice. Sonia's head jerked up spontaneously. She could barely decipher what the man was saying. But the quality of his voice made her step into the outer office.

"What are you watching?" she asked Jatin curiously.

"A new series. A documentary on Pune," he replied.

Sonia seated herself beside Jatin and viewed the programme with interest. The camera panned from verdant hilly slopes to a tall, good-looking man, who was commenting smoothly and effortlessly. He was standing atop Hanuman Tekdi, the hill behind F.C.Road. The sun was dipping along the horizon behind him and the camera panned again, as he indicated the sprawling city with his hand. Patches of lush green were beginning to dull as the sun disappeared and the lights began to twinkle amidst the stretches of uneven, concrete structures. The presenter continued to drawl into the mike.

"This is Pune, spread out before us. A city of green trees, hills, rivers and of course masses and masses of unplanned buildings. But that can be expected with a population of four million and a land size surprisingly larger than neighboring Mumbai! And yet, Pune, which is India's leading industrial, educational and research cities, has retained forty percent area under green cover. Pune is one of..."

As he continued to elaborate on the richness of culture, Sonia realized that she most certainly liked the Presenter's voice. It was clear, resonant and deep, but not deep enough to echo jarringly into the ears. It had a musical feel to it. And she also liked his face. It was an interesting face, well-defined features—

The telephone shrilled into her thoughts and Sonia gestured to Jatin to reduce the volume of the TV. She returned to the inner office and picked up the receiver.

"Sonia!" boomed the familiar, friendly voice of Inspector Divekar.

"Jeevan Uncle!"

"Smart guess. You have my horoscope before you, right?"

"How can you poke fun at something so serious! Do I ever mock you about the methodology the police use?"

"Hey, just kidding, you know. Even though it's worth considering the possibility that you may throw us out of business. Perhaps you could succeed where we police have failed, like in catching the Owl."

"The Owl?"

"Haven't you heard of our world famous thief, nicknamed the Owl? An intelligent international crook, who has managed to slip from the long arm of justice for a very long time. If you do manage to trap him, it will be a feather in your cap!"

"There you go again." Sonia sighed. "Believe it or not, Uncle, I'm up to my eyes in work!"

"I get the hint. I just called up to say I liked your ad. Keep it up!"

His patronizing tone rankled a little, as she hung up. Inspector Divekar, her father's dear friend, meant well but tended to go overboard with his sense of responsibility toward her.

A coconut vendor was passing by the window, shouting loudly in Marathi, "tender coconuts!" Sonia was tempted. This hot weather was giving her an unquenchable thirst. She popped her head in the outer office.

"Jatin, why don't we treat ourselves to some coconut water?" she asked.

"Good idea. How about stocking our little fridge for this summer?" Jatin responded with a grin.

"Only if our official budget for the month permits it," Sonia said primly.

"Well, in that case, I can buy just two more!"

"Oh, are we in that bad a shape?" Sonia looked astonished.

"Quite, but I'm also being careful! I have my responsibilities. We need to pay the rent on this office, remember?"

"Don't remind me. I know we need to get a case, fast, or we may have to close up office," Sonia said, with a grimace. "But let's not get our spirits down. Go fetch our coconuts!"

Jatin switched off the TV, flew out of the office and hailed the coconut vendor. Within minutes, he was back with four tender coconuts and straws. He placed two coconuts in the fridge.

"It's awful out there! The sun! Boss, as soon as we have some money, we need to get an air conditioner," Jatin announced, handing her a coconut.

Sonia accepted the fruit and sipped the cool, sweet water. "Don't I know that?"

"An air-con and also a computer, a bigger office, two cell phones, one for you and one for me—" Jatin continued.

"Right. But first we need a case—a real money-sprouting case!" Sonia finished. She returned to the inner office and sat behind her table, sipping the coconut water. The ceiling fan whirled overhead, with fits and squeaks and she glared at it.

"Don't you break down on me!" she warned aloud.

As if on cue, the fan slowed down, swinging noisily. She watched the reducing speed with alarm. A hot and dry summer without a fan? What misery! She focused on the fan and muttered, "Go on, move, you're not failing me. I rented this office with you. You better last out until the end of the season!"

The fan chugged and squeaked again, and much to Sonia's amazed relief, picked up speed with a loud groan.

"Wow! I just experienced what positive thinking can do!" she exclaimed. Then she raised the coconut to the ceiling. "Thank you for being considerate."

She settled down, to enjoy the coconut. The tasty fruit water was refreshing and she immediately felt replenished and energetic. She had just eaten the soft tender coconut and tossed the empty shell into the dustbin, when the connecting door opened and Jatin walked in.

His eyes were gleaming. "There's a man who says he'd like to meet you. A Mr. Mohnish Rai. And you're not going to believe this…." he said in an excited voice.

Sonia picked up her ears. "A prospective client?" She raised an inquiring eyebrow.

The expression on Jatin's face snuffed her hope. "I doubt it! But…" Jatin paused dramatically, "He's the man we just saw on TV, on the Pune show."

Sonia was startled. What a strange coincidence! "Are you sure? I mean, you know your TV loses colors and gives distorted images from time to time!"

"Of course, I'm sure!" Jatin was indignant. "And my TV set is the best piece you can get in the market for the price I bought it at. It just—"

"All right, I get it." Sonia hastily curbed his flow of indignation. "Send him in."

She threw a pleading look at the ceiling fan. *Don't ditch me*, she prayed silently. Then she hastily flicked open her appointment diary and sat with her pen poised. The door opened and a man entered, shutting the door behind him. Looking up, she saw a man throwing a casual glance around her neat, discreet office. In one sweep, she took in his spotless, creaseless white shirt, clean blue jeans and polished leather shoes. *Well-to-do,* she made a note. *And definitely the presenter from the show.*

"Yes, Mr. Rai. What has brought you here?" she enquired in her best business tone.

His gaze had passed over the music system with its display of cassettes and CDs and lingered on the set of astrology books, lined systematically on a shelf. An almost imperceptible change overcame him. A smile plucked at the corners of his mouth and his gaze shifted to her.

"Curiosity. And you can call me Mohnish," he replied, drawing out a chair and seating himself.

"Pardon me?"

"I said, curiosity." He smiled.

Sonia stared at him. Actually, Mohnish Rai looked much better off-screen than on-screen. He was a handsome man, clean-shaven, with intelligent brown eyes and a straight nose. The smile produced a rather attractive dimple in his right cheek. The crop of well-trimmed hair with a straying flick falling over his forehead made him look young but actually, he seemed to be in his late twenties. He exuded confidence bordering on arrogance and was certainly no client. She extinguished her wilting hopes by closing her diary with a determined bang.

"Nice place. Kind of stimulates you to work, I guess. Look, let me explain, Miss Samarth. I am a reporter—a freelance reporter—you may have read my articles or seen me hosting shows on local Television." Mohnish Rai paused, expecting an acknowledgement from her, but Sonia deliberately maintained a dignified silence.

"I read your advertisement in the *Times,*" he continued. "I simply could not resist it. I had to meet you!"

"Why?" Sonia asked bluntly.

"Well, it's kind of bizarre isn't it? Combining investigations with astrology! In an age where science has made tremendous progress, it amazes me that there are still people who rely on what I think is propagated by quacks. Moreover, you claim to solve cases with the help of this… this illusion? It's a rather bold commitment, you know. I thought, if nothing else, it would certainly make an interesting feature. Tell me, Miss Samarth, how many cases have you solved blending intellect and facts with the cosmic powers? Do you really believe that astrology can substitute for facts? Are your clients happy with your style of operation?" He flung his questions at her, in an almost jocular manner, in the very same voice she had appreciated just minutes before.

Sonia steeled herself against the fusillade of his questions, which didn't seem any less crude because of the quality of his voice. She took a deep breath and remarked without revealing a vestige of anger, "Since you mentioned quacks—let me fill in the gaps. Quacks are a product of half knowledge and are found in every respectable field, astrology being no exception. Vedic astrology is a science like any other. And no science can be censured and held responsible for man's incapacities, his inability to research, his deceptions and his natural inclination to greed and scheming. What you call illusion is the result of this interaction of science with man. And yes, I do claim to use the science and knowledge of Astrology to solve the cases which come to me. Because, I firmly and irrefutably believe, that a horoscope is an X-ray of a person! You can even label it an almost metaphysical representation of the `real you'. The point is not to substitute facts with the `cosmic powers' as you called it, but to use the planetary positions to guide the facts. And finally, Mr. Rai—"

"Interesting! I'm beginning to catch the drift of your reasoning. And please, call me Mohnish!" he interrupted magnanimously. "Do you think it would prove useful in catching international crooks or criminals like say the Owl? Please elaborate, Miss Samarth, I'm highly impressed by your theory."

"Thank you, Mohnish. But I don't recall consenting to give you an interview. Do you?" she asked sweetly. The ceiling fan spurted and squeaked in approval.

The dimple staged another appearance. "There's always a right moment. Like the present. So, to continue, what do you attribute—""

"No, I'm not interested," she stated flatly. "I'm sure you can find other satisfying avenues to quench your curiosity!"

"Oh, I see that you're hurt. I'm sorry I didn't mean to..."

"Look here, Mohnish. I'm a busy person. I have loads of work piled up and I'm fighting against time. You really must excuse me!" She stood up pointedly.

His eyes swept appreciatively over her. Tall, healthily slim with straight hair in a non-fussy blunt cut, creamy skin, searching honey-brown eyes, faint pink lipstick, a pleasant yellow cotton *salwar kameez*—short in keeping with the latest fashion—neat nails on shapely hands with a single-stone ring on her right ring finger—perhaps a diamond. She seemed efficient, intelligent and fired with remarkable purpose. A pastiche of beauty and brains. But *Astrology?*

The intercom buzzed.

"Yes, Jatin?" Sonia asked.

"The cat is here again."

"Okay... ask her to sit... !" The flush crawled all over her face an instant after the blunder.

Mohnish raised an eloquent eyebrow.

"Cat... cat... short for... Catherine!" she explained haltingly. Then, remembering that she need offer no explanations, she gathered her scattered wits and held out her hand. "Goodbye, Mohnish."

He stood with slow deliberation. "I'm not done yet. And this isn't the last you've seen of me. I'm extremely motivated to take this interview and you'll give it to me, Miss Sonia Samarth."

"Don't forget to take an appointment," she returned coolly.

Mohnish smiled enigmatically, then strode out of the room. At the reception area, however, he paused. Jatin was totally absorbed in feeding milk to a beautiful golden cat. Chuckling to himself, Mohnish Rai stepped out into the street. *Interesting, very interesting indeed!*

Sonia sighed. Surely only the beginning. Adverse remarks, criticism, biased estimations were undeniably a part of her profession—especially if it was tainted with a rather suspicious brush! It was true that people found it difficult to understand how the innocuous looking square called a horoscope could inhabit twelve houses, the twelve zodiac signs with the positions of the planets and influence our entire life! What they didn't care to acknowledge was that it required a detailed study to comprehend the intricacies of this science. In any event, she wasn't here to debate on the pros and cons of astrology and thrash out their pet aversions. She had set up a business. She wasn't going to compel anyone to pursue her line of thinking and she wasn't going to be persuaded otherwise either! This was her free world and no one had the right to intrude on her liberty of thought and action!

Sonia strode into the outer room and lifted the cat, stroking the silky head fondly. It meowed in acknowledgement. "You funny little thing. You're as regular as the sun and yet we don't know where you come from and where you go! You do have a family, don't you?"

"I think she's a stray," Jatin guessed.

"I'm not so sure. She's well-fed, tame and too friendly. Look at the way she insists on sitting on my lap. She's used to people. And don't miss this fancy leather collar with the steel studs. She's a pampered one."

"In that case, her owners ought to care where she vanishes to for days altogether, don't you think so? I would if she were mine. I would be worried sick if I didn't see her for every meal!" Jatin said indignantly.

"Actually so would I," Sonia agreed. "I say, I've an idea! Let's try to find out where she lives. I mean, her owners. She must belong to someone in this area."

"Great, then we can tell them a thing or two about caring for mute animals!" Jatin retorted, still heated up in his role of animal saver. "But how do we go about it?"

"Well, let me think… we could tie a note round her neck. Hold on a minute."

She tore a strip of paper from the pad and wrote neatly on it—*if this cat belongs to you, contact us at Stellar Investigations. Contact No…* She handed the paper to Jatin.

"If it doesn't reach the actual owner, it will at least be mobile publicity for us!" she laughed, and the cat purred in agreement.

Jatin secured the note round the golden neck, tucking it inside the collar. The soft head rubbed against Sonia's hand, purring noisily.

"Go find your people, cat. You're a good girl, aren't you? Then come right back again. Run along now." Sonia patted her and shoved her lightly toward the door.

The cat turned around and stared at her with glowing eyes, meowed intelligently, and then, with a swish of her abundant tail, vanished down the corridor.

"Now let's bide our time!" Sonia experienced a sudden wave of excitement. Then she grimaced. Life must be in a pretty bad shape if she could feel thrilled at the thought of finding a cat owner. The indisputable truth was that she itched for something to happen. It was definitely time for her to emerge out of her inertia and prepare herself for some action—any action.

CHAPTER II

The Return of the Cat

In the outer office, Sonia lit some joss sticks before the idol of Ganesh. She bowed her head, clasping her hands together in a silent, reverent *namaskar*. It was a brand new day of hopes and wishes and she prayed for a case—some work. Then Jatin switched on the TV and much to Sonia's annoyance, Mohnish Rai appeared on the screen, on Cable-News.

"The Kerkar jewels—the pride of the Kerkar clan—which were reported missing about a month ago, have been confirmed to be stolen by the family. The family had been hesitant to reveal the loss to the public. And suspicion rests on the renowned international crook, popularly known as the Owl. The jewels were in the custody of the Kerkar family, locked in the vault of their Mumbai residence. Unfortunately, no place is secure and no jewels safe, where the Owl is concerned. Provided of course, that the police prove that the jewels were indeed stolen by the Owl! This is Mohnish Rai for Cable Television."

"Wow! Mr. Rai is active!" Jatin whistled.

"Pushy is the more appropriate word for him," Sonia corrected. "I'm going to do some reading now and you should use your time too. If the cat returns, call me immediately."

Sonia settled down at her table. She was determined to put the day to good use. The fan swung overhead with valiant rhythmic creaks, fighting to serve its tenure, as she flicked open a book on astrology.

It was then that loud earsplitting meows announced the arrival of the cat!

Jatin burst into the inner office.

"She's returned and the note's gone!"

Catching his infectious excitement, she hastened to the outer room. The cat had comfortably ensconced herself on the softest and warmest chair and was treating herself to a thorough lick and bath!

"The note was too tightly secured for it to have fallen off. Which means someone removed the note," Sonia observed, fondling the golden head. "Give her some milk, Jatin."

"It's got to be the owner," Jatin predicted, moving to the small refrigerator Sonia's parents had loaned her.

"Perhaps. Whoever it is will undoubtedly call us."

"Not if they think we wish to complain!" Jatin grinned, as he splashed a generous helping of milk into a bowl. He placed it on the table and the cat immediately settled down to her business of lapping the bowl clean!

"I guess you're right," Sonia agreed. "If my note was removed last evening, we ought to have heard from the owner by now. But if the note was delivered this morning, then we should wait and see..."

As if on cue, the telephone rang shrilly, and Jatin galvanized into action. "That's her now!"

"Or him!"

"Stellar Investigations? Yes, please hold the line..." Jatin covered the mouthpiece with his hand and whispered, "it's a him!"

Sonia accepted the extended receiver. "Hello?"

"Hello! This is Ajay Patkar. I… I read the note tied round the cat's neck," a polite voice said.

The name rang a bell. "Good. She belongs to you then?"

"Actually I… would like to meet you. I… need to talk to you. May I come over to your office?"

"Of course!" She gave him the address and hung up, her eyes alight with excitement.

"What happened?" Jatin asked anxiously.

"Nothing happened. He seemed kind of evasive. In any case, he's coming over straight away. So we shall finally get to see the famous anonymous owner, if he's the one, that is!"

An hour later, Sonia was facing a tall man in formal clothes. A navy blue coat hung over a boy's figure. In fact, Ajay Patkar appeared to be in his early twenties. But although his attire and the expensive cell phone in his hand implied money and success, his appearance suggested a distracted mind. It was the clouded expression on his stubbled face that really caught her attention.

"Yes Mr. Patkar. You came to discuss the cat?" Sonia prompted.

Patkar shifted uncomfortably in his seat. "Yes… I mean no. Let me be honest. The cat doesn't belong to me. Last evening I was relaxing in the Model Colony lake park—you could call it a vain attempt at finding refuge with nature—when this cat came along and rubbed against my legs. I rather like animals, so I stroked her. Then I noticed the piece of paper round her neck and curiosity got the better of me. I took it and read it and should actually have replaced it. But I was so relieved that this detail slipped right out of my mind! It was almost as if the cat had brought an answer to my worries."

"What do you mean?" Sonia asked, intrigued.

"I've been so confused and disturbed these past few days, feeling low and kind of worthless. Floundering… not knowing which way to turn. I just didn't know what to do. And then I found that note, which seemed like a message from heaven! The idea just clicked. I… I know that this is normally not a routine approach… I mean accepting cases… on the pretense of being a cat owner…"

The young man was so obviously confused and embarrassed that Sonia, whose heart had begun to thud with optimistic bangs, decided to assist him. It was a do-or-die situation!

"Are you implying that I do something for you Mr. Patkar?" she suggested, her casual tone as simulated as her lack of understanding.

"Yes! Will you please… I mean, I need your services, I can pay your charges whatever they are. But I need your help!" Patkar rushed on, relief flooding his face.

Sonia could barely control the surge of happiness that threatened to disclose her unprofessionalism! But she harnessed her feelings with admirable control and instead threw a grateful look heavenwards. She caught sight of the ceiling fan swinging and creaking awkwardly and hastily rang the buzzer.

Jatin popped his head in.

"Two *chai*, please, Jatin!"

The assistant's eyes lit up at the code words. *Chai*—tea—meant business. At last!

"Right, boss!"

"And Jatin, you can join us with your notebook."

Sonia leaned against her cushioned chair, set her face in a pleasant encouraging mask and began, "Well, Mr. Patkar. I believe you're the son of the famous Patkar Industrialist?"

He nodded. "My father expired six months ago, leaving me the sole in-charge of his empire!"

She detected that he didn't seem too happy with the responsibility. Perhaps it was too much for his barely adult shoulders.

"Yes, I read about that in the papers. His death must've been a great shock to you."

"It was. He had a massive heart attack. I wasn't at all prepared… I mean, we are never prepared to lose our loved ones…"

She was discreetly silent for a minute. Jatin reappeared, armed with paper and pen, and drew a chair near his boss.

"So, are you ready to tell me what's bothering you?" she asked Ajay Patkar gently.

"Yes. I'll put it as briefly as possible. Last Wednesday, a friend of mine—Satish Mali—came to live with me for a couple of days. Satish and I have been school friends and we'd been in touch over the years. In fact, though we met on and off, I've always considered him my closest friend. He's the only friend, I've shared all my deepest thoughts with. Last Wednesday, I'd invited him over to my house but on the same night, he was… murdered… in his bed! It was terrible! My best friend dead! And in my home! I… I just couldn't believe it! I curse the moment I invited him. I felt as if I had issued summons for him to be murdered, as if I handed him to death myself, with my own hands! I… I'll never forgive myself…" His eyes moistened and he fumbled in his pocket for a handkerchief.

Sonia allowed a few seconds to elapse before she prompted him. "The police have been called, of course."

"Yes, they're working on it but I'm not satisfied. I want to take no chances. I need to be completely assured that justice will be done. I want the culprit to be caught, no matter what!"

"And he will be," Sonia assured, with quiet confidence. "Do you live with your family?"

Ajay Patkar nodded.

"Can you give me the details of the house members?" Sonia asked.

"My Mother—Alka Patkar—you may have heard of her. She is a social activist. I'm the only son. Mahesh Uncle, my Dad's brother, and his son Naresh are recent additions to our house. Mahesh Uncle lost everything in a fire in our native place in

Konkan and became quite destitute. So my Dad took him and my cousin under his wing. Naresh is a couple of years older than I am. There's a family housekeeper-cum-everything, Yamuna Maushi—who has looked after me for years! That's the lot, I guess."

"You haven't left out anyone?"

"No. Unless you count the gardener but he too has been with us for ages!"

Jatin's pen was flying as he jotted down these details in shorthand.

"Now can you describe exactly what happened that day?" Sonia requested. "Please don't leave out any details, not even the least important one."

Ajay Patkar took a deep breath and began, "I'd been feeling very low since dad passed away. And I thought I would ask Satish over for a few days. We could chat like old days and it would be a good change for both of us. You see Satish was an orphan, poor but a real gem of a person. He wasn't too happy with his part time job in an ad agency and I felt that I could get him absorbed in Dad's company. Though I never actually got down to doing it. Anyway, he came over in the evening and we had dinner together..."

"Who was present at dinner?" Sonia interrupted.

"Just my cousin Naresh and the two of us. Mother was out, attending a meeting, and was to be out till late. And Mahesh Uncle did not come in at all."

"Go on."

"After dinner, we chatted for a while. Then I took him to the guest room, but it was smelling awful, so I offered him my bedroom and decided to bed down with Uncle."

"Smelling? You mean that the room wasn't aired and smelled musty and unlived?" Sonia confirmed.

"No. It's a room we use frequently for our guests. It's always in good shape actually. But Yamuna Maushi later discovered a dead rat in the room, which had caused that repulsive odour."

"I see," Sonia said, reflectively. "Continue. What time did this... incident occur? I mean, when was Satish murdered?"

"The police predict it was between two and three in the morning. But not a soul heard a sound. It was only in the morning, when I went to awaken Satish for a morning walk that I saw this ghastly sight! Satish had been stabbed to death and the blood was all over the bedsheets!"

"Stabbed with a knife?"

"A paper cutter." An almost imperceptible change crept into his voice, which Sonia's sharp ears detected instantly.

"The paper cutter belonged to someone in the house." She hazarded a guess.

Patkar nodded. "It was Naresh's paper cutter."

"Oh, your cousin's," Sonia remarked thoughtfully. "But usually paper cutters are designed to be harmless—"

"Not this one. It was a bronze family heirloom given to my cousin by my dad."

"And where was this article normally kept?"

"In Naresh's room. But he claims that he couldn't find it the last few days."

Sonia digested this bit of information, slowly, glancing at Jatin. "You slept in Mahesh Uncle's room that night, with him, didn't you? And neither of you heard... ?

"I did sleep in his room but not with him. Mahesh Uncle was away all night...."

Sonia raised an eyebrow. "That's interesting. Where was he all night?"

Ajay Patkar shrugged. "I wouldn't know. Often, he goes to our farmhouse, a few miles away and spends the night there. I assumed that's what he'd done when he didn't turn up all night. He was present for breakfast, though."

Sonia was silent, as she observed Jatin's pen fluttering across the paper. Then she said, "You and Satish were close, you say.

Do you have any idea why someone would want to harm him?"

"I've absolutely no notion! I simply cannot imagine anyone wanting to hurt a person like Satish. He was an introvert—quiet but extremely intelligent and friendly. I've never known him to turn his back on a needy person. There's no earthly reason why anyone would wish to harm him!"

"Someone bearing a malice against him?"

"Not that I know of."

"Have the police checked the paper cutter for fingerprints?"

"They are doing it now though I haven't heard from them as yet."

"If this is an outside job, can you give me one reason why someone would choose your house for the murder?"

"No," Patkar said firmly. "I've been thinking about it but it beats me." He sighed.

"Satish was killed in your house, in your bed and with an envelope opener that belonged to the house—never mind who it belonged to. I think it's pretty obvious to me that someone from the house—I won't say family because it's a little too soon to come to conclusions—is responsible for this hideous crime. Someone, perhaps, who bore malice towards Satish. You do understand the implications of such a possibility?" Sonia asked carefully.

Ajay Patkar looked unhappy. "I've been assailed by these same doubts the last few days and that is precisely why I'm here. The thought had crossed my mind that in all likelihood, the search would result in turning inwards, towards my family. But when I think of poor Satish, my blood boils! Why him? No one—except for Mother and Yamuna Maushi, our housekeeper—really knew him! And they've always liked Satish and encouraged my friendship with him. It all seems so pointless!"

"What about Naresh?"

"Oh, Naresh met Satish for the first time that evening. It was a spur of the moment invitation, so he had no idea I had a guest staying over. In the beginning, I thought Naresh looked a little distracted but then they did exchange some views on advertising and it was an enjoyable dinner on the whole. I'm sure Satish felt good all evening. At least that's a solace to me—he was happy and content for his last ever meal! We had absolutely no inkling that something so frightful would happen, so immediately after a pleasant dinner! It seems almost impossible that one of my family members could have..."

'But it is a strong possibility that we cannot afford to ignore," Sonia interposed.

The *chaiwala*—the boy from the tea stall—arrived just then and served the hot liquid. They sipped it in silence.

"Will you take up this case, Miss Samarth? Even though the police are already handling it?"

"I will, but first you ought to understand how 'Stellar Investigations' works. You may have seen our ad in the Times, yesterday?"

"I'm afraid not."

"Never mind. It's important for you to know that we operate differently from other investigators. We combine criminology with astrology. Do you believe in astrology?"

He looked confused. "I... guess so. I don't know. I mean I've never really chased astrologers to read my future!" he added with a sheepish grin.

"But you believe in it enough to have your horoscope made? Well, your father maybe, if not you?"

"Yes. As a matter of fact, just last month I discovered a whole bunch of horoscopes, when I was sorting out my father's cupboard. He must've got the horoscopes made, when I was a kid."

"Good. Can you get me those of your family members?"

"Of course, but what do you plan to do with them?" he asked curiously.

"Right now, it may suffice for you to know that I need them to deliver my goods!" She smiled. "I'd also like to take a look at your house and possibly speak to a few people. Perhaps right away?"

"Mahesh Uncle may be in the office but you can meet the others."

"Good enough. You can give me your address and I shall follow you. Also, I'd like you to jot down the details of Satish's ad agency and house." She pushed a pad towards him.

Patkar quickly scribbled the addresses on the paper and then left.

Sonia turned towards Jatin with sparkling eyes. "Well what do you make of it all?"

"It's Naresh, of course! The cousin. And I can bet they will find his fingerprints on the paper cutter," Jatin foretold confidently.

"But why would he wish to kill a perfect stranger? That is, assuming that he really met Satish for the first time that night. Remember that a crime is investigated on three 'Ms'. Motive—why the crime was committed; Modus Operandi—how the crime was committed and Material—what weapon was used to implement the crime. There's got to be a motive for Naresh to kill Satish. Besides there's Mahesh Uncle. We don't know anything about him. And then Ajay's mother and his Yamuna Maushi. And of course, it wouldn't do to overlook the odd chance that Satish did really have enemies that Ajay Patkar knows nothing about! Someone may have wished to settle an old score! This case is not as straight as it looks, Jatin. We have to examine beyond the surface and we'll have to do a great deal of scratching at the top to get to the bottom of the matter!"

"Are we going over to Patkar's house, with a magnifying glass? We'll need it and I've done a lot of reading up on forensics and..." Jatin's eyes shone with anticipation.

"Hey, hold it! I'm sure you've done your homework but I'd

rather work with my brains and horoscopes than magnifying glasses. Besides, the police must've already covered that ground!" Sonia chipped in quickly, before her eager colleague could expound on his novel-earned pages of knowledge.

"Oh!" His face fell.

Sonia almost felt sorry for him. She'd better handle him well, or she would loose her best and only assistant. "But there's something else that you can do." she added.

"Right!" He whipped out his pad again and the smile was back on his face.

"Listen carefully. I'd like you to go to Satish's ad agency and make some discreet inquiries. Speak to his associates; find out about his office life, friends, enemies if any, relations with everyone. If they're reluctant to talk, tell them you're authorized to question people. Visit his house, meet his neighbors, have a chat with them."

"Right, boss."

"And Jatin—while you're out, see that you buy a lovely, soft cushion for Nidhi!"

"For *whom?*"

"Nidhi—the cat. Nidhi means wealth and our Nidhi is here to stay. She's earned her home in this office!"

"Right, boss!" Jatin grinned appreciatively.

The ceiling fan groaned and creaked. Sonia glanced up and smiled. "And yes, find an electrician and see that that the fan is in top condition today!"

Jatin stared at the fan bewildered and shrugged.

CHAPTER III

The Clue from the Past

Koregaon Park was on the other end of Pune and Sonia drove slowly through the heavy traffic. Her second-hand Maruti van hiccupped over bone-shaking speed-breakers. Hot air through the windows fanned her already flushed and perspiring face. At a traffic signal, she swept a cotton hanky across her face, as she waited for the red signal to change to green. A carrier truck, with a huge slogan printed on its back—Love Thy Mother—blocked her route. An auto on her right, displayed a lingerie ad and Sonia couldn't help grinning. Anything for a little extra money. The signal turned green and immediately cars honked impatiently. Cyclists and two-wheelers cut recklessly through her path. Considering the manner in which the busses and the rash two-wheelers raced at high speed, you'd think that the Pune roads were empty. Instead, the roads pulsated with life, not only with vehicles criss-crossing dangerously, but also two and four-legged animals lazing casually on the streets. It was a wonder that the city's traffic accident rates were lower than the fast moving developed world. Sonia sighed. Heat or no heat, with every passing day, the traffic was getting unbearable.

Finally, she drove into Koregaon Park—a residential area for the upper crust of society, which also housed one of the major attractions of Pune, the Osho Commune—the international meditation centre of Osho Rajneesh. Sonia observed the Westerners—the followers of Osho Rajneesh—couples strolling about arm-in-arm, attired in long maroon robes—the dress code of the Commune. Vendors lined the street, selling colorful silk scarves and an array of white and maroon robes. Sonia had always found the Commune fascinating and one day, hoped to study what lay behind its walls. But right now, she had to concentrate, on her first major case in hand!

The Patkar house was a grand, two-story affair, off the main street. Sonia passed two constables, deep in discussion, outside the bungalow. A well-maintained lawn was a treat to the eyes, as she led her van down the drive. She had just pulled up her vehicle, and taken a swig from the water bottle she made it mandatory to carry with her, when Ajay Patkar strode towards her, with a hospitable smile. If he noticed how flushed and sweaty she looked, he was tactful not to mention it.

"I'm glad you could make it so quick. Would you like anything? Something to drink before we begin?"

"No, let's get started."

"Fine, where would you like to start?"

"The guest room, I believe."

He nodded and indicated the way. A quaint red brick path, led to the back of the house past a small rock fountain, which had a wonderful cooling effect. Sonia paused for a second, pretending to observe the house and allowed the fountain to transfer its cool moisture. Then, feeling refreshed and composed, she followed Patkar to the guestroom. They stopped at a door and Patkar unlatched it.

"There are two entrances to this room," he explained. "One from inside the house and the other from the garden, in case any of my guests need the privacy."

A faint odor, mingled with the scent of an air freshener, whiffed into Sonia's nose, as they stepped in. She sniffed it.

"The stench must have been pretty bad," she observed.

"Yes, it was awful. Yamuna Maushi hunted out a dead rat the next day, from under the bed."

"Do you usually find rats around here?" Sonia asked, curious.

"No. Yamuna Maushi and our gardener make absolutely certain of that. You know, placing poison balls to get rid of the mice, for the monthly housecleaning."

"And this was not the housecleaning time of the month? I mean, maybe one of the servants had placed poison balls to get rid of the mice."

"Not that I know of. But you could ask Maushi later."

Sonia moved quietly round the room, her keen eye observing the smallest detail. A bed, a cupboard, table and chair were the sole occupants of the space. The cupboard was empty. She opened the bathroom door and her eyes swept over the clean toilet. A cupboard in the corner of the bathroom, caught her attention and she moved towards it. She opened it and frowned. An odd collection of articles lined the shelf. An inkbottle with some liquid in it, a piece of cloth and a tiny glass stick. She picked up the bottle and read the label on it: "cashewnut juice." Strange and yet she sensed something familiar about it all. Something she ought to know.

"Is this room secluded from the rest of the house?" she asked, closing the toilet door behind her.

Patkar was leaning against the bedpost, waiting patiently for her, and he straightened at once. "That's right. I told you, it was to serve a dual purpose. Freedom of movement and privacy. Where to next?"

"Your room, please."

This time, they took the inner door, which led down a corridor into the main hall. The entire décor of the house was ornate and each room they passed was populated with a large collection of valuable antiques. Bronze statues of Lord Krishna in different positions, blackened with age, stood on display in the grand hall. Patkar explained that his father was an avid collector of old statues and they reached the landing,

"My parents and I have rooms in this wing and Mahesh Uncle and Naresh have rooms on the other side," he explained. "This is my bedroom here."

The room where Satish had breathed his last, was beautifully done up, with money poured with a free hand into its decorations. Lush blue carpet, thick embroidered curtains, a wall-to-wall wardrobe, and a sprawling bookshelf lined with gold-gilded volumes and books. Apparently, Ajay was a much-loved son.

"I shudder to come in here. It's too soon to sleep in this bed," he said in a low voice.

"I can understand," Sonia agreed, sympathetically. "It must've been an awful experience to find your best friend, lying dead in your bed!"

She approached the window and glanced down. No ivy or pipeline ran along the wall. It would be difficult for an outsider to climb up that way. Her gaze skimmed over the room. It was thoroughly cleaned up, leaving absolutely no trace of any gory incident. Obviously, the police had finished with the murder scene.

The door opened and a plump woman in her mid-fifties bustled in. Draped in a printed cotton sari with her hair casually bundled in a bun, she wore a big, round bindi on her forehead.

"Here you are, Ajaybaba. These are some letters for you."

"Thank you, Maushi." He took the letters from her and quickly scanned through the return addresses.

"Yamuna Maushi," Sonia smiled at the woman. "You've been with the family for years, haven't you?"

"Oh yes, ever since Ajaybaba was a year old," the woman

replied. “I was living in Goa at that time and they were in Mumbai. Ajaybaba’s mother was finding it difficult to look after a baby, so his father called me over from Goa to take care of the child. Ever since then, I have been a part of this family, taking care of all of them and looking after the house.”

“She loves me like a son,” Patkar explained with an affectionate smile at the plump lady.

“I believe you found a dead rat in the guest room?” Sonia questioned.

“Oh yes, God! What a shameful thing to have happened. I particularly see to it that every nook and corner of this house is properly dusted and cleaned. Never a cockroach or mice will you find! Then out of the blue, this rat! And to think that I didn’t notice it! It was terrible!”

“Then you hadn’t put poison balls or anything of the kind?”

“Certainly not! I don’t know what is happening to this house! The tragic death of Satish the other night—poor, poor boy—such a wonderfully sensitive boy, so quiet and nice—to think that such a horrible thing could happen to someone so decent! And then this rat! I found it under the bed, the next day. I keep telling Ajaybaba that God is angry with us! These incidents do not augur well. It’s necessary to do *shanti*—a ritual to sanctify the house. I’m going to light incense sticks in every room to expel the evil spirits!” She left the room, still muttering under her breath.

“She’s a dear,” Ajay Patkar remarked, grinning fondly, as they stepped out into the corridor again. “She’s been more like a mother to me than a governess. Of course, my parents have always been there for me when I needed them,” he added hastily. “But building up a business in industrial products, is no easy matter. It took up a lot of their time, and I was naturally left in Maushi’s care.”

“How did Mrs. Patkar take the news? I mean, a murder right next door!”

"Oh, my mother was so greatly shocked that she nearly fainted! She hasn't been feeling well and is in bed. She always approved of my friendship with Satish and liked him a lot. I'm not surprised that the news upset her."

"Do you think I could meet her for a minute? Or would I be intruding on her privacy?"

"I'll have to check. Will you wait here a second?"

Sonia nodded. Patkar knocked on the door opposite his own and stepped inside. She could hear muffled voices, and then he reappeared.

"You can go in," he told her. "I have some phone calls to make, if you'll excuse me. And I'll find those horoscopes for you. Feel free to look around, as you please."

"I will, thanks."

Mrs. Patkar's room was exactly as Sonia had imagined it. Large and spacious, with the distinct touch of femininity. Dreamy pink walls with a framed mural of Ganesha, printed curtains, bedspread, and a huge wardrobe aligning the entire left wall of the room. The elaborate dressing table with its multiple mirrors undoubtedly reflected the personality of the owner.

A woman in her late forties, attired in a fashionable, dainty nightie, sat up in the plush bed. Flawless skin that glowed in spite of the dark circles under the eyes, manicured fingers nervously twining and entwining into each other, and a faint sad smile on lightly brushed pink lips. A woman with expensive tastes and money at her fingertips to satisfy those tastes! But Sonia was also aware, having seen her often on television, that Mrs. Patkar was a philanthropist who gave away a lot of money to the needy and to charity. It raised her respect for the lady.

"Hello Miss Samarth. I'm so glad you're here. I can't wait to see this whole messy business cleared up!" Mrs. Patkar spoke in a soft, refined voice.

"I understand the feeling," Sonia replied, sympathetically. "And I'll do my best to solve matters. But what I really need, at the moment, is all the information I can get my hands on. Any bits and pieces of knowledge, however unimportant, could prove to be useful links in this case!"

"Absolutely! Please, ask me whatever you need to ask," Mrs. Patkar remarked in a pressing tone.

"Can you tell me what time you came home on Wednesday night?"

"I was very busy that evening," the older woman said immediately. "You see, I socialize a lot—social commitments of all kind. You can never say no to anyone—not when you are in my position!" She sighed. "Women councils, board meetings, Chief Guest at functions—all that lot. I think it must've been twelve-thirty when I returned that night. I went straight to my room. I was so tired that I slept like a log! And the next morning I heard this terrible news. I couldn't believe my ears! Poor Satish! He was such a good friend of Ajay's, such a nice boy. We've known him for years! Why would anyone want to kill the poor soul! Sometimes destiny—life, is so cruel, so inconceivably ruthless that I begin to feel quite uneasy!"

"I can imagine," Sonia agreed with a thoughtful expression. "Did you hear any kind of disturbance in the night? A sound, perhaps or a door opening, or even a cry for help?"

"Absolutely nothing. I told you, I slept like a log."

"Thank you, Mrs. Patkar. I won't interrupt your rest any more."

"But you will get to the bottom of this matter?" she asked anxiously.

"Rest assured, I will." Sonia smiled and left the room.

She regained the corridor, deep in thought and crossed over to the other wing. She tried the first door and it swung open. Here was a room in keeping with the rest of the house, announcing the strength of money. An ornate writing table stood in a corner. A photograph of a young, smiling face stared back at her as she rummaged through the articles on the table.

A writing pad, envelopes, a laminated driving license bearing Naresh's name, ballpoint pens. So, this was Naresh's room. Sonia took the license and read the expiry date. Nine years from now. A new license. She replaced it on the table, observing mentally that it would be easy to lift any one of these articles to incriminate Naresh. Sonia lifted the photo and studied the youthful smile. Naresh was as good-looking as his cousin was. Why would anyone wish to frame him for murder? Especially since he had never met Satish before? But what if that was just an act and Naresh did nurse a private grudge against Satish? Did Naresh have a secret agenda? Had he, in fact, killed Satish?

Sonia was deep in thought as she stepped out of Naresh's room and opened the door to the adjoining room. It was a neat, simple room minus the Patkar pomp, almost as if the owner wished to be declared as different. A mattress on the double bed was neatly rolled up, while the other half was covered in a pristine white bed sheet. The room evidently belonged to Mahesh Uncle. It was obvious that he wished to use minimum facilities provided by his brother's family.

Sonia stepped out of the room and nearly collided into Yamuna Maushi. The governess handed her a bunch of booklets. "Ajaybaba asked me to give you these."

Sonia accepted the horoscopes, held together with a ribbon. "I'm glad we met again, Maushi. You've known the family for years. Can you describe them to me? Tell me about Naresh."

"Oh, he's a nice sort. Quiet and barely talks. Very interested in keeping fit. In fact, he's working out in the gym right now."

"But what does he do?"

"Helps Ajaybaba out at the office. But otherwise he's really very secretive about his life."

"And his father?"

"Oh Mahesh Uncle is quite different—very much like Patkarsaheb, I mean Ajaybaba's father, but without that urban polish of course. He loves his native place and misses it. How often he has said to me that he will go back and replant the mango tree plantations on his land. He is willing to work at it all over again rather than lose his old, familiar life. He truly loves his land!"

"Maushi, do you honestly think Naresh murdered Satish?"

"No." The plump woman's answer was prompt and decisive.

"Even if it was his paper cutter that killed Satish?"

"Even if that were true, I would still find it immensely difficult to believe that Naresh is capable of such a crime!"

Sonia was silent for a moment as they moved towards the staircase. Then she said, "Do you remember seeing any strangers hanging around the house on Wednesday, the day of the murder? Or any visitors perhaps?"

"Not that I noticed. Uncle had a visitor but that was on Tuesday. I particularly remembered him—or rather them, there were two of them—because I thought they were kind of odd, the Hindi film goonda type. I showed them into the study where Uncle asked me to call them. But they didn't wait for long. I know because when a few minutes later I went to ask if he wished me to serve any refreshments, they were gone. Mahesh Uncle was sitting very still in a chair. I asked him if anything was the matter and he said there wasn't."

"And you didn't see these guests again, anywhere near the house on Wednesday," Sonia confirmed.

Maushi shook her head. "No. I'm quite certain about it."

"Oh well, I suppose they're of little consequence." Sonia shrugged. "But in other words, you feel that no outsider would have had a chance to steal Naresh's paper cutter? Or for that matter, even attempt to kill Satish. That any stranger would have been immediately noticed by you?"

"I think so."

"Thank you, Yamuna Maushi, you've been tremendous help! Can you show me the way to the gym please?"

The family gym was behind the house. Sonia walked out of

the front door, wondering how anyone could work out in forty degrees heat, when she almost collided with a tall, lean man. He was dressed in a white cotton shirt and khaki trousers and threw her an unconcerned look.

"Oh hello! Mr. Patkar? Mr. Mahesh Patkar?" she ventured.

"You are…" He frowned.

"Sonia Samarth. I'm investigating Satish's death."

"You mean officially?" he asked sharply, the unconcern vanishing and the frown deepening.

"Of course!" Sonia blinked at his aggressive tone. "Do you mind?"

"Yes!" he replied, quite fiercely. "I mind very much! I object to outsiders meddling in our house! Taking it to pieces and exposing it to public humiliation!"

Mahesh Patkar glared at Sonia, then strode past her with long purposeful strides. Sonia stared after him, surprise rapidly turning to indignation. Then, within seconds, she was back to normal, shrugging off the man's insolence and belligerence as lack of culture. Or was it, perhaps, simple insecurity? Mahesh Patkar certainly held no semblance to the rural, sensitive guy, Yamuna Maushi had sketched. Was it merely his concern for his family, in the light of public disgrace? Or was it fear—fear that sprung from secret knowledge of the truth? Thoughtfully, she made her way toward the gym.

It was well-equipped and installed with the latest machinery. A lone figure was huffing and puffing on the treadmill. Clad in a vest and shorts, Naresh looked young and impressionable. Sonia approached him with a smile and he faltered, a little abashed.

"Hello, I'm Sonia Samarth. Mr. Ajay Patkar has asked me to look into Wednesday's unpleasant incident."

"And I'm Naresh, Ajay's cousin. Excuse me." He hastily picked up his towel from a pile of things, gave himself a thorough rub, and pulled on his jacket. But not before Sonia had noticed a deep brown mark on his upper arm. Her gaze narrowed. That mark rang a bell. As if, she ought to recognize it. She frowned as she jogged her memory for the intangible answer!

"Yes Miss Samarth, what can I do for you?" Naresh asked, zipping up his jacket.

"Let me come straight to the point. You know that it was your paper cutter that killed Satish. Can you enlighten me on how it happened to be used as a murder weapon?"

Naresh shrugged. "Would you believe me if I said I don't know? I couldn't find that particular cutter for the past few days and I thought that I'd misplaced it. It's a crazy situation! Why me and why Satish? I'd never even met the guy before!"

"But you do understand that the evidence of the cutter could be incriminating, making you the prime suspect."

"I know. But why would I kill somebody I've never known? And with my own paper cutter, for God's sake! And leave it as positive evidence for the whole world to discover? Damn it, I'd use more cunning than that! This seems like a desperate, hasty job—premeditated perhaps—but certainly not with the intention of hushing up the entire matter! In fact, I'll go so far as to claim that someone is deliberately out to frame me!"

"I'm sorry that logical as it may seem, the police may not take that view. They go by facts and evidence. Look at it this way. The paper cutter was yours. Chances are that it has your fingerprints on it. You knew Satish was in the house. And most important, you have a suspicious background since you belong to the Rebel Cross gang!"

Naresh looked as startled as if she had knocked a punch into his nose. Sonia's unblinking gaze observed the conflicting, transient expressions on his face.

"I'm right, am I not?" she emphasized, softly. "I saw the cross on your arm and also the cashewnut juice you use, to make that mark with. The moment I saw the cashew nut juice bottle in the guestroom cupboard, I linked it with your tropical and humid Konkan background and the cross confirmed my suspicions.

You deliberately put a dead rat in the guestroom, because you didn't want Satish to sleep there. Because..."

"Yes, I did put the rat in the room, but I did not kill Satish!" Naresh's face changed color and his skin seemed tautly drawn over the bones.

"I know. You placed the rat there because you have your Rebel Cross meetings in the guest room every Wednesday night," Sonia continued calmly. "But the police won't believe you. As far as they're concerned, the case would be as straight as a line. Mr. Patkar, I think you may very soon need a good lawyer and I suggest that you start looking for one right away!"

"But..."

Before he could utter his protest, sudden hasty footsteps crunched loudly on the gravel outside. Two uniformed men burst into the gym, their faces grim and non-committal.

"Inspector Divekar!" Sonia exclaimed.

'Mr. Naresh Patkar, I have an arrest warrant for you!"

"My God! The case is over then! Naresh did it, just like I thought!" Jatin whistled.

Sonia threw her purse on the table and fondled Nidhi who curled comfortably on a soft, blue cushion.

"Did you find anything worthwhile at the ad agency?" she asked Jatin.

"Nothing much. Everyone was shocked to hear about Satish's death. Satish was a liked guy. No, he had no quarrels with anybody, neither office colleagues nor neighbors. But all this information is redundant, now that Naresh is caught!"

"Accused but not convicted," Sonia reminded. "I can't help thinking that this case is a little like pedaling downhill. Often when you cycle down a slope, you barely have to pedal. And you enjoy the effortless ease of the ride so much that quite often you miss the signboards! To all appearances, everything is so painlessly clear-cut and dried in this case. But that, in itself, leaves plenty of room for doubt! I have this recurring suspicion that the police have missed a signboard along the way, Jatin, and I have every intention to find it. Something is not right here. Something I ought to see, but cannot. Will you please leave me alone for a while? You can switch on the music while you go out and order some lunch for us in the meantime."

Jatin nodded as Sonia settled in her chair. He switched on the music system and loud drumbeats rocked the room. Jatin grinned to himself. His boss never failed to surprise him. She insisted on blaring music to motivate her thought processes. She'd once told him about her 'I formula' and when he'd looked bewildered she had added, "Nothing like music and dance to *inspire insight* into *intuition,* and *instigate investigation!*" Her source of inspiration was anything from soul-searching and philosophical non-filmy Hindi ghazals, romantic Hindi film songs, to hard rock and jazz. The priority, in each case, went to the volume, which had to be almost ear-splitting. Only then did the music flow meditatively deep through the body. Jatin closed the door, which mercifully dulled the sound. He had no relish for his boss's preference of volume.

Sonia stared into space, her mind working in unison with the quickening rhythm of the drumbeats. A finger absent-mindedly twirled a lock of hair, as was her habit. The other hand distractedly fondled Nidhi's silky head. Voices of the people she had met, repeated their dialogues in her mind, like characters in a film.

She stood up abruptly and began swaying to the drumbeats, then began dancing. Her eyes were closed meditatively, as the music took hold of her body. Then all of a sudden, she stopped. With renewed resolve, she took the bunch of horoscopes Ajay Patkar had given her and spread them out before her. Each horoscope was subjected to the minutest observation. One by one, she set each booklet aside, until she stared at the last one in her hand. For a moment, her expression was that of bewilderment and then impulsively she exclaimed aloud. She got up and took one of the almanacs from the shelf, referring to it with a great deal of interest. Then once again, she immersed herself in the horoscopes, particularly the last one, simultaneously scribbling furiously on a pad.

The serviced fan worked noiselessly overhead, efficient in its muteness and just an occasional squeak, betrayed its age.

Half an hour later, to Jatin's surprise, the musical jing-bang was abruptly turned off.

He peeped into the room. "Lunch's arrived!" he announced.

Nidhi immediately meowed her approval. But Sonia stood up, slinging her handbag on her shoulder. "You go ahead and eat it. I'm going out!"

Jatin and Nidhi watched, amazed as she zipped past them and was gone. What had happened? He ought to be kept abreast of the latest, Jatin felt. Grumbling silently to himself, he poured some milk in Nidhi's bowl. Then, together, they set down to accomplish the important business of polishing off their respective lunches. Nidhi finished off the milk in seconds. Jatin, however, took his time enjoying the delicious fried bread and mixed vegetable, the famous *pav bhaji* of Pune. Fortunately, his boss's high-handed manner did nothing to interfere with the justice he usually did to his meal!

After lunch, Nidhi returned to her new bed and Jatin settled down to wait for his boss to return. Instinctively he sensed that the music had worked and something was on.

An hour elapsed before Sonia returned, a pleased, triumphant smile radiating on her face.

"Come in, Jatin, let's talk!" she said and waved him into her office.

"Have some good news?" he asked cautiously, following her inside.

"Yes, I do. But the first thing you do, after we finish our talk is to stock the fridge with fresh coconuts!" Sonia declared and

Jatin grinned.

"But boss, the details, please!"

"You know, Jatin, we've been such naïve fools. Trying to eat the raw dish before us without making any changes to it—either additions or subtractions! The result was that all along we'd been barking up the wrong tree!"

"How's that?"

"There's this scene from a Hindi film that I vividly remember. The hero wishes to call the heroine for a date. So he sits in a college classroom, writes a note, and aims it at the seat where the heroine normally sits. Unfortunately, the heroine and her friend have changed places that day and his note falls straight into the friend's lap, creating a lot of comedy and misunderstanding! This sequence has been at the back of my mind for some time now. It's funny how these films affect your mind and thinking!"

"Boss—which is the wrong tree?" Jatin asked patiently.

"You'll see soon enough! This afternoon I set about the case in a most systematic manner. It was time to turn to the horoscopes and try to find out if I could peg down a particular horoscope. So first, I checked out all the horoscopes to find out whose horoscope matched that of a criminal's. And sure enough I found one which showed me all the traits of a murderer! It amazed me because at that point that made no sense! But I did realize that I'd chanced upon a most vital lead, one which had plenty of potential to be explored. The next step was to go sequentially backwards from what I knew happened. What do we know? I mean what really happened?"

"Satish was murdered."

"Now the next logical question : where was he murdered?"

"In Ajay Patkar's room."

"In Ajay's bed, to be precise. Who normally sleeps in that bed?"

"Ajay of course!"

"Right. So if Satish hadn't been in the house, who would have been sleeping in that bed?"

"Ajay… my God, are you suggesting…!"

"You got it! Conclusion—that paper cutter was meant for Ajay Patkar and not Satish as everyone presumes! It was pure bad luck that Ajay invited Satish on the same day as Naresh's gang meeting. Naresh, as a desperate means, placed a dead rat in the guestroom, so that the smell would drive Satish away. Accordingly, Ajay offered Satish his bed and in the bargain, placed his best friend straight into the hands of destiny! The murderer was unaware of the change. And thinking that it was Ajay in the bed, struck him with the knife!"

"In that case, the murderer has to be someone, who did not know that Satish was sleeping in the room that night," Jatin pointed out.

"Good deduction. Now, who are the people who knew about the change of rooms? Naresh himself, since he was responsible for it, and Yamuna Maushi. And who did *not* know about the change? Mahesh Uncle and Mrs. Patkar. After I realized that, I went back to the horoscope I had singled out. It was Mrs. Patkar's horoscope that revealed the criminal traits!"

"But how's it possible? How can a mother try to kill her own son?" Jatin protested.

"Exactly! I asked myself the same question and the answer again came to me from her horoscope! I won't go into details, but Jupiter in her fifth house is in conjunction with Rahu. Saturn, with Ketu, does not aspect the fifth house favorably and to make matters worse, the *swami* or the lord of the fifth house—a house which governs children—is with Saturn. To make this technical jargon simple, such a woman will never conceive and will never have a child of her own. And even if she did, on the odd chance, it will not be a son!"

"But she has a son!"

"That had me floored, too! But only for a while. The world

knows that Ajay is her son but her horoscope denied the fact. Which made me think—was he really her son? I mean, did she give birth to him? If my line of thinking was correct, then our whole perspective on this case would change! The issue was remarkably sensitive but I had to find out! Because only the answers to these questions would throw light on this case and it was vital to tackle Ajay. I paid him a visit and put forth my argument in the most persuasive manner possible. He was naturally quite upset by my suggestion that he was not his mother's son. Ultimately, I did succeed in convincing him and he was willing to co-operate. It was their family gynecologist, from Mumbai, who furnished the information we needed.

"Ajay is not the present Mrs. Patkar's son but the son of Mr. Patkar's first fiancée who died in childbirth! After he remarried, the matter was hushed up, because Mr. Patkar always wanted his son to feel that this was his real mother. But that is exactly what Mrs. Patkar could never be—a real mother! She despised him, because he reminded her of her husband's first love and because she knew that she could never have a child of her own. So she threw herself into social activities, parties and mounting debts, leaving the child in the care of Yamuna Maushi."

"Whew! How did Ajay take the news? I'm sure I would have been shattered to discover that my mother was not my own!"

"Oh, he'll come to terms with it, I suppose."

"But what about the motive? Why would she want to kill Ajay? And with Naresh's knife? What enmity could she possibly have with Naresh?"

"The age-old greed for money. Inheritance. The old Mr. Patkar, knowing his wife's squandering capacity and dislike for his son, left everything to Ajay and after Ajay to Mrs. Patkar. But he made a joint nominee in Naresh, whom he liked and trusted. Mrs. Patkar was neck deep in debts and her debtors were constantly hounding her. She had no control over her husband's money and she hated asking Ajay for it. So she decided to go the whole hog—to kill Ajay with Naresh's paper cutter so that she could kill two birds with one stone or to put it literally—with one paper cutter! Then the inheritance would all be hers! On Tuesday, when two of her rather unpleasant debtors paid Mahesh Uncle a visit and threatened her life, she decided to act fast. She knew that Mahesh Uncle would be at the farm that night. She decided to seize the opportunity. Unfortunately, her plan misfired and her knife took the wrong life!"

"But what about proof? And are you going to inform Inspector Divekar about this?"

"Inspector Divekar is at the Patkar house right now. He's positive that he'll get the truth out of her. As for proof… a deep and vicious stabbing always leaves some stains on the clothing of the killer. I am sure a thorough search of her room will reveal a spotted nightgown!"

There was a knock on the door and Inspector Divekar, a tall broad man with a receding hairline, attired in a brown uniform, strode in, a beaming smile on his lips.

"I can't believe it, Sonia, you did it! A little pressure and Mrs. Patkar went to pieces, confessing everything! And we found that nightgown too! Brilliant work! And you mean to tell me that it was a 'horoscope' which gave you the lead?"

"Absolutely, Jeevan Uncle, believe it or not!"

"I'm beginning to believe it!" Inspector Divekar smiled.

"Gosh, I'm hungry. Jatin, I thought I told you to order lunch!"

"In a jiffy, boss," Jatin remarked with a grin.

"Where's Ajay Patkar?" Sonia asked the Inspector.

"Struggling with hard truths. But he'll be all right. He should be here soon. Hello! Who's this on the cushion?" Inspector Divekar stroked the cat.

"Nidhi—my lucky charm!" Sonia laughed and Nidhi meowed in agreement.

CHAPTER IV

Confessions of the Night

Lightening streaked across the darkness, ripping the sky open with its brilliance. The thunder followed with such an earth-shaking rumble that Sonia shuddered. Jatin, too looked a little startled, pausing over his meal. Inspector Divekar merely concentrated on his Chicken Biryani. A light drizzle fell outside the restaurant, like soft fountain water.

"What a night!" Sonia remarked. "Though I do hope it pours. It's been such a dry season this year that we almost feared a drought situation in parts of the country. But not anymore, I hope. We need the rain for the crops and the economy."

Inspector Divekar nodded. "For the first time to-night, I can see some signs of our famous monsoon rains coming on. Are you sure, you won't try some of this Biryani? It's delicious!"

Sonia smiled. "No thanks, I'm a strict vegetarian. And as it is, I'm full! Thank you for a wonderful treat in this charming place!"

Sonia glanced around at the beautifully decorated restaurant. Located along the curving green banks of the Mula River, the restaurant was aptly called 'Mula Retreat' and served traditional

Maharashtrian food along with other choices. The decor was rustic, with coir mattresses adorning the mud walls, in criss-cross patterns. A bullock cart rested in the corner of the huge hall, where children played, creating sounds with sticks on the wooden wheels. Waiters in white dhotis—loin cloth—kurtas and small white caps, moved around, with food placed in cane baskets, matching the Maharashtrian mood and ambience.

Sonia and Jatin had thoroughly enjoyed the food—*bhakri* made of sorghum flour and crushed chilies along with curds and the spicy gram gravy called *pithla*. Inspector Divekar had insisted on taking the two of them out to dinner to this new restaurant. They had arrived a little early, so as to enjoy the idyllic location and the cool evening breeze. 'Mula Retreat' was sandwiched between sugarcane and sorghum fields on one side and an open grazing plot on the other where cows and sheep grazed. The metal bells of the cows tinkled melodiously. Local fishermen, in their tiny red and blue wooden boats, who had thrown in their nets for fishing in the rippling water, were now returning home with their haul. The river and the Babul and Neem trees bathed in the golden-pink glow of the setting sun, had sparkled with a dreamy, almost surreal effect. *An ideal evening for meditation and romance,* Sonia had thought. But, without warning, the weather had changed and a cold black blanket had enveloped the entire city.

Thunder rumbled again and Jatin remarked, "The weather's perfect for this kind of spicy food."

"Also perfect to commit crimes," Inspector Divekar added, as he polished off his *biryani*. He looked quite distinguished in a comfortable sky-blue cotton shirt and black trousers.

Sonia smiled. "Trust you to equate a beautiful romantic night with crime!"

"Romantic? This is a setting for criminals! On a night like this, criminals find their way easily and effortlessly to their victims and their loot! I'm positive we'll have a whole list of new cases tomorrow morning at the police station."

"You're right, I suppose. But good criminals, like good investigators can strike anytime, any place," Sonia reminded.

"Absolutely. Take the Owl for instance."

"The international crook—who's supposed to have stolen the Kerkar jewels," Sonia recalled. Mohnish Rai's voice and face, delivering the news on TV, rose in her mind as a sequel to the recollection. And she didn't at all appreciate the way her mind automatically supplied these images!

"Yes, the Owl. I'm sure he has the Kerkar diamonds. He's an amazing man, though I've never had the good fortune of interacting with him. You never know when he'll display his skill and talent. He's so perfect in the implementation of his 'schemes', that he has successfully evaded being caught by the police."

"So far," Sonia added.

"Going by his track record, I doubt if he'll ever get caught. He's going to be one of those criminals, who just fade away, I mean simply vanish—a closed file. Never to be seen or heard of again. But, of course, that won't be for a long time still. I'm sure he has yet to accomplish many more feats!" Inspector Divekar prophesied.

Sonia shrugged. "I'm afraid I'm no authority on the Owl. I doubt that our paths will ever cross."

The waiter arrived with the bill and the inspector dropped a five hundred rupee note on the tray. Then all three of them hastened to the car park, where Sonia's van was parked. Soon they were out on the street, the tar road sparkling white in the dim streetlights.

"I wouldn't like to be caught out on such a night! I'm glad we finished dinner and are returning home in time," Sonia said, as the vehicle sped toward the city. The headlights, like elongated, golden ribbons on the wet glistening road, pierced the way into obscurity.

They drove in silence for a while. The, suddenly Inspector Divekar said, "Jatin, please stop the van by this gate!" He pointed out the concrete shadow which was looming up on the left.

"Are you getting off here, Jeevan Uncle?" Sonia asked, puzzled.

"As a matter of fact, *we* are getting off for a few minutes. I'd like you to meet some people Sonia. They live in this really smashing bungalow, you simply must see!"

"Jeevan Uncle, it's late and it's going to pour! Don't you think we should pay this… er… visit some other, more appropriate day and time?" Sonia suggested, glancing at her wristwatch.

It was past nine. The dinner had been wonderful and it had filled her with warmth and lethargy. And now she looked forward to cuddling up in her warm bed.

"It won't take long and, frankly, the Tupays will profit by your visit," he replied, enigmatically.

Sonia stared at him in bewilderment. But his plump face was closed. Without awaiting her response, he ordered Jatin to park the vehicle and follow them inside the bungalow. With a strange reluctance of heart, Sonia trailed after Inspector Divekar up the flight of stairs to a wooden double door. He rang the bell, which clanged through the house like an echo of the rumbling thunder. The double doors opened, to reveal a man in his late forties. A streak of white wove through his thick mass of jet-black hair.

"Inspector Divekar! I'm sure glad you could make it!" he exclaimed, his face breaking into a welcoming smile.

"I said I'd come, didn't I? Meet the daughter of my best friend, Sonia Samarth. Sonia, Mr. Tupay."

"Do come in, Sonia, its much warmer inside," Mr. Tupay said and waved her in.

The hall was like a mini studio, with theatre-like sets, all ready for recording. A Rajasthani seating arrangement in one corner, complete with bead pots and handmade long curtains of tiny stuffed toy animals and beads. Low cane chairs, in another corner, with a revolving swing to go with it. A plush, heavy sofa formed a ring in the center of the hall.

There were four people seated on the sofa. Three women and a man. Sonia was introduced to each one of them. Mr. Tupay's wife Medha, their daughter Revati, her friend Gaurav, and Mrs. Tupay's sister Pradnya Joshi. Sonia observed them all with a sudden stirring of interest within her. It was second nature for her to slip into the role of an observer and discover little secrets that no one was aware of. And she was certainly beginning to notice and make strange discoveries.

The similarity between the sisters was striking. Both Medha and Pradnya had single, long, thick plaits and were clad in Calcutta off-white cotton silk saris. The passing years had lent a few lines to the two attractive faces, but the hint of a frown on the brow was more than a mark of age. It was worry. The two sisters had obviously been deep in conversation before Sonia's arrival. However, the interruption had not dispelled the heavy tension in the room. Something wasn't right here. Sonia sensed it and remembered what Inspector Divekar had remarked a moment ago—"the family would profit by her visit." He had deliberately brought her here, at this late hour—but why?

"Do join us, Sonia, we were just having coffee," Medha Tupay suggested, a smile lighting up her rather tired face.

"Coffee would be a treat on such a night," Sonia surprised herself by saying. She caught Inspector Divekar's eye and was satisfied with his approving nod.

Lightening lit up the room in a flash, throwing a bright blue tinge on all the faces. The thunder rumbled as if on cue and the downpour began suddenly, rattling the wide windows. Jatin entered, barely in time, shaking off the drops at the door.

"Terrible weather, isn't it?" Inspector Divekar observed, relaxing on a sofa and Mr. Tupay joined him.

They were all now sitting, facing each other like some

round table conference. Almost as if they were ready to begin a game or a drama. Like something was about to happen. The impression was so powerful that Sonia felt strangely excited. It was odd and most mystifying. What exactly did Uncle Jeevan have in mind? Her gaze shifted to Revati. A pretty girl, slim and fair with hair swept up in a pony tail, looking young and vulnerable, in jeans and a green T-shirt. She was leaning on the arm of her mother's sofa, her eyes restlessly darting to the wall clock and then seeking those of Gaurav. But he sat, head bent, his gaze fixed on a spot on the red carpet. Gaurav interested Sonia. Of medium built, dusky with a becoming stubble, his quiet reserve placed him as an outsider. But at the same time, he was comfortable enough to completely ignore her presence in the house.

Pradnya Joshi laughed. "It's a night for ghost stories!"

"Don't, Aunty!" Revati exclaimed. "Please, no ghost stories!"

"No need to get hyper, Reva," Mrs. Tupay admonished her daughter. "Here's the coffee. Thank you, Kaki," she smiled at the sari-clad, tall housekeeper. "Did you give some to Sushil?"

"Oh yes, he's sitting right there, having it," Kaki indicated with her head.

For the first time, Sonia noticed that there was another person in the hall. A thin, dark figure, sitting unobtrusively in a shadowed corner of the hall. It was the manner in which he held his cup, in an awkward grip, as if it might fall off any minute that puzzled her. He appeared to be staring straight ahead of him, into the wall.

"What do you do, Sonia?" Mr. Tupay broke into her reflections.

"Sonia and Jatin run a detective agency," Inspector Divekar explained. "And, to say the least, it's not an ordinary agency. The interesting part is that she's an astrologer too and uses her knowledge in her cases!"

"How unique!" Pradnya exclaimed spontaneously.

"Yes, isn't it?" Inspector Divekar continued. "And she's really good with her predictions, although reading the future is not her profession!"

Sonia waited, patiently and vigilantly. Her sixth sense told her that Uncle Jeevan was treading a slow and deliberate path in a preordained direction. She had to only bide her time, wait for the Inspector to unwrap his purpose and watch out for the next cue. Which came soon enough.

"I have my horoscope in my drawer, would you mind reading it, please?" Revati asked, her voice, a peculiar combination of request and appeal.

"Really, Revati…" her mother began in protest.

Sonia flashed the inspector a glance and noted the almost indiscernible nod. "Well, to be honest, I don't usually do this kind of a thing. However, tonight can be an exception." She smiled at the girl.

"Oh great!" Revati exclaimed. "Thanks a ton! I'll be right back!"

"I'd like mine read too," Pradnya spoke up.

"Get all the horoscopes!" Inspector Divekar called after Revati. He turned to Sonia with a slow half-wink.

In a trice, Revati was back. She handed a bunch of booklets to Sonia and settled down.

"It's really good of you to do this, but…" Mr. Tupay demurred but the inspector raised a hand.

"Relax, Ritesh. This is simply for fun and it will hone Sonia's skills, won't it *beti?*"

Sonia laughed non-committally. "Before I begin, I ought to tell you the rule. Never lie to the doctor and astrologer! Like I say very often to my clients, a horoscope is an X-ray of a person. It can tell a lot. Astrology is a science but I combine it with intuition. So if a prediction is correct, no matter what it is, you have to admit it. Sometimes facts—well-guarded secrets—come to the surface. You have to make a clean breast of them. There's no point continuing with this, if any one of you is planning to play a hide and seek game," Sonia remarked in a professional voice, softening the words with an encouraging smile.

"I accept!" Revati said, promptly, "and I'm sure the others do too! Right, Dad?"

"I see no reason to disagree." Mr. Tupay shrugged but Sonia intercepted the glance he flashed at his wife.

Gaurav moved and she immediately sensed his change of stance. Gone was the reserve. Now he was observing her with frank curiosity. She unfolded Revati's horoscope and studied it carefully. The others waited and the silence was palpable. Revati leaned eagerly over her shoulder, trying to see what Sonia could see. Her childlike excitement was refreshing. Finally, Sonia looked at her and smiled.

"You're in love and plan to get married soon, don't you? I mean this year—January to December—before Jupiter changes from your seventh house."

Revati's pretty face glowed. "Yes! Gaurav and I are getting married! Could you really read that in my horoscope?"

"Yes, but I also see a problem. I don't wish to discourage you, but it's not going to be smooth sailing. And I don't mean your married life. I mean your *getting married.* I can see a lot of drama... publicity..."

Revati glanced at her parents. "You're absolutely right, Miss Samarth. Inspector Divekar could tell you all about it. You see there has been a problem, a very serious one."

"Really? Can you tell me about it?" Sonia asked with interest.

"I'll tell you." The deep voice spoke for the first time. It was Gaurav. "Revati and I have been seeing each other for the past eight months. We were in love and told our families about it. Fortunately, there is no reason for anyone to object, so we decided to get engaged. But out of the blue, Revati began receiving anonymous letters. Crude and threatening letters asking her to break off her relationship with me! At first, we thought it was some kind of a joke, but as the frequency of the letters increased, we realised that this was not to be treated lightly. It was some detrimental mind's crude idea of fun!"

"That is when they contacted me. Ritesh is an old friend of mine," Inspector Divekar explained to Sonia. "We are working on it, but it's been difficult to trace the source of these letters. Look at this latest one."

He extracted a sheet of paper from his pocket and showed it to Sonia. It was a message composed of letters cut from a newspaper. The message was brief and clear. CHUCK HIM BEFORE THE TENTH OR FACE THE CONSEQUENCE.

"But today is the tenth!" Sonia exclaimed.

"And tomorrow is our engagement!" Revati said, gloomily.

"I see..." Sonia remarked. The grave and tense atmosphere in the house now became a platform of understanding for her. What she'd sensed was a cringing anxiety against an anonymous and faceless threat.

"I'm so scared. I keep feeling something dreadful is going to happen tonight." Revati shivered. Lightening flashed through the room and crashed far away. But the sound made her jump. "Someone just walked over my grave! Literally, look at these goose bumps!" She indicated the prickled skin of her arm.

"Revati, enough!" Mrs. Tupay snapped. "We're all here. Nothing is going to happen to you. Right, Inspector Divekar?"

"Absolutely. You have no need to worry," the Inspector confirmed in a reassuring voice.

Sonia glanced at Revati and said with a smile, "If it's any comfort to you, your horoscope shows that this matter will be sorted out eventually and you will get married soon."

"It certainly is," Gaurav affirmed. "I don't like this business one bit and shall certainly be relieved when we get engaged tomorrow. It's a small ceremony. No guests, no pomp. Just family."

Sonia took up the next booklets. The horoscopes belonged to Mr. and Mrs. Tupay. She easily reeled off the combinations of the stars and what they implied. They were an obviously devoted couple and were very impressed with the way she predicted some important incidents from their past.

"But Mrs. Tupay. You have this habit…a restless nature, which never leaves you in peace. You worry a lot and at the moment something is weighing heavily on your mind."

Medha Tupay nodded. "You're absolutely right. I am basically a nervous-natured woman and I feel responsible for all the matters in my house. I am fidgety and often discontented but there's always a good reason for it. Take this business of the anonymous letters. One can't help worrying about something so serious. And then, there's Sushil."

"Sushil?" Sonia's gaze shifted involuntarily to the still figure in the corner. Sushil was sitting upright, with a napkin on his lap, staring into space. The coffee mug rested on the table.

"Who is he?" Sonia asked.

"A family member now. I guess there's no harm in telling you, since half the world already knows about it. Sushil is actually an orphan someone left at our door, an absolutely brand-new baby left in our care. I didn't have the heart to turn him over to some orphanage, so I handed him to Kaki, our housekeeper. She's like a family member too and gladly took charge of the little baby. He grew up with Revati—a healthy, intelligent boy—and both were inseparable friends. He had a good education and lacked for nothing. But somehow bad luck seemed to have followed him after all these years. A strange incident occurred about six months ago."

"What happened?" Inspector Divekar asked curiously.

"Sushil had an accident. He crashed straight into a car on the street when it halted abruptly and he was thrown off his scooter. It wasn't very serious, but he knocked his head. An oldish stranger brought him home. What was really remarkable was the manner in which Sushil, who was babbling strangely, clung to this old man like an unreasonable child. He refused to allow the man to depart. It was most embarrassing and ultimately we had no choice but to request the man to hang on for a while. Fortunately for us, he was looking for a job, so we offered him the gardener's post. Only then did Sushil relax. But ever since then, he has kept to his room. He has to be led to the dining room for his meals or for a breath of fresh air. Kaki looks after him. But he recognizes no one, talks to no one. The whole affair is really tragic!"

"Except the gardener. Sushil talks to him, but only once in a while," Kaki spoke up. "The rest of the time he stays in his room, behaving so strangely, almost like an insane person."

"Is he violent?" Sonia asked.

"Oh no! In fact, he's like a small child, lost in his dreams and fantasies. He's quite harmless, but it really is sad. I was going to ask you if you could read his horoscope and tell me if he will ever get well. You see, he's like a son to me, I'm so worried about him!"

"Do you have his horoscope?" Sonia could not hide her surprise.

"Yes. His birth details and certificate were tucked in the shawl he was wrapped in."

"How extraordinary!" Sonia murmured reflectively. "Well, of course I shall! I'd like to take a look at his horoscope myself."

Kaki hastened away to fetch the horoscope. Sonia glanced at Sushil. He sat like a statue through all the talk, the wooden expression like a face set in a coin. What did he think of? What did he see, Sonia wondered. Was he aware of them, could he hear them talk? The thunder suddenly crashed and her skin jumped. Sushil's shoulders shook for a fraction of a second. Then his figure froze again.

"Why don't you read Pradnya Aunty's horoscope in the meanwhile? Until Kaki hunts out Sushil's horoscope? I'd love to know if she will ever marry!" Revati enthused, spontaneously hugging her aunt.

Pradnya Joshi blushed, embarrassed. "You're crumpling my cotton sari, dear. And at my age I should devote my life to God, not to any earthly human being!" she remarked dryly, patting Revati's cheek affectionately.

Sonia smiled at the bantering and took up the last booklet. She opened it and stared at it a long time. Kaki returned with Sushil's horoscope and she accepted it absent-mindedly. Her eyes didn't leave the marked squares in her hand. When she did glance up, she found Pradnya Joshi's eyes transfixed on hers. Her light smile was replaced by an anxious gleam.

"Miss Joshi… I would rather like to speak to you in private." Sonia matched her gaze and her tone was grave enough to silence the background murmuring in the hall.

"Why?" Revati exclaimed tactlessly.

"Why…" Pradnya's question was a mere whisper.

"Because I may speak too much and I don't know if I *ought* to!" Sonia remarked.

Sudden fear flashed across Pradnya's face, so fleetingly, that Sonia thought she'd almost imagined it. Then tranquility stole over her entire body and Pradnya seemed to relax. Reconciled, Sonia guessed.

"Go ahead and say what you ought to. I guess, I'm ready for it," Pradnya replied, her voice controlled. She rearranged the pleats of her sari and settled against the sofa.

Mr. and Mrs. Tupay exchanged surprised glances. Inspector Divekar leaned forward, curiosity written all over his face. Revati looked hard at her aunt but she ignored her. The figure in the corner stirred, the empty coffee mug turned in restless hands. The rain pattered noisily on the windowpane like a steady pelting of stones.

"If that's what you wish." Sonia drew in a deep breath. She felt as if she was treading on hidden land mines. "Your Venus and

Mars together in the first house indicate an artistic personality. You are a lover of arts but you are also an incurable romantic. A minute ago, you said that you never married. I suppose it's true in the official sense of the word. But something happened long ago, you were in love once but it didn't work out, did it? In fact, it could have culminated into marriage but I think—no, I can *see*—that he tricked you! Am I right?"

The hall hushed. Only the crackling of the rain outside intruded on the loaded silence. All eyes were focused on Pradnya, awaiting her reaction. She looked steadily at Sonia and replied, without flinching, "Yes, you're absolutely right!"

"Pradnya!" her sister exclaimed. "What are you saying?"

Pradnya turned to face the impact of her sister's shocked expression. "You were in the last year of college then," she said, dispassionately. "I guess I was lonely. No parents to talk to, you at college… and he came into my life, when I needed a friend badly. We fell in love. He was a frequent visitor at home and we decided to get married. But the night before, he vanished along with all my jewels! I couldn't believe it. He'd always claimed that he was ambitious and wanted to be a rich man one day, but I never thought it would be with my money! He was nothing but a handsome thief!"

"But why didn't you tell us? Why didn't you tell me?" Mrs. Tupay looked hurt.

"You were engaged to be married immediately. I didn't wish to create complications," Pradnya explained briefly.

"But, Aunty, to live all these years without marriage… in memory of a man who deceived you—" Revati was shocked.

"It wasn't in memory of him!" Pradnya broke in harshly. "It was in distrust of all men! He turned out to be a rascal, going to jail several times and later even hounding me for more money!"

"You mean you met this man again?" Mr. Tupay asked.

"Several times. I can't imagine how wrong I could have been in my judgement of him. The last time I met him was some months ago. After that day, I haven't set eyes on him. Today I came down from Mumbai for the engagement, so..."

A window crashed open behind Sonia and Pradnya turned a startled face towards it. Her attention was riveted to the open window and all color had drained from her face. Seeing Pradnya's reaction, Sonia instantly whipped around, but empty space met her eyes. The glass pane shivered and groaned against the pitch darkness. When she turned around, Pradnya had recovered, her pale face composed and set in its normal mask. Her gaze rested on her manicured hands, subjecting them to a minute examination.

"But Pradnya, no marriage, don't you regret it all?" Medha insisted, unaware of any interruption.

"No, the only thing I miss in life is a child. I always wanted one but I guess fate had other plans." Her sister sighed.

"Yes, you always loved children and you paid special attention to them. You took them for outings—it was understandable, I suppose. It must be difficult not to have a kid when you love kids and always wanted one so much," Medha remarked meditatively.

"And that's why..."

Sonia cleared her throat eloquently. "Excuse me, but I haven't quite finished yet. There's something else, more private." She took a breath, then, without economizing on her words, she continued, "Miss Joshi, there are subjects which perhaps you would not wish me to discuss as evening chatter. Things which you may want to hold back from the others. Believe me, I derive no pleasure in raking up the past and making your secrets public. You may stop me now. If you wish to close the subject, do so now."

An avalanche of emotions broke loose on Pradnya's face. Sonia watched her in immense fascination. Pradnya's hands shook as she covered her face, wrestling with guilt for a moment. Then she drew them away, steadily. The dredges of conscience proved powerful enough to force the moment of truth. Pradnya knew what Sonia had to say and she was not going to turn her back on the truth.

"It's inevitable, isn't it?" Pradnya replied, with forced nonchalance. "Perhaps Providence sent you here today, to unravel the truth that I never had the nerve to admit. This is my chance to bury the past once and for all, and I intend to take it. You will be my spokesperson!"

Everyone in the room stared at them, intrigued at the enigmatic communication between the two women. Inspector Divekar frowned, then glanced at Sonia but her entire attention remained on her confessor. She held the woman's gaze and there was something bordering on admiration in her eyes.

"You said that you miss a child in your life," Sonia began, with slow deliberation. "That was partly true. You do miss him, but not because you don't have a child but because you *have* a son whom you cannot claim as yours!"

Her words fell like a bomb in the hall. Medha drew in her breath sharply and her eyes darted wildly to her husband. Revati's face registered shock and even Jatin, who was inconspicuous until then, turned in his chair.

"This is utter nonsense!" Medha raised her voice, offended to the extreme. "You are insulting my sister..."

But Pradnya raised her hand. "Sonia is absolutely right, Medha. Yes, I have a son I've never been able to call mine. When... When that thief ran away, I... I was pregnant, though I didn't realize it until later. You were married and I was against abortion. I went to a place where there were no prying eyes and delivered my baby!"

"Pradnya! You... you don't know what you're talking about!" Medha remarked faintly, clutching her husband's hand wildly. Her voice shook uncontrollably.

Her sister turned to Sonia. "If you could read so much from my horoscope, perhaps you'll be good enough to tell me where he is right now." She leaned towards Sonia and asked almost defiantly, "Where is my son?"

Sonia smiled at the older woman's challenging look. "I don't need to read your horoscope for that. I'm already aware of the identity of your son, and his whereabouts! Your son is right here, in this house and he's Sushil!" She paused, enveloping everyone with a cruising gaze.

Pradnya looked across at the figure in the corner and smiled sadly. "Yes," she admitted softly. "Sushil is my unfortunate son."

As the words were uttered, all pandemonium broke loose. Medha screamed a loud, hysterical, "No!" Kaki, the housekeeper, stood frozen like a statue at the kitchen door. Thunder clapped so deafeningly that everyone jumped, startled. Simultaneously a cup crashed, the sound drowned in the sudden clamor, which gripped the house. And then, like a masterstroke, the house was plunged into darkness.

"Oh God!" Revati exclaimed. "Gaurav, where are you?"

"Right here!"

"Kaki, get the candles please."

"Yes, sir."

"It's all your fault, Pradnya! You lied to me! You..."

"Sh... not now, Medha. Pull yourself together."

"Is the fuse this side of the hall?" Inspector Divekar asked.

"In the kitchen. I'll check," Mr. Tupay replied.

As the multiple conversation criss-crossed across the hall, Sonia rose, allowing her eyes to get accustomed to the darkness. Lightening flashed, illuminating the room for a brief moment. Shadows molded into solid shapes and casually Sonia's eyes moved to the corner. The remote figure sat in its dazed state, like a blind man, his hands placed on the table beside the napkin, a pitifully, melancholy outline. She was about to move when someone banged into her. An apology sprang to her lips but was curbed by a sudden ear-splitting sound. The shot was followed by an agonized scream of a woman.

"What happened!" someone yelled.

"Don't move anybody! Ritesh show me the main electricity switch. Jatin move towards the kitchen," Inspector Divekar snapped orders.

A cold gust of wind made Sonia shiver. Minutes later, the hall was flooded with lights and she blinked at the sudden glare.

"Pradnya Aunty!" Revati screamed.

All eyes were riveted on Pradnya, who lay in a crumpled awkward heap, on the sofa. A dull red mark was soaking her off-white blouse. Inspector Divekar pushed his way through the horror-struck family members and checked the pulse.

"Alive," he observed tersely. "The bullet grazed the right shoulder. The impact and pain made her faint. Someone call the doctor immediately."

While Sonia and the Inspector did their best to arrest the flow of blood, Ritesh Tupay telephoned the family doctor. It took a while for the doctor to make his way through the stormy night, but soon Pradnya was driven away in an ambulance.

As the ambulance disappeared in the night, Medha dissolved into bitter tears. "What in heavens is happening in this house! I hope to God she lives! I really don't care if she lied or kept secrets, but she must live! I must go to the hospital…"

"She'll be fine, dear. Just stay calm. And you will go to the hospital once this matter is cleared up," her husband drawled consolingly.

"But who shot at her? And why!"

"I hope Inspector Divekar will have an answer to that most crucial question."

The Inspector glanced at Sonia, who was staring at the door, where Kaki stood.

"This is the kitchen, adjoining the hall, isn't it?" she asked. "Can I take a look?"

Sonia headed toward the kitchen, followed by Inspector Divekar and Jatin. Kaki made way for them to pass through into the huge room. An oval jute rug was thrown in the centre of the stone slabs of the floor. On the wall opposite to the entrance of the kitchen, closets curved round a long cooking platform. A dining table was placed beside another door, along the right wall. Sonia opened the door and immediately a gush of wet wind swept into the room. She shut the door at once, shivering. Her gaze glided along the floor and caught a small pool of water, at the bottom of the wall on the immediate left. Just above the puddle of water was the electric main switch of the house.

The water trailed out of the kitchen and with a frown of concentration, Sonia followed it to the corner table, in the hall. Another puddle glistened under Sushil's chair. He sat motionless, his eyes closed and the napkin on his lap. Nonplussed, she returned to the kitchen and stood in the middle of the room. Inspector Divekar was studying two coffee mugs on the table. He touched them. They were warm.

"Kaki, did someone have coffee in the kitchen a while ago?" he asked.

"Yes, the gardener came in, wet and shivering, so I offered him some coffee. Then I went out into the hall to collect the empty cups and the lights went out. "

"But he wasn't in the kitchen when the lights were switched on?"

"No. Actually, I didn't even think of him. My first thought was naturally for my poor Sushil. But he was right there, as unconcerned and detached as ever. I guess the gardener must have left to check if everything was okay outside."

"Yes, quite likely," the Inspector agreed.

As Inspector Divekar continued his inspection of the kitchen, Sonia took her place on the sofa, meditating silently. Medha was sobbing softly now and the two lovers were talking in low tones. Jatin took the seat beside hers.

"Anything I can do, boss?"

"Any ideas?"

"The gardener?"

Sonia nodded briefly. She wished she was back in her office with the music blaringly eliminating the unnecessary details. Quite unexpectedly, a scene from a film knocked on her mind. The hero is travelling in a train and a blind beggar passes him, singing an old song. The hero listens for a few minutes, then drops a coin in the beggar's extended palm. The coin is not a reward for the quality of the man's singing but because the song has triggered some hidden memory. It has deeply touched a core, a sentiment… she recalled. The scene stuck in her brain…

Her hand casually riffled through the horoscopes lying on the glass centre table and she flicked them open, one by one. Suddenly she stiffened. A finger twirled a lock of her blunt cut, as she bent her head over a single horoscope. The seconds ticked by. Jatin waited with bated breath, an expression of awe and respect on his face. He knew his boss's mind was racing and calculating. Her foot was tapping with a mental rhythm and her shoulders swayed so slightly that only Jatin detected it. Finally, she raised her head and he caught the full impact of a triumphant glitter.

"Jatin. I need to speak to everyone. Not Sushil of course and Kaki can stay with him. I mean the rest of them and Inspector Divekar. But not here. Find out if we can meet in a quiet room. Perhaps a study?"

Minutes later, Sonia, Jeevan Uncle and Jatin were shown into a spacious, thickly carpeted study. Maroon velvet cushioned armchairs, surrounded a huge teak wood table. Mr. and Mrs. Tupay seated themselves opposite the Inspector and Jatin. Gaurav settled himself behind the table, while Revati leaned casually against it. Sonia paced the floor, lines etched on her brow.

"Are we just going to chew over the issue?" Ensconced in the deep chair, Inspector Divekar raised an inquiring eyebrow. "Or do you have an answer to this riddle?"

"Possibly, if I can straighten the muddle in my head," Sonia replied. Her cruising gaze took in each member of the family. "That's what I'm going to do, try to clear the muddle and I want you all to listen and help me. One thing puzzles me immensely. Something was expected to happen tonight—I mean everyone was waiting—subconsciously—for some kind of incident, but it was on Revati's account." Sonia stopped pacing and glanced at the girl. "She was getting the threatening letters and that was the reason why you were here in the first place, Jeevan Uncle."

"That's true," Inspector Jeevan acknowledged.

"But it was Pradnya Joshi who turned out to be the victim! Why? There are several theories to that. First, the culprit had planned this attack all along. Second, someone entirely different pulled this stunt, capitalizing on the already strained situation. And third, it was a spur-of-the-moment change of plan on the part of the culprit. If you choose the last option, then the question arises—what made the culprit change his mind? Obviously something did—was it something that transpired during the evening? Something that he or she *heard?*"

"My theory is that this is an outside job," Inspector Jeevan stated firmly. "After all, we cannot ignore that puddle of water, under the main switch and near the table."

"You mean the gardener?"

"On pretense of getting a cup of coffee he came inside, switched off the lights, then approached the table, fired at Revati as was his intention all along, but missed in the dark."

"And then left through the kitchen door," Sonia completed, nodding. "I did feel a cold gust of wind, while I was trying to gauge Sushil's reaction in the dark. But someone also banged into me a split second before I heard the shot. Someone in direct range of Pradnya with a deliberate intention of harming her!"

"So you mean…"

Sonia faced the assembled group of people. "I am merely trying to piece together a distorted picture, trying to make it a whole with some sense. We have some pretty good evidence of what happened here tonight, though at the moment it seems to have no bearing on each other! Someone banged into me, a gust of wind, and pools of water in two different spots. Now let's rearrange the course of events in the form of a story.

"Actually, it was when we were discussing Pradnya's horoscope that I got the first hint of something being amiss. She was talking about her marriage when she halted and stared at the window. She seemed shocked, as if she'd seen a ghost. She clearly saw something or someone outside. I believe it was the gardener, looking in at the window. He came in to have a cup of coffee. He waited until Kaki went out into the hall and then he quickly moved to the switch and turned off the lights. He came into the hall, banged into me, fired at Pradnya, then escaped through the kitchen door."

"But why Pradnya?" Jatin asked. "I mean what motive could he possibly have to shoot Pradnya?"

"Because Pradnya *recognized* him when she saw him at the window," Sonia replied. "He was her husband, the thief who made off with her jewels and left her pregnant!"

"What!" Jatin exclaimed.

"Her husband! What would he be doing here?" Medha Tupay asked incredulously.

"You could be right," the Inspector accepted, thoughtfully.

"But there's a hitch in this story. A point which had been bothering me," Sonia added, reflectively. "If the gardener did it, what about Revati and those threatening letters? It was obvious all through the evening that Revati was supposed to be the main target tonight. Could that mean that there were two different people involved in this business? But this incident seemed too hinged together to be played a coincidental part by two strangers. Then there's also that pool of water at Sushil's feet. How could it have got there? It surely was an important clue. Therefore, I reconsidered the evidence. There's only one way that puddle could have found its way under the table. Unless Sushil himself went out in the rain and returned to his seat…."

"That's impossible!" Revati ruled out.

"Sushil does not go unattended anywhere at all," Mr. Tupay explained.

"He has to be led everywhere. How can he just get up and go out in the rain like a normal person?" Medha protested. "Don't you see, he's unaware of what's happening around him. He's like a child, lost in his own world, he's unsound of mind."

Sonia quietly absorbed the spontaneous defense of the family members. It was obvious that they loved Sushil a lot and felt deep sympathy for him.

"Yes, I know," she agreed. "That leaves us just one other solution. Someone who had been out in the rain had taken the same position as Sushil. To be precise, *sitting* in Sushil's chair!"

"But Sushil was there all along. You saw him and so did Kaki," Jatin argued.

"Precisely. And that was how I began thinking, I mean really thinking. All evening I had this odd feeling that I was participating in some kind of charade, a drama being enacted before my eyes. There were characters in the foreground and in the background. Initially I concentrated on those who were obviously active. But gradually, others—the subtle ones screened either by their absence or immobility—came sharply into focus. I had been seeing things, hearing them, gathering disjointed information from voluntary expressions and forced confessions. The links were available, ready to be gleaned and put in a logical sequence of a composite whole. Revati and Sushil growing up together as close friends, Revati's engagement, Sushil going crazy, the threatening notes. Facts which could be coerced into a sensible whole. And that's exactly what I'm going to do now. Reconstruct another story."

Sonia's gaze swept across the room, resting fleetingly on each of the family members. Mr. Tupay—dignified and composed;

Medha—nervous and anxious; Revati—excited and restless; and Gaurav—alert and sharp. For a second, Sonia sensed a deep wave of sympathy for all of them.

"Sushil and Revati grew up together," Sonia began. "Sushil was in love with Revati, but she was unaware of it. When she decided to marry Gaurav, Sushil almost lost his mind in sorrow. Rejection gave rise to ungovernable jealousy. One day, in his distraught state, Sushil met his father, who fed him a lot of poisonous crap about the mother he'd never known, without disclosing her name. The two decided to join forces. His father stayed on as a gardener. Under his father's criminal influence, Sushil sent the threatening notes to bust up the engagement. Together they planned this evening, which would be a sort of poetic conclusion to his rejected love for Revati. Revati was totally unaware, that her life was hanging on a thread of decision. She had to either not marry Gaurav or face Sushil's bullet. Yes, I'm quite sure, that was his intention." Sonia faced Revati, who stared at her with wide frightened eyes. The young girl's face was pale. Gaurav immediately grasped her hand in a comforting grip.

Sonia swiveled back to face the others in the room. "However, when astrology forced some startling revelations, Sushil discovered his real mother. I remember how the cup slipped from his hands and crashed to the floor when Pradnya admitted that Sushil was her son. Her revelation startled him. His hate for her was stronger than his love for Revati, so instead of using the gun on Revati, he fired at Pradnya."

"I don't believe all this," Medha muttered, incredulously. "Sushil would never do something like that. Apart from the fact that he cannot!"

"Hm... interesting," Inspector Divekar remarked. "But I foresee some major problems. The first one being that Sushil *couldn't* have been in two places at the same time, since you and Kaki saw him in his place. Kaki can bear witness to that—" he reminded her.

"We both saw a figure sitting in the dark, at the table. Our eyes were only recollecting what the brain had already stored in it. We both *thought* it was Sushil on the assumption that he'd been seated there all evening. Neither of us went close enough to really vouch for his identity!"

"But how…" Mr. Tupay began.

"Let me explain," Sonia interrupted. "All evening whenever I glanced towards Sushil, he was sitting with his napkin on his lap. When the lights went out and my eyes gradually grew accustomed to the dark, I noticed that his hands as well as the napkin were *on the table*! And when the hall was illuminated again, his hands and the napkin were *back in their original position*! Why should the napkin change positions unless it was deliberately moved to unveil something—a pistol, for example? And who would change the position of the napkin without being conspicuous? Sushil, of course. But Sushil had sat like a statue, right under my nose. He hadn't even moved! Then how could the whole drama have been enacted? Something must have transpired in those few, confusing minutes immediately after the lights were switched off. What had transpired? Then quite out of the blue, the roar of confusion ceased and the answer streaked across my mind." Sonia paused to inhale a deep breath. "The man Kaki and I saw was not Sushil!"

Inspector Divekar and Jatin exchanged startled looks.

"What exactly do you mean?" Jatin exclaimed, clearly bewildered.

"This is ridiculous!" Medha complained querulously, glancing at her husband for support. But Mr. Tupay was studying Sonia intently. Gaurav and Revati stared at her curiously.

"I think you need to explain yourself," Mr. Tupay suggested.

"Let me complete my story. According to plan, the gardener entered the kitchen on the pretext of wanting some coffee. When Kaki left the room, he switched off the lights, then moved swiftly to Sushil's table. There, under the cover of darkness, they quickly exchanged places, because it was Sushil who was supposed to do the firing. But at the same time, if anyone checked, he needed to be found seated in his place. So the gardener took his position at the table, pretending to be his son. Sushil took the pistol from under his napkin and in the dark banged into me. He shot at Pradnya, hastened to his seat again, and his father slipped out through the kitchen door. That's when I felt the cold gush of wind. When the hall was again illuminated, it was as if Sushil had never budged an inch. The deed had been done, but Sushil, for all appearances, had all along remained in his chair. A most infallible and perfect alibi!"

A loaded silence ensued. The Tupays seemed stunned and even Mrs. Tupay, who had vehemently repudiated all accusations against Sushil, was at a loss for words. Gaurav was regarding Sonia with a look of respect on his face.

Inspector Divekar frowned deeply into his reflections, staring hard at Sonia.

"The pistol?" he finally asked.

"Still under the napkin," Sonia replied.

"And the fact that he is claimed insane by a good many people?"

Sonia smiled and held up Sushil's horoscope. "Moon—the controlling planet of the mind and Mercury—the planet related to brains and memory—are both in excellent and auspicious conjunction with Jupiter. You wouldn't find a clearer, more logical person with total control over his mind and body!"

Inspector Divekar stood up, taking in Sonia's confident stance. Then his eyes flashed his admiration and he gave a nod of acceptance. He wheeled around and with Jatin and the others in tow, marched out into the hall.

Sonia heard the action rather than saw it and with a sense of immense satisfaction, she relaxed into the study armchair. The case had been solved.

CHAPTER V

The Right Map

College boys whizzed past on mobikes, shouting "Happy Independence Day!"

Sonia, driving along in her van, waved back at the beaming, youthful faces. Patriotic songs were booming on the loudspeakers all around the city, adding to the heightened national sentiment in everyone's heart.

The morning sun filtered through a light drizzle, spreading a heavenly glow on the city. What a beautiful day it was! Sonia breathed in the air deeply. It felt fresh and clean and smelt of wet mud. She smiled with satisfaction. She loved peaceful Pune!

At her office gate, Sonia halted, as a group of teachers, attired in creaseless white saris, walked past. Uniformed school boys and girls trailed obediently behind them, chattering noisily. Each one of them carried a miniature paper flag of India. *These children are the future of our country,* she thought idly. *Do they really understand what freedom means and what it cost us,* she wondered. As the crowd disappeared, Sonia turned the van into the parking. She took a minute to examine the rose buds in the garden, listened to a cuckoo sing melodiously, then climbed the three steps to her office. Television sounds emerged loud and clear from the inside. Jatin had begun the morning well! Sonia let herself in and stared at her assistant. He was dressed in a ceremonious spotless white khadi kurta and pajama and even matching foot wear of Kolhapuri chappals.

"Happy Independence Day, boss!" Jatin greeted Sonia cheerfully, handing her a plastic saffron-white-green flag.

"Thank you, Jatin! You look fresh and different today." Sonia smiled, accepting the tricolor flag which was pasted on a stick.

He glanced down at his clothes with pleasure. "The occasion deserved special effort—khadi kurta. It's Independence Day after all. I even attended flag hoisting in our housing colony."

"Good. I'm going to place this flag on my almanac shelf!"

"And I'm going to put it on my tele, so as to remind me that I owe my present democratic existence to freedom fighters who lost their lives for a free country!" Jatin announced.

"Good idea. What are you watching?" she asked, glancing at the TV.

"The 15th August Independence Day celebrations at the Red Fort, in Delhi."

Sonia stood beside Jatin and viewed the stiff, alert figures of the Navy, Army and Air force battalions standing in attention, awaiting the arrival of the Prime Minister. He arrived soon enough, responding to the guard of honor with a salute. Then, amidst a reverent silence, he hoisted the flag. The tricolor fluttered gracefully in the wind as the crowd began the national anthem—*Jana Gana Mana*. Then the Prime Minister took his place behind a bulletproof dais and began his speech.

Celebrations were in full swing all over the country amid tight security, which had been spiked because of suspected terrorist attacks. Going by the enthusiastic thousands that had gathered to watch the flag hoisting at the Red Fort—terrorists or no terrorists—it was apparent that nothing dampened the festive spirit of the Indians.

"Isn't it wonderful? I experience such immense thrill to watch all this—look, I have goose bumps on my arms." Jatin showed her his prickly skin. "I never miss the Red Fort flag hoisting. It reminds me—"

"I know," Sonia interrupted. "Free spirit, duty, what you owe this country—"

"You got it!" Jatin nodded. "And that's exactly why I also attend office, on 15th august, when the whole of India has a holiday!"

"You're a good boy, Jatin," Sonia conceded. "But I thought it was more the fear of loosing a likely case that made you refuse to stay away from this office even on Sundays, than your spirit of vacationing! And it was your choice to come here today, not mine."

"I know, boss." Jatin grinned sheepishly.

Sonia smiled back at him. "And that's why I shall allow you to continue viewing the celebrations for a while."

"Thank you," Jatin acknowledged. "You're a good boss too. And I'm not the only one who thinks so. There is a special bouquet and a newspaper write-up on your table." His impish grin spoke volumes.

Sonia raised an eyebrow enquiringly, then stepped into the inner office. Immediately Nidhi demanded attention with welcoming meows and Sonia had to put her curiosity on hold, until the cat was fondled and was sufficiently satisfied. Then she turned to the bunch of roses, placed on the table. The card said—Happy Independence day! From Mohnish. A newspaper write-up lay beside the bouquet and Sonia quickly scanned through the article. With every word, her amazement increased. It was a glowing report on Sonia Samarth's excellent investigative capacities. Courtesy Mohnish Rai.

Sonia perched on her chair thoughtfully. Her eyes inadvertently swept over the article again. She didn't know what to make of this approach. What did Mohnish have in mind? It was a kind gesture, of course and she had to appreciate it, without any doubt. The report on the Tupay case was pretty accurate. She had to give Mohnish his due. Besides, the article was a ray of hope amidst the recent spate of news write-ups on Stellar Investigations. There were no names mentioned but the jokes on astrology and disrespectful comments on how people treat criminology rankled. The remarks were most unfair, biased and unjustified. At least Mohnish had tried to represent her side of the story and given an unprejudiced view of her technique in the Tupay case. Sonia touched the beautiful peach-colored roses and rising, placed the vase near the window. Nidhi meowed, rolling lazily on her pillow. Sonia sat down beside her and fondled her.

"Yes, my lucky charm. What next?" she whispered to the cat, adjusting her leather collar.

Nidhi stared unblinkingly up at her mistress, held out her paw, and drew Sonia's hand to her face. She laughed. "I get it! You want me to take a break so that I can give you some attention, don't you? But can I afford breaks?"

In response, the cat licked her hand lovingly.

The intercom rang and she spoke automatically. "Yes Jatin?"

"Mr. Mohnish Rai to see you," came Jatin's crisp reply.

Sonia straightened with a start and then blushed at her own uneasiness. Now what? She ought to see him and thank him for the article, she told herself sensibly. However, she wouldn't let him cajole her into an interview if he behaved as high-handedly as the last time, her stubborn side decided. Her feminine side quickly set into action, passing a comb through her already immaculate hair, adding a touch of pink lipstick and glancing critically but not without satisfaction at her reflection in the little mirror. The ice-cream pink *salwar kameez*—delicate but not impractical—sat well on her trim, fit body. She looked efficient and professional. The only thing she wasn't pleased about was the eager, anticipatory look in her honey–brown eyes.

Sitting in her chair, she took a deep steadying breath and asked Jatin to send Mr. Rai in. The door opened and Mohnish strode in.

"Happy Independence Day!" he greeted brightly. "I'm glad you're working today and consented to meet me." The dimple in his cheek was already on exhibit as he took a chair.

"Well, I had to thank you for… for… this." Sonia waved her hand at the roses and the newspaper article. "Though, why you went to all that trouble…"

"No trouble whatsoever!" Mohnish brushed her words away. "It's my duty to report anything exceptional—whether it's an individual, an event or both! And I specifically wanted that article to be published today because I think it goes with the basic concept of independence—a unique representation of the real free and emancipated woman of India."

Sonia smiled, feeling awkward. "And the flowers?"

"That is my instinctive response to someone beautiful and intelligent!"

She could do nothing to prevent a blush from stealing over her face! "Thank you," she responded with a smile.

She observed his gray–and–yellow checked shirt, blue jeans, and the leather pouch round his waist. He was certainly good-looking and very charming. And his voice was exceptional. He was perfect in the role of reporter and television presenter. But what drew him to this office, she wondered.

"What brings you here today?" she asked, leaning back against her chair. "More curiosity? I can satiate that right away—I love to read, meditate, go for long walks," she spieled off. "I love listening to music, sometimes I dance all night! I celebrate Christmas and I believe Santa comes on Christmas Eve with gifts."

"Christmas? You're a Hindu, aren't you?" Mohnish asked instantly, then grinned good-naturedly. "Thank you, I'm highly enlightened. And curiosity *is* a long-lasting reason—I admit I'm very curious about you. In fact, you *intrigue* me. But I'm afraid your brief bio-data is not going to easily douse my interest in you. In fact, it has now fanned it. However I shall tackle my personal issues at a later, more convenient stage—today I am here on business!"

"Really?" Sonia's eyes instantly flared with interest.

"Yes. Recognizing your inherent talent at solving mysteries, I have brought you one myself," he replied.

Sonia searched his face for sarcasm but finding none, allowed herself to relax into her natural professionalism. "Do you mean a personal case—a problem?"

"Well yes, but that we shall tackle later, when you're less busy. This is a different mystery."

"What kind of mystery? Something to do with the Owl?"

"No—though that too is definitely something else we may discuss one day. Have you been reading about the Kapoor case in the papers?"

"Yes. And I've heard about it from Inspector Divekar."

"A most interesting story. You may be aware of the details but I'll just run through them, since it's important to do a little revision. A month ago, Mrs. Kapoor went to the police station to report her missing husband. They had had a fight and Mr. Kapoor had walked out in the middle of the night and vanished for a whole week. He had this habit of walking out on her and returning after several days, so she didn't worry initially. However, after a week had elapsed, Mrs. Kapoor began to fret and thought it wise to report his absence. "

"Unfortunately, the very next day, Mr. Kapoor was found dead on a railway track. An apparent case of suicide. Mrs. Kapoor claimed that he was constantly threatening her that he would one day commit suicide and unlike others, he'd actually done it!" Sonia completed the story.

"But that's not all. She gave an obituary in the paper with Mr.

Kapoor's photograph. Now, this is where I come in. Another woman saw this photograph. She claimed that the man in the photograph was her missing husband! Now what do you make of it?" Mohnish observed Sonia with narrowed eyes.

She tapped her pen reflectively on the table. "How long have you known this second woman?"

"She's a perfect stranger to me! In fact, she's a stranger to this city. When she—her name's Neha Gulati—saw the photograph, she was at a loss what to do. Apparently, she feels some kind of distrust for the police, so she went to the nearest social service Nari Kendra, you know that home for homeless women. The owner happens to be a friend of mine and I was sitting with her when this lady arrived."

"I see… And you thought this would be a perfect case for me?" Sonia arched a dark eyebrow enquiringly.

"I thought that woman needed a fair hearing and representation. Will you take her case on my behalf?"

Sonia held Mohnish's penetrating gaze without blinking. "Are you convinced that she was not lying?"

"There isn't the least bit of doubt in my mind. I 'm convinced that she was speaking the truth. Poor, though she obviously appeared, she seemed absolutely genuine to me. But of course, you have to trust my judgement on this." He shrugged eloquently.

"I think I'll try my hand at that—I mean trusting your judgement!" Sonia smiled and he grinned.

"Thanks! Can I call Neha in?"

Neha Gulati was in her early thirties, short, clad in a crumpled cotton *salwar kameez* which had seen better days. Her hair was rolled untidily into a bun; a red bindi clung crookedly to her forehead, which already displayed a smear of *sindoor,* and she continually fidgeted with her dupatta, wrapping it around her head. She carried a small cheap suitcase. But for all the signs of poverty, there was a real dignity about her, which struck Sonia.

Mohnish introduced the two women, requesting Neha to sit down and narrate her story again.

"I live in a small town in Uttar Pradesh," she began in Hindi and with a tiny start of surprise, Sonia realised that she was literate. "My husband—Tusharji—did all sorts of odd jobs, but he could never settle on anything permanent. One day, he told me that he had bagged a fantastic job, one which would change our fortune. The only hitch was that he would have to go to Pune. I was unhappy about this job but I had no say in the matter. In our community, we women simply obey orders. My husband went off and wrote to me occasionally. But he never once mentioned his job, where he was working or living. This was almost six months ago. For the last two months, I've had no letter from him, no news, and I began to get worried. I thought perhaps he'd been thrown out of his employment and that he was ashamed to tell me about it. So I set out to bring him back home. But... but... the moment I arrived in the city, I bought some potato-vada to eat, wrapped in this newspaper... and I saw... this—" Neha's voice broke as she indicated the photograph in a soiled local newspaper.

Jatin immediately produced a glass of water and she accepted it gratefully. Sonia and Mohnish glanced at each other. His face held a questioning look. Sonia took the newspaper from Neha, studying the obituary.

"I understand your predicament, Neha," Sonia sympathized, "but tell me, are you positive that this man is Tushar Gulati?"

"I can swear on God that this man is my husband!"

The silence that followed was only broken by Neha's occasional sniffs.

"And do you know why this photograph has been printed in the paper?"

Neha nodded. "Mohnish *saheb* has explained to me. But how is it possible? How can my husband be in any way connected with this Kapoor woman and they... they say he is dead? I don't understand! I simply don't understand! Oh, what am I to do? I'm so terribly confused!" She choked over her tears.

Sonia did her best to comfort Neha but the woman seemed inconsolable. Finally, she gestured at Mohnish to come out into the outer room, leaving Jatin to do his bit as she carefully closed the door behind her.

"What do you think *now?*" Mohnish asked.

"I'm glad I trusted your judgement," Sonia replied with a half smile. "That poor woman is almost crazy with frustration and misery. Where will she live, while we adopt our course of action?"

"At the Nari Kendra of course!"

"Good, because this may take a few days. I shall have to consult Inspector Divekar since he handled the Kapoor case. It could be a rather unpleasant situation—finding out if the dead man was indeed Tushar Gulati. Bigamy is not uncommon these days, you know, but proving it, especially when the man is dead, could be extremely disagreeable!"

"Do you think this is what it is—bigamy?" Mohnish asked curiously.

"It is a possibility one must consider. However, if it's my intuitive opinion that you are seeking, then no. I suspect foul play. But my suspicions, until proved, are quite baseless."

"So what's your next line of action?" Mohnish asked, folding his arms.

"Meet Mrs. Kapoor, find out what I can about her married life, if she permits me to, of course. In the meanwhile, I think you should take Neha to the Kendra."

"But what about her horoscope? Don't you need it to proceed on the case?" he asked, a trace of innocence in his tone.

For the first time, Sonia burst out laughing—a healthy, bubbly youthful laugh that chimed liked a bell. Mohnish waited patiently for the peal of amusement to subside.

"Well?" he asked. "May I share the joke?"

"Actually—I'm sorry—I didn't mean to be rude." She looked up at him with twinkling eyes. "It's just your assumption ..."

"But you're the one who works with horoscopes!"

"Yes, I do," Sonia said in a more sober tone. "But it's not as if I *hunt* for horoscopes before I *look* for facts, at the first scent of a crime! I treat astrology like a map when I arrive in a city—a map that will guide me and help me navigate myself in the desired direction. However, before I embark on the journey to that city, I need to gather information—facts, knowledge about the journey as well as my destination. Initially I work with facts and investigation. Then if I reach a deadlock or a fork in the road, I use my map—which shows me the precise route or alternate options. At the moment I am still at the pre-destination stage and I have no intentions of vaulting over facts!"

"Got it!" Mohnish grinned sheepishly.

"I'm not saying I may not need Neha's or Tushar's horoscope," Sonia pointed out. "I may resort to astrology, at a later stage, after I have given enough opportunity and scope to my fact-finding, investigative capacities and when I need to reconfirm or reconstitute my findings!"

"You're trying to tell me that astrology is not the magic wand most people might make it out to be. In your policy, astrology goes hand in hand with the facts."

"Precisely. Some may regard my technique of solving cases with a great deal of suspicion and perhaps even disbelief, because they don't believe in the science of astrology. But to tell you the truth, such an attitude bothers me the least. They are unaware that the Vedic Astrology principals and predictions are the outcome of thousands of years of statistical study of the magnetic cosmic forces and their effects on our lives. Anyway, my total belief in the science of astrology sanctions my modus operandi. To put it plainly, astrology delivers the goods to those who believe and study it and I believe, study and practice it!" She did not add that she'd been rewarded with results. She had seen her mental confusion dissolve, her arguments keel over, and answers emerge out of a blank horizon. No, she wouldn't tell him about it. Words would merely undermine the value of her personal experience—a premise secluded from prying eyes. Instead, she turned to him and smiled. "Let's not waste any time. 15th August, our independence day, is an auspicious day to knuckle down and begin cracking this problem!"

Mohnish straightened with alacrity. "Right! I'll be on my way. And you'll keep me posted on your progress? I'll call you up from time to time."

Sonia nodded.

Mohnish hesitated. "Thank you," he said simply.

"Actually, I ought to thank *you* for trusting me to find Neha's husband," she responded.

"That was not a problem. Surprisingly, I do trust you," Mohnish stared at Sonia, as if gauging her reaction. Then he smiled. "Well, see you later then."

Sonia stood still for a moment, feeling his presence after he'd left. Which was odd…

Jatin stepped out into the outer office. "Neha is okay now," he informed Sonia. "But boss, I was right, wasn't I?"

"Right?" Sonia looked a little confused.

"About not taking a holiday on Independence Day? We have a new case!" Jatin pointed out, unable to contain his excitement.

"You were absolutely right!" Sonia agreed whole-heartedly.

The auto rickshaw—a three-wheeler scooter—trundled over the speed breakers, on the long stretch of Sinhagad road. The smell of diesel seemed to fill the auto, as it chortled and grunted noisily. Seated on the brown cushioned seat which had a big tear in the middle, revealing the stuffed cotton, Sonia glanced outside. Her eyes flew from the piece of paper in her hand to the passing buildings. Although Inspector Divekar had taken a day to ferret out all the details of the case for her, he had given her exact directions to the Kapoor residence.

Vehicles zipped past, unruly and uncontrollable in the morning rush, but the rickshawala nonchalantly managed to avoid brushing sides with his road-fellows. He whistled, unconcerned, as the vehicle, jumped and steadied over small ditches.

"Slow down a bit please," Sonia told the driver of the auto rickshaw. He slowed down, passing a bakery, a laundry, a chemist and a vegetable mini-market. "You can stop here," Sonia said, as she spotted the Kapoor house.

The auto jerked and stopped by the side of the road.

"How much do I pay you?" Sonia asked, as she rooted around in her handbag for a copy of the tariff card.

The driver, in a khaki shirt and a handkerchief tied around his forehead, glanced at the meter.

"Thirty rupees," he replied casually.

"Thirty!" Sonia exclaimed. "Are you sure? Where's your tariff card? It's supposed to be pasted on the back of your seat."

"What Madam, have some trust," the rickshawala remarked a little indignantly, in Marathi. "Children tear it off, so one can't put up a tariff card."

Sonia found her card and checked the rate. The fellow was charging two rupees more than the normal rate. "It's twenty-eight rupees!" she told him sternly.

The unabashed rickshawala smiled carelessly. "What Madam, everything is so expensive, can't afford anything and then, what is two rupees to people like you?"

"Why, do I look as if I grow money on my head, instead of hair?" Sonia asked him sweetly. She slapped the exact amount on his hand and stepped out of the auto.

The rickshawala shook his head and drove away muttering at the miserliness of rich people. Sonia threw a resigned look after the receding auto. Basically, she hated haggling over trivial matters. But this was more a matter of principle than just two rupees. Anyway, with her van gone for maintenance servicing for the day, she had little choice but to travel by public transport. With a sigh, Sonia turned to the Kapoor residence.

For a few minutes, she observed the house, before passing through its small, black rusted gate. It was a ramshackle building, looking almost as if it had been hit by a gigantic hammer. The walls were discolored and revealed damages. Certainly a very old house in need of serious repairs.

Sonia walked up the overgrown path and rang the doorbell. Immediately a melodious tinkling, most incongruous with the dilapidated structure, receded into the house. Footsteps hastened towards the door and it was opened by a house cleaner.

"Madam is not at home," she explained, in Marathi, before Sonia could utter a word.

"When will Mrs. Kapoor be back?"

"She's gone out with Jaidevsahib and said she would be back soon."

"In that case, I'd like to wait for her," Sonia replied, stepping into the sitting room.

The maid shrugged and silently made way for Sonia to enter. The girl was attired in a red printed cotton sari with the bottom half of the pleats tucked in at the waist to avoid hindrance. Apparently, she was sweeping the house.

The room was small—a neat sitting room with relatively new furniture. A small two-seater sofa set, a thick red square rug and a landscape on the wall comprised the decorations of the room. On the wall opposite to Sonia, hung a garlanded photograph, which revealed an unlined, smiling, near-profile of a man. A backlight shone on his shining hair. It was obvious that the photo was taken in a professional studio.

"This is Mr. Kapoor, isn't it?" Sonia indicated the photo with a hand.

"Yes, he passed away just recently, poor man," the maid responded sympathetically. "Did you know him?"

"No—but I'd like to know about him. You see I am an investigator and—"

"You mean *jasoos*—like in films!" The maid excitedly tucked her sari around herself and seated herself comfortably on the floor. "But you don't look like a *jasoos,* an investigator."

"No, I guess I don't," Sonia agreed, with a rueful smile. "Have you been working here for long?"

"Ever since Madam arrived here. She and Sahib were looking for a *bai*—a maid, so they spoke to the Kulkarnis, who told their maid, who told my sister. She said to me—Rama, you've lazed around for long, here's a nice job, take it. So I accepted it! And I've been so fortunate, both are such wonderful people!"

"And when did you first come to this house—I mean how long ago?"

"Sometime in March. I remember, I asked Madam, if she wanted me to help her make pickles or anything else but she wasn't interested. She never made jams or pickles, like the rest of us women. I think all the time she simply thought about Kapoorsaheb."

"Was Mr. Kapoor unwell?"

"Oh no, he was a fine sturdy man and healthy. But alcohol can ruin a person!" Rama spoke knowledgeably. "Not that he used to drink all day. He drank occasionally but when he did drink, there was no controlling him. They had loud quarrels so that all the neighbors could hear them shout and screech at each other. We fight too—my husband and I—but even we maintain a kind of decency. At least my husband never goes to other women with his worries!"

"You mean that Mr. Kapoor was in the habit of going to other women.?"

"Oh no!" Rama exclaimed hastily. "I meant that he would behave funny. You won't mention this to anyone? You look like a decent woman, yourself, so I can tell you the truth! He would come to me and blabber a lot of strange things—I blush to tell you what he would say in his drunken state! He told me that I reminded him of someone. That he had lots of money and would give it to me. It was very indecent talk for a man of his stature and class, with a beautiful wife like Madam and me just a poor house cleaner. But he was a nice man. I'll never forget what he did one day. He came into the kitchen after one of those terrible fights, held my hand and slapped some money onto it, asking me to use it all on my children. It was very wonderful of him, but of course, I didn't take his money. I gave it to Jaidevsaheb. After all, it isn't right to take advantage of an intoxicated man. Poor though we are we have our principles!"

"Yes of course," Sonia agreed with a smile. "But how was he when he was sober?"

"Oh a fine man—spoke in the most respectful and dignified manner, never even glanced in my direction. What a difference drinks made to his personality—it was shocking!"

"And did you ever hear him mention committing suicide, when Mr. and Mrs. Kapoor quarreled, for example?"

"Suicide?" Rama's eyes flickered thoughtfully to the photograph. "Only once. I'd just come in and I heard Madam telling him never to mention suicide again. She was awfully upset and sobbing and I felt quite sorry for her. But he was a strong man, Kapoorsaheb, and I never thought he would take his own life. But he did, didn't he?"

Sonia nodded thoughtfully. "Tell me about Jaidevsahib. Is he Mrs. Kapoor's brother?"

Rama burst out into laughter. "Hardly! He's their family friend—the only friend I saw around here—apart from the neighbors of course. A decent, polite man, highly educated and always around to help the Kapoors."

"How did Mr. Kapoor and he get along?"

"Oh, famously. Quite often, it was Jaidevsaheb who would resolve their quarrels and put sahib to bed. They slept in separate rooms, you know." Her voice dropped to a whisper.

"And I've noticed..." She halted abruptly and stood up swiftly. "Madam is here! Would you like something to drink?"

"No, thanks." Sonia turned to meet the tall, slim lady who stood at the door, staring at her in surprise.

A pair of light brown eyes flashed a curious mix of hostility and bafflement. Clad in an off-white sari, Mrs. Kapoor approached Sonia with quick strides. The widow's straight hair fell in a loose, silky curtain on her back. A tiny mole on her right cheek added a hint of mystery to the beautiful, flushed face.

"Who are you and what do you want?" she demanded softly.

Sonia quickly introduced herself as Inspector Divekar's niece. "I'm here on routine enquiry," she explained, carefully masking her quickened interest. From the corner of the eye, she noticed that Rama had slipped away.

Mrs. Kapoor instantly dropped her unreceptive attitude and smiled sadly. "I'm sorry—I mistook you for one of my pestering neighbors. Kind though they are, they do overdo the condolence bit. Please, sit down. How can I help you?" She took the armchair opposite Sonia's.

"I won't take much time. I simply need to ask a few questions. I know you must be upset and I really don't wish to intrude on your privacy anymore than I must!"

"It's a trying period, you know. Apart from the grief, there is the melancholy picture of a long dreary, lonely life..." Mrs. Kapoor's eyes moistened.

"I can imagine. But I understand, that you—if I may say so—didn't exactly share a cordial relationship with your husband?" Sonia asked, cautiously.

Mrs. Kapoor sighed. "You must've heard reports from the neighbors," she stated simply. "And I cannot blame them. Dhiresh—my poor husband—did exhibit a massive temper from time to time and he had no qualms about expressing it loud enough to shake the earth. But I love him a lot and he loves me too. However, he would sometimes go through bouts of depressions. He would frighten me—talking about suicide, about walking away from my life forever—and…and.. he went and…and… did it! I still can't believe it!" She lapsed into sudden silence and Sonia allowed her to compose herself.

"You have recently moved to Pune?" she ventured, after a respectable interval had elapsed.

"Yes. We lived in Delhi—my husband changed his job and so we came to Pune. He… he had a tendency of changing his jobs, rather too often for my liking—but I suppose it was his flaring temper and his reputation—anyway, this was the only decent place we could afford. The rent was reasonable and the area good. Besides, Mr. Jaidev—my husband's friend who'd offered to take him up as a partner in business—lived in the same locality. Mr. Jaidev has been of invaluable help to me!"

"In Delhi, what did he do? I mean, where did your husband work?"

"In a bank. He was the manager," Mrs. Kapoor said briefly.

Sonia paused before she remarked softly, "Mrs. Kapoor, I need to ask you an important question, please do not take it wrongly. Did Mr. Kapoor have a girlfriend? Or if I may put it crudely, another wife back in Delhi?"

"That's preposterous!" Mrs. Kapoor's beautiful eyes flashed in anger. "Whatever may be his reputation otherwise, Dhiresh is the most loyal husband I ever saw! He never looks at another woman and inspite of everything, he loves me a lot!"

"I'm sorry, I didn't mean to upset you." Sonia rose to take her leave. "Thank you for your co-operation, I hope I don't have to bother you any more."

Mrs. Kapoor was struggling to control her fraught emotions, her color slowly returning to normal. She nodded but did not rise. Sonia stood looking down at her for a moment. She did not have the heart to tell her that another woman had claimed her husband. She walked out of the house with a meditative expression on her face.

"How did your interview with Mrs. Kapoor go yesterday? Any theories?" Inspector Divekar asked, on the telephone.

"Actually yes, a working theory… But it's rather premature and I'd rather keep my own counsel for the moment. Jeevan Uncle, will you do me a favor?" Sonia asked. She was at her table, scribbling notes on a pad. Nidhi sat on her lap, curled awkwardly, but refusing to leave her mistress's lap despite the discomfort.

"Shoot!"

"Can you ask Mrs. Kapoor for documents, papers of identification? Anything from her marriage certificate, to ration card and of course horoscopes!"

"Is this another `routine check-up' or are you really on to something?"

Sonia heard the smile in her Uncle's voice and grinned. "Too soon to confirm either. And yes, I'd like Jaidev's horoscope too. After all, he is very closely connected with the family."

"Oh! Do you suspect some kind of a love triangle? Wife wants to marry the friend, so she gets rid of the inconvenient husband?"

"Why not? It does happen, everyday, all around us. Although Mrs. Kapoor seemed genuinely in love with her husband, but you can never tell! And to say the least, it pays to be skeptical in our line. Anyway, the horoscopes will help establish the relationship, if there is any!"

"I get it. Papers of identification are an excuse to get to the horoscopes." Inspector Divekar laughed. "My dear girl, trust your instincts, never mind what the world says! Be bold enough to demand what you need! You really have to walk rough-shod over a lot of egos, opinions, jokes, criticism and ill-humour to reach the ultimate goal—results matter, never mind what the process of achievement is!"

"Jeevan Uncle, thank you for that pep talk!" Sonia remarked sincerely. "I'll remember your advice every time I falter in my steps!"

"Good, but what if the Kapoors haven't got their horoscopes made?"

"Quite unlikely, unless they are total atheists. But if that's so, you can ask for their exact birth date, time and place."

"Right. The horoscopes will be with you within the next hour!"

Sonia replaced the receiver just as Jatin walked into the office. "What have you found out?"

"The reports are identical. The neighbors are well-versed with the Kapoor arguments, since those two never restrained themselves. But when sober, he seemed to care for her. To all appearances, a normal pair of husband and wife—the usual round of fights and then making up. But he did have a tendency to leave her in the lurch and vanish for a few days."

"Hm…socializing?"

"In the neighborhood mostly—birthday parties."

"Standard of living?"

"Comfortable."

"Any doubts raised or hints pointing towards Mrs. Kapoor and Jaidev?"

"None."

Sonia pondered this information. Nidhi uncurled and stretched on her lap. Then, sensing her mistress's obvious unconcern and unresponsiveness, she reluctantly jumped on to the windowsill. Sonia followed her actions absent-mindedly, her thoughts on a different plane. A vision rose involuntarily before Sonia's eyes. Her neighbor's child speaking to her mother. Mother talking to someone else. Impatient child deliberately drawing her mother's face towards herself to demand attention. The image was momentary and gone in a flash. Now what on earth had brought that incident back to her? Sonia sighed. Her mind had an eccentric and incomprehensible existence of its own!

"How about Neha Gulati?" she asked Jatin. "Did you ask her if she can produce Tushar's horoscope?"

"I did, but naturally enough, she did not have it in her possession. In fact, she doesn't seem to remember seeing it in years! And she cannot remember Tushar's birth details either."

"Her mother-in-law? She will most undoubtedly remember her son's birth details."

"She lives in the village up north. Difficult to get to her on phone and a letter would take too long," Jatin explained matter-of-factly.

"But what about a telegram? That will be quick enough," Sonia pointed out.

"I hadn't thought of that! In the age of emails, a telegram seemed to be farthest from my mind!" Jatin conceded with a sheepish expression.

"In a vast and complicated country like ours, you have to conform to any means of communication! Delay does not hamper dependability! Send a telegram immediately asking for the son's birth date, time and place. And in case, there still remains a problem of literacy, I'm sure the village postman will be useful—they normally are!"

"Very well. Anything else, boss?"

"Nothing for the moment."

Just before noon, a small packet was delivered to Sonia's table. Inspector Divekar had been true to his word. A note was attached to the three horoscopes, written out on separate sheets of paper. *She was hesitant to part with the originals, so she made out copies which I am sending. Since my man gave her a very natural and valid reason, she suspected nothing. He also got them written in front of him, so I think it is safe to assume that she didn't try any hanky-panky!* Sonia smiled at the note. Jeevan Uncle was a gem.

She turned on the music and romantic instrumental piano filled the office. It was a tune she liked. The horoscopes lay on her desk and a ripple of excitement ran through her. She experienced a heady feeling every time she touched a horoscope. It was like the thrill before a journey—only, at such times, the journey was into a person's psyche, making inroads deep into the mind of an individual, reading his secrets as clearly as if he himself had bared his heart to her. She enjoyed the power that strode straight into her hands. The power to gauge and to study human nature for an undeniably excellent cause. Certainly, no amount of displeasure and criticism was going to demoralize her or cramp her style. She had a gold mine in her hands and she knew perfectly well how to put it to good use. The music was already encouraging and stimulating the most positive thoughts within her, she realized with a smile. She swayed with the romantic soft notes, closing her eyes, allowing the music to envelop her in a magnetic cocoon. Ten minutes later, she opened her eyes and approached the desk, her whole body tingling with anticipation.

Sonia placed Dhiresh Kapoor's horoscope on the left, his wife's in the center and the third paper on the right. For the next forty-five minutes, the next piece of piano filled the room, first with slow cautious notes, then rushing on with full, powerful bangs. Nidhi, yawned, strolled, rubbed against her mistress's legs and finally meowed in protest at being ignored. It was only when a hand passed over her with a casual disregard for her mood and affection that the protests ceased into low murmurs of perplexity. What could be so important as to occupy her mistress's attention when she, Nidhi, was around?

Sonia stared in fascination at the first two horoscopes. The Moon, Ketu and Uranus in Mr. Kapoor's first house. And Neptune in Mrs. Kapoor's first house, face to face with Uranus in her seventh house. A strange couple but most ideally suited! Eccentricity bordering on cruelty! Capable of almost anything—even murder? Sonia frowned, but it was Mr. Dhiresh Kapoor who was dead; he had committed suicide, not murder. Her eyes flicked to the third horoscope. Jaidev's horoscope. Nothing extraordinary about his career, a clean chit on the character front and the normal ups and downs in life. Jaidev seemed a safe type except for the extreme bad phase on the health side. Instinctively she felt that she ought to warn him—it was a period for accidents, sudden happenings, he needed to look after himself.

Sonia's gaze reverted to Kapoor's horoscope and she frowned. Here was a horoscope which showed a distinctive, shady past. The cloud of doubt in her mind began to take the shape of a singular idea. The more she thought of it, the more concrete it seemed to grow! She felt an instinctive distrust for this man. Mr. Kapoor deserved to be checked out.

She rang the buzzer and Jatin came in immediately. He put his hands expressively on his ears and hastened to turn off the music system! "I thought you would never call a lunch break! I'm famished," he admitted, cheerfully. "Should I order lunch for you?"

"Lunch?" Sonia asked absent-mindedly. "No no, not yet. I want you to do something for me before that!" She barely noticed her assistant's fallen expression as she rasped the instructions at him.

"But why dredge up information on Dhiresh Kapoor? He's dead and of no use to us!" Jatin objected.

"Existence is not a precondition to knowledge! Anyway, Dhiresh Kapoor may be dead, but he didn't live in a void. He had a past, a life that was as real as yours or mine. Moreover, the law of nature dictates that our past always overtakes the present to affect our future and the future of our near and dear ones. Mr. Dhiresh Kapoor needn't be an exception to this rule!"

Jatin nodded as he jotted down her instructions. The pen weighed heavily in his starved, weak hand! It was unfair working on an empty stomach. He would have to make this objection clear to his boss in their next official meeting! Feeling most disgruntled, he returned to his table and picked up the receiver, dialing 183 for telephone enquiry. How in heavens was he going to trace the bank numbers!

Nevertheless, half an hour later a very different Jatin rushed into the inner office. His eyes gleamed with satisfaction as he burst into the room.

"Your hunch proved right, boss! I spoke to the manager of the bank of Delhi and he gave me a detailed report on their ex-manager Mr. Kapoor! You'll love to hear this! Kapoor was accused of embezzling money from the bank! And the amount is huge! About 2 crores!"

"Wow!" Sonia exclaimed. "So what happened?"

"Unfortunately, nothing happened. Before any legal action could be undertaken, Kapoor vanished from Delhi. The police searched high and low for him, but he did a clean disappearing act!"

"Obviously, he came here to Pune, with the noble intention of starting a new life all over again! But the guilt wouldn't permit him to live peacefully. That's why he committed suicide..." Sonia remarked contemplatively. "You know, Jatin, crime is a little like drinking liquid in a moving vehicle. It's very tricky business. You may succeed in drinking a sip or two but invariably, some of the liquid spills on the ground, or on the dress, leaving telltale marks. Sooner or later, those marks are discovered! How did the manager react to the news of Kapoor's death?"

"He did not mince words! He thought the man deserved a prison sentence! They had some rather incriminating evidence against him."

"Did *you* tell him about Kapoor's suicide?"

"Oh no. He read about it in the papers."

Sonia paced the floor of the office, meditating deeply. "I

wonder if his wife knows anything about the money, now that Kapoor is dead. I'll have to meet with her again."

"But boss, what about Neha Gulati? Where does she fit in all this mess? Is he or isn't he her husband Tushar?"

"Honestly, I'm as much in the dark as you are! However, I *have* formed a vague, foggy picture from the statements of Rama the maid, Neha and Mrs. Kapoor. The common features were that he frequently changed jobs, was educated, dignified when sober, but spoke of lots of money when drunk. It is now pretty obvious to me that the man who embezzled the money and Mr. Dhiresh Kapoor are one and the same. But is Dhiresh Kapoor Neha's husband Tushar? There's also the fact that he kept telling Rama, that she reminded him of someone—if it was not his wife, then who could it be? It could be Neha, but then it could be someone else. So, there's a possibility that he could be Neha's husband but I am not confident enough to publicize my conclusion. Something's holding me back—obviously a lack of concrete proof—and I simply can't seem to conquer the feeling that I'm way off the mark!"

"But you *are* gaining ground, boss!" Jatin smiled encouragingly.

Sonia returned the smile. "Of course we are! Goodness, I can hear hunger rumbling inside me! Why haven't you ordered lunch? How many times have I told you, not to skip lunch for work? My brain simply refuses to respond on an empty stomach!"

"Right away!" Jatin hastened out of the room, hiding a smile.

Sonia gazed across the room at Mrs. Kapoor and Jaidev. The latter was of medium height, an almost hefty man in his late thirties with a few gray hairs immediately above his forehead. But it was his ever-shifting gaze that struck Sonia. Jaidev's small coal-black eyes seemed to be constantly searching, without focusing on anything particular.

"It's true that my husband was accused of embezzlement," Mrs. Kapoor conceded, in a low voice. "But he didn't do it!"

"How can you be so sure?" Sonia asked gently.

"Oh because I know my husband!" Mrs. Kapoor exclaimed with sudden spirit. "He would never do anything like that! He told me so and I believe him!"

Sonia frowned. "But if you were so convinced of his innocence, why did you both suddenly leave the city and come to Pune? Why didn't you fight it out and get his name cleared?"

Mrs. Kapoor flashed an appealing glance towards Jaidev, who sat placidly at her side with a non-committal expression on his face. Receiving no aid from him, she turned to Sonia with a sigh.

"Will you believe me if I tell you that I had absolutely no idea why we suddenly left Delhi? My husband simply announced the change and all I did was follow. It was only when we came here that I realised, by and by, that something was not right. My husband had become an entirely different person. One evening, in a moment of acute depression, he confided in me. He was bogged down by the hounding unjust accusations and couldn't face the injustice of it all! I think that was the main reason why he committed suicide. He realised that the *badnami*—the bad name—would follow him wherever he went!" Mrs. Kapoor said in a sad voice.

Sonia folded her arms. "I'm afraid I still fail to understand why he fled from the accusations instead of taking them by the horns, so to say!"

"You don't understand because you didn't know my husband. He was a weak kind of person, unable to cope with the pressures of life, kind-hearted, who wouldn't hurt a fly! He found life unbearable if he saw a mother hitting a child or if he saw a child throwing stones at a dog! He was a total misfit for this hard and cruel world. That's the reason why, when the world turned against him, he took the chance of leaving it forever!" Mrs. Kapoor spoke with a distinctive reverence in her voice.

"Mr. Jaidev, do you agree with... this character sketch of your friend?"

"She couldn't have expressed it better. Mrs. Kapoor has described my friend perfectly," he replied, gravely.

"Thank you, both of you," Sonia remarked, picking up her handbag hastily. An idea was beginning to juggle in her mind, and she realized that she had to get out of the confines of this location. The stagnant atmosphere of the house and the overhanging feeling of death suddenly seemed to suffocate her.

Without preamble, she headed towards the gate, opened it and for a moment, turned around and glanced at the building. The house, she thought, looked like a stale cake without its icing and crumbling at the corners.

"Here's the telegram! With all the details you need!" Jatin handed his boss the paper.

Sonia almost snatched it in her eagerness. "It's taken long enough! I've been waiting for this bit of information for three days. And I had to keep all my theories suspended in the meanwhile! From this information, I can write out Tushar's horoscope."

Without further ado, Jatin inserted a cassette and a ghazal floated soothingly into the air. Sonia immediately turned to the shelf. Her hand traveled along the almanacs of different years, paused on the one she was looking for, then carried it to the table. She looked up the month and referred to the time. On a plain paper, she began drawing the horoscope. Her pen plotted the chart with the numbers which represented the different zodiac signs. It was when she began filling the squares with the constellations that her heart began an unexpected tattoo. She'd seen this combination before! In fact, she'd seen this horoscope several times in the past week. Hastily, she completed plotting the horoscope. Then riffling through the documents on her desk, she produced the other three horoscopes. With an almost feverish anticipation, she brushed aside the mess on the table. Her trembling hands carefully laid out all the horoscopes side by side. Mr.Dhiresh Kapoor, Mrs. Kapoor, Jaidev and… the fourth and final one—Tushar! Her gaze moved back and forth, a stunned expression on her face. There wasn't an iota of doubt. This was Jaidev's horoscope all over again, number by number, star by star! And with the clarity of lightening, the pieces of the puzzle converged into a shocking truth.

Sonia leaned against her chair, fighting to compose herself. The wave of excitement at the sudden discovery of the truth—stark and horrible—was ebbing slowing, leaving her cold and weak. She had to act quickly before it was too late.

She rang her buzzer and Jatin popped his head in.

"Yes, boss?"

"Jatin, you have to leave immediately—I want you to fly to Delhi—today. You have work to do!"

"Fly!" His eyes shone. "I've never been in a plane before…"

"There's always a first time!"

"Yes but can we afford it? Five or six thousand one way… that makes it twelve thousand rupees! What's so urgent?" he asked sensibly.

"Everything! We don't have a moment to loose! As for the money—this is a risk I must take! Now listen very carefully and make no mistake about it! You have to work fast and efficiently!"

Jatin caught the infectious streak of anxiety mingled with excitement and without another word, whipped open his pad. Her instructions followed one after the other.

"And remember, the moment you lay your hands on it, call me directly! I shall be near the phone all of tomorrow morning!"

"Right boss! I'm going to love this!" Jatin rubbed his hands together, an anticipatory gleam in his eyes.

"If all goes well, I'll be glad too!" Sonia remarked, on a more sober note. "Now get going."

Sonia paced the room, her eyes shifting restlessly from the telephone to the wall clock. It was past ten. The offices in Delhi should be open by now. Why hadn't Jatin called? She slowed her frenzied steps, shaking her head. There was no need to get panicky. She couldn't change the past but she had done all she could for the present, to see justice done. She had rung up Inspector Divekar and he had promised to follow her lead. The rest would have to wait until the proof was in her hands.

The phone shrilled like sweet music into her reflections. Sonia rushed to pick it up.

"Boss? I've found it! You hit the nail dead on the head!" Jatin's excited voice rang into her ear.

"Excellent work, Jatin! I promise you a raise for this case!"

"Wow, thanks, boss! It took me some time, going through all the newspapers, contacting their offices. But I found it ultimately!"

"You can fly back now and don't forget to bring the paper with you! In the meantime, I'll set the cat on the mice!"

"I can't believe it! You did it again! With the same technique—I wonder what the critiques will have to say about this one!" Inspector Divekar asked with a guffaw.

"Wait a minute! I'm still in the dark about a lot of things," Mohnish interrupted.

They were all sitting in Sonia's office—Inspector Divekar, Mohnish, Jatin and Nidhi—the privileged one—on Sonia's lap.

"I have yet to be told the whole story," Mohnish insisted. "All I know is that Mrs. Kapoor and Jaidev have been arrested for murder. So those two *were* romantically involved and had to get rid of the husband?" Confusion was written on his handsome face.

Jatin glanced at his boss, candid admiration in his expression. "Boss, why don't you explain the hows and whys of it? I'd love to hear it too!"

Sonia smiled a little bashfully. "Sure!" She caressed the cat with a loving hand. "But first let's have some *chai* with plenty of milk!"

After Jatin poured out the hot beverage, Sonia continued, "On the face of it, this did seem a very simple case of bigamy. Until I met Rama the house cleaner and Mrs. Kapoor. They narrated some rather contradictory things about Mr. Kapoor, which sometimes rang true and often rang curiously made-up. Dhiresh Kapoor kept referring to another woman whenever he was drunk and with Rama—that made me wonder if he was indeed referring to Neha. But then again he also claimed that he had money and that did not fit the description, since Neha's husband was a poor fellow. I realized later that what he meant was that he *would be getting a lot of money!* What was also strange was the way Mrs. Kapoor moved from the present tense to the past tense whenever she spoke about her husband. She seemed confused and at the time, I excused her, thinking that she was prostrate with grief and a distraught person and was finding it really hard to cope with her husband's death!

"Then I had the opportunity of going through the three horoscopes and I got a clear insight into the natures of each person. It was when I saw Mr. Kapoor's horoscope that I noticed the inherent crookedness of character and something stirred in my mind. I decided to check up on his record at the bank, where, true to my suspicions, we discovered that he was involved in a fraud of 2 crores! When I confronted Mrs. Kapoor with the accusation, she gave me such a graphic and pathetic description of Mr. Kapoor that she almost managed to convince me! She would have been successful too but for the fact that the devoted and glorified image of her husband that she created for my benefit was in direct contrast to my readings of his horoscope. That was the point where this whole business began to ring entirely untrue and I began to have serious doubts about the couple.

"Also, keeping in mind the fact that Dhiresh had embezzled money from the bank, I wondered why the couple had not changed their name when they came to Pune. I mean, that would've been the obvious thing to do. Change their names and settle in another place, so as to start life all over again. Especially, if you are guilty. But what really clinched the matter were Tushar's birth details! When I charted his horoscope from the almanac, I got a shock. Neha had claimed that Mr. Kapoor was her husband, so going by her claim, Mr. Kapoor's horoscope should have *matched* her husband's horoscope! But that was not what happened. It was Jaidev's horoscope, that was an exact duplicate! This mix-up floored me for a moment until truth dawned! I had two options before me. If Jaidev's horoscope matched Tushar's, then Jaidev ought to be Neha's husband, which he *wasn't*! And if Mr. Kapoor was Neha's husband, then his horoscope ought to have matched Tushar's, *which it hadn't*! Since both these calculations misfired, I decided to approach the problem from another angle. Keeping Neha's claim as the right hypothesis—that Mr. Kapoor was actually Tushar—I matched *the horoscope with the face—Mr. Kapoor's face*! And realized that that was exactly what Mrs. Kapoor had done! She had refused to give the original horoscopes and had copied them down for us. Only, while doing so, she had changed the names, or should I say, she had left the original names intact. She labeled Jaidev's horoscope as Dhiresh Kapoor and put Jaidev's name on the other horoscope!"

"But why would she do something like that?" Mohnish demanded.

"Because she wanted to take no chances. She realized that we had begun to suspect something. At the same time, she dared not tamper with the horoscopes, perhaps because she was aware that a good astrologer can figure out if anything is amiss with the horoscopes. So quite ingeniously, she changed the names to confuse us."

"But you *read* the horoscopes, found out the natures and even got the lead of the bank fraud! Neha's husband was not involved in any of that," Mohnish pointed out.

"True, though I didn't get the bank lead from Jaidev's horoscope—which is also Tushar's horoscope—I got it from *Mr. Kapoor's*!" Sonia accepted.

"Hold on a minute! I can't seem to follow this..." Mohnish interrupted.

"Let me explain," Sonia put up her hand. "When Mrs. Kapoor put her husband's name on Jaidev's horoscope, all she did was *put the right name—or the real name—on the right horoscope*!"

"What! You mean..."

"Exactly. Jaidev is the real Mr. Kapoor and that means Mr. Kapoor is alive!"

"Then the other Mr. Kapoor...I mean, the man who died?"

"Was Neha's husband, Tushar!" Sonia disclosed. "It was an infallible, premeditated plan. But for a few chance loopholes, they would have been successful! Mr. Kapoor—I now mean Jaidev—embezzled money from his bank. To shake off the constant threat of the police they devised a brilliant plot. Kapoor met Tushar one day and found out his penchant for changing jobs and his weakness for money. They offered him a good deal. Tushar was to impersonate as Mr. Kapoor in Pune, so that everyone recognized him as Mr. Kapoor. They offered him a great deal of money against total secrecy. Tushar accepted. The poor chap had no idea what the Kapoors really had in store for him. As per their strategy, they would get rid of him—which they did—then they would announce the death in the papers and put an end to Dhiresh Kapoor and the bank fraud! In due course, they would have moved to another town and lived happily ever after with their loot!"

"But what about the photograph in the obituary? Surely, that would give their plan away. After all, people in Delhi recognized the original Mr. Kapoor even if the Puneites did not!"

"Yes, I thought of that, too. So I sent Jatin all the way to Delhi to check out the newspapers. To my great delight, the proof we needed fell straight into his hands. The obituaries in the Pune papers, given on a different date, had Tushar's photo in them. But the Delhi papers had *Jaidev's* photos on them! It was a daring plot but the Kapoors obviously banked on the Delhi-Pune distance and the short memory of human beings! It was sheer bad luck that Neha recognized her husband from the newspaper," Sonia finished with a satisfied smile.

"Brilliant! Absolutely brilliant detective work!" Inspector Divekar enthused.

"Yes, but I have a question. What was Tushar's horoscope doing with Mrs. Kapoor?" Mohnish interposed.

"I think it was simply good thinking on the part of the Kapoors. They'd clearly worked out their plan to the last detail. They knew that there certainly would be a police enquiry once Tushar was found dead. Some kind of documents would be needed—which they were—"

"But wouldn't it have been simpler to say that the horoscope was lost or got misplaced in the Delhi-Pune transit?"

"I don't think so. Even today, we treat the horoscope with respect. People may not entirely believe in them or find them indispensable, but that does not stop them from getting their horoscopes made. Impulse and curiosity betray the so-called scientific and logical mind. The urge to find out more about our future proves stronger than common beliefs and rationality. Human beings live with this paradox all their lives! So, in this case, a refusal to give the horoscopes under any pretext would have perhaps roused suspicions. It was safer to give the horoscopes, since it bought them some time, and the Kapoors like the majority of our lot, under-estimated the power of the stars. They also saw no reason to worry since they planned another vanishing act soon enough!"

"Yes, you were absolutely right there. Your warning prompted fast action. I put two constables on guard outside the Kapoor house. And sure enough, a van did arrive to pick up their luggage! That was good foresight! Fortunately we were on the spot to put a spoke in their wheel," Inspector Divekar chuckled. "So, all's well that ends well!"

"Poor Neha. It really pains me to pass on this bad news to her," Sonia said with a troubled expression.

"I'll do it for you, if you like," Mohnish offered, then added gently, "it's not just bad news that you deliver to her. It's also justice done! You've managed to catch her husband's murderers—I think that would satisfy Neha!"

"I hope so." Sonia sighed.

"I'd better get going, Sonia. I have loads to do! But I'll keep in touch." Inspector Divekar took his leave and Jatin went to see him off.

Mohnish observed Sonia quietly. She wore a pure white chikan salwar kameez with a string of fake pearls round her neck. Her face was bent towards Nidhi. An inner glow of tranquility was reflected in her expressions and actions. A lock of silky hair swung loose and covered her profile and absently, she tucked the errant strand behind her ears and glanced up, meeting his candid gaze. For a second, their eyes locked, then she turned away, a slow blush crawling over her neck.

Mohnish smiled and raised an inquiring eyebrow. "Well? Your map—your horoscope—took you to your destination?"

"Yes, my ever-faithful map!" Sonia smiled. "What will poor Neha do now?"

"I think she has plans to stay on at the Nari Kendra. They find her very useful, doing odd jobs and helping around with the work. I can assure you that she will be perfectly happy there!"

"That at least relieves my mind!"

"Good, because I want you to relieve my mind too! I've been waiting anxiously for this case to get over so that I can make you a request," Mohnish said, with a cheeky grin.

"You mean you wish to discuss your case?" Sonia remembered.

"Well, not quite. It's something else."

"I'm not going to give you any appointment for an interview!" Sonia laughed.

"Then how about an appointment for dinner?" he asked, with a twinkle in his eye.

Sonia blushed again. "Just the two of us?"

Mohnish nodded, his dimple prominent in the right cheek.

"And we won't discuss cases?"

"Anything but that!"

"And we'll go to a lovely, cozy place?"

The dimple deepened. "Paradise on earth!"

"Sounds fine to me, but first I shall have to ask Nidhi! What do you say dear?" Sonia fondled the golden fur and the cat meowed her response. "Oh, I'm afraid she's given her permission!"

"She knows what's best for us!" Mohnish laughed and Sonia joined in.

CHAPTER VI

Marriage Jitters

"I don't believe it!" Sonia laughed.

"You better believe it!" Mohnish replied.

The evening sun on the Shaniwar Fortress, made the old stones glisten and shimmer. The 1736 historical monument, partly destroyed in a fire, stood in the centre of the city and still drew tourists in large numbers. It was a place synonymous with Pune and its cultural heritage. In front of the grand entrance, stood the magnificent statue of the eighteenth century Maratha General Bajirao Peshwa I. People still admired this undefeated general, who had brought the downfall of the Moghul Empire at Delhi.

On the right of the spiked gates, the fast food stalls made good business. The *bhel puri* and *ragda patties* stalls were mobbed by children and parents, in their best holiday mood. Laughter rang out among the clusters, attired in colorful saris and salwar kameezes.

Sonia observed Mohnish minutely, as they stood in front of a *paani puri* stall. Was he joking or serious? She couldn't tell with Mohnish. In a lemon yellow t-shirt and cream trousers, he looked the picture of innocence. And the dimple in his right cheek, which now staged an appearance, was so disarming that she knew she would believe him if he said the earth was square.

"You mean you have a flower shop *and* a photo studio?" Sonia confirmed..

"Yes." He nodded solemnly. "And I don't think it's funny that you doubt it!"

"Okay. I'm not trying to be rude. But you?" Sonia emphasized exaggeratedly. "This sophisticated, classy freelance journalist, with a cell phone—in a flower shop—the picture just doesn't fit!"

"You'd be surprised if I revealed all my activities to you!" he shot back.

"You mean there's more?" Sonia's eyes widened in amazement. "You'd better tell me all—I really don't want to be staggered with shock!"

"Okay then, don't say I didn't warn you. I own a flower shop, a photo studio and a garage!" Mohnish announced.

"And yet you need to earn your living as a freelance journalist and reporter!"

"Not quite. I freelance as a hobby—not as my bread and butter!"

"Well, I won't believe you until I find out for myself. Or until I read your horoscope! By the way, what is your zodiac sign?"

"Can't you guess? I thought you guys could look at a person and predict such things?"

Sonia pushed her plate forward for another round of *paani puris*. The vendor added the boiled potatoes and sprouts to the puris, dipped them in the tamarind water, and placed each fat, round *puri* on her plate. Sonia always had a problem stuffing the whole *puri* in her mouth without spilling the tamarind water all over her dress. But the mouthwatering dish was too tempting to be considered a means of indignity! Mohnish was more adept, she noticed, as he neatly popped a *puri* into his mouth, without displacing a single drop! He savored the burst of spicy liquid in his mouth.

"So, can you guess my zodiac sign?" he repeated.

"I think I can take a guess. Your ascendant is Scorpio, "Sonia stated emphatically.

Surprise flickered on his face, but he dipped his head and polished off his last *puri* before saying, "Justify, please."

"Are you ready to take the good with the worst?" she asked, with a grin.

"Oh–oh that doesn't sound too good for me," he chuckled, as he paid the paani-puri vendor.

They strolled down the road and over the bridge, oblivious to the jostling crowds and the traffic whizzing past. A light drizzle began and Sonia raised her face to meet the fine rain. She was glad she'd agreed to take the evening off. Mohnish had proved to be a most interesting and intriguing companion. And the evening had granted more than promised, to say the least. They walked leisurely over the bridge, the cool wind riffling up Sonia's silky blunt hair.

The Mutha - a major tributary of the Mula river - river flowed silently below them. Pune city flourished around their confluence. Several bridges joined the two sides of the town and in the fast dimming evening glow, the bridges appeared like a group of thin arches fading into the horizon. Pune city stretched on either side of the river—a wild, unruly combination of the very old, quaint rickety wooden structures with the ultra modern concrete buildings; of natural fauna, tropical trees and parks; and temples, mosques and churches signifying the curious and amazing mix of religions and castes. Pune, with its *gallis*—small alleys, which were the adventurous walker's delight—was an eternal source of fascination for all visitors. And for die-hard Puneites like Sonia. She threw a look of appreciation at the sprawling city, soaked in the drizzle of the setting sun. She glanced at Mohnish, who was staring at her with a faint smile on his lips.

A group of street dogs followed them, wagging their tails. Sonia threw some of the biscuits that she always carried in her handbag. The tails wagged harder in appreciation, as the dogs gobbled down the biscuits within seconds, then curled up on the uneven pavement contentedly. Sonia smiled at Mohnish.

"What were we talking about?" she asked casually.

Mohnish grinned. "You were telling me about my zodiac sign," he reminded.

"Oh yes! You're a Scorpio. Scorpios are dynamic, loyal and family-loving..." Sonia began.

"That I am," Mohnish agreed promptly.

"But they are also vindictive, shrewd and cunning!"

"That I'm not!"

"Scorpios are dangerous people to cross; they always remember a wrong done to them."

"Hey, that's not fair," Mohnish protested.

Sonia laughed. "I can perfectly understand how you feel, sometimes astrology can be pretty cruel!"

"Right! And what is your zodiac sign? Gemini? I believe they're the most flighty!"

"That's a myth. I'm a Sagittarius—and please spare me the boredom of a character sketch! I still have to learn to accept the crevices in my character gracefully!" Sonia smiled.

Mohnish's glance flickered to her curved lips and then to her twinkling eyes. Her sense of humor was appealing. As was her unselfconsciousness. She was refreshingly unconcerned about her looks—which made her seem like wild flowers dancing with the wind...

"Is it true? Can you deduct, looking at a person's face, what his zodiac sign is?" he asked suddenly.

"Sometimes."

"Suppose the Owl were to stand before you, would you be able to recognize that this guy's a criminal?"

"The Owl—you mean the crook?"

"Not just a simple crook. He's a genius. Light with his fingers, agile on his feet, and I heard that he possesses a super IQ."

"Wow, sounds like an interesting man. Have you seen or met him?"

"As far as I know, no one has met him. He's so well–hidden and disguised that he could be the next guy on the street and you would never know. But there are speculations about him—that he's stolen some of the best heirlooms in the world, he's handsome and dangerous and has houses strewn everywhere, travels in his own jet…"

"All stolen money."

"Some of it. The rest is well-invested and well-distributed. He's even rumored to have made generous donations to social organizations!"

"I really must meet this man."

"But would you be able to pin down his zodiac sign?" Mohnish persisted.

"I really couldn't say. It's not as if, if you're a criminal, you've got to have such and such a sign or if you're not, vice versa. Astrology is far more complicated. But yes, sometimes you can take a guess. Sometimes your star sign is so imbedded in your personality, that you can immediately spot the sign. But there's no rule."

A marriage procession trailed down the crowded street and Sonia and Mohnish's attention was riveted on the cavalcade. A live musical band, consisting of a keyboard, trumpets and drums played the latest Hindi film number. The youngsters of the group danced along with the music, leading the bridegroom on a heavily decorated white horse, while the more elderly family members, followed him sedately. It was a grand procession, a display of sparkling clothes and jewels. Someone burst firecrackers and they exploded into a thousand diamonds against the sky. Sonia tried to take a peek at the groom's face as he passed her. But a huge garland of flowers covered him from top to bottom. With a shrug, she turned to Mohnish and grinned.

"I love weddings! And I love to watch the groom's face when he's on horseback—sometimes enjoying it, sometimes feeling terribly out of place!" She laughed.

"Tradition can make you feel equally good and foolish," Mohnish agreed.

"I guess that's true. Going with the changing times, tradition can either enrich or embarrass. It all depends on the way you look at it." Sonia glanced at her watch. "I'm afraid I have to leave. I promised my Mom that I would go to a friend's place with her."

"But we still have to discuss my case. Remember I told you about it?"

"Yes, I do, but there's a snag. I don't mix business with pleasure. I'm afraid you'll have to take an appointment and come to the office, one of these days." Sonia shrugged exaggeratedly.

"Oh, but this won't take more than a minute..." Mohnish deliberately added to the light banter.

"I've never been accused of being partial to anyone before. And I would be called that, if I break my own rule. So, no business with pleasure!" Sonia laughed. "Unless it's so important that you've lost sleep, appetite, and weight over your problem. And I see no signs of any such changes in you."

Mohnish chuckled. "So, I'll reserve my case for a rainy day, right?"

"You got it," Sonia agreed.

For a moment they looked at each other, the intimacy of shared pleasantries soaking into their friendship.

"Need I say that I thoroughly enjoyed myself today and that we must go out again?" Mohnish remarked, on a more serious note.

"No, you needn't," Sonia replied. "And I too look forward to another evening like this."

Mohnish watched her climb gracefully into her van and drive away. She really was unique. And with every passing moment, his need for her company was forming into something more long-lasting and permanent. Which was good, wasn't it? he asked himself. And for the first time, doubt uncoiled in his mind. Was he heading the right way? With a troubled sigh, Mohnish turned toward his car.

Sonia stroked the silky head of Nidhi as she curled in her lap. She glanced at the roses on the table and frowned. The card displayed the words "Secret Admirer". Was this Mohnish's idea of fun? If it was, she should tell him to stop squandering his money on flowers. There were other ways of impressing her.

The door opened and Jatin popped his head in.

"There's a lady here who says she simply must see you," Jatin informed.

"So send her in," Sonia remarked.

Jatin hesitated.

"What's the matter?" She stopped cuddling Nidhi, who immediately busied herself with cleaning her face. Sensing that more was on the way, Sonia turned her full attention on her assistant.

"Should we allow her to just barge in and meet you? I mean, without either appointment or a call? And you with a cat on your lap?"

"Jatin…"

"After all, boss, you're quite famous now and you should demand such formalities!"

"Jatin."

"An appointment, maybe a week later, a little display of work pressure—all these things go a long way in creating a good impression! It would help prove how busy we are. Busy is the keyword for success and increased clientele. Besides, you rarely discuss money! You should permit me to take care of that important detail in the outer office. Each client should pass through me..."

"Hey, hold it right there!" Sonia raised her hand, struggling to hide her amusement. "You've been reading that 'How to be Successful?' book, right?"

"How did you guess?"

Sonia sighed. "I am an investigator, aren't I?" she mocked, then, seeing the hurt on his face, added quickly, "I've seen you reading that book, hour after hour, so it was no big deal. However, I wish you wouldn't follow the advices as golden rules. It helps to bend our all–busy schedule for an urgent case, okay?'

"Okay!" Jatin grinned and pivoted on his heels toward the door.

Sonia sighed again. Jatin was so uncontrollable at times. But also indispensable...

Minutes later, he returned with a tall, slim girl, in a Salwar Kameez. Her shoulder-length hair was confined to a rubber-band. The white Lucknow Kurta was creaseless but her good–looking face was flushed and her gaze very anxious.

"Miss Sonia Samarth? I'm Aarti, Aarti Vaze. You simply must help me!" the girl exclaimed.

Sonia indicated the chair. "Do sit down and tell me how I can help you." She nodded at Jatin, who whipped out his pad and drew another chair.

Aarti opened a brown handbag, delved into its depths and extracted a sheaf of papers. "These are the horoscopes of my family. You need them, right? I've heard so much about you!"

Jatin sought his boss's eye. Distraught women always left him floundering. But Sonia remained cool. She accepted the horoscopes without glancing at them.

"Miss Vaze, I think you need to calm down. Take deep breaths and count till ten. Go on, do it..."

Aarti looked taken aback, but she obeyed. She took a deep steadying breath and closed her eyes. When she opened them, she appeared more composed.

"Now, start at the beginning and tell me what's bothering you," Sonia commanded gently.

"I'm a teacher at H.A. School. I teach the primary classes. Two months ago, we had a school function and Pradeep Gupte—a well-known painter—was invited as chief guest. We chatted over the official lunch for a few minutes. He was young and handsome and quite charming. The next day, he arrived at my door-step—I live in the school premises—with flowers. From that day, we met regularly and fell in love with each other. We felt so good together, so right that it wasn't at all surprising when he proposed. I was the happiest soul under the sun! Pradeep introduced me to his family—his parents, their adopted daughter Meera and his sister Beena. They were all very nice to me. It was wonderful. Here, I was—an orphan with no family—and all of a sudden I was going to have a whole brand new family who genuinely seemed to like me! I thought that finally life was really being fair to me. But…." She paused.

"What happened?" Sonia prompted quietly.

"A few days ago, I overheard an argument between Pradeep and his parents. I gathered that they—Aai and Baba, Pradeep's parents—had been very keen on his getting married to the daughter of a family friend. She comes from a cultured, rich family and is well-suited for Pradeep in every possible manner. But Pradeep has refused. He claims that he loves me and that he will marry no one but me!"

"How nice of him," Sonia said.

"Yes, I loved him all the more for it. But that conversation told me enough—that all was not as well as it seemed. That I was not a natural choice for Aai and Baba and that they were not really happy with the match. They were simply playing along for their son's sake."

"Yes, I guess that's pretty common in our society," Sonia agreed. She was watching Aarti worriedly. So far, the young woman hadn't divulged any real, serious reason for her distraught state.

"We're getting married two days from now. For the last week, I've been living with the family. Aai and Baba insisted that since I have no one, I should stay with them and enjoy all the preparations."

"That was very kind of them, wasn't it?"

"Yes. I thought so, too. But of late, I've been having this strange feeling that something's not right. I can't place my finger on it—it's just a gut feeling that something strange is going on. And I'm frightened!"

"Have you seen or heard anything? What is it exactly that you fear?" Sonia probed.

Aarti shook her head energetically. "Just low voices in conversation, Beena and Meera and sometimes Aai and Baba and even Pradeep and Meera. And I've been getting these headaches, which make me very dizzy. I found some powder at the base of my coffee cup. I couldn't help wondering if I was being drugged!"

"Why would anyone do such a thing?"

"I haven't the faintest notion! I told you, I've nothing concrete to tell you, it's just a feeling."

Sonia rested her hand on Aarti's and pressed it reassuringly. "Do you know what I think? I think these are marriage jitters. You've spent a childhood and youth nurtured on loneliness. Fending for yourself in this wide world has been your major task, taking up all your energy. And out of the blue, a whole new life and possibilities are unfolding before you. I think anyone would be more than a little overwhelmed by so much happiness. Too much of anything, all at once, especially since you've rarely had it, can be pretty damaging. Especially if you fear that it's all too good to be true! What you need is to keep your mind on an even keel. Just relax, stay calm and enjoy the feeling of getting married. You deserve all the good things happening to you, Aarti. So don't let anything worry you," Sonia advised, smiling.

But Aarti looked doubtful. "Are you sure? Just marriage jitters? Nothing else?"

"As of now, I'm quite sure. But leave these horoscopes with me, since you've brought them. By the way, how did you manage to get hold of the entire family's horoscope? I mean, it's not as if one can find horoscopes strewn around the house, for all to see?"

"The family astrologer—Guruji—had been over to fix the wedding date. I quickly copied them, when no one was around. It would have looked mighty suspicious if I'd asked for the horoscopes openly."

"And extremely awkward to explain," Sonia agreed, sympathetically.

Aarti leaned forward impulsively and clutched Sonia's hand. "Will you at least do me a favor? Will you attend the wedding? I'm getting married two days from now. Will you please come?"

"Aarti..." Sonia began patiently.

"Please say that you'll come!" the girl pleaded. "I'll feel so much safer!"

Sonia looked into Aarti's moist brown eyes. Could this be more serious than it appeared?

"Okay, if you think it'll make you feel better, I will. But believe me, you'll be fine," she reassured with a warm smile. She felt a sudden affinity for this orphaned woman, who was little more than a girl. Something about the honesty in her face appealed to Sonia.

"Thank you! I'll send you the wedding card, so you know where to come." Relief had flooded over Aarti's face. "And... And if I discover something concrete, can I pass it on to you?"

"Of course, anything of the slightest importance. Goodbye,

Aarti, and all the very best for your future!" Sonia proffered her hand.

"Thank you for seeing me. I'm already feeling better after talking to you." Aarti took Sonia's extended hand with a nervous smile, then quickly departed.

Sonia gazed absent-mindedly at the closed door. It was some time before she realized that Jatin was staring curiously at her.

"Boss, did you mean that?" he asked. "I mean the explanation about marriage jitters?"

Sonia flopped down on the window seat beside Nidhi and stroked her. "She'd nothing to tell us, Jatin, absolutely nothing—no incident, no proof, no tangible fears. Unless she can pinpoint what's worrying her, it'll have to be put down to marriage jitters, I'm afraid."

"But she seemed so positive about her fear," Jatin reminded her.

"Yes, but who can vouch for its gravity? It could be a figment of her imagination, stemming out of the excitement of the latest incidents in her life."

"You could be right," Jatin mused, sounding disappointed. "So the case is closed?"

Sonia laughed. "We never had a case!"

"And will you read those horoscopes?"

Sonia glanced at the papers, bound by a rubber band, on the table. "I may..."

"And are you going to attend the wedding?"

"Yes, since I promised. That's the least I can do to allay her fears."

"How about some chai?"

"That's exactly what I need."

Jatin closed the door behind him, leaving Sonia alone with her thoughts. Her glance rested on the stack of horoscopes. Should she? It could be a waste of time. But it was not as if she was buried under an avalanche of work. And no urgent matter was hankering for her attention, either. On the other hand, what if she found something worthwhile? Could Jatin be right? Had she taken Aarti's fears too lightly? Should she have been more circumspect? Well, there was a huge possibility that the answers to her questions could be found in the horoscopes. In any case, it was her duty to reconfirm.

With renewed resolve, Sonia rose and approached her table. Releasing the papers from the band, she aligned the six horoscopes on the table. Her eyes flicked over each, calculating. Aai. Baba. Beena—the sister. Meera—the adopted daughter. Pradeep and Aarti. Interesting family, artistic, rich—her eyes traveled along the horoscopes, picking and discarding. And then, suddenly, she took a sharp breath. She stumbled into her chair and separated three of the horoscopes from the rest. Her heart began a familiar tattoo, of understanding, of excitement. Was it possible? Could it be true? Sonia sat back against the chair, her hand twirling a lock of hair, her mind locked in confusion. Dare she meddle with people's lives on the basis of unsubstantiated suspicion? How could she be certain that her horoscopic revelations were not colored by Aarti's hysterics? A peccadillo, encroaching on the rights of human beings, could be detrimental to her practice and career at this point. But the antithesis to the worry reproached her. Ethics were fine. But where did they stand pitched against stark suspicions based on scientific calculations, backed by Aarti's gut instinct? Her mind was in a tailspin. As her thoughts swirled on, like a potter's wheel, her finger twirled faster, until finally she shook her head in frustration.

Sonia sighed and stood up. She selected a popular Hindi film wedding song and inserted the CD. Her feet began tapping, as the song began playing at high volume. Soon she found herself dancing to the words and music of the song. The melodious number was rendered by two of the best voices in India. It lifted her spirits immediately, making her feel happy.

As the song ended, Sonia felt perspiration trickle down her forehead. She wiped it off carelessly with her hand, feeling relaxed and tension-free. Nothing like good music and dance to disentangle the mirage from reality, duty from ethics, and action from illusion!

The sharp, almost sad notes of the Indian oboe-like instrument—*shehnai*—filled the huge hall with music. Trust the *shehnai* to create a wedding atmosphere in a traditional, usually grand Indian wedding, Sonia realized. She settled down comfortably in her cushioned seat, adjusting her silver-sequined black kameez. Children ran in groups, their merry laughter ringing through the hall. A pretty girl in a frilled dress approached her with perfume. Sonia allowed the child to rub the essence on her hand, then accepted the rose and pedha—a sweetmeat—with a smile. She observed the marriage rituals taking place round the fire. The buzz of voices, the floating notes of *shehnai*, the flower-decked stage ready for the couple, the holy fire around which the bride and groom would presently take the *saptapadi*—seven rounds that would bind them for life—it was all so satisfying and inspiring. Sonia sighed in contentment. Each wedding ceremony she attended brought into sharper focus her need to enjoy all the pampering that went inherently with the Indian marriage customs. One day. Not the splurging of money though. For herself, she would rather have a simple wedding with just a few close friends and family...

Aarti looked beautiful in her yellow sari with gold adorning her wrists and throat. She must have waited all her life for this special occasion. The bride sat now, with his head bowed, following the commands of the pundit. Pradeep looked handsome in his silk kurta. His adopted sister, Meera, dressed in a jazzy red and green sari, hovered protectively around Aarti, heeding to her needs. A little distance away, Beena and her parents were mingling with the guests, urging them to proceed to the lunch hall where the buffet awaited the crowd. Sonia glanced at her watch. It was almost one. Hunger rumbled in her stomach. She'd done her duty of attending this wedding. All was going well and now she deserved some food inside her. But where was Jatin? He was supposed to meet her at the hall.

The pundit requested the couple to take the seven rounds and Aarti and Pradeep stood up. Sonia watched as the young couple made their way in clockwise direction, slowly round the fire. Aarti glanced up and looked at Sonia, who flashed her a warm smile.

Finally, the rounds were over. The couple was declared religiously married. The *shehnai* played voluminously and a musical band struck up notes of a movie song, to celebrate the bond. The bride could now go and change for the reception. Aarti rose, and made her way to a room specially retained for the bride. Meera followed her with some *prasaad*—special food offered to God—in her hand. At the door, Aarti half turned and glanced at Sonia, but Meera hustled her new sister-in-law inside the small room and the door shut. Minutes later, the door opened and Meera walked out, shutting the door behind her again. Sonia waited. Any minute now, Aarti would emerge, resplendent in her reception sari, glowing with happiness and renewed confidence. And then Sonia would feel free to sample some of the exotic food and they could both laugh at Aarti's 'marriage jitters'. She relaxed, observing the teeming crowds as they drifted toward the buffet section. Where was Jatin? He ought to be hear by now. As if on cue, her assistant appeared at the end of the hall, hastened through the people festooned with jewelry and glossy clothes and headed straight toward her.

"Whew, I did it!" he sighed, slouching down on the seat beside her.

"And just in time. The ceremony's over and I'm hungry!" Sonia smiled at him. "Aarti's changing. We can congratulate her, eat and then leave."

A terrible scream tore across the hall. Startled, Sonia and Jatin jumped to their feet. The guests too halted in their tracks. Meera stood still at the door of the changing room. Her face was white.

"Something's happened to her! Something's happened to Aarti!" she stammered.

Sonia galvanized into action, as if she possessed lightening instead of feet. Followed closely by Jatin, she streaked to the little room, then stopped. Aarti lay sprawled on the bed, motionless. A piece of paper was clutched in her hand. Sonia immediately checked the girl's pulse. Then she plucked the paper out of her hand and opened it. A single line was written on the page: *I do not wish to live, so blame no one for my death.*

"Jatin, shut the door and let no one in! And call Inspector Divekar and a doctor immediately!" she rasped and Jatin instantly flew into action.

The contrast was shocking. Within moments, the glorious festivities had become drastic tragedy. Aarti was no more. Her body had been taken away for a postmortem. Sonia wondered if anyone in the room was more shocked than she was. She hadn't believed Aarti, had labeled her instinctive fears as mere marriage jitters. It almost seemed funny now! Only, death was not funny. It was serious and irreversible. And she'd spent hours agonizing over stupid arguments, arguing about choosing ethics over life and death issues. She certainly had a long way to go as a detective, she chided herself. Because it wasn't important, just to be a good investigator, it was also important to be able to sift instinct from illusion. And, if worst comes to worst, to trust illusion as one trusted instinct, if only so that you left no stone unturned. And that's where she'd been weak. Guilt tore through her like a jagged knife. A glacial hand clutched at her heart. What if… What if… The words clamored through her brain in ceaseless, remorseless repetition.

Gradually the sobs and mutterings of the family members seeped through her numbness. The guests had all left. Pradeep sat, paralyzed with shock, his head in his hands, looking a lonely figure. Aai and Baba were silent and Beena was sobbing freely, heedless of Meera's comforting words.

"Why did she do it?" Baba kept muttering. "I just don't understand it!"

"She seemed so happy, so excited to get married," Aai agreed.

"She wasn't happy, I told you that," Beena spoke up suddenly. "I told you the other night that Aarti seemed distracted, and reluctant and terribly unhappy. But you told me that was normal. It wasn't normal, was it? Look what she did! And now we shall never know what was worrying her!" Beena burst into sobs.

"I don't understand.... They wanted so much to get married." Aai sounded flustered. "Why would she commit suicide?"

"Do you remember what Guruji told us?" Meera spoke up. "He'd predicted that something like this would happen! Do you remember, when we matched the horoscopes, Guruji said that they didn't match? That Pradeep and Aarti had better not get married?"

"Yes, I did." A gruff voice interrupted them.

An old man with a balding head drew up a chair. "I'm most sorry about what happened here today. I did say that Aarti and Pradeep are not suited, but nothing in her horoscope would've prepared me for this. Yes, I warned Pradeep that he had a very unique combination in his horoscope. That his first wife would die and then he would remarry. But even I couldn't predict that his wife would commit suicide! And on their wedding day! Life is too complicated and unpredictable, isn't it?"

"Pradeep said at the time, that he didn't care, he loved Aarti too much to bother about such predictions! And now look what's happened! A poor innocent girl has lost her life!" Beena cried, in a harsh voice.

"She didn't loose her life, she took it herself," Aai corrected sharply. "Let's not blame each other for what's happened, Beena. Be careful what you say. Aarti was obviously the suicidal type."

"It's all right for you to say such things, Aai!" Pradeep interrupted, suddenly. "But I've lost the love of my life and I shall never know why. Oh, why did she do it? Why didn't she talk to me?" His shoulders shook as he bowed his head in grief. Meera moved instantly to his side and pressed an understanding arm around him.

Sonia cleared her throat. "Excuse me, I've been listening and I really must introduce myself to you."

The others looked at her in surprise, as if aware of her presence for the first time.

"I'm Sonia and I run a Detective Agency. Aarti came to me two days ago, feeling thoroughly lost and frightened."

"Frightened?" Baba questioned amazed.

"Yes, unfortunately I didn't believe her at that time because she had nothing concrete to tell me. But I wish I'd probed, that I hadn't acted so pompous and self-assured. I wish I'd let her talk to me—but I didn't. Can any one of you tell me why she was feeling so fearful, just days before her wedding?"

"We have absolutely no idea! I wasn't even aware that she'd sought your help." The bridegroom looked even more distraught than before Sonia spoke.

"She was over-excited and over–sensitive to issues," Beena replied. "But I wouldn't have imagined in my wildest dreams that she was so desperate about something!"

"I know—I couldn't either," Sonia agreed. "Anyway—whatever her reasons, Aarti's gone."

"I can't believe it," Pradeep murmured, in a dead voice.

Sonia stood up. "I'm really sorry—for everything. I wish I could've prevented this from happening. And I wish I could've been of more help. Goodbye."

She headed to the entrance of the hall. At the door she

turned. The family was huddled together, grieving and crying. Sonia felt an intense urge to burst into tears herself—for lost causes, for lost love and for death, which is the final parting.

"It's been four days since the incident and you're still grinding the memories to powder. You know you can't blame yourself," Mohnish repeated for the nth time. "Superfluous guilt will lead you nowhere. And there's no point moping, you can't change the past."

Sonia was pacing the floor, restless and disturbed. Mohnish was leaning against the table watching her, his arms folded, his eyes sad. An attentive Nidhi sat beside him. Both he and the cat watched, their heads swiveling along with Sonia's pacing.

"I'm not moping and I know I can't change the past. But I *can* learn from the mistakes I've made, can't I?" Sonia pointed out.

"I think you're being too hard on yourself. Everyone makes mistakes, it's normal—it's a human right!"

"Not when it involves a person's life."

"Aw… come on Sonia! You couldn't possibly have known that Aarti planned to commit suicide. Not you, not anyone! You said so yourself, she had nothing to tell!"

"Yes, but I should've persisted, read between the lines, helped to sort out her jumbled fears—I don't know," Sonia shrugged eloquently. "Done *something* to relieve her burdened mind. I just let her walk out of that door saying she had the marriage jitters. Marriage jitters, for god's sake! Unforgivable!"

Mohnish was silent. He'd never seen Sonia in such a mood. Anger, guilt, retribution—all directed towards herself—stuck into her customary serene logic like splinters. Perhaps it was best if she purged herself of all these negative feelings. At length, her blazing face lost color and she slumped into a chair.

"Where's Jatin?" Mohnish asked casually, hoping to change the subject.

"Out. I've sent him on some errands."

"He wasn't here the last time I dropped by either."

"He was reading too many books and falling into a habit of preaching to me! So I sent him on some real practical jobs. It'll keep him away from his books and protect me from his intelligent advice," Sonia replied with a faint smile.

"That's better. You do look quite beautiful when you smile," Mohnish remarked.

"Thanks and you make me feel better too," she admitted.

Another silence ensued as both looked awkwardly at each other. Mohnish stepped forward and placed his hands on her shoulders. His deep gaze bore into the honeyed depths of her eyes.

"You know that you can always rely on me, don't you? Whatever the situation, Sonia, however silly or dangerous, if you ever need me, you know I shall be there for you…"

Sonia nodded, suddenly tongue-tied. A wave of bashfulness swept over her.

Propitiously, the phone shrilled at that moment, drawing a physical wedge between them. Sonia almost sprang to the instrument and hastily lifted the receiver.

"Hello? Yes, I'm listening… Oh good! You know what to do, don't you? Go ahead and contact him, I'll talk to him later." She listened for another minute, then hung up.

Mohnish watched her with a great deal of curiosity. When she turned to him, her eyes were twinkling.

"You said, you'd be there for me, right? However silly or dangerous?" she challenged.

"Yes, though I didn't know you planned to take me up so instantly on the offer."

"That will teach you never to take risks with me!" she laughed. "So? Are you game?"

"Well, since I said it, I'm not one to back out on a promise. Name the situation, place, act and time!"

"Great, I like your spirit!"

The night was cool and a wind swept the dry Banyan leaves off the road. The Zen drove down the road, turned a curve and halted in front of the Gupte Residence. It was a modest bungalow of red bricks. The moonlight bathed the house and the tree-lined drive, pooling in at the gates. Meera hit the button on the remote and the well-oiled gates swung silently open. Pradeep accelerated and was halfway through the gate, when he halted so abruptly that Meera was almost thrown against the windscreen.

"What the… !" she cursed, turning to Pradeep.

The young widower was staring straight ahead, his eyes wide, shock and fear written all over his handsome face. Meera slowly turned in the direction of his averted gaze and gasped. Aarti stood at the entrance to the residence. Dressed in her bridal yellow sari, decked in jewels, she stood motionless as the wind tugged and pulled at her pallu. Her shoulder-length hair blew wildly about her face.

"No….!" Meera screamed.

"Stop it! Stop screaming!" Pradeep yelled.

"It's a ghost! She's come back, Pradeep, she's come back! To take revenge!"

"Shut up and get out of the car!"

"No! She's coming towards us!"

Aarti walked slowly to the car. The headlights threw her figure into harsh shadows and the moonlight created a contrasting halo around her slender form. She stopped at the bonnet of the vehicle and raised an accusing hand towards Pradeep. He stumbled out of the car. The wind seemed to blow stronger, throwing him off balance.

"I'm sorry! Forgive me! It was all her idea, believe me! I loved you, I truly did!"

"Liar! Liar! You planned it, you never loved her, you killed her!" Meera screeched, scrambling out of the car, now hysterical and out of control.

Aarti turned to her. The venomous hate on the dead woman's face made Meera step back in fear. Wildly, she turned around and fled.

Pradeep stared after his adopted sister, uncertainty and fear clogging his brain. At that moment, hard lights went on and he winced at the brilliant impact.

"Mr. Pradeep Gupte, you are under arrest for the attempted murder of your wife!" Inspector Divekar's voice rang out through the darkness, cutting into the fog in his head.

The grieving bridegroom turned a confused, hazy gaze at the sudden crowd gathered around him. Inspector Divekar, Mohnish, Jatin and some constables—their faces hard, accusing and unforgiving. And at the back of group, Sonia, holding Aarti's hand. Aarti was sobbing uncontrollably.

"I can't believe that you played such a dirty trick on me!" Mohnish said indignantly, but there was a twinkle in his eyes.

"The first rule in investigation, is never to reveal all your cards. Right, Jatin?" Sonia chuckled.

"Right boss, though I didn't know you were reading the same book!"

"I wasn't, but that's immaterial."

"But it still doesn't justify the fact that you didn't treat friends as real friends." Mohnish looked hurt.

"The second rule is not to reveal your cards, even to friends!"

Mohnish grinned. "Okay, I give up. Now tell me exactly what happened! I'm still so confused. I truly believed that Aarti had committed suicide and that you just could not get over your guilt trip."

"Okay, let me start at the beginning. You know that Aarti came over with all her anxieties and fears and I sent her packing with my confident and immature advice. But after she departed,

I checked out the horoscopes she'd left with me. And I realized that Pradeep's Venus and Mars were in the same house as Meera's. Without going into astrological jargon, it was enough to tell me that those two were strongly attracted to each other and were having a relationship. But Pradeep claimed to be in love with Aarti. Somehow, that did not seem to add up, since Aarti's horoscope revealed no such bonds with Pradeep. Then I began wondering where Aarti fitted into the picture. There are usually two reasons why couples marry—love or money. Since Aarti was an orphan and with no inheritance lined up in the sidelines, the motive for this marriage had to be love! I began wondering if it was love for Aarti, as Pradeep declared or could it be love for Meera?

"Another interesting detail was that Venus and Mars in Aarti's horoscope were so placed, that they showed that this girl was going to be badly tricked. I kept running in circles, trying to decipher the workings of three loving hearts! And then I stumbled on to another star combination in Pradeep's horoscope. There were traits of a criminal mind and there was an extremely strong possibility that his first wife would die and only then could he lead a married life. Somehow, that set me thinking. What if Pradeep loved Meera and was aware of this troublesome hindrance in his horoscope? The idea took such a strong root, that I thought I must investigate it. But there was a problem. Did I have the right to pursue a hunch, based entirely on my astrological knowledge? I debated with myself and argued that I had no right to malign people with criminal plans that might well be the product of my own imagination. But finally, the Investigator in me won. I knew that if there was even the remotest possibility of something fishy going on, I would be saving a life. It was a risk I had to take.

"So Jatin and I made some background checks. Jeevan Uncle, of course, went all out to help me. And sure enough, we found that Pradeep Gupte had been sentenced to a three-month jail for a minor crime. He was also reported to have been seen with Meera in the coziest of joints. Some of his friends even expressed surprise that he was marrying Aarti instead of Meera. It was then that I knew that something was surely cooking. Aarti had spoken about Guruji, their family astrologer. So I contacted him. He confirmed that he'd advised Pradeep against the marriage for the same reason—that their horoscopes were not suitably matched and that his wife could die. At that time, I called up Aarti and warned her to be on the alert.

"It was the afternoon before the wedding that Aarti came to the office with some real proof. Fortunately, she'd overheard Pradeep and Meera talk in the garden. The only words she heard were Meera's, who said, "this would be her last *prasaad!*" That set me thinking. Which *prasaad* was Meera talking about and which day would it be given? The most difficult part was to figure out when they would try to get rid of Aarti. After all, anything could happen anytime! I tried to place myself in the shoes of Pradeep and Meera. If I were so passionately involved with Pradeep would I allow him to get married and consummate that marriage? No—I would be too possessive to take such risks. But, if Pradeep tried to kill Aarti away from home, it would draw suspicion. I realized that it had to be done in the public eye after the marriage had taken place but before it could be consummated!

"After that, it didn't take me long to figure out what their plan was. After the Saptapadi, Aarti would go to her room to change. Meera would take some God's *prasaad* for her—you know, *shira,* a sweet dish made of semolina. Only this concoction would also have a generous amount of poison in it! Aarti would eat it and instantly fall dead. Meera would then remove the tell-tale *prasaad* and stick the suicide note into her hand and declare that Aarti had killed herself."

"That was some plan!" Mohnish whistled.

"Yes, quite ingenious but we decided to come up with a

better plan, didn't we, Jatin?"

Jatin grinned. "You bet!"

"We decided to defuse their excellent trap and sponge a script of our own from their crooked scenario! Aarti was warned that if she was brought anything to eat—specially *prasaad*—she wasn't to touch it. She had to send Meera out of the room, pass the food to Jatin through the window and pretend to die. When Meera returned, she believed her plan had succeeded. Hiding the empty *prasaad* utensil, she slipped the note into Aarti's hand and raised a hue and cry that the poor girl had committed suicide. Uncle Jeevan, who was with us in the plan, was ready for action. He was waiting round the corner for just the right moment. Within minutes, Aarti was huddled into a police car and taken away for postmortem. Meera and Pradeep had no reason to believe that their plan had not succeeded!"

"And was the *prasaad* tested for poison?'

"Yes, Jeevan Uncle spared no time in taking it to the lab. It is positive evidence of their heinous act!"

"Wonderful! But then you backed out. Why?" Mohnish reminded.

"Have you ever noticed what happens when you drive a two-wheeler very close behind a car? You never see the potholes the car is going over and you end up falling into those potholes. Even though we had the poisoned *prasaad* as proof, it wasn't sufficient evidence to incriminate Pradeep and Meera for attempted murder. I gave them plenty of space, allowing me to spot their potholes, so that I could circumvent them and lay another trap. Since the couple was entirely unaware that their plan had misfired, they were unguarded. And unaware that Jatin was keeping a close watch on their activities. Initially they kept their distance from each other but eventually love outstripped decency. We didn't need further proof of their attachment to each other. They were obviously a devoted couple. We had to await the right moment, to spring the next trap. Not too soon but also not too late, because it would've been difficult to retain the "body" for long under the pretext of "post mortem". At some point, Pradeep would surely lay claim to his beloved wife's body. Besides, Aarti was in hiding at Inspector Divekar's house and was getting restless. When Jatin called up yesterday to say that Pradeep and Meera would be returning from a friend's place late night, we finally had the perfect opportunity to enact our little drama. Since we were prepared beforehand, everything went off smoothly. I thought Aarti was brilliant, wasn't she?" Sonia chuckled.

"I think *you're* brilliant, boss!" Admiration shone in Jatin's eyes.

"Thanks, Jatin, that's sweet of you! And I thought you were good too!"

"Hey, before this mutual admiration goes any further, I have one question to ask," Mohnish interrupted with a broad, dimpled smile. "What if the poison had been administered before Aarti went for a sari change?"

"That wasn't possible. The whole point of the plan was to get married, remember? Pradeep wouldn't dare kill Aarti before they got married. The sari change was the only time when Aarti would be alone with Meera. Meera would definitely act at that moment and Aarti knew it. The moment Meera arrived with the *prasaad,* Aarti had the sense to set our plan in motion."

"Gutsy girl," Mohnish applauded.

"And also perceptive. I almost got her killed, by disbelieving her," Sonia admitted.

"Yes, what was all that about—the self-recrimination?" His brow knitted in a frown.

"That was just that—a brutal introspection! Residual guilt. When you came to the office, I was engaged in a skirmish with myself. I couldn't stop myself from reliving the horror of what would've happened if I hadn't read those horoscopes and trusted Aarti's and my instincts. The image of a dead Aarti kept hounding me. I was sore and mad at myself because I'd almost goofed up the case, ranting about ethics and stuff when the paramount thing in life was—*life!* I'm sorry if I misled you—but if it's any consolation to you, I truly and really was mad at myself for being such an overconfident, pompous ass in the beginning. If I'd really labeled it all as the proverbial marriage jitters, Aarti would be dead and I would've never forgiven myself!"

"I understand." Mohnish nodded sympathetically. "What about Aarti?"

"She's gone back to her school but she's now the official daughter-in-law of the Gupte house. I guess she'll take some time to decide about her future. She has some major decisions to take. Poor girl." Sonia sighed. "I think this whole episode has really taught me a lesson."

"We've all learnt a lesson," Jatin added magnanimously.

Sonia turned to him and quirked an eyebrow.

"I better fetch us some chai," Jatin mumbled, hastily beating a retreat.

Mohnish and Sonia laughed.

"He's incorrigible," Mohnish said.

"But the best assistant I could have. And I wouldn't repeat it to him," she said.

"You don't have to. I just heard it!" Jatin popped his head through the door and grinned from cheek to cheek. "Thanks." He was gone again in a flash.

CHAPTER VII

Invited by Horoscopes

Anand Gandhi trudged along the gravel path, engrossed in thought. He was perspiring freely, but that was the least of his worries. The late afternoon sun cascaded gold over the glistening Mulshi lake as the hills converged straight ahead to form a sharp V. The letter would have reached her today, he thought. It would've entertained him immensely to watch her reaction. But she would come, he was certain of that. He was looking forward to this evening's rendezvous, which, if he had any say in the matter, simply had to go well! Everything was planned to the last 't'.

A sigh escaped him. He experienced an unusual wave of fatigue and loneliness. But he couldn't. feel either tired or lonely. Not now when the end was so translucently close. He'd set out to achieve his goal, with a crystal clear logic and mind. And he'd gone through a lot. He couldn't afford to succumb to meaningless protests of the body now! Besides, he had Maya, his wife, and his son Swapnil, not to mention the entire cotton empire he'd worked so hard to raise to stupendous heights. No, he'd forsaken a lot for his end, which was now so within reach that he could almost touch it! All he needed was a little patience and then he would be free from all the entanglements of life! And he would most certainly have the last laugh. As usual, excitement of the approaching events caught up with him and he smiled. He was going to enjoy himself very much.

He straightened his broad shoulders, encased in an expensive khadi silk shirt, and headed toward the sprawling house ahead.

Reema frowned deeply as she observed Anand Gandhi's slow progression down the path. How tired he looked, she thought. He certainly didn't come anywhere close to resembling the successful, ruthless businessman that he was. The sun glinted on the pane and she stepped back hastily. She couldn't risk being caught watching. This window had served her well these past few months. Not that her watch had yielded much. Time was short and she had to be prepared. It could be any moment now.

All the anger and hate built up inside her was like a volcano, ready to erupt. *Today,* she was certain, it would be *today*.

Reema turned from the window, as Anand Gandhi entered his study from the side door and vanished inside. Instinct told Reema to stay on her watchful post. It *had* to be today!

Swapnil Gandhi lounged about the terrace watching his father move in the direction of his study. Such a dynamic man, so successful, so unscrupulous. Swapnil had so much to learn from him—if only they could interact like normal beings. But of late, it was getting more and more difficult to communicate with his father. Swapnil was sure that something was on his mind. But it was unlike Anand Gandhi to confide in anybody—not even his wife. Specially not his son, whom he trusted as he would a stranger. This pained Swapnil. He'd tried very hard to please his father. But somehow, he always ended up making a mess of things. The reason was quite obvious. Basically, they were different in principles and he was no match for Anand Gandhi's quick mind. And now, despite the interest Swapnil had displayed in the business, Anand took his own decisions—mostly financial ones. Especially after he had discovered his son's expensive habits. The uproar that followed immediately after that still rang painfully in Swapnil's mind.

Well, he had to have another talk with him soon—unpleasant though it would undoubtedly be. Swapnil winced at the prospect, but he had no choice. He must talk with his father—today!

Sonia attentively watched the live telecast of the Gokul Ashtami celebrations on the Cable News. Mohnish's voice drawled on effortlessly in the background with a steady flow of comments. The festival rejoiced the birth of Lord Krishna at midnight and the next day celebrated his childhood love for curd and butter in the form of a game for the public, called Dahi Handi. Usually a pot of curd was tied about fifty feet high, between tall buildings in the centre of the street. This time it contained a spectacular amount of money for the winning team. The game took place in different parts of the city as the public—Hindus, Muslims, Christians, Jains and other communities—all gathered together to have a great time.

A group of boys formed a large circular chain, arms outstretched and holding each other by the shoulders. Lighter boys climbed on the shoulders of the first circle, forming another narrower circle on the top. Swarming crowds cheered encouragingly and *dhols*—large cylindrical drums—played loudly, as another group of boys climbed onto the second circle. Sonia watched in fascination as the human pyramid grew amidst rhythmic cheering and drumming, narrowing on the top to allow one tiny boy to climb. On the top of the human tower, he reached out to grab the pot of money. But he was too short. He leaned further up in the sky and the group below him rocked. The crowd screamed wildly and Mohnish voiced his comments excitedly. The human pyramid swayed dangerously, lost balance and crashed down. The boys toppled, one on top of the other, like the cards of a card-house.

"Oh no!" Jatin exclaimed. "They were so close!"

"One weak link and the whole pyramid topples," Sonia observed.

"Here's the next team now."

"Jatin, ten minutes and you get down to work," Sonia commanded gently.

Jatin grinned. "Right, boss!"

Sonia returned to the inner office and immediately her attention was drawn to the lush bunch of roses there. The card read 'Secret Admirer'. The bouquet had been delivered by the florist that morning. This was going too far. Who was sending these bouquets, week after week? Mohnish had flatly denied having anything to with the roses. Who was her secret admirer and what did he want of her? Why didn't he reveal himself? It was really quite tough trying to solve the mysteries of the impenetrable and inexplicable human mind. With a sigh, Sonia turned to Nidhi and straightened her collar. The little cat really did look quite royal, with her golden coat and black leather collar.

Absently she took up the newspaper and once again read the brief news on the Owl. The police had finally found a trace to his latest whereabouts. He was last reported to be in Mumbai. Mumbai of all the places! So close—Sonia sensed a thrill of excitement. What could an international crook like the Owl want in Mumbai, Sonia wondered. On the other hand, why not Mumbai? It was, after all, one of the most happening spots in the world. But also so huge that it supplied hundreds of hiding places for crooks. Would the police ever be able to capture the Owl?

Jatin opened the door and walked into the inner office. "Boss?"

Sonia glanced up at him. "What happened? Has a team finally won?"

"No boss. TV is not the only thing on my mind!" he protested indignantly.

"Really?" Sonia raised an eyebrow expressively.

"Well, OK, I admit it's a good source of entertainment and information but not when we have work to do," he explained with dignity, holding up an envelope. Without another word, he set it on the table.

"What's this? Something interesting?" she queried.

"Very!" he replied.

Puzzled, Sonia dropped the newspaper and examined the contents of the envelope. The first paper was a letter—a computer print-out. It was short and addressed to her. *Dear Madam, I'm sending you two horoscopes. Two people plan to meet today and I'm afraid, something terrible is going to happen to one of them. Please come to the following address before night falls—if you think you can prevent it from happening. With due respect, Anand Gandhi.* The address printed below was a Mulshi address.

"Well?" Jatin ventured.

"Fascinating," Sonia murmured as she took up the other two sheets of paper. Each contained a neatly drawn out horoscope.

"I thought so, too. But does it mean anything? Like a real client? Should we take it seriously or treat it as a joke?" Jatin remarked. "I mean it does seem as if someone's trying to pull our legs!"

"Yes, it does seem so," Sonia admitted. She stared thoughtfully at the horoscopes, then glanced at the envelope. "This arrived by courier?"

"Yes, just now."

She looked at her wristwatch. "It's five just now. If we leave straight away, could we reach Mulshi by seven?"

"You don't plan to take this note seriously, boss?" Jatin asked incredulously. "It's obvious that something isn't right here."

"I know that. But doesn't the name Anand Gandhi ring a bell?" There was a meditative expression on Sonia's face. "Isn't he the guy who brought the best cotton designs along with the cheapest rates in the market, but who's still the most private public figure around!"

"The cotton king!" Jatin gasped. "You mean, this is *that* Anand Gandhi?"

Sonia nodded. "Unless this whole thing is a sham—which we'll discover soon enough—I believe this is from the same Anand Gandhi. As far as I remember, he lives in Mulshi."

"So you think this is serious business?"

"Not only is it serious, it's a challenge! Can't you detect that 'if you dare' tone in the letter? Anand Gandhi may be just playing a game or he may sincerely intend it to be a challenge. I don't know which it is—a game or a challenge, the what or why—yet! But I intend to find out!" Sonia said, with grim determination. "Because if this is a deliberate, malicious stab at my respectable profession and practice, I'll return it with full justice and vigor. And if this is indeed a harbinger for a crime about to be committed, then I must do my best to prevent it!"

"But what I don't understand is why he doesn't come out with it straight? I mean, if he knows something, why not just speak up and tell you what he knows? Why be so *odd* abut it?"

"To rouse our curiosity, for one, and to ensure that we accept his invitation."

"*We?*" Jatin raised an eyebrow. "You expect me to come along?"

Sonia smiled pleasantly. "Of course. And don't forget to carry an overnight bag, in case we have to stay over."

"But your parents, if they object…."

"My parents have given me a free hand to do as I please. And Jatin—I do the worrying here, *you* follow orders!"

Jatin grimaced. "I know. But once in a while... I should show some sense, shouldn't I? I can't always allow you to just pick up your bags and go off somewhere. I feel responsible for you!"

"Thank you, but I don't need you as a chaperone. I need you as an assistant," Sonia reminded pointedly, amused at the gallant, protective role young Jatin had taken up.

"Besides," Jatin continued, ignoring her, "what would Mohnish say?"

"What would *who* say?" Her eyes narrowed .

Jatin shrugged. "Mohnish. He asked me to keep an eye on you."

"Mohnish! And since when did he start giving you orders?"

Jatin grinned, unabashed. "He cares for you, boss. It's only right that he should make such a request!"

"Hold it, hold it! I don't need anyone ladling out advice to me, certainly not you, and most certainly not Mohnish!" Sonia raised a hand. "And anyway, this conversation is going way out of control. No more discussions. I want you back here in half an hour, ready to leave."

Jatin shrugged again, realizing belatedly that he'd gone too far. But he was only trying to do his duty. His boss ought to have taken it in the right spirit. Sometimes he simply couldn't understand the woman.

Sonia was fuming. How dare Mohnish say such things to her assistant! He'd no right to meddle with her professional life. She'd take it out with him when she got back, she decided, still bristling with resentment. Right now, she had to calm down and think about the case in hand.

She picked up the two horoscopes and glanced at them. There was something about them, something she ought to recognize. But what was it? One horoscope had Gemini as its ascendant and the other had Cancer. But the rest of the planetary positions were quite similar. If she could find out which year they belonged to, she would get the precise age of the two people and a general description of their looks.

For the next half an hour, Sonia studied several almanacs, looking for different combinations. She was so engrossed in the job that she barely noticed Jatin performing his duty, albeit a little belatedly. He slipped into the room quietly, slipped a CD into the player, and melodious strains of flute loudly filled the air. At the door, he glanced back and observed with satisfaction that his boss seemed less agitated and more concentrated on the horoscopes.

At last! She had it. With a feeling of triumph, Sonia jotted down the date of the first horoscope. Her eyes sparkled with excitement. The person in the second horoscope had been born just a few minutes after the first. What a remarkable coincidence! Suddenly questions swamped her mind. Did the two people whose horoscopes these were know each other? Were they friends or enemies or simply strangers? Were they even aware of each other's existence? How was Anand Gandhi connected with these two people? Did one of the horoscopes belong to him? And what was his motive for sending her the information?

There was no point tossing ideas around in a void. There was only one way to divest herself of her sharply piqued curiosity. Reach Mulshi as soon as possible. Which was what she intended to do. She quickly gathered the almanacs, the letter and the horoscopes and stuffed them in her handbag. Then, fondling Nidhi, she sloshed ample milk for her in a bowl and slipped out of the office.

Sonia drove the van slowly through the crowds gathered in each square. Everyone was engrossed in the game of Dahi Handi. She inadvertently searched for a TV crew, then realized that Dahi Handi was on in various parts of the city. Mohnish could be absolutely anywhere!

Beside her in the van, Jatin almost hung out of the window in his eagerness to soak up the atmosphere. Passers-by halted to contribute to the rising wave of encouragement, clapping along with the *dhol,* as different teams tried their luck at reaching the pot. As the van crawled through the crowd, their attention was riveted by an astonishing sight. A girls' team! Sonia couldn't resist it. One look at Jatin's eager face and she stopped the van round a corner. Jatin flashed her a grateful smile and they climbed out of the vehicle.

Dressed in shorts and t-shirts, they formed the pyramid, planting a firm foundation of tall, hefty girls. The lighter, nimble ones went next, until the last girl climbed agilely on the top of the eighth column. Sonia and Jatin watched, with bated breath as the girl reached the pot and hit it with all her might. The pouch of money fell straight into her arms! Delight rippled through the human pyramid, as the mob screamed in appreciative frenzy. Sonia and Jatin joined the thunderous applause, enjoying the excitement.

"Wow! Girls! This is the first time I've seen girls play Dahi Handi! That was some display of discipline," Jatin remarked with admiration in his voice, as they returned to the van.

"Yes, a perfect example of good planning and organization of human resources; unity and discipline, which works in any situation of life—be it work place or at a personal level," Sonia agreed, as they set forth again.

She edged the vehicle out of the crowd and toward Mulshi. "Everyone is equally important in the achievement. Each one of the group has to put in his or her best. A single weak link can pull down the whole pyramid."

They drove silently as the van ate up the miles—Jatin still reflecting over the amazing girls' team. He was sure lucky to witness this new revolution, he thought gratefully.

Dusk was falling fast, when the vehicle finally climbed up the hill, throwing up dust from the road. The Mulshi Lake loomed large and dark on the right, the hills surrounding it like large, shapeless patches of black.

"This must be it," Jatin announced, as a large gate rose ahead of them.

Sonia nodded as she drove past the lampposts on either side of the gate. She half-expected a watchman to arrest their progress but much to her surprise the area appeared deserted. A short drive led straight to the front of the two storied-house. She pulled into the drive and the two of them stepped out of the van and into the porch. Jatin hitched his overnight bag over his shoulder, as his boss pressed the doorbell. A merry tinkling filled the depths of the house. Immediately the door was flung open. An oldish woman, clad in a sari, gaped at them in bewilderment.

Sonia quickly introduced herself. "Is Mr. Anand Gandhi in? He's invited me—"

Before she could finish, the old lady gasped and clapped her hand over her mouth. Still mute, she turned and hastened into the house. Sonia raised an eyebrow at Jatin. Now what was up?

"I think that was an invitation to have a free run of the place!" She grinned and the two of them stepped into the hall.

The lush, almost ostentatious furnishings, done with taste and style, bespoke of money and elegance. Evidently, no expense had been spared on any corner of this home. Sonia didn't doubt that the house boasted an excellent view of the lake too. A perfect recluse for a rich businessman, one who led an extremely private life.

"Can I help you? I'm Swapnil Gandhi." A refined voice broke into her observations.

Sonia whirled around to face a boy just past his teens. Fair good looks. Tall and boyish with a refreshing innocence in his face. But at the moment, the frown lines on his face betrayed annoyance.

Sonia cleared her throat. "I'm Sonia Samarth and this is

Jatin. I'm here on an express invitation by Mr. Anand Gandhi. May I meet him?" she asked politely.

"You mean..." The boy's eyes widened. He stammered, struggling to speak, and then shut up.

Sonia observed him with a great deal of interest. What was happening here?

"What is it?" She couldn't help asking.

The boy was pale and his hands were trembling. He sat down abruptly on the plush sofa.

"Dad's...Dad passed away... I just found him! I think it's not natural..." he burst into tears.

Jatin stared horrified at the sobbing figure, then looked helplessly at his boss, awaiting instructions! Sonia steadied her quickened breath and counted till ten, then sat down beside the overwrought boy, allowing him to vent his feelings. Finally, his sobs tapered into hiccups.

"Tell me what happened," she said gently. "I'm an investigator, maybe I can help?"

Swapnil nodded, blew into his kerchief and glanced up at her with reddened eyes. "I think someone...killed Dad. I've called the police, they should be here any minute. I also called the doctor."

"You did the right thing, but tell me exactly what happened," Sonia insisted.

"I'd something important to discuss with Dad, so I went to his study—he's always there at this time of the day—but I found... there was blood all over... someone hit him on the head... I think..."

"Have you touched anything?"

"No... No, I couldn't! The blood..."

"Good. Do you mind if I take a look?" Permitting Swapnil no time to protest, Sonia rose expectantly.

The boy hesitated for a fraction of a second, then led them through a passage, to a room on the left. At the door, he stepped aside, allowing Sonia and Jatin to pass through. At first sight, the man inside the room appeared to be sleeping. But closer inspection revealed the details. Anand Gandhi lying with his head slumped on the table, his head battered by something heavy. Sonia's eye scouted round the room and immediately spotted the big metal flower vase lying upturned on the floor. It was covered with blood. No points for guessing what struck the poor man! A half-burnt paper on the carpet caught Sonia's attention. She bent and spotted the smudged words. It was a letter. She straightened, without touching it. The entire left wall was lined with tall windows with a door at the other end of it, which led into a garden. Before Sonia could turn to Sawpnil and ask any questions, the wail of a siren pierced the evening. The police had arrived.

"I've heard of you, Miss Samarth. Inspector Divekar holds you in high esteem and I hold his opinion in high esteem." Sub-Inspector Ganesh Inamdar was surprisingly forthright.

"I'm flattered and glad. Does that mean we can work together on this case?" Sonia asked, with a smile.

"Apart from the fact that your contribution would be advantageous to me, I understand that you've actually been hired by Mr. Anand Gandhi. So that does give you the official right to be here, doesn't it?"

"*Hired* wouldn't be the exact word I'd use, but I guess it would come close. Actually I've been dragged into this murder, whether by coincidence or design, is what I need to find out."

"Good. So should we begin?" The sub-inspector rubbed his hands together in anticipation.

"Could you tell me what you found in the study?"

They stood in a medium-sized room adjoining the hall. The room had a table with a computer on it, and a sofa set arranged near a large window which overlooked a garden. Jatin was on standby, ready for any action his boss desired. Sub-Inspector

Inamdar held out two half-burnt sheets of paper, in gloved hands. There was scrawled handwriting on both sheets.

"I believe it's a letter. Unfortunately we don't know who wrote it to whom," Inamdar remarked.

Sonia ran her eye over the pages. The first sheet read. '*...I am trapped and all because of.....you've got to understand..... don't be fooled...I need to get out......*' The remaining words had curled up into ashes.

"This obviously seems like some sort of a plea," observed Sonia. "The paper's quite yellow so it's an old letter. Unlike this one, this small slip, which seems pretty recent."

The handwriting on the smaller sheet of paper was darker, bolder and more forceful but indisputably the same as the first. These words too had an ominous ring to them. *'I'm coming. It's payback time!'*

"Well?"

"Definitely a threat, perhaps to Anand Gandhi. Perhaps it was the threat that made him approach me, albeit unconventionally," Sonia concluded.

"But someone tried to burn these letters. Was Gandhi doing it or someone else? And why?" Jatin frowned.

"To destroy evidence? Or... to create evidence?" Sonia mused.

"You mean these were deliberately left in the study to mislead us?" Jatin asked.

"I don't know. I'm just thinking aloud." She shrugged.

Sonia was thoughtful, staring at the words, trying to coerce some meaning into the half-expressed emotions. Strong emotions but of very different natures—one a plea and the other a threat. The words *retribution* and *justice,* flashed through her mind. But *who* had written these two notes? And to whom? And why?

All three of them stepped into the hall, where the whole family had gathered, sitting idly, talking in low voices to one another. The body had been taken away but Sub-Inspector Ganesh Inamdar had hung back, wanting to talk to everyone. Maya Gandhi—looking shocked and dazed, grappling with the truth that her husband was murdered. Swapnil—tear-stained and red-eyed. The house maid—or Daaima as Swapnil called her—with swollen eyes and sniffing ceaselessly. And Reema—Anand's secretary who lived at the mansion.

It was Reema, the secretary, who intrigued Sonia immensely. Medium-height, wheat-complexioned, she appeared young and fresh—not at all secretary material. In fact, she distinctly lacked the poise and confidence of a businessman's personal assistant. What could she be doing in a place like this, Sonia wondered with a frown.

And more baffling, where did she, Sonia, fit into this scene? Why had Anand Gandhi *really* invited her to the house? His invitation seemed more nebulous than ever now. Had he known that he was in danger? Had he sensed something that he'd wished to convey to her? And who did the horoscopes belong to? For a moment, Sonia experienced an acute wave of annoyance which she tamped down immediately. This was no time for expressing personal frustrations. The man who had issued her the invitation was murdered and she was going to forge ahead with her investigation and find out who killed him.

Sub-Inspector Inamdar cleared his throat, securing the desired effect. Everyone instantly glanced in his direction.

"I'm quite sorry about what happened here this evening. And I—we—would certainly like to get to the bottom of this sordid affair. But we need your co-operation. Miss Samarth and I need to ask you some questions, individually and in private. We'll be in the next room. Miss Reema?"

Reema flashed Swapnil a nervous glance. His reassuring half smile, Sonia thought, spoke volumes.

As the other three settled down around a table, Reema chose the single sofa seat, sitting on the edge, her hands twisting a kerchief. Ganesh Inamdar raised an eyebrow and Sonia nodded in understanding. Jatin pulled out his notebook.

"Reema, how long have you been working here?" Sonia asked the girl casually.

"Six months," the secretary replied, in a husky voice.

"And did you like your job?"

"I'd nothing to object to."

"Are you officially qualified to be a secretary?"

"No. I'm an MA in Sociology, but since I needed a job desperately, Swapnil offered me this post and I had no choice but to accept it," Reema offered.

"You and Swapnil are good friends."

The young woman blushed. "Not exactly. I mean, we were in college together but..." She halted, looking confused.

Sonia threw a glance at the others. The sub-inspector was leaning over the table, listening intently, and Jatin was busy with his shorthand. She said, "I'd like to hear, in your words, what you were doing this evening and exactly what happened."

Reema nodded. "I was in the office writing out some cheques which Mr. Gandhi had to sign. I saw him go for his usual walk and then return to his study. The road from the garden leads into the study and I can see it from the office window. Mrs. Gandhi was gardening and—"

"What time was this? Do you remember the exact time when Mr. Gandhi returned from his walk?" Ganesh Inamdar interposed.

"I can't be sure but I think it was around six."

"Right. Go on."

"Mrs. Gandhi was in the garden doing some work, but when her husband returned she followed him inside. I took the cheques to him a few minutes later and she was still with him. I think they were in the midst of some... discussion but they stopped when I entered the study."

Her hesitation did not go unnoticed by Sonia. "Do you

know what they were talking about?" she pressed.

"I haven't a clue." Reema's response was prompt. Too prompt. "Mr. Gandhi signed the cheques and I returned to the office," she concluded, on a note of relief.

"And after that, did you hear or see anything fishy?" the sub-inspector prompted.

Reema considered the question seriously. "No, though I was in the office for a while. But, I've been thinking, something wasn't right—it was different, something odd..." She paused, frowning.

The other three waited, expectantly. Reema continued to concentrate, apparently unaware of the silence fallen in the room.

"Yes! No wonder it registered unconsciously!" She looked at Sonia triumphantly. "Mr. Gandhi is—was—ambidextrous. Meaning he would use both his hands for activities but he always signed his cheques with his right hand. Now I remember what puzzled me all evening. This evening he signed the cheques with his *left hand*!"

"Are you sure?" Sonia asked, surprised.

"Positive! I couldn't miss such an overnight change in habit."

Sonia nodded, her face thoughtful. "Anything else?"

"No, not that I can think of."

"In that case, thank you, Reema. That will be all for now though we may need to talk to you again later." Sonia smiled at the girl, who stood up readily. "Oh by the way, is it possible for you to bring me your horoscope?"

"Horoscope? I'm afraid I don't have it here. It could be at home."

"Home is..."

"In Mumbai."

"Well then, you better ask your family to send you the birth details, or better still, fax it to you immediately"

"Yes, I can do that. But, why do you need my horoscope?"

Reema couldn't hide her curiosity.

Sonia shrugged. "Operative technique."

The secretary nodded, unconvinced but Sonia merely smiled and said, "Could you please send Mrs. Gandhi in?"

Reema slipped out of the room. Sonia exchanged glances with the other two.

"A smart woman," Jatin remarked.

"And an excellent actress," Inamdar added.

"Do you really think so?" Jatin countered. "I thought she was so genuine!"

"He's right, you can never know…" Sonia responded absent-mindedly.

A knock on the door preceded the arrival of Mrs. Gandhi. The widow was short and plump, clad in an expensive silk sari. The tears had dried, leaving a mottled pattern on her cheeks. She seemed too absorbed to care. A woman unconscious of her looks. Kind? Now why had she labeled this woman as kind, Sonia wondered. But she had a distinct impression that this woman would put the needs of others before her own. Sometimes her intuition played havoc with her reasoning, Sonia decided. She had to curb it, especially when a murder case was concerned! She needed hard-core logic, not instinctive emotional responses to people which could capsize rational thought, she chided herself severely.

"Please sit down, Mrs. Gandhi. We know that this is tough on you, but you understand that this is standard procedure… ?" Inamdar began.

The lady of the mansion nodded. "I don't know how I can help you. I don't know *anything* at all.! I'm just too stunned to talk. Memories of the days spent with him, the intimacy, the loneliness, the life we led together—all that seems so pointless now. I feel so deceived, so humiliated, so betrayed by… by everything! Why did this happen? *How* did this happen? I'm so confused, I don't know what is right from wrong anymore! I don't know anything myself, how can I explain things to you or anybody else, for that matter?"

The tears were coursing down her cheeks, her control buckling under emotional pressure. Sonia left her seat and spontaneously covered the woman's shoulders with her arms. Mrs. Gandhi's agitated sobs finally receded and she rubbed her eyes angrily.

"I'm sorry, I'm a fool! I should learn to accept what's happened but somehow I can't. All those wasted years, the irreversibility of it all—it's a shame, I just don't know how to cope!"

"I understand, Mrs. Gandhi. And let me tell you, it's okay to vent your feelings. Death is a strange thing. Irreversible, yes, and final. But not the end of the world for those staying back," Sonia supplied in a quiet voice.

Silence ensued as Mrs. Gandhi tried to get a grip on her emotions. Sonia glanced at the woman sympathetically. Why did she get the impression that she had entered the climax stage of the story, Sonia wondered. So many episodes may have elapsed in the lives of Gandhis; episodes fraught with secrets left to be unearthed in the final climax scene. And would she be successful in leading the story to a successful, satisfactory end?

"I'd like to ask you just one question. Do you think you could answer that?" Sonia asked the widow.

Mrs. Gandhi nodded, producing a kerchief and sniffing into it.

"You were in the garden when your husband returned from his walk. You went inside and then you two had a talk. Could you tell me if you were arguing?"

Mrs. Gandhi looked a little startled and caught Sonia's kind gaze on her. For a second, the myriad expressions on her face evaded capture and then her face froze into indifference.

"Arguing or discussing—it's the same with us. We usually had our tiffs. But we hardly spoke because Reema arrived with some cheques to be signed and then I left too."

"And did you notice something different, or odd, while your husband was signing the cheques?" Sonia persisted.

A thoughtful expression flitted across her face, as she shook her head slowly. "No..."

"Thank you, Mrs. Gandhi. That's all for now, but we may wish to speak to you later, when you're more inclined to talk."

The widow rose and walked toward the door, her silk sari trailing behind her, and her troubled thoughts already far away from the room.

"Hmm... Intense!" Jatin expelled a sigh. "And definitely genuine." he insisted.

"And extremely in love with her husband," Sonia added, with a sigh.

She leaned against her chair, feeling disturbed. And upset. Was it the woman's helpless ramblings, she wondered. The human mind was a labyrinth, so cryptic. The detours that thought processes took made it an impossible task to peg down fiction from fact. Not to mention the bulwarks that the mind had set up. It wasn't so easy to turf out the fabrication, if there was any, from the morass of all that hurt.

Out of the blue, an idea began cavorting around the conscious edge of her mind, but she couldn't grasp it and pin it down. Well, later, she would think about it later.

Swapnil Gandhi was more in control than his mother and more willing too, to answer any questions. But he hadn't much more to contribute from what he'd already told Sonia the first time they'd met.

"You said you had something important to discuss with your father," she reminded him. "Can you tell us what it was about?"

Swapnil hesitated for a minute, then shrugged. "Well, okay, you're bound to find out sooner or later anyway," he remarked, matter-of-factly. "I needed money. I've run into some heavy debts and needed money from him."

"You're a gambler," Sonia confirmed.

"Not an accomplished one. I just had bad luck once, that's all, but Dad refused to help me. I had to talk to him and convince him to pay up for me, one last time, but I never got the chance. He… H…" Swapnil stopped abruptly. His carefree tone and façade slipped, revealing raw pain.

Was it the pain of the loss of a father or frustration at facing the hounding debtors, Sonia wondered. Swapnil excused himself and quit the room. Sonia sighed and turned to her assistant.

"Jatin, I think it's time to begin our modus operandi—to collect the horoscopes from the family. Could you do it now?"

"Yes, boss." Jatin stood up with alacrity and headed out of the room.

Inamdar excused himself, saying that he needed to question the servants. Alone in the room, Sonia couldn't help but feel a little lonely. Odd. No case had ever elicited such a reaction from her. Like a personal loss. Like a core being slowly and deliberately removed! She felt pinioned to this case and even responsible! That was absurd! Or was it something more? A moral responsibility, a human responsibility?

She stared out of the window, into the night. Then impulsively, she extracted the two horoscopes sent to her by Anand Gandhi, placing them side by side on the table. Two minutes, just two minutes… The squares with their constellations suddenly focused before her eyes, defining new statements. Was it possible? My God, if that was true… Why hadn't she thought of this before?

Jatin returned with three horoscopes and a fax. So Reema had managed to obtain hers from home.

"Thank you, Jatin. Now I need some quiet. Could you just hang around in the hall, while I go through these? Keep your eyes open and if you see anything of the slightest importance or suspicion, get right back here," she instructed.

"Right, boss!" Jatin grinned. He wished he could provide her with some music, but that would certainly be in bad taste in a house where a death had occurred! "We still have Daaima to talk to," he reminded her.

Sonia nodded absently. "After I finish with these. And Jatin—I think I shall want to make some phone calls and can you find out if they have internet facilities attached to this computer?"

"Straight away!" He returned a few minutes later. "You can use the phone and the computer in this room."

Sonia nodded, as Jatin left the room, shutting the door behind him. Automatically her favorite music began playing in her head and she closed her eyes, swaying slowly. Then as the tempo in her head increased, she moved across the room, with slow swirling movements. Jatin popped his head in and stared in astonishment. What in heavens was his boss up to!

Sonia appeared to be dancing in the silence. No, not quite, he realized with a start. The totally absorbed expression on her face with a faint smile touching her lips and her graceful rhythmic hand and body movements seemed to penetrate into the silence, and elicit a melody entirely of a different kind. The feeling was so compelling that Jatin could almost pick up the rhythm in her head! He shook his head in amazement, then slowly withdrew, leaving his boss alone with her brilliant experiments.

Slowly Sonia opened her eyes, smiling to herself. If anybody saw her, he would think she was quite mad! But this refreshing feeling of energy was so invigorating, that it was worth being called batty, she decided as she turned to the horoscopes.

Sonia sensed the uncoiling of an inner excitement as she unfolded the booklets. She placed the two horoscopes sent by Anand Gandhi on the top. Right below them, she placed

Mrs. Maya Gandhi's horoscope. Virgo as zodiac sign as well as the ascendant; Venus in the seventh house in the zodiac sign Pisces; Sun, Neptune and Uranus in the fifth house…Sonia stared at the horoscope, her breath quickening. Mrs. Gandhi's horoscope told a story, a very sad story. Lacerations of the past! She flicked open Anand Gandhi's horoscope and gasped. It was an exact duplicate of one of the horoscopes which had been posted to her. Gemini in the ascendant. The Moon, Sun and Rahu in the eighth house and the seventh house accumulated with Mars, Saturn, Mercury, Venus, Uranus and Neptune! What a unique combination! Her eyes traveled along the squares, calculating and judging. Her hands suddenly felt clammy and automatically she rubbed them against her dress. Had the night suddenly turned cold, or was it the cool breeze through the open window? She turned her attention resolutely to Swapnil's horoscope, simultaneously consulting Reema's. Certainly something on between the two of them. Harmless? Not quite, but nothing that could not be controlled. Reema's horoscope, her parents… She needed to check that out, she decided. Sonia stared contemplatively at the four horoscopes on the table and then the fifth one, disconnected and isolated, sent to her by Anand Gandhi. What had he mentioned in his letter? That the two people were going to meet and one of them was going to be hurt! Did he mean himself? Had he known that he would die? And who was the second person? If her assumptions were right… An image of a group of people sitting on a joint wooden bench rose in her mind. When one person moved or shook his leg, the whole bench moved and all the rest of the people moved… Wasn't it exactly like that? The repercussions of a deliberate act influenced the actions of others…

She picked up the receiver and quickly dialed Inspector Divekar's number. He was the only person who could help her at this hour. After a brief discussion with him, in which she outlined the details of her requirement, she hung up. The

Inspector would certainly call as soon as he had the information. Next, she logged on to the internet. Fifteen minutes of surfing and she had all the answers to her questions—well almost all. No sooner had she disconnected than the phone rang. It was Jeevan Uncle.

"You're on the right track, Sonia. Here's what you need," Inspector Divekar boomed.

Sonia quickly jotted down the information and her hand shook with excitement. Finally she had all the pieces to this puzzle, she sighed as she replaced the receiver. And what a mess it was. What a clever plot! Here was an example of how an intelligent mind could use the human pyramid to his advantage. Perfect planning, perfect implementation and exploitation of a human chain, climbing on to the shoulders of others, to achieve one's goals. But which was actually more the manifest meandering of an insensitive, warped and invidious mind! Well, luck had finally backlashed. Retribution?

A cold gust of wind made her shiver and she instantly wheeled toward the window. And gasped. A figure in a black coat, a black hat drawn low over the face, was framed against the window. A motionless, ominous figure! Her mouth went dry. It was Anand Gandhi staring back at her! In an instant the figure had vanished.

"Who's that!" she called out sharply, but silence met her ears.

She rushed out into the hall, calling out to Sub-Inspector Inamdar and Jatin.

"What happened?" Jatin asked.

Sonia opened her mouth to speak, then froze. The man in black stood at the entrance of the hall. The bearded face had an uncanny resemblance to Anand Gandhi. A thinner, more hollow-cheeked than the original but definitely the same face.

He stepped forward, his eyes boring straight into Sonia's.

"I've come to make a confession," he said in a rough voice. "I killed Anand Gandhi."

"No!" Mrs. Gandhi gasped, collapsing on to the sofa. Daaima ran to her aid.

Reema glared with bright eyes at the stranger, her fists curled into balls. Swiftly, Swapnil strode to her side and his hand covered hers.

"You can arrest me right away, Inspector, I'm ready to go," the man said.

"But who are you? And why should you kill Anand Gandhi?" Inamdar asked, nonplussed.

"I don't wish to say anything more. I've said all I have to!" the man retorted harshly.

"Sub-Inspector Inamdar, could we talk for a minute?" Sonia interposed.

The Officer nodded, looking confused. The others watched in bewilderment as Sonia led him aside and spoke to him in urgent, hushed tones. Surprise flickered on Inamdar's face. Jatin sat on a chair, his admiration for his boss, showing through the anticipatory gleam in his eyes. His boss was at it again! The phone rang and Jatin answered it, handing it over to Inamdar. The conversation was one-sided, but Sonia noticed that the Sub-Inspector seemed startled. Some new revelation? When the officer hung up, he immediately turned to Sonia.

"I have some news about Anand's death," he murmured and continued in muted tones. A sparkle of satisfaction rose in Sonia's eyes.

"What's happening here!" the man in the black coat rasped angrily. "Why are you wasting time?"

"I'd like to know what's happening, too," Sawpnil spoke up for the first time, throwing anxious glances in his mother's direction.

"I'm ready to explain. But just two at a time. Mrs. Gandhi, will you please join us in this adjoining room? And you, sir?" Sonia requested.

Mrs. Gandhi rose and followed Sonia, Jatin and the Sub-

Inspector, as if in a daze. She stumbled and the man's arm shot out to support her. If Sonia had any doubts before, they were quite resolved now.

"Let me start at the beginning," Sonia began, looking directly at the widow and the stranger sitting opposite her, on the sofa. "This afternoon I received these two horoscopes by courier and a letter from Anand Gandhi. Let me read the letter aloud to you." Sonia read the letter, then paused. "I was of course quite curious. We arrived here, only to find that Anand Gandhi had been murdered. After having spoken to each one of you, I studied the horoscopes and this is what I arrived at. One of the horoscopes sent to me by courier belonged to Anand Gandhi himself. The second horoscope belonged to someone born just two minutes after Anand Gandhi. The horoscopes were too similar to be a mere coincidence, I realized. So that left me with the one and only logical explanation. The two horoscopes belonged to *twins*!"

Jatin gasped, wonderment written all over his face. Mrs. Gandhi sat like a statue, her tear-blotched face all swollen and pale. The man beside her remained stiff with anger.

"Now without going into a lot of technical jargon, let me explain what I deducted from the horoscopes that I had. Two horoscopes of two brothers—One with Gemini as ascendant and the other with Cancer. For the sake of ease, I shall call them Gemini and Cancer. Being twins, the two ought to have had similar destinies, but the difference of two minutes changed the course of their lives drastically. Gemini had a whole lot of planets in the seventh house, which revealed him to be a dramatic, eccentric, cruel personality, even sadistic to an extent. And his eighth house had the Sun and Moon along with Rahu in Saturn's favorite sign—in short, he would prove to be his brother's biggest enemy! Now Cancer—basically a good person at heart, but Saturn in the sixth house in conjunction with Uranus, Mars and Venus, aspecting the house of siblings, turned him into his brother's victim. And this is the tough part—the lord of the seventh house Saturn and the planet of siblings Mercury, are both in the sixth house in conjunction with Uranus, Mars, Venus and Neptune—reveals that his wife would have relations with his brother!"

An audible gasp escaped Mrs. Gandhi and she rose unsteadily.

"Please sit down, Mrs. Gandhi. I haven't finished yet," Sonia warned gently.

"I don't want to listen to any of this! I won't listen!" the woman exclaimed.

"I'm afraid you'll have to," Sub-Inspector Inamdar insisted.

Mrs. Gandhi sank down heavily, the tears beginning to stream down her cheeks again.

"And now I come to the third horoscope. The lady's horoscope with Virgo as the ascendant. A victim of happenings entirely beyond her control. A pawn in the hands of destiny. Sun and Uranus together indicate melodramatic incidents with regard to her husband. But worse, the ninth house is also the brother-in-law's house. The planet of the zodiac sign Taurus in the ninth house, is Venus which is in her seventh house, which means that the lady had a relationship with the husband's brother! An extremely complicated charting of the horoscope and I admit that it startled me. But it also made the whole story stand out like a clear, rain-washed landscape.

"And so now I shall tell you a story which began several years ago and which shall lead us to what has actually transpired in this house this evening. I may be wrong, some parts may be totally construed, but I'm trying to string together a sketch of reality!

"Anand and Jayesh Gandhi are identical twins. Jayesh is Gemini and Anand is Cancer. Maya and Anand are happily married and they have a son. They live in Mulshi. Anand is constantly away on business, mostly to Mumbai, where his brother Jayesh handles the headquarters. One evening Maya's husband calls her up and tells her that Jayesh has been arrested for murdering a client. It's an open-and-shut case and Jayesh has been sentenced to fourteen years in jail! It is a while before Anand returns home, subdued and changed, and Maya puts this down to the heartrending experience of seeing his twin convicted. What Maya doesn't know however, is that the man who has returned to her is not her husband *but her husband's brother!*"

The shocked gasp from Jatin was like a gunshot. Mrs. Gandhi's face now revealed a resigned expression. The man beside her stared unblinkingly at the floor.

"Jayesh has used their identical looks to fool the law and his brother. It was so cleverly enacted that not a soul suspected that Jayesh had switched places. Not even Anand's wife! Anand writes from jail to his wife, explaining the mess, but the letter never reaches Maya. At least not then. Fourteen years pass and finally Anand is released. His first impulse is to write a threatening note to his brother warning him that he's coming home to take his revenge. But Jayesh now has other plans. He's so used to being Anand, the soul of the Cotton Empire, that he's loathe to relinquish his hard-acquired identity. He decides to keep it forever. His plan is simple. He asks his brother to meet him at the cliff—perhaps at Sunset Point—where he plans to dispose off his brother once and for all. But first, he decides to reveal his true identity to Maya, the woman he has deceived all these years. He would then head toward the cliff, get rid of his brother by perhaps pushing him over the cliff or shooting him, and then return to the house as the indignant Anand Gandhi, returned from jail!

"His plan was perfect. Jayesh sent out two horoscopes to me, to ensure that I would land here as witness to the whole drama. Then he deliberately showed Maya the two letters that his brother had written. To say that it was a great shock for her to discover that the man she'd been living with was not her husband but her husband's brother is an understatement! Reema arrived at that very moment to get some cheques signed and Jayesh deliberately signed them with his left hand, so that Reema, as an additional witness, would help him re-establish his identity as Jayesh. It was after all necessary for him to re-establish his identify, then kill his brother and return as Anand. However, he hadn't bargained for two things. One, that Maya would be so incensed that she would threaten to disclose his identity—"

"Only threatened, but *I* took his life! I killed him! He was insane and he deserved to die!" The man in black spoke up heatedly.

Sonia turned to face him and smiled. "No, *Mr. Anand Gandhi*. You did not kill him. And neither did your wife Maya, for whom you are understandably trying to cover up. Though she did hit him with the vase in her rage. Tell me, Mrs. Gandhi. Did you go out into the garden, after Jayesh revealed his identity to you?"

"Yes…" She looked puzzled.

"And you stormed back into the room, furious and determined not to allow Jayesh to get away with his scheme?"

Mrs. Gandhi nodded.

"Did something strike you as odd? The way he was sitting, perhaps?" Sonia prompted.

Mrs. Gandhi frowned. "Yes, he'd burnt up one of the letters he'd shown me. And suddenly he was leaning over his table. I remember thinking that it was odd—a moment before he was laughing so cruelly—his laughter is still ringing in my ears! And the next moment, he was quiet and reflecting, with his head on the table. But that didn't stop me from picking up the vase and hitting him hard over the head like a crazy woman!"

"He wasn't reflecting. He'd just had a massive heart attack. He was dead!"

A thundering silence ensued. Maya's face blanched and then she turned wildly to her husband. They stared at each other and hope flared in their eyes.

"Does that mean…?" Anand stammered to Sonia disbelief tainted with sudden longing.

"Now listen carefully. This is what really happened and this is the story you shall repeat. Jayesh Gandhi had a heart attack and in his struggle for survival, he knocked the vase, which fell on his head. But a spilt second before that, Jayesh was already dead! In Mrs. Gandhi's horoscope, Mars aspects the ninth house which has Saturn in conjunction with Jupiter. This indicates that she will be *tempted* to murder him but Jupiter will not allow such a thing to happen! And this means that there's no murder and hence no case. And what passed between us in this room was mere speculation, on my behalf. I was simply trying to outline a story out of the horoscopes that were sent to me! I may be wrong, of course, but I don't want any corrections!" A faint smile touched Sonia's lips.

She turned away discreetly as Mrs. Gandhi burst out sobbing and fell straight into her real husband's arms. Anand held her close, then the two rose and he led her out of the room.

"Boss, there's something I don't understand. Why send us the horoscopes?" Jatin asked.

"First, I think it was Jayesh's idea of fun. Second, he wanted to have written proof that the fake Anand really wanted to get rid of his brother. He wanted to return as Anand from jail, remember? Just as he did his best to recreate his original identity with Maya and Reema, he left proof with us so that we could vouch for the fact that he indeed had ulterior motives! Then as per his plan, he would arrive on the doorstep as the real Anand Gandhi and claim that his brother either ran away or committed suicide!"

"Whew! What a fantastic idea! How very clever!" Jatin whistled.

"And also cruel, wreaking havoc with the lives of so many people… Jatin, I'm exhausted. Do you think you can handle Swapnil and Reema?"

"Sure, boss, but what do I have to do?"

"Reema is the daughter of the man Jayesh murdered years ago. I think she's been acting as a secretary, with some poetic notion of avenging her father's death. She's young and immature and I'm certain Swapnil will take good care of her. Do you think you can manage?"

"Right, boss! I'll be right back!" Jatin grinned, thrilled beyond words at this added responsibility.

Sub-Inspector Inamdar came forward with a warm smile on his face. "I'm speechless—truly, I don't know what to say!"

"Then don't say anything at all. Remember, we agreed on this decision together," she remarked.

'Yes, but it was your idea to give them a second chance, not mine," he reminded her gently.

"They deserved it. Fate has played some cruel tricks on them; it was only fair to back off now. But let's forget it! This case is closed. We all need a goodnight's sleep, it's well after midnight!" Sonia yawned.

"I'll ask a constable to drive you back to town," Inamdar offered, as the phone shrilled into attention. Inamdar lifted the receiver. "It's for you," he told Sonia.

Surprised, she took the receiver. Inspector Divekar again?

"Hello Sonia, I've been worried, where in heavens are you?" The familiar deep drawl echoed into her ears.

"Mohnish!" Sonia exclaimed. "You've been worried about *me?*"

"Of course!" he retorted and in a flash her earlier anger and loneliness were a distant memory.

She listened to him for a few minutes and then hung up. Her fatigue too had vanished. She picked up her handbag and with a light spring to her feet headed out into the night.

CHAPTER VIII

The Last Dance

The September sun was on the horizon, painting the sky in golden-pink shades. There was still plenty of time for the famous Panchgani sunset, but already the glow in the sky was a treat to watch. Sonia's eyes feasted on the golden ball as it tilted over the tableland—a flat top of one laterite rock—which was the second largest plateau in Asia. Every single time she visited this hill station, she marveled. Panchgani was an idyllic hilly town on the crest of the Sahyadri mountain range, which derived its name from the five hills surrounding it. A favorite choice of tourists and also the perfect location for film shootings.

A cool breeze ruffled up Sonia's silky blunt cut. She tore her eyes from the beautiful sight and again observed the scenario around her.

Three large, red and blue striped garden umbrellas were set up on one side. Sonia along with Jatin, relaxed under one of these, watching sixty people bustle around them. A spot boy approached them and served them hot chai in two disposable thermacol cups. Sonia smiled at the shy kid.

"Silence, please!" A voice boomed on the hand held speaker-cone. Chirag Mehta, the producer and director of the film titled 'Ek Paheli' (The Puzzle) issued crisp orders to his team and everyone immediately fell into position. The cameraman on top of the crane, the light men with the huge HMI lights, the makeup man and junior artists hovering on the sidelines—all ready for action.

"Roll camera!" Chirag bellowed.

The clapper boy slipped in front of the camera, clapped the board and said, "Ek Paheli, Sequence 70, Scene 3, take 1."

"Music! Action!" Chirag ordered, as he observed the scene from his monitor.

The fast beats of the tabla in western fusion, rolled loudly on the Nagra, the spool recorder. Sonia watched in admiration as Nimisha, the famous actress and her friend, danced with perfect tempo and grace on the beats before a huge ornate set of a temple. The camera, raised high on top of the crane, whirred, as the crane swung smoothly in tune with the music. The light boys trained the huge reflectors and the lights on the beautiful actress. There was no doubt. Nimisha was a star—in the real sense of the word. Attired in a sequined, traditional blue and gold Bharat Natyam dance sari, her tall willowy body showed off perfect curves. Her personality emanated magic, poise and a sense of vitality. In front of the camera, she was just great.

The group on the sidelines watched in absolute silence, appreciation on their faces. Except one face. Jay—the hero of the film, was positioned at the foot of the crane and the expression on his face, startled Sonia. He was staring at Nimisha, a long fixed gaze filled with agony and misery. Whatever could cause such intense emotion in the man, Sonia wondered. Was he in love with Nimisha?

"Cut! Perfect!" Chirag boomed, pleased.

Jatin expelled a slow whistle of approval. "Wow! She's good, isn't she?" he whispered.

Sonia agreed. "The best. What perfect rhythm, and she's

supple, like a cloth in hand."

The music was switched off and the shot was okayed. Immediately a flurry of activity commenced, as trolley tracks began to be laid for the next shot. Lights changed position around the set of the temple and the entire crew including Chirag and the twelve light boys, swung into action. The make-up man ran to Nimisha to touch up her make-up. She patiently allowed her face to be dabbed and puffed, then, smiling, walked toward Sonia and flopped down on the empty chair beside her.

"How do you like it?" she asked in a cultured, husky voice.

"A wonderful experience. I'm so glad I came," Sonia expressed warmly.

The spot boy offered Nimisha a cup of chai which she accepted gratefully.

"I told you you'd enjoy the change. Sonia, we've known each other since school days and I wanted you to see what I actually did. I'm so glad you accepted my invitation, even if it's on the last day of the shoot. Just one more small sequence and we shall be done with this schedule. Then we can attend the small party at the cottage."

"And then we'll leave," Sonia reminded her.

"Are you sure you won't stay for the night?"

"No, I have work tomorrow. And it's only a three – hour drive to Pune."

"Okay, I should be consoled by the fact that at least you could come today," Nimisha flashed her famous million-rupee smile, which had lodged into the hearts of the Indian public.

"I had to. I thought it was time to brush shoulders with the great Nimisha Raikar," Sonia teased, then added warmly, "You've come a long way haven't you?"

"You mean from the time in school, when I'd been so desperate to act, that I had been on the verge of committing suicide?" Nimisha asked, memory bringing on an intense look in her light eyes. "I remember how sick I was of school and how

I longed to act, but had no permission from home. If it hadn't been for you, I would have committed suicide, Sonia."

"No, you wouldn't have. It was just that—desperation and frustration. But you were strong and managed to overcome that silly urge of taking your own life. And look at you now! Successful, sought after, highly paid with an adoring fan following!"

"You're right. It was tough. It was really tough, reaching this stage, without compromising on my principles." Nimisha rested against her chair, a reflective expression on her beautiful face. Her eyes followed the film crew hastening to organize the next part of the dance sequence.

"Look at those people. Chirag—the director, Jay—my co-star and the hero of the film, K. Kusum—my choreographer and the woman, who in a way, is responsible for my meteoric rise to success. If she hadn't choreographed dances which showcased my dancing skills, I would still be a starlet. Kusum getting on in years now. You know Sonia, each one of those people and the rest of the crowd out there—each one of them—has a secret, a skeleton in the cupboard. Jay made me a scandalous proposition, which shocked me. I instantly gave him a piece of my mind and he apologized profusely. Now we pretend as if nothing ever passed between us and we are cordial to each other. As for Kusum, each dance step of hers has a history… I think this will be my last dance with her. Believe it or not, the world of films is a quagmire. Before you realize it, you're sucked into the swamp of lies and deceit, gilded with the gloss of glamour and creativity. Too late, you realize that you're trapped. I almost wish that I wasn't here, between these people, trying to act normal. But I am here and I have to admit, if I didn't love the work, I don't know how I could've handled this feeling of being trapped."

Sonia's concerned gaze rested on Nimisha for a moment. Did she seem depressed? No, just resigned. Then as Nimisha continued talking, Sonia's gaze moved to the others. The director, with a Panama hat on his head, was discussing with the handsome Jay—heartthrob of the masses. K.Kusum listened on, offering suggestions. She was a tall, elegant lady, past her prime but carrying herself with immense dignity.

An old man offering baskets of strawberries and mulberries accompanied by a young boy, approached her. Kusum tasted the fruits and seemed to like them. Sonia watched in amusement, as the choreographer spoke in a raised voice to the man, who was apparently a little deaf.

"Panchgani is famous for its berries!" Nimisha remarked unnecessarily. Then, suddenly she leaned toward Sonia and whispered. "I have some real damaging proof. It can ruin someone."

Sonia blinked. Immediately Nimisha straightened and resumed in a normal tone. "If you needed story material for a film, I can promise you that each one of them can boast a background, far more colorful and fascinating than fiction! But then I think you can deduce that from their horoscopes, can't you?" she asked, interest glimmering in her light eyes.

Sonia shrugged. "I probably could tell."

"Good, I specifically asked Chirag, Jay and Kusum to bring their horoscopes, on location. I hope you haven't forgotten your promise of reading our horoscopes, have you?"

Sonia particularly disliked a general reading of horoscopes. However, she didn't want to hurt her friend and she'd agreed to keep time for a reading session.

"No, I haven't. But just a quick run through, okay?" she conceded.

"Oh, good! After this sequence, it will be pack up time and the whole film unit will leave for Mumbai. Just a few of us are staying back for the night, because the hotel manager insisted on inviting us for a party he was throwing this evening. You and Jatin will of course join us and then we can have a small horoscope reading session."

The next shot was ready and Nimisha excused herself. Sonia settled against her chair once more, to be entertained by the high power activity of the film scene. Idly her eye roved from the scene of action to the sidelines. A few other vendors and tourists were hanging about, giggling and enjoying the trials and errors of the rehearsals. Sonia made a mental note that she had to buy a basket of strawberries and some jam for her parents. Later, when the shoot was over, she'd stroll around the pretty town and do some shopping.

The rehearsals for the take were taking longer then expected, but Jatin watched with full concentration. Sonia picked up the newspaper she had bought that morning, on the way to Panchgani, but which she hadn't had a chance to read. Her eyes flicked over the headlines, her feet tapping absently along with the music on the Nagra. At a particular write-up she paused, her pulse quickening. The Owl! It was reported that he was last seen in Panchgani! How very odd, she thought. He had moved from Mumbai to Panchgani and the police were once again on his trail. But would they be able to catch him? And if they didn't, what would be his next destination? Pune? Sonia couldn't help but experience an unusual, rather childish thrill at the thought.

The shot was ready for the final take, so Sonia folded the newspaper and concentrated on Nimisha.

The sun was setting over the horizon in blazing colors. Sonia drank in the glorious sight, as the film unit packed up. The huge lights, their stands and long cables with the extension boards were loaded into a van. Others were pushing boxes of hired set property like table lamps, sofa cushions, kitchenware, paintings into another van. Earlier, the set of the temple was dismantled in such record time, that Jatin had gaped in amazement. As one by one, the loading completed and the generator van, the buses and cars crawled out of the town, Jatin sighed. It had been a great experience, being in close quarters with a real film crew and trying to understand first-hand the technique of film production. If his career as a detective didn't work, he could easily take to filmmaking!

"The film unit has left," he reported to his boss, unnecessarily.

Sonia nodded.

"What about us? When do we leave?"

"Late evening. I'm just going to have a brief horoscope reading session with Nimisha and her friends, then we're free to return to Pune."

"Boss, I thoroughly enjoyed myself today. Thank you!"

"Thank Nimisha, not me."

"Do you really mean that? Wow, I'd love to talk to her and take her autograph!" Jatin exclaimed, starry eyed.

Sonia laughed. "Go ahead, before she returns to her cottage. She's right there beside her car! In the meanwhile, I'm going to the market. Catch me there after you're done with the acknowledgments!"

The market was a small quaint place consisting of a single, long street. Shops selling leather goods, footwear, hand-woven multi-colored mattresses and fruit products, lined either side of the street. The whole market road had a charming, magical feel to it, as tourists flourished in an array of colors, in the crepuscular light. Sonia and Jatin strolled along, checking out the items on display. Jatin had bought a walking stick with a carved dog head and Sonia's shopping bag was almost full with mixed fruit and mulberry jam and two baskets of strawberries.

She paused at a shop selling hand-woven cotton carpets. The striped carpets were piled high, one on top of the other, inside and outside the shop. Sonia ran her hand over the carpets and picked out the jazziest one.

"I hope that's not for the office," Jatin commented over her shoulder.

"Actually it is," Sonia confirmed.

"But boss, you can't! It's too… too *feminine*!" Jatin protested.

Sonia raised an eyebrow. "And what's wrong with it being 'too feminine'?"

Jatin hesitated. "Think about the image of the office! It's Stellar Investigations—a detective agency—"

"Run by a woman—a very feminine and stylish woman, I hope," Sonia completed and her tone brooked no argument.

Jatin shrugged. "Don't say I didn't warn you!"

Sonia turned back to the carpet, shaking her head, in mild annoyance. The vendor, a strapping young fellow, in a thick multi-colored shirt which appeared to be stripped off the mattresses, smiled encouragingly at her.

"How much for it?" Sonia asked him in Hindi.

"Nine hundred rupees."

"Nine hundred! That's too much!" Sonia brushed him off.

"Ok, how much are you saying?" The vendor seemed ready to bargain.

"Four hundred rupees," Sonia stated.

"Boss, that's too cheap," Jatin whispered in her ear and Sonia frowned at him.

"Four hundred rupees!" the vendor exclaimed visibly shocked. "That is not even my basic purchase price!"

"Four hundred rupees," Sonia insisted, firmly.

"What Madam! Quote something reasonable."

"Ok. Four hundred and fifty and that's my last price," she conceded.

"Seven hundred."

"Boss, Seven hundred seems reasonable to me," Jatin whispered again.

Sonia threw him her worst frown. "Jatin, go away!" she hissed fiercely.

The vendor watched their exchange with a great deal of curiosity. "Seven hundred?" he asked hopefully.

"Four hundred and fifty." Sonia unsympathetically and

firmly stuck to her price.

"No, Madam, too cheap." The vendor looked downcast.

Even the most hard-hearted purchaser would've melted at the vendor's dejected expression. Jatin did. But not Sonia.

"Fine!" She shrugged and turned to leave.

"Ok, take it!" The vendor intervened hastily. "But, mind you, you are getting it dirt cheap and please don't tell anybody at what price you bought it." He stuffed the carpet into a plastic bag, accepted the money and turned to the next customer.

Both he and Sonia looked quite pleased.

She clutched Jatin by the elbow and led him away from the shop. "The next time I'm bargaining, don't you dare whisper advice into my ear!" she warned him.

"But I was only trying to help!" Jatin protested.

"Of course!" Sonia grimaced.

Jatin couldn't help grinning appreciatively. "But I must say that you did a good job. That was a good bargain. Well done!"

"Thank you," Sonia smiled, sweetly. She thrust the carpet into her assistant's hands. "You may as well go keep this in the van," she told him, then added on a friendlier note, "And don't worry, the moment I lose a case because of the carpet, it goes straight home."

Jatin grinned. Tucking the carpet under his arm, he trudged to the van, whistling tunelessly. Sonia smiled after him. He was such a child at times!

She resumed her stroll down the street, glancing at the leather goods displayed in the well-lit windows. She spotted some hand-knitted cardigans on the other side of the road. It was while she was crossing the street that she had an uncanny feeling. Like someone was staring at her. She whipped around, her gaze probing the crowd for a familiar face. But the passers-by, mostly tourists in groups, were engrossed in their own shopping and merry-making. Sonia shrugged. Her imagination was playing tricks on her! She continued down the street, her ears extra sensitive to the sounds around her. Suddenly the skin on the back of her neck prickled and she wheeled around again. No, this was no imagination. Someone or something was definitely following her. But who was it? Her cruising gaze yielded no results, and perplexed, she turned toward the van. She may as well return to the cottages where the party was to take place.

She was half way across the street, when a hand clasped her by the shoulder. Sonia was startled.

"Hi!" a familiar voice drawled.

"Mohnish!" Sonia exclaimed. "What in heavens are you doing here?"

Mohnish grinned from ear to ear. He looked quite handsome in a lemon yellow cotton shirt and ink blue jeans. Dark glasses shielded his eyes from the evening sun. He threw an appreciative glance over Sonia's sleeveless, black Top and cream trousers. "I'm here to do a feature on Chirag Mehta."

"On Chirag! Are you sure?" Sonia couldn't hide the suspicion in her voice.

"What do you mean?" A frown puckered his brow.

"I mean, isn't it too much of a coincidence that we both should be in Panchgani on the same day?" Sonia asked. "Are you positive you're not following me?"

"Following you!" Mohnish couldn't have looked more surprised. "Why would I follow you?"

"I don't know," she admitted. "Ok, forget it! I'm just a little hyper." She brushed off further conversation and began walking toward the van.

Mohnish fell in step with her. "I can see you don't like coincidences. You're not happy to see me here."

Sonia stopped. Crowds jostled around her, making a discussion difficult. "I'm sorry. I didn't mean to be rude. It's just that it is a real coincidence. Forget it. Are you going directly to Chirag for the interview?"

"I think I will. So I'll see you in Pune, tomorrow?" Mohnish asked her seriously.

"Of course!" Sonia smiled, holding out her hand. "Goodbye."

Mohnish grasped her outstretched hand in a warm handshake. "Bye."

It was dark outside and merry sounds of laughter and spoons clinking against glass plates, drifted into the cottage. Jay was pacing in the room, an expression of deep worry marring his good looks. Chirag swirled the drink in the glass, hiding the exasperation he felt. Jay was intelligent and urbane but sometimes he got a little too panicky.

"You've got to stop this at once, Jay. What's done is done. You can't really undo anything can you?"

"No I can't," Jay exclaimed. "But I've got to do something! What if she goes with the knowledge to the police?"

"Police? You're crazy! She wouldn't do something so foolish!" Chirag laughed. "Anyway, she has no proof."

"She can tell them what I said to her."

"What *did* you say to her?"

Jay looked at Chirag. "What do you mean? I was very clear, wasn't I?"

"Were you?" Chirag raised an eyebrow. "Can you repeat what you said to her?"

"Of course. I said, 'Nimisha, there's someone very special who desires to interact with you. Someone who wishes to shower you with love and everything you've ever desired in life.' That's what I said to her."

"Right. And what does that indicate? You took no names, you made no unpleasant requests. Don't you see? You simply implied and hinted. She can't go to the police with hints and suspicions!"

Jay stared at Chirag for a moment and his brow cleared. "Put like that, it does seem rather...outrageous, doesn't it? So for the moment I'm safe? I don't need to do anything about it?"

"You don't need to do anything about it, ever!" Chirag grinned. "Just tuck that idea away for good. And think about what you have to tell him. Your main concern now ought to be facing him. I can imagine his reaction, when he hears that Nimisha turned him down. A powerful man—a dangerous man... He'll ask for a replacement—someone equally attractive."

"I hate this whole business!" Jay burst out.

"I know, but it's too late for your conscience to pop up, isn't it? This is the price you have to pay for opportunities, success and money. Focus on these goals and everything seems tolerable." Chirag advised kindly. "Come on, let's freshen up and join the others. I want to meet this astrologer Sonia something, Nimisha's friend!"

K.Kusum glanced at herself in the mirror. She smiled grimly, studying her reflection—tall and graceful, draped in a plain black, glimmering *salwar kameez.* She ought to have become an actress. She had the looks—oh not the light eyed, classic, fine features of Nimisha—but a face with character and strength. Yes, she had plenty of strength. She knew that had an opportunity presented itself, she would've been good as an actress. But destiny had led her down the path of choreography. And God alone knew how difficult it had been to establish herself in this world of cut-throat competition. She had barely survived, at first and then a stroke of luck had cleared the way to success. She had never looked back. Until now. Suddenly she felt afraid. She couldn't afford to lose all that she'd achieved in life. She'd struggled too hard and for far too long to let it slip out of her hands. She couldn't give it up all now, at the zenith of her career. Not for anyone!

K.Kusum straightened, squaring her shoulders. She was the best, no matter what. A faint smile of satisfaction crossed her lips.

There was a knock on the door.

"Come in!" she called.

The door opened and an old, dhoti-clad man stepped in with four baskets, each a combination of strawberries and mulberries.

"The berries you had ordered, Madam," the old man spoke gruffly.

"Oh yes!" K.Kusum automatically spoke loudly in Hindi. "Keep them on the table, by the window." She indicated with her hand, just in case, he didn't hear her.

The old man nodded, placing the baskets on the table.

"Good." K.Kusum picked up the basket of red and purple-blue, luscious fruits. She loved strawberries and mulberries. They were fitting goodbye gifts to give her friends. Jay, Chirag and Nimisha would certainly understand her emotions behind the gesture, she thought with a faint smile on her lips.

Jay swung a comb through his already immaculate, gelled hair and flashed himself a disarming smile. His talk with Chirag had lifted his mood considerably. Now he could look forward to this last evening, with his friends. Tomorrow would be rest day and then again, his nose would be to the grindstone.

A knock on the door, preceded the arrival of an old man with a basket of berries.

"*Kusum madam ne phal bheja hai.*" Kusum Madam has sent fruits.

"*Shukriya,*" Jay thanked him in Hindi.

The old man handed him the basket and shuffled out again.

Jay glanced appreciatively at the berries. A green satin ribbon was tied in a beautiful bow, over which a card read, 'To Jay, from Kusum.' Jay smiled. Kusum's way of saying goodbye? She really had the knack of doing it in style.

Nimisha shut the suitcase she was packing. She threw a

quick look across the neat tidy cottage and was about to leave, when there was a knock on the door.

"Who is it?" she asked, picking her purse.

"Berries for you Madam! Kusumji asked me to hand you these."

"Thanks. Do I have to pay you?" Nimisha accepted the basket.

"She's paid for it."

The old man retreated and Nimisha watched him leave. Then raising an eyebrow, she glanced at the basket, which she placed on the table, near the window. Kusum presenting her with berries? What exactly was she playing at? Surely not peacemaking? She picked up a purple-blue fruit.

"Madam, there's a call for both you and Kusumji at the reception," a hotel boy announced from the open door.

"A call for me? Can't you connect it here?"

"It's in the manager's office. That phone isn't connected to the PBX."

Nimisha dropped the berry into the basket, picked up her purse again, shut the door and followed the hotel boy to the main reception area.

The cottages were more like row houses, small and red-roofed. Tidy in their arrangement and yet pretty with pink lace curtains adorning the grill-less wooden windows. Glasses clinked as the small circle partied on the lawn adjoining the cottages, where the film personalities and other hotel guests were housed. Sonia sat in a chair, a glass of juice in her hand. Even though the majority of the film unit had departed, the others had a good reason to rejoice. The shooting was over and the film would now be promoted to the editing stage. These people, who had spent over a month together like a family, in this last schedule of the shooting, were now going to part—perhaps forever or until the next film. Whatever destiny chose.

She saw Jatin, circulating amid the guests and helping himself to a plateful of salad. It had been a good treat for him. After his unfailing loyalty to Stellar Investigations, he deserved a change. Her gaze moved to the cottages. Nimisha must be busy dressing. Actresses were usually very conscious of the way they appeared in public. Nimisha would be no different.

Sonia watched the strawberry vendor go to different cottages, delivering the goods and heading out of the premises. Leaning against the warm cushioned seat, Sonia allowed the breeze to relax her body.

"Enjoying yourself?" a low voice asked, startling Sonia.

Jay looked extremely handsome, in a white silk kurta—casual yet elegant. His smile was warm and friendly.

Sonia smiled. "Very much, thank you."

Jay seated himself beside her. "You're an old friend of Nimisha's, aren't you? But I've never seen you before."

"That's because this is the first time I'm attending a shoot of hers."

"So, how do you find it?"

"Exhausting!" Sonia grinned.

Jay threw back his head and laughed heartily. "You're absolutely right. Film work is tedious though exciting. Very few know what effort goes behind filmmaking. Sometimes I feel that it would help, if they knew. At least they would stop a minute to think before they pan a film!"

"The reverse could also be true of course. I mean, going by the supreme effort and amount of work, how many filmmakers truly stop and think before they make films? Could that be one of the reasons for the devolution of films?" Sonia asked.

Jay looked taken aback. "Oh, are you the type who prefers art cinema to commercial, song and dance mainstream films?"

"No. I'm the type who prefers to be entertained with sensible, wholesome films. And that is *not* arty cinema. That is logical, middle-of-the-stream, intelligent cinema. Songs and dance included."

"Fair enough," Jay conceded with an abashed smile. "But creativity cannot be typecast."

"Do you know what I believe is the main function of anything creative—be it performing arts, fine arts, films or books? It is *to heal.* Creativity has the power to heal—the creator as well as those exposed to it. A good creation can be therapeutic. It may ruffle your beliefs, challenge your intelligence and instigate your thought processes, but ultimately it must soothe. It must mend broken spirits, touch a core and harmonize the turbulent highs and lows of the agitated human mind. The process and the product must automatically trigger a process of healing. That is what creativity means to *me.*"

Jay stared at her, his eyes widening in amazement.

"Hey, what're you two talking about?" Nimisha slipped into the chair on Sonia's left.

"Nothing special," Sonia shrugged.

"In that case, why don't we start our horoscope reading session?" Nimisha asked.

"Here?" Sonia indicated the swirling crowds.

"Oh. They're all drunk and happy. They won't bother us. Jay, have you your horoscope on you?"

Jay nodded, a little sheepishly.

"OK, you first," Nimisha ordered.

Sonia ran an eye over the handwritten horoscope and felt a familiar tingling of excitement. Horoscopes—x-rays of people. Honest revelations of deep dark secrets. In a way, she enjoyed the power she experienced the moment she began analyzing the twelve squares with their star combinations. Wasn't this another kind of creativity, intended to serve and to heal?

As she studied Jay's interesting horoscope, another chair was drawn on Jay's right. K.Kusum flashed her pleasant smile. Sonia acknowledged the gesture, then concentrated on the horoscope in hand. Full of dramatic twists and turns, mired with love affairs and a dangerous streak… As she began a narration of Jay's past, she sensed his restlessness. It was always like that. The desire to know. And then the distinct feeling of having too much revealed.

"You are getting more and more embroiled in something unpleasant," Sonia concluded.

"Unpleasant?" Jay asked, unnecessarily.

Sonia fixed an uncompromising gaze on him. "Need I put it in black and white?"

"Well," Jay hesitated and Nimisha watched him curiously. "No, I… I think I know what you're talking about. But is there any way, I mean any chance of getting out of this… situation?"

"Yes. This year, before Jupiter changes. A clean cut before it's too late."

"It's already too late," Jay murmured and Sonia felt a little sorry for him.

"Don't worry. You will get out of it," she assured with a smile and handed him the piece of paper.

"Now my turn!" Nimisha said, with an almost childlike glee.

"And mine, after that," K.Kusum added, with a smile.

"Oh well then, you first Kusum. In fact, I'll go last." Nimisha offered grandly.

Sonia glanced from one woman to the other. The two women were smiling at each other, but Sonia detected something. Hostility? Friction between the actress and the choreographer? She shook her head off the fancies and turned to K.Kusum.

"By the way, thanks for the berries, Kusum," Jay said pleasantly.

"Oh yes, thanks a lot," Nimisha remarked.

Kusum smiled. "Just a gesture to express my pleasure at the wonderful time we shared together.'

"Same here. We worked with perfect co-ordination for this shoot," Jay agreed.

Sonia waited for them to finish, then glanced at K.Kusum.

"You first," she said.

Kusum handed her a booklet, a traditional plotting of the stars. Sonia turned to the ascendant horoscope. From the corner of her eye, she noticed Chirag emerging from behind the cottages and heading toward them. Another chair was drawn and she glanced up fleetingly. Chirag nodded a hello and completed the circle of interested listeners. Cool night air swept around them and laughter and drunken voices mingled with the atmosphere. The smell of kebabs and curries pervaded the night scents and Sonia sighed. She sensed it. Something strong and unexpected. Something inevitable.

"You've come a long way, haven't you? Hard work, plenty of it and you still had to struggle to get your due," Sonia began.

"Absolutely right," K.Kusum agreed.

"Oh, she's worked hard enough," Nimisha agreed and K.Kusum glanced at her sharply.

"You'll be doing at least two things at a time. Both creative.... do you also have a business?"

"Yes. I'm in the jewelry business. I design and produce semi-precious jewelry. But my first love will always be dance," the choreographer explained.

"That's understandable. You're good at your work," Chirag agreed.

Sonia was silent for a moment. Then she continued, on a more sober note. "You've had a tough childhood. Your siblings... do you have an invalid in the family?" she asked abruptly.

K.Kusum looked startled. "How did you know that?"

The others glanced at her, astounded. All except Nimisha. The expression on her friend's face, took Sonia by surprise. An arrogant, almost hateful smile curved her lips.

"A horoscope can be a source of many surprises," Sonia explained but waited for the choreographer to speak.

"Yes, my younger sister. She's always unwell, can barely get out of the house..."

"You never mentioned her," Chirag interrupted.

"I didn't feel the need to."

"Yes but….." Jay spoke up.

"Look, let's drop it, okay? I don't want your sympathy!" K. Kusum's sharp brush-off took everyone by surprise.

"As you wish!" Chirag shrugged. He extracted a cigarette and lit it nonchalantly.

Only Nimisha maintained a steady, unblinking gaze, her eyes hard and cruel. The choreographer met her stare with defiance.

"Who's next?" Sonia asked and Chirag promptly forwarded his horoscope.

She opened the booklet and spent a studied moment over the star combinations. Then she glanced up at Chirag and her eyes betrayed compassion. "You have success and fame and money, but there's one thing missing in your life. Or should I say someone?"

Chirag's face registered candid astonishment, then a pained expression flashed in his eyes. It was obvious that this was the last thing he expected Sonia to mention. "Hit the nail on the head," he remarked dryly.

"You experienced real love a long time ago, didn't you?" Sonia continued and the others glanced at him expectantly.

"Yes, a very long time ago. We were in the film institute together, madly in love and dreaming of growing rich, famous and old together. She was very talented. But one fine day, she simply vanished! I've never gotten over her!" The deep agonized look in his eyes surprised Sonia. The man was still madly in love with the girl!

"How sad!" Nimisha exclaimed.

"Now I know why you never married," Jay said sympathetically. "Obviously you must've tried very hard to search for her?"

"I moved heaven and earth, looking up all her friends, going to places she had mentioned even casually. I tried everything but to no avail." Chirag sighed, puffing on his cigarette. "I guess what has to happen does. After all everything happens for a reason, doesn't it? Some call it destiny."

K.Kusum was silent.

Sonia glanced at the horoscope again and remarked, "But you will meet her again. One day."

Chirag looked startled. "Are you sure?"

"Positive. Since Jupiter has entered your seventh house. Since last July."

The director stared at her, a contemplative gleam in his eyes. Not a pleased, happy look, Sonia observed. Which was odd… .

K.Kusum turned to Sonia, a sudden enthusiasm on her face.

"Do you think you can read my sister's horoscope and tell me a few things?"

"Of course," Sonia replied a little hesitantly.

"Good, I'll go fetch it."

"In the meanwhile, I'm next," Nimisha remarked dryly.

Sonia watched K.Kusum leave the table and head toward her cottage. What a strange woman! One moment she was most unwilling to talk about her sister and the next, she was anxious to show her horoscope. She wished she had more time to read Kusum's horoscope. There was something in it which she had meant to explore… something she'd meant to say but was interrupted. What was it…

But before she could spare it another thought, a chill ran down her spine. K.Kusum staggered out of her cottage. She was lurching and fighting for breath, holding her throat in agony. Sonia started, throwing her chair backwards. "Call a doctor!" she yelled.

The others turned, as she sprinted, just in time to catch the falling, gasping woman. Her face was changing color. She was spluttering, trying to say something.

"What is it, Kusum… what happened?" Sonia urged.

"I.....*he can't read....*" K.Kusum took a last gasp and was still. Her hand slid to the ground and a mulberry rolled on the lawn.

Sonia stared at the woman. Kusum's face was contorted. She sensed rather than saw the crowd gathering in fast motion around them, shocked murmurs and stifled screams thickening the atmosphere. She rose and someone hastened forward, stooping over the dead woman. Dazed, Sonia glided aside, as someone took charge of the situation, and found Jatin beside her. Solid, steady Jatin.

"Boss, are you all right?"

She nodded. Poor K.Kusum. Concerned about her invalid sister one moment. And dead the next! *This was life?*

The police sirens sounded shrilly and the next half hour was buzzing activity. K.Kusum's body was taken away before a stunned audience and her cottage was cordoned off. The crowds were ordered to stay off the premises while the rest of the film unit was advised to stay on for a couple of days, in case the Police needed to question anyone. An atmosphere of ominous anxiety settled on the merry-making group of people.

Sonia stepped forward. "Sub-Inspector Pawar?"

"Miss Samarth! What are you doing here?" The Sub-Inspector, a huge man, hefty in frame, turned toward the Investigator. A faint frown plucked his brow.

Sonia explained briefly.

"So you saw her first. Odd isn't it, this business?" Pawar frowned.

"Most definitely. If you don't mind, I'd like to help."

"You mean—all that horoscope stuff? You must be joking. This is probably murder ma'am. Murder of a famous personality, even if she's just a Choreographer. I really wouldn't like anyone messing around here. Anyway, you need to be hired first to work with us."

"I've hired her," a deep voice spoke up.

Sonia turned astonished eyes on Chirag.

"I'm in charge of this set-up and I want this terrible mess cleared up at once. I'm sorry for K.Kusum, but I can't keep my artists hanging out here endlessly. A lot of money is at stake. So I want as many forces working on this as possible."

"Thank you. I appreciate your concern for all." Sonia smiled at Chirag. Turning to Pawar, she raised her eyebrow. "I guess you have no objections now?

The Sub-Inspector shrugged, grudging acknowledgement on his face. "As you wish, Miss Samarth."

"Do you know what her last words were?" Sonia recalled. "*He can't read*! Does that make any sense?"

She and Jatin were having breakfast in the cottage. They had stayed the night after all. Jatin in a room in the main hotel and Sonia had the Cottage. Now as they finished a breakfast of Upma and coffee, Jatin glanced across the table at his boss. Her face held a frown.

"He can't read? How odd..."

"I know, all night, I've been trying to figure out what she could've meant. I mean, if someone was dying... their last words would probably be—*help, save me,* or even that *I'm poisoned,* but, *he can't read,?*"

"Poisoned?" Jatin repeated, startled. "Is that what you think?"

Sonia nodded. "Positive. Cyanide—I'm quite sure of that. Same symptoms. And besides, she was fine, when she left us. Something transpired in that cottage in those few moments she was inside. She came out instantly. It is definitely a case of poisoning."

"But boss, murder? I mean despite what the police said yesterday, I was still under the impression that this was a natural death." Jatin looked almost shocked. "Murder, in a film unit?"

"You'd be surprised at the kind of jealousies and hatred that run through this film industry. I'm surprised that we don't hear of tempers flying every moment." She thought of Nimisha's words. 'The world of films is a quagmire…'

"But who would want to kill a choreographer? I mean I can understand, strictly for filmy reasons of course, an actress wanting to kill another actress, or an actor or a director doing the same. But a choreographer, who apparently seems to be no threat to anyone's ego?"

"Yes, it's worth thinking about, isn't it? Why would anyone wish to kill K.Kusum?" Sonia spoke, almost to herself.

A knock sounded on the door and Pawar, stepped inside.

"Oh hello, Sub-Inspector Pawar. Any news?" Sonia welcomed him with a smile.

"The reports will come in soon. But we suspect murder, all right."

"Cyanide poisoning?"

"So you guessed," A faint gleam flickered in his eyes.

"I don't need to check horoscopes for what my eyes can tell me," Sonia replied sweetly.

Pawar flushed. "Look, I'm sorry. I spoke to Inspector Divekar of Pune and he said you're brilliant. I'm sorry I underestimated you." He looked a little uncomfortable.

"Oh forget it!" Sonia brushed off his apology. "Would you like to have some breakfast?"

"Oh, no thanks, I've just had mine," Pawar declined.

"Fine, let's get down to work. You searched Kusum's cottage last night, didn't you? Can you tell me what you found?"

"The room was pretty untidy. A chair and the waste-paper basket were upturned, probably in her struggle to steady herself. There was a basket of berries and her purse contents on the table."

"Yes, but what did you find?"

"Bits and scraps of paper—nothing apparently important in the waste bin. The berries have gone to the lab. We suspect that the cyanide was swallowed"

"Do you know, she's the one who sent the fruits to everyone," Sonia pointed out. "As goodbye—how fateful! How sad..."

"I heard. But then someone tampered with her berries for sure," Pawar said.

"But when? When and how did anyone have the time to tamper with the berries, provided of course, that's the way cyanide found a way into her body. How was the cyanide inserted into the berries? And of course, most importantly why?"

"The three 'Ms' of investigation," Jatin interposed with understanding.

"A good many questions and we hope to find the answers to them all," Pawar assured confidently.

"Did you go through her handbag? What was in it? Did you make an inventory?"

"Of course! All the lady stuff—compact, lipstick, a small tin of talcum powder, some papers, a horoscope, phone diary, some tissue papers, a cheque book, that's all."

Sonia was thoughtful. "You know what fascinates me most? The timing. And the fact that someone has been extremely clever and intelligent, in using Kusum's gifts against her. This has to be an inside job—someone from the film unit who had good reason to kill the choreographer, had access to the cottages and who could move about the place without rousing suspicion."

"But the film unit had left by then, except for... Do you mean one of the three to whom the berries were gifted?" Jatin asked, a little surprised.

"Possibly," Sonia replied thoughtfully.

"Rest assured. By evening we shall have found out who poisoned K.Kusum," Pawar wagered.

Admiration shone in Sonia's eyes. "I like your confidence Sub-Inspector."

Sonia glanced around the tiny makeshift shack of corrugated sheets, which had a prime location in the market place. The boy sat behind a wooden table along with his grandfather, the old man with the dhoti who sold strawberries. Bouquets of exotic local flowers and crates of berries lined the iron shelves. Jatin lolled on a tall stool, as Sonia tried to get some information out of the son.

"What's your name?" she asked in Marathi.

"Ganu," the boy, who was in his teens, replied. "What is it, what did we do wrong?" he asked a trifle anxiously.

"Nothing, absolutely nothing wrong." Sonia reassured immediately. "But I want you to tell me exactly what passed between that lady who bought the strawberries from you and your grandfather. I mean what did she say?"

"The filmy lady—Kusumji? She asked us to deliver four baskets to her cottage in the evening. So I chose the best fruits and Nana took them to her."

"Do you recognize these film people?"

"Of course! I've seen all their films. I know them by heart. I love Chirag Mehta's films. I think Jayji is okay, though. Could do better films. And Nimishaji—who doesn't love her? She's just great. All my friends think she's the most beautiful actress in the industry! Even Nana here likes her!" Ganu laughed, nudging his grandfather. "Don't you, Nana?"

Nana's wrinkled face creased into a smile of general understanding.

"Nana, you took the baskets to Kusum?" Sonia asked in a raised voice.

"Yes. I took them to Madam but she said she'd like some ribbons put on each basket. And she asked me go to the general store and buy the ribbons. Pink, blue, red and green, according to the cards."

"And did you do as she told you?"

"Of course," Nana spoke slight irritation grating his voice.

"I bought the ribbons and put them on the cards, just as she told me."

"And then what did you do?"

"Madam had informed the hotel Manager that I would be delivering the fruit baskets, so I had no problem moving about the premises. First, I kept Kusumji's basket—she had ordered one for herself too—on her table. Then I went along and delivered the other fruit baskets—to Jayji and Nimishaji and then Chiragji, but he wasn't in his cottage."

"How long did it take you to deliver all the baskets?"

"Just a few minutes. All these people are put up in four cottages in a row. It hardly took me any time at all."

"And did Jay and Nimisha say anything to you?"

"They thanked me."

Sonia smiled at Ganu and his grandfather. "Look, if you remember anything else—anything at all of the slightest importance—please contact me immediately at the cottage. And thank you for your help."

Nana and Ganu nodded.

Jatin looked at his boss.

"Where to next, Boss?"

"Nimisha Raikar."

Sonia glanced around the cottage, while Nimisha freshened up in the bathroom. The cottages were identical. A small sitting-room and a bedroom with attached toilet. Neat and cosy. On the table stood a basket of mulberries. Sonia fingered the slightly withered fruits, past their glory, her hand traveling down to the card. It simply said Kusum. A pink satin ribbon adorned the bottom of the bouquet in the shape of a bow. A coffee pot filled with steaming hot coffee, was awaiting consumption.

"Sorry to keep you waiting, Sonia. But I like to sleep in late and last night was such a shock. I still can't believe it!" Nimisha was in her nightgown, with a woollen wrap-around thrown casually over her shoulders.

She poured herself a cup of coffee, then settled down in the chair opposite Sonia and Jatin. "You wish to ask me something, don't you?"

"Just a few questions."

"Okay, shoot." Nimisha sipped delicately from the steaming cup.

"Do you have any idea why anyone would want to kill Kusum?" Sonia asked.

Nimisha shook her head. "Absolutely no idea. I mean who could do this to Kusum? In fact, I'm truly shocked."

"Are you?" Sonia asked a trifle sharply and Nimisha stared at her with wide eyes.

"You don't mean to imply that I actually *know* something about this business?" the actress asked incredulously.

Sonia matched the stare, with a contemplative glint. "All I *know* is that, something was not right between the two of you, last night. I sensed the friction and heard your snide remarks. What is it Nimisha? Tell me. You were so different with her last night. Why were you so... hard... so cruel, so unlike you, with her?"

Nimisha blushed. "So you noticed."

"Of course! Something was going on between the two of you and I need to know what it was. It may be unrelated to Kusum's death, but I would still like to know. You've got to tell me, Nimisha, whatever it is!" Sonia urged.

Nimisha rose gracefully and poured herself another cup. Then still standing, she faced Sonia. "Yes, there is something but I'm positive that it has nothing to do with Kusum's death, which according to me was just something she ate wrong, or perhaps even a heart attack. And right now, I'm not even sure I should repeat the knowledge. Now that Kusum's gone, I do not wish to reveal the skeletons in her cupboard."

"But earlier, you wished to do so," Sonia said shrewdly.

Nimisha nodded. "I thought it was the right thing to do—then."

"But if it's important you've got to tell me!"

Nimisha dithered, then sighed. "Well all right. I'd discovered a secret of Kusum's that no one, not a soul was aware of. I think you almost discovered it yourself last night."

Sonia and Jatin passed each other quick looks, but maintained a silence.

"More than a month ago, Chirag and I were returning from a day's shoot and our car broke down near Malewadi, a village which is about two hours from here. We had to take help from the locals. While the village mechanic was inspecting the vehicle, I strolled around and came upon a very pretty cottage. A thin, pale woman was sitting in the garden, being attended to by a nurse. She recognized me at once and invited me inside. I got chatting with her. She seemed to know so much about me and mentioned all my films and dances that had become a hit. I was led inside the cottage for tea and there on the shelf I saw photographs of Kusum and this woman. I was astounded, when she admitted that she was Kusum's sister Geeta!"

Jatin turned a quick surprised look toward Sonia, but she was concentrating completely on her friend.

Nimisha shook her head reflectively, then continued. "It was while Geeta went to her room to fetch something that the nurse bared the real relationship between the sisters, to me. A stroke had left Geeta very ill and weak, years ago, and she rarely left the house, but her mind functioned well and she could illustrate what she thought. Geeta was a most, exquisite dancer and chorographer before the stroke. But after the illness, it was her sister who took advantage of her talent. The nurse told me how, after a year when Geeta recovered sufficiently to walk around, Kusum—who was always aware that her sister was the more talented of the two—had brainwashed her into thinking that she would always be too weak to pursue a career and she

Kusum would have to take care of her all her life. Not wanting to be a burden on her sister, Geeta, despite being an invalid, had wanted to assist her. She continued to be extremely creative. So creative, in fact, that each step of Kusum's that took her up the ladder of success was a product of Geeta's brain. Kusum realized that she had finally found her gold mine under her very roof! Without being overtly tyrannical, Kusum had subtlety applied emotional pressure on the weak sensitive Geeta; deliberately kept her talented sister under wraps for fear of exposing her own lack of expertise and managed to stay in the limelight herself. When Geeta showed me her illustration book on which she etched all her creativity, I was thoroughly moved and upset.

"I knew that I had met Geeta purely by chance and learnt this most extraordinary and fascinating truth. But I couldn't let it go at that. I liked the soft-spoken Geeta a lot and was convinced that what I'd heard was the real picture. I advised her to rebel against the domineering Kusum and to crawl out of the woodwork, but she was too reconciled to her non-existence. She had no strength to go against her sister, who was at least providing her with a comfortable life."

Nimisha sighed. "I was really shocked. If anyone realized that the brain behind Kusum's famous dance steps—even those that tipped me and her to stardom—was her sister, what a downfall it would be for Kusum! All her success, everything that she'd achieved in her life, would seem fake. She would be an object of ridicule and pity and her position in the film world would be lost for good."

"And did you tell Kusum all this?" Sonia inquired.

"Yes. I was hell bent on seeing justice done. I felt that if Kusum had a shred of decency she would give Geeta her due, even if she could never make use of the acclaim. Kusum and I argued a lot. I asked her to give Geeta her credit, but she refused brazenly. Do you know what she said to me? *'Upon my dead body!'*—that's what she said to me. No remorse, no regrets. Just plain cold denial. Sometimes I wonder if this wasn't suicide after all. Perhaps Kusum thought it was the best way out—to die instead of face the humiliation and stigma of rejection."

"Suicide," Sonia repeated reflectively. "Yes, I know what you mean. K.Kusum must not have taken your "suggestions" kindly. You were a threat to her existence as a choreographer. Perhaps the only way out for her was death."

Jatin flashed Sonia a look. Something about her manner made him speculate. What was running through her mind? he asked himself.

"But this wasn't suicide, was it?" Nimisha asked astutely. "Was Kusum really murdered?"

"I personally think so. Nimisha, what did you do before you joined me at the lawn?"

"I was getting dressed, of course. Then since we were all going to leave the next day, I got busy with some packing. I had almost finished when the vendor appeared with a basket of berries from Kusum, which surprised me. But then, I felt that she was trying to pacify things between us, so I accepted the gift. I think almost immediately, the hotel boy came calling me, saying there was a phone call for Kusum and me. But when we both reached the Manager's cabin, the line was blank."

"Is that unusual?" Sonia asked with piqued interest.

"Not particularly." Nimisha shrugged. "Usually fans try this kind of stuff. They obtain the number from somewhere and are content to simply hear your voice."

"And then what happened after that?"

"I joined you and Jay."

Sonia nodded. "I guess that's all for now. Nimisha if you remember anything unusual—anything at all—please pass it on to me, okay?"

"I will," Nimisha promised.

Jatin helped himself to *kofta* curry and *puris,* tucking in with relish. The sound of the television was a little too shrill for his taste, but his boss was working and her musical taste took first precedence. Personally, he would have opted for a soft, romantic instrumental while he ate his lunch. This rock band screeching out harsh vocals would certainly wreak havoc on his digestion, giving him a stomach upset. But he would bear that. It was up to him to see that his boss worked in the most conducive surroundings away from home!

Sonia sat on the bed, four horoscopes spread out on the mattress. Chirag, Jay, Nimisha and K.Kusum. The raucous singing seemed to grate into her head, deep down, creating abrasive scratches on her thinking. She needed to rack her brains. Fast. And the hard rock helped, with the fuzzy guitar lead etching subliminally between her numb grey cells, jogging them into attention. Chirag. Gemini on the ascendant in conjunction with Venus, Mercury, Uranus and the Moon. A director of great class, a little theatrical and melodramatic in his treatment of films perhaps, but totally committed to cinema, in his own unique way. His horoscope revealed a very talented man, willing to do anything for his goal. Mars aspecting inauspiciously on the seventh house indicated dramatic twists on the love scene. Would he be willing to do anything for love?

Jay's horoscope, she had already seen. She spent a thoughtful minute over it, before turning to Nimisha's. Complex, creative and constructive. Certainly not destructive. But then there was that streak—that wild streak and that constant obsession with suicides. Finally, Sonia lifted K.Kusum's horoscope and stared at it. Ascendent—Scorpio. A complicated plotting of the planets. Uranus in the eighth house indicated a possibility of poisoning. But what had it been last night that she had almost discovered in her horoscope? Something that had been on the tip of her tongue?

Drumbeats had now joined the guitar lead, strings reacting melodiously to the fast moving fingers of the guitarist and suddenly Sonia's mind began vibrating. Her feet began tapping and her fingers drummed on the table. She closed her eyes, absorbing the music and opening her mind to the wave of revelation she sensed was coming. As the music reached its peak, Sonia's eyes widened, her thoughts reaching a crescendo. My God! *"He can't read!"*

Jatin glanced at her flushed face, his hand freezing in mid-air. He recognized that look on his boss's face.

"Jatin can you call up Sub-Inspector Pawar and ask him if there was a card on Kusum's basket? And, if he can't bring it along, could he tell you what was written on it?"

"Right, boss!" Jatin pushed his empty lunch plate aside and quickly washed his hands.

As he sped to follow instructions, Sonia lifted two horoscopes, gazing at them sadly. This whole business reminded her of the carrom board game, where pocketing the wooden pieces was such an art. In an attempt to strike right, sometimes you flicked the striker so slow that the piece barely reached the pocket and sometimes the timing and pressure of the flick on the striker was so perfect, that the piece slid smoothly into the pocket. But very often, you flicked the striker so hard, that the piece popped into the pocket and popped right out again, or the piece and the striker both fell into the pocket! Sonia sighed. That was exactly what had happened with this murder. Not only had the piece jumped right back but the striker had been pocketed!

Jatin returned, with the Sub-Inspector in tow, looking puffed up and important. Sonia looked at them expectantly.

"Here's what you need," Pawar said and handed her a piece of paper. "I copied the words out for you, though why you need it beats me!"

Excitedly, Sonia read the words and said, "Thanks, this is just what I need. Have you any other news?"

"Yes, it was definitely cyanide that killed her. In the mulberries."

"I know," Sonia spoke in a resigned voice. Suddenly the glow of knowledge had left her face.

"You know?" Pawar asked.

"I'll explain in a minute. But will you excuse me a second? Jatin, can you come with me?"

"Of course!"

At the door, Sonia paused. "Sub-Inspector Pawar, can you do me a favor? Can you send a constable to invite Jay, Nimisha and Chirag here? I believe they are all sitting in the hotel lounge. I think we need to talk."

To Pawar's great amazement, Sonia and her assistant hastened out of the room. Pawar stared uncomprehendingly at the open door. He momentarily wondered if he should leave, but then decided against it. Inspector Divekar had spoken highly about this girl, and something told him, that he should hang on. Witness her investigating techniques with his own eyes. He gesticulated to the Constable standing outside and issued instructions. Minutes later, Nimisha, Jay and Chirag trooped into the cottage.

"What's up? Do you have news?" Chirag asked the Sub-Inspector, who shrugged.

"I guess so," Pawar said.

Silence ensued as they awaited Sonia's return. She arrived minutes later, followed by Jatin. The deep flush on her face betrayed her excited mood.

"Did you find it?" she asked Jatin.

"Yes, this card from Jay's fruit basket says *'To Jay, from Kusum'*," Jatin handed her card.

"And this one from Chirag's basket says *'To Chirag, from Kusum'*," Sonia completed. There was a glitter in her eyes, as she held up another gift card. "And this one from Nimisha's room says *Kusum* and the card from Kusum's room says *'To Nimisha, from Kusum'*! It all seems as clear as rain now."

The others stared in confusion at Sonia.

"What is clear as rain?" Jay asked, frowning.

"What does all this mean?" Pawar asked.

"It means that K.Kusum was killed because of cyanide injected into the mulberries," Sonia explained dryly.

The others gasped, but Sub-Inspector Pawar raised a plump hand. "We already know that."

"Boss," Jatin began patiently, "let's start at the beginning. Who killed K.Kusum?"

Sonia looked from one expectant face to another. Nimisha—anxious, Jay and Chirag—curious, Jatin—eager as always to know the truth. Pawar—a curious blend of annoyance and impatience. Worried that she had indeed got to the bottom of the matter, before him.

"K.Kusum killed herself," she announced.

"What!" Nimisha exclaimed. "Suicide?"

Sonia shook her head. "No. It wasn't suicide, Nimisha. I think it's time you braced yourself to hear the plain truth."

An ominous silence ensued as Sonia seated herself on a chair opposite the others.

The Sub-Inspector leaned forward. "What makes you so sure she killed herself?"

"Partly the horoscopes, partly logic and partly her dying words—*he can't read*." Sonia passed him a brief smile. "I think it won't be difficult to surmise that it all began when Nimisha discovered that Kusum had an invalid sister, who was far more talented than her. Also, that each dance step of Kusum's which had led her to stardom, was actually Geeta's. Nimisha told Kusum about her discovery and demanded that justice be done. But she refused. In Kusum's own words, '*upon my dead body*!' Right Nimisha?"

Nimisha nodded. She seemed nervous and jittery. Jay stared at the actress, digesting this bit of news. Chirag's face looked grimmer than ever. Sonia concentrated on the actress.

"What Nimisha did not know was that in demanding justice

for Geeta, she was actually imperiling her own life!"

Nimisha gasped. "What… what do you mean?"

"You threatened to expose Kusum, to make the world aware of her incapacities, to undo whatever Kusum had achieved in her life. It was a life and death matter for a woman, hard-driven with ambition. She had no choice. It was your death and her life!

"She planned it all carefully, leaving it until the last day. Her goodbye gifts. Strawberries and mulberries. To all of you, including herself. When Nana, the old man arrived with the baskets, she deliberately asked him to buy satin ribbons. Then she quickly injected small doses of cyanide into some of the mulberries in one basket and put a card with Nimisha's name on it. When the old man returned with the ribbons, she asked him to put the ribbons as per the names on the cards and then deliver them. She made very sure that Nana understood what she said, even though he was slightly deaf. But what she hadn't bargained for was the fact that he couldn't read! Nana did not reveal to her that he was illiterate. He put a pink ribbon on Kusum's own personal basket and delivered it to Nimisha's room. But the basket with the poisonous fruits, which was actually meant for Nimisha was left on Kusum's table, absolutely without her knowledge."

"You mean…" Jatin began, comprehension dawning on his face.

"You got it. That basket was meant to kill Nimisha not Kusum."

Nimisha paled, her knuckles turning white under a tight clutch. "Oh my God!" she whispered.

"Now this is what I think happened. Kusum left us to fetch Geeta's horoscope. Without the least doubt that all the baskets had been delivered as per instructions, she casually popped one or two mulberries into her mouth. In a flash, it had hit her that something had gone wrong. She realized that she hadn't long to live and had stumbled out into the open. Too late. She died, her last thought being the shocking realization that the baskets got interchanged because Nana could not read. All along, I've been wondering what she meant. And then it struck me that she probably said what was on her mind as her last dying thought! That *he can't read*!"

A stunned silence seemed to fill the room. Nimisha looked dazed. Jay and Chirag amazed. Pawar was trying his best to hide his admiration.

"Sounds fantastic, but not impossible. But an important question is how did Kusum get hold of the cyanide? We need evidence, you know," the Sub-Inspector said.

"And we shall have it. First, let's talk about the cards on the baskets. These are the words on the card found on Kusum's basket. They say, *'To Nimisha from Kusum'*. And Nimisha's basket, in her room had a card with *'Kusum'* written on it. When I first saw it, I found it a little odd that instead of saying *'from Kusum'* the card simply said *Kusum*. Of course, it did not strike me at that particular point that basket was never meant to reach that room. If it hadn't been for Nana's blunder, Kusum would've been alive by now and Nimisha would've been dead!"

Nimisha shivered, looking as if she was really being forced to taste some cyanide!

"Kusum used to design and produce jewelry," Sonia continued. "Cyanide is often used in this business. I'm positive that the small tin of talcum powder that you found in her handbag contains liquid cyanide, not talcum powder! What remains is the syringe that injected the cyanide. I believe that a real thorough search of Kusum's cottage would probably reveal crushed glass and needle."

Sub-Inspector Pawar stood up, rocked on his feet with his hands in his pant pockets, indecision written all over his face. Then with sudden resolve, he nodded briefly and whisked his huge bulk out of the cottage. Jatin glanced at his boss, smiling warmly.

"Boss, how did you guess? I mean to find that Kusum got caught in a web of her own making?"

"Her horoscope. Something about her configuration had been bothering me. Last night and all of today, the idea kept niggling at the back of my mind—that I ought to have noticed what it was. And finally, I struck the right note. There were unique combinations in Kusum's horoscope. The lord of the first house, Mars was placed in the ninth house with Cancer—an unfriendly star or a debilitated star—afflicted by Saturn, which also aspected the third house—the house of siblings—very unfavorably. In short, Kusum would benefit from a very talented but ill sister. Besides, Moon and Neptune facing each other; Uranus in the house of death; Sun in the twelfth house in conjunction with Mercury, with another debilitating zodiac sign Libra—all indicated that Kusum would be responsible for her own destruction. I discovered that not only was Kusum a danger and threat to others, but she was also a potential death trap for herself.

"That made me look at the matter entirely differently. I mean, Nimisha's story very clearly revealed that between the two, she made a better target for murder. Kusum had more reason to kill Nimisha than Nimisha or anyone else had to kill Kusum. Then why had Kusum ended up being the victim? Then it all suddenly unraveled like lightening. Kusum's elaborate plan had backfired."

"But what if it had worked? Wouldn't Kusum have been the prime suspect?" Jay asked.

"I doubt it. Firstly, except for Nimisha, not a soul was aware of Geeta's existence, so the seed of the murder would have been buried forever. Lack of motive automatically makes the case weak. Besides Kusum had sent the strawberries and mulberries to all of you, including herself. She could always claim that she had no idea how the cyanide reached the fruits.

After all, the baskets were placed on the table near these wide-open windows. Anyone could have just hopped in and injected the cyanide. And not a soul would've noticed, since the rest of you were at the party on the other side of the lawn. And, at an appropriate time and place, Kusum would've disposed off the talcum powder tin and the syringe."

A minute ticked by—a minute loaded with the churning thoughts of the people in the room. Then Chirag remarked slowly. "If it hadn't been for you, no one would've ever discovered that Kusum had, in reality, planned to kill Nimisha."

Nimisha shivered again. "I can't believe it! That she could have gone to such great lengths, for such selfish reasons. Poor Geeta. I wonder what she would do now. No sister, no creative satisfaction, lost in some remote village."

"It needn't be like that at all," Sonia said quietly and Nimisha looked at her in surprise.

"What do you mean?"

Sonia leaned forward and took her friend's hand. "You wanted justice, didn't you? So do it. Give the unsung Geeta her due. Find her, give her publicity and if possible use her as your personal dance instructor. Who knows, with your support, she may bounce back to energy. And your actions may give a new lease of life to someone almost non-existent so far!"

Nimisha stared at Sonia, understanding gleaming moistly in her eyes. "Sonia, you're a gem, you know that?"

"All I know is that there's someone up there who is constantly watching us. Call it a super power or call him God, but he has his own, singular way of seeing justice done. Perhaps he has chosen you as his means, to save Geeta from the clutches of oblivion. Perhaps, that's why you are still here, hale and hearty—for a reason?"

Nimisha nodded, her eyes filmed over with tears. "I'll see you later," she said huskily and left the room.

Sonia was silent for a moment, then she glanced up at the

others. Chirag sat staring at the carpeted floor, deep in thought. Jay rose.

"Does this mean that we are free to leave now?" Jay asked.

"I think that's up to Sub-Inspector Pawar. He may have some formalities to wind up," Sonia replied.

Chirag straightened and took Sonia's hand in a warm clasp. "Thank you. You have done us all a great favor. I can't tell you how glad I am that I hired you! Will you please send your bill to my office? This is my card." He removed a plastic visiting card from his wallet.

"I will. Will you be leaving immediately?"

"My production manager has arrived from Mumbai this morning and as soon as we settle our accounts, we shall leave. Thanks again."

"You're welcome." Sonia was formal. She watched the two men quit the cottage—Jay with a happy bounce in his step and Chirag looking weary.

Jatin smiled at her. "Boss, there's so much to learn from you!" he remarked.

Sonia turned to him and the sparkle in her eyes took him by surprise. "Oh yeah?" she asked.

The evening light was fading, as Chirag headed toward his cottage. It had taken all day to settle the accounts and his production manager had finally left. Jay and Nimisha had departed from the hotel ages ago. But he'd hung on, feeling loathe to leave the hill-station. He had dealt with the money matters, with an uncharacteristic impatience, longing to retreat into his world. He felt upset and angry, as he opened the cottage door. Without bothering to switch on the lights, he strode straight to his half-packed suitcase. Riffling intolerantly through the clothes, he extracted a photograph. Then slumped on the bed, sudden tears coursing down his cheeks, his head in his hands.

"I'm sorry, I'm sorry" he muttered. "But it was the only way!"

The street light fell on the bed, and on the smiling face of the photo. He glanced at it again, intensity raging through his body. "Why did you leave me? Why didn't you contact me? All this hurt and pain and anger! How did you expect me to cope? And look what's happened now! I had to save *her!* I had no choice. I had to save her, you have to understand!"

"I think she will understand," a quiet voice spoke and Chirag almost jumped off the bed in shock.

"Sonia!" He rose unsteadily, as if drunk.

Sonia emerged out of the dark corner of the cottage. Her face was grave, but a sympathetic gleam shone in her eyes.

"You saved her all right. If it hadn't been for you, Nimisha would've been dead by now. You switched the baskets, didn't you?"

"Yes I did! I hated Kusum! She had taken my love away from me! My talented, beautiful Geeta—hidden in some dark village, away from the world by her sister! A sister who used Geeta's illness as an excuse to her own selfish gains! I saw Geeta after years, the day Nimisha and I were returning from the shoot and I couldn't believe my eyes. I hadn't even known that she was Kusum's sister. I overheard everything from the garden window and I felt as if my heart would burst. What agony to discover her—her soul and body shrunk with time. My immediate instinct was to go up to her and take her in my arms. But then I stopped myself. I realized that love was no more enough. The past years had created a huge valley between us. I had to cross that valley carefully and handle her with a tender care; get to the bottom of the matter and return to her with answers—solutions that would set her free from her past. I said nothing to Nimisha either. But I felt helpless. I knew I ought to do something but what? I was simply looking for an opportunity to mend matters somehow—anyhow!

"These last few days, I'd constantly overheard Nimisha

confronting Kusum about Geeta, and was grateful that Geeta had a champion. I thought it was wonderful of Nimisha to take up for the poor girl. Last night, while the rest of you were at the party, I was lurking around Kusum's window and saw her injecting poison into the berries. She kept swearing under her breath. When she specifically asked Nana to deliver that particular basket to Nimisha, I was stunned. It struck me that Kusum planned to kill Nimisha! I acted on impulse—without bothering to pause and think. Only one thought clamored in my head—that I had to prevent Nimisha from eating those mulberries. From my cell phone, I called up the manager's office. When both Kusum and Nimisha left their rooms to attend the call, I quickly climbed through the windows and switched the baskets. I waited until everyone had gathered for the horoscope reading session, then joined the group on the lawn. It was only a matter of time before Kusum fell into the trap of her own making!"

He fell silent, hugging the photo to his chest. Sonia stepped forward, took his hand and nudged him gently into a chair. She drew another chair and sat down beside him.

"Chirag, you could've simply taken the basket and gone to the police," she pointed out softly.

"It didn't even occur to me!" Chirag shook his head. "And even if it had, I wouldn't have wanted to. She didn't deserve to live after all that she'd done. The last straw was trying to kill Nimisha, who was doing her best for my Geeta. That really got me. I'm glad that she's dead! My only concern now is Geeta."

"Don't worry about her, Nimisha's going to take good care of her," Sonia assured. She leaned forward and her voice was calm and controlled. "Listen Chirag, listen carefully to what I have to say. You did what you have to do. Right or wrong, is really very debatable. But now, there's only one course of action left for you. You must square up to the situation and take responsibility. You must confess. If you own up to the switching of baskets, a good lawyer will get you off with a light sentence. After all, you did it to save Nimisha. She owes you her life and she will say so in court!" Sonia searched his face for a reaction—either acquiescence or refusal. But there was nothing.

"And," she added on a gentle note, "after you serve your sentence, you can rebuild your life with Geeta."

Chirag's blank stare dissolved into myriad emotions flitting across his face. Then glancing back at the photograph in his hand, he remarked resignedly, "There's no other way, is there?"

"Unfortunately no. But in the present circumstances, this is good enough, believe me," Sonia squeezed his hand.

"But what if she doesn't want me? What if she hates me—what if Geeta hates me for what I did?" he asked suddenly, fear stamped on his face.

"She won't," Sonia replied confidently.

"How can you be so sure? It's been years since I met her, what if she despises me?" Chirag held his head again with sudden frustration.

A hand rested on his shoulder and a soft voice spoke. "Every second of those long years had been filled with memories of you!"

Chirag looked up wildly. "Geeta!"

The frail, weak woman smiled wearily at him, but her eyes were overflowing with love. Chirag enveloped her in strong embracing arms and they clung to each other, the dam of tears bursting and sweeping away years of accumulated, stagnant sorrows.

Sonia quietly and discreetly slipped out of the door, into the cool night. Sub-Inspector Pawar, Nimisha and Jatin, who were standing outside the cottage, flashed her eager, questioning looks. Sonia brushed a hand over her moist eyes and sighed contentedly.

"You were right, Nimisha. Facts can be far more fascinating than fiction and real–life romance more romantic than in films!"

The van headed out of Panchgani, winding down the idyllic mountain road, the valley dipping into a green and colorful landscape. The pink light of dawn stained the horizon, the tender golden rays slowly enfolding the entire world in their beauty and warmth.

Jatin yawned but Sonia appeared fresh and energetic. She hummed a song, as they left Panchgani behind them.

"But boss—" Jatin began.

"I know what you want to ask me," Sonia interrupted. "But try to figure it out for yourself."

"I can't. At least not this early in the day. Tell me, could Nana read or not?"

Sonia smiled. "Yes, he could read."

She maneuvered the van skillfully down the twisting road. "You know what first set me on to Kusum, apart from her horoscope? The basket cards. If someone had indeed murdered Kusum, why would Nimisha's basket have Kusum's name on it and Kusum's basket Nimisha's name? Which meant that at some point something had gone wrong. And what was that point? I worked my way backwards in logic. Taking Kusum's dying words *"he can't read"* as a basis, my first step backwards was Nana and his delivery. Kusum's belief that he couldn't read, meant that the baskets had indeed been wrongly delivered. And who would know this best? Obviously the person who was aware of the existence of poison in the berries. If Kusum, who had eaten poisoned mulberries, noticed the muddle, then she also had to be aware of the cyanide in the berries. Which meant, in turn, that not only did she know *how* the cyanide got into the berries, but also *who* had put it in there! Had it been someone else, she would've tried to drag that person's name in. But she didn't, because she herself was her own victim!"

"But you're saying that Nana *could* read," Jatin pointed out.

"Yes, but *Kusum* didn't know that! She'd no idea that Chirag had switched the baskets. She assumed in those last few moments that Nana had made a mess of the names. In fact, that was what really gave me the next lead. If Nana could read and had assured that he had delivered the right baskets, why did the cards belie the fact? In short, if the baskets were not muddled up because of Nana, as Kusum thought, *then how had they been exchanged?*"

"But what made you suspect Chirag?"

"I didn't suspect him immediately. My first thought was that if someone had deliberately set out to murder Kusum, he would've at least taken the precaution of removing the telltale cards. It only proved that this was a hasty unpremeditated job. Then, I remembered seeing Chirag coming from behind the cottages, when the horoscope reading session was on. He was the last to arrive and had plenty of opportunity to create mischief. But why would he want to kill Kusum? The motive eluded me.

"At the same time, I hit upon Chirag's horoscope. Venus, Mars, Uranus and Moon in the ascendant Scorpio indicated a talented man, with dramatic highs and lows in his love life. But Mercury was trapped between the Sun, Saturn, Mars and Rahu which clearly showed that he could be propelled toward some dangerous mistakes, even committing murder. It set me thinking. Did his love have to do anything with Kusum's murder? And then suddenly, I recalled that he was with Nimisha in the village, when she met Geeta. Could Geeta be Chirag's lost love? Seemed far-fetched but it definitely provided a motive for him to kill Kusum, even unintentionally. After all, if Geeta was his love, he could've been incensed to realize that Kusum had achieved success at Geeta's cost.

"The idea took firm hold and I simply couldn't shrug it off. There had to be a connection between Kusum and Chirag. And the link could be Geeta. Chirag's love vanishing and Kusum's sister living in oblivion, no one even aware of her existence—somehow it seemed to add up. The more I thought of it, the more likely it seemed. But I didn't know for sure. I knew that I had to be certain before I publicized my theories. When we both departed to fetch the basket cards from the respective cottages, I deliberately went to Chirag's cottage. His suitcase was open on the bed and I quickly riffled through its contents. I didn't know what I was looking for at that point of time. It was sheer luck that I found a set of kerchiefs tucked in his bag. All the well-worn cotton kerchiefs had a beautifully embroidered message on them—'to my darling Chirag from Geeta'! It confirmed all my suspicions that Kusum's sister was Chirag's long lost love.

"But I still had to validate my theory with definite proof. I knew that I had to somehow get him to confess his involvement in this whole affair. So I pressed ahead with my specious logic of how Kusum got trapped in a web of her own making, which was mostly true. Knowing fully well that Nana was not responsible for the basket switch, Chirag was a little puzzled and confused. Unquestionably, he was not a thoroughbred killer and I took advantage of his vulnerable state of mind. I waited for Chirag to relax and expose his feelings in the privacy of his cottage, then tried to persuade him to come clean. Fortunately, not being a veteran murderer and acting solely at the spur of the moment, he was more manageable than I thought he would be. I'm glad he confessed."

"It was a good idea to ask Nimisha to bring Geeta here," Jatin acknowledged.

Sonia nodded. "The village was two hours away. I thought it would be wonderful if Chirag could finally meet her—it would change his perspective on the whole issue. Somehow it was important that she be present to boost his morale and help him regain the straight path again."

"But, boss," Jatin asked, "why go to so much trouble? Why not just hand him over to the police?"

Sonia smiled, as she drove the vehicle down the hill. "Because this was not a normal crime. Not a deliberate, cold-blooded attempt to kill the choreographer. Chirag, paradoxically, killed as well as saved. Despite his hate for Kusum, I would even go a step further and say, he really did kill to *save* Nimisha. And that made him eligible for a humane handling of the situation." Sonia paused and added almost to herself, "A life and death situation created a criminal out of a normal, ordinary man. But that had also triggered the beginning of a whole new healing process…"

"You really did a great job with him, boss," Jatin said warmly. "There's really so much to learn from you!"

"Who's that in the middle of the road?" Sonia asked abruptly.

The vehicle slowed, as a figure stood on the narrow tar road, hitching a lift.

"I don't believe this!" Sonia muttered, astonished.

She pulled up the van. Sonia and Jatin stared as a grinning Mohnish popped his head in through the window.

"Hi! My car broke down! Can you give me a lift?"

CHAPTER IX

In the Shadow of the Stars

"Sonia Samarth!" a voice hailed, over the hum of loud voices.

Sonia, who was in the process of stuffing some shopping bags in the back of her car, froze. The busy Mahatma Gandhi Road was packed full on a Saturday evening. She turned to see a familiar face emerge out of the group of youngsters.

"Rita!" she exclaimed. "How wonderful to meet you after so many years!"

"Yes, isn't it? I'm surprised you even recognized me. If I'm not mistaken, you're a pretty well-known investigator now." Rita grinned and hugged Sonia.

"Stop kidding. Tell me how you've been and what you've been up to all these years?"

"Oh, I've been fine!" Rita's eyes twinkled. "What a whole lot of purchasing! Are you getting married?"

"Of course not!" Sonia laughed. "I'm shopping for the Diwali festival. My Mom is so fed up of my non-feminine professional life that she insisted I go buy myself traditional Indian clothes—specially a sari! And I'm supposed to wear the sari this Diwali, even if not a soul visits me!"

"Wow, what a mom! But it's just the beginning of October now, Diwali's at the end of the month."

"I know, but I thought I'd finish it off, just to please her. Then she'll leave me in peace to tackle my next case, whenever it happens along." Sonia grinned.

"Good planning. I wish my mom financed such ventures!" Rita laughed. "By the way, let me introduce you to a good friend of mine." Rita drew a woman in her early thirties to her side. "This is Kamini Rane. We live in the same Colony, though she lives in a classy bungalow and I—"

"Live in a classy apartment. Not much difference," Kamini added good-naturedly.

Sonia liked her instantly. Five foot three, small build, and average-looking, but it was the sweetness in her face that was arresting.

"A lot of difference, I'm afraid," Rita declared. "Kamini's the proud owner of 'Elegant Furnitures'—the designer name in wooden furniture. And her husband Ravi Rane runs the big show. And I just run a small-time Beauty Parlor. No comparisons whatsoever."

"Will you stop it?" Kamini nudged her friend playfully.

Sonia noticed that there wasn't an iota of snobbishness in her. She was genuinely unconcerned about her wealth.

"Oh, I forgot to tell you an important detail, Sonia. Her cousin, Vivek, is an excellent astrologer, so you two have something in common. As far as I know, very rarely have his predictions gone wrong."

"All his predictions have come true," Kamini added loyally.

"That's interesting, I would love to meet him one day and exchange notes," Sonia enthused.

"Look, why don't you two catch up on old times? I've got to go, I have an appointment with the doctor," Kamini suggested.

"Are you sure I won't be ditching you?" Rita confirmed.

"Not at all. Go ahead and have a good time."

Rita raised an inquiring eyebrow at Sonia, who nodded.

"Let's go have some coffee and chat at Dosa Palace," her old friend agreed readily.

Kamini stepped out of the elevator, her heart soaring with joy. Finally, finally Vivek's prediction had come true. She was pregnant! There was another tiny heart beating inside her body. She couldn't believe it! The extraordinary phenomenon of another life existing inside her. It was finally happening to her. Motherhood was no longer just a dream, it was a reality. The big reality that she had yearned for, year after year.

She climbed into her Tata Indigo and suppressed the urge to drive like crazy back home. To disclose the great news to her husband. Ravi would go mad with happiness. She could see him now, jumping with delight. He was such a boy at times. Like his son would be, or his daughter. It didn't matter. Boy or girl, she would love her child like no mother had. This Diwali would be a special one for all of them. She would fill the whole house with lanterns and lights, so that the mansion would attract all the joys and prosperity in the world.

Her sunny thoughts whirled on in a glorious flurry of activity, eating up the miles to her house. She parked in the drive and hastened inside the bungalow. Seeing the study door ajar, she headed straight to it, her steps buoyant and light. She was about to step into the study when she heard low voices inside. Ravi was talking to her cousin, Vivek. Not wanting to intrude, she turned away but stopped. Ravi's words floated clearly up to her.

"I just don't know what to do! I wouldn't dare reveal such a horrifying truth to her."

"I know, I know. But she's going through a bad patch in her life. She needs to take care. Don't you think you should warn her about it?"

"No. She's such a softhearted woman. Just imagine what it would do to her if she were to realize that you've predicted this terrible thing. That this is probably the last month of her life. It would kill her on the spot!"

"I guess you're right. You shouldn't. It would destroy her for sure," Vivek agreed, sympathetically.

Blood froze in Kamini's veins. Only a month to live? She couldn't believe her ears. Why now, when she was finally becoming a mother? Could Vivek have read her horoscope wrong? No, he never did. He was always right. He'd predicted the pregnancy, hadn't he? And here she was, on the very threshold of motherhood. Desperation coursed through her body. Why *now?* Why *her?* Oh God! The world suddenly swam and darkness enveloped her in a big welcome wave.

"So, am I actually going to see you in a sari during Diwali?" Mohnish asked, falling in step with Sonia.

"What's such big deal about a sari? It's just another form of attire," Sonia replied, casually.

"Not just *any other attire*. A sari is beautifully feminine and fetching, and I have never seen you in one."

Sonia was taking an evening walk in the picturesque Agriculture College, close to the Stellar Investigations office. Three tree-lined, long stretches of tar roads, from opposite directions joined in the centre to reveal the commanding castle-like stone structure of the College. A well-maintained lawn provided relaxation to the lounging students as well as the general public, in the evenings. Sonia loved to walk along the road—the prolific tamarind, mango and hundred-year- old banyan trees forming a tunnel of thick foliage overhead. The sunrays forced their way through the gaps in the branches, in checkered patterns on the road. Further on, a rough path led into sorghum and sugarcane fields. Cool wind rustled through the thick, gnarled deep brown branches, transferring the dead leaves to the ground to form a rust carpet. Sparrows chirped noisily, filling the evening with natural musical sounds.

Sonia took a deep breath, raising her face to the warm golden rays and the nippy breeze.

"This is true Diwali weather. I can feel the festival in the air," she sighed, as leaves crackled and crunched under her feet.

"I know what you mean," Mohnish agreed, "But you haven't answered my question! Will you meet me during Diwali?"

"Only if you tell me what you were doing in Panchgani last month, during the film shoot," she countered, with a grin.

"Ah, the moot point." Mohnish sighed. "Look, let's go sit down on the lawn. Then maybe we can talk some sense," he suggested.

"Fine, but just for a few minutes."

They selected a dry, sunny spot on the green lawn opposite the sprawling college building with its huge spires. Brisk walkers of all ages marched to the three ends of the College and then took a break on the lawn, which was also a rendezvous for friends and pensioners. White fluffy clouds formed patterns and pictures in the deep blue sky.

"Okay, let's get this straight, once and for all," Mohnish began. "I did not follow you to Panchgani, even though you strongly suspect so. I was there to interview Chirag but unfortunately the interview did not take place and you can imagine why! He just wasn't in the mood, so I spent some time enjoying the hill station. It was pure chance that my car broke down and I had to take a lift from you!"

Sonia studied the intense look on his handsome face. "You want me to believe this tale?"

"Yes," he stated flatly. "Why would I follow you, Sonia?"

Sonia shrugged. "I don't know. I've been getting these 'Secret Admirer' bouquets and the worry is beginning to gnaw at me. And then I had this strangest feeling when I was in the Panchgani market that someone was either observing or following me and then you turned up!"

"I can see your point," Mohnish conceded. "But you have

to believe me when I say I don't send you those bouquets. I'm not your 'secret admirer'—I believe that my admiration for you is transparently clear. I am proud to know someone like you."

Sonia blushed. "Thank you," she said simply.

"Good, that's out of the way." He looked relieved. "Now can we talk about something else?"

"Some other time!" Sonia stood up. "I have to go home and our few minutes are up."

"Hey, that's not fair!" Mohnish protested. "I want to have a long hearty talk with you. Don't tell me I have to take an appointment for that?"

Sonia dusted her dress and smiled. "Fortunately no. Honestly speaking, I'd like to have a long talk with you too! I know nothing about you and it's really time for you to reveal some of your dark secrets."

"Name the place and the time, and I'll be there!" Mohnish agreed with alacrity.

"Fine." Sonia smiled.

"That's a promise?" He fixed her with a steady gaze and she nodded.

Amiably, they strolled out of the college.

Jatin critically studied the colorful paper lantern, swinging by a hook outside the Stellar Investigations office. It looked bright and cheerful—a true representative of the approaching Diwali festival. Jatin loved Diwali and all that it signified in the tradition and culture of the Hindu Indians. Diwali—or 'Deepawali' in the Sanskrit language, which meant a row of lamps—brought out the best in him. But wasn't that what the festival was supposed to do? The five-day celebration, which had a traditional mythological story attached to each day, was today significant because of its relevance to the Indian values. Each day glorified different relationships, from mother and child, brother and sister, to husband and wife, uniting the whole family as never before. In the basically agrarian economy of India, the festival originally celebrated the harvest period of the farmers. This had set off the tradition of worshipping Goddess Laxmi to welcome wealth and prosperity into the house. It was also a time to visit friends and relatives with sweetmeats. Jatin had a long list of friends that he'd had misunderstandings with the past year. Diwali was the perfect festival, he decided, to patch things up.

The hexagonal lantern was simple but charming. It had taken him a great deal of juggling on a high stool, before he could secure the lantern a place of honor. If only his boss could appreciate the effort he took over every single task, she entrusted to him!

Jatin carried the stool inside. Then, dusting his hands, he went up to his boss. Sonia, he noticed, was as usual busy playing with the cat in her lap. Jatin frowned.

"Boss, the lantern is in place," he informed.

"Good, I'll take a look at it as soon as Nidhi is ready to sleep," Sonia responded.

Jatin's frown deepened.

"Boss, I need leave."

"Leave?" Sonia was so amazed at the request that she almost dropped Nidhi. "Did I hear you right? Did you say *leave*?"

"Yes, I need leave."

"Why?"

"Diwali's next week. It's the festival of lights—I have to buy new clothes, help my family cook delicacies—Okay," he added hastily, as Sonia's expressions changed, "at least, place orders for them. My little cousins are coming down from Mumbai, I need to burst crackers with them. Besides, we're not doing anything great right now. I mean we don't have a case at the moment and I don't have much work..."

"Oh yes you do, you're supposed to feed in all the details of our cases into the new computer," Sonia reminded him. "And as for not having a case at the moment, I've been thinking of taking up Mohnish's case. He's been after me for some time now and I think it's high time I paid heed to his problem."

"Yes, but do you need me for that?"

Sonia frowned. "Why wouldn't I need you?"

Jatin shrugged. "I don't know. Of late, I've had this feeling that I'm kind of redundant and useless."

"Are you fishing for compliments?" Sonia asked suspiciously.

"No but actually it would help tremendously to know that my work and contribution are appreciated."

"Your work and contribution are appreciated, Jatin. Period." Sonia suppressed her amusement.

"But you never really listen to me!" he protested.

"I don't?" Sonia was surprised that he'd noticed.

"No. I've been telling you that you need to create an *atmosphere*. Show clients how busy you are by delaying appointments, maybe give a few press interviews, and not seem so desperate for work!"

"If we don't grab cases as soon as they materialize, I may have to shut down this agency. And then you'd have to go home for good," Sonia reminded him gently.

"I know, but..."

"Jatin....how many days' leave would you require?"

"One."

"One day. *One day*? You mean you plan to eat ladoos and chaklis, burst crackers, meet your cousins and family all in one day? Haven't you heard of labor rights? Diwali lasts for five days and you're entitled to lots of leave and—"

"I prefer not to regard myself as a common laborer," Jatin interrupted primly.

Sonia hid a smile. "Fine, which day?"

"Monday—first day of Diwali."

"All right. Take Monday off but I want to see you here at nine sharp, on Tuesday."

"And you won't solve any cases before I return, right?" he asked uncertainly.

"Of course I will. You can't expect me to stop functioning and keep everything on hold, just because you decide to take a day off?" she asked incredulously. Really, Jatin needed to be checked. He was getting more out of hand with every passing day.

"But, boss, it's *Diwali,* you can't work during the most celebrated festival of the year?"

"Who says I can't?" Sonia demanded. "Do you know what Diwali means to me? Not just cleaning of houses, cooking fatty, sweet and spicy food and bursting crackers to welcome health and wealth into our homes. I love the thought behind it, of course, but actually I'd like to implement what it represents. I like to remember that Diwali also means the triumph of good over evil. And so I'd like to clean my mind and help others clean theirs, so as to keep everyone healthy. I'd like the light of inspiration, love and caring to shine in my heart. And I'd like to do my *karma,* my investigative work, so that good truly triumphs over evil. I'd also like to work to welcome wealth in the form of experiences which would make me a better human being. And, of course, I hope that money happens along the way." She smiled.

"In that case," Jatin remarked, hastily. "I think I'll decide on Monday which shall be my day off."

"Suit yourself," Sonia returned her attention to Nidhi, but she couldn't help chuckling. She would have to be a fool to ever really be angry with her assistant. He was inimitable and as committed to investigation as his complex and absurd principles permitted him to be and she suspected that he was going to completely drop the idea of taking leave.

He left but returned almost immediately. An entirely different Jatin, flushed and excited.

"Boss, a client!"

Sonia's instinctive reaction was to quickly place Nidhi aside. Then, she deliberately slowed down. Jatin was right. She had to behave like an investigator. A mature, experienced detective with active grey cells. Not a bumbling amateur out to impress. She could afford to take five minutes to straighten out her table, close the earlier case, allow herself time to relax before plunging into another case. The prerequisites of a professional. Jatin watched Sonia's deliberate slow actions with appreciation. His boss was learning, he nodded in satisfaction. *Better late than never,* he thought as he left the room.

When Sonia was convinced that sufficient time had elapsed, she buzzed the intercom. Her pen and notebook were on standby. The door opened and a tall lady bustled in. Sonia opened her mouth for a formal greeting and stopped, astonished.

"Rita! What a pleasant surprise! I was expecting a client."

"I *have* come to seek your investigative services," Rita replied gravely.

Sonia's brow puckered. "What's the matter? You sound so serious."

Rita seated herself. The troubled expression on her face was at odds with her usually cheerful personality.

"Sonia, do you remember Kamini, the woman I introduced you to some weeks ago?"

"Of course I do. Kamini Rane, Elegant Furnitures. What about her?"

"I've only just got back from Delhi, I'd been away for several days. So I thought I'd go and check on her. But when I went to her house, I got the shock of my life!"

Sonia leaned forward, steeling herself to hear the worst.

"Kamini was in bed—but such a different Kamini, I almost didn't recognize her. Thin with dark circles under her eyes, listless, disinterested and pregnant! At first, I thought it was her pregnancy which was causing all the trouble. But I'm wrong. There's something else but she wouldn't tell me. Sonia, if you saw her, you would realize that she's wasting away. Dying, slowly but surely. We've got to do something about it!" Rita had tears in her eyes.

"Of course we will. And I will go and meet with her. But first, brief me on all you know about her. You've known her for long, haven't you?" Sonia automatically buzzed the intercom and Jatin hastened in with a pen and paper in hand.

"Several years. I knew her before she got married. We went to the same post-graduate college. Her parents died in an air crash when she was in school and she's been raised entirely by her maternal Uncle, Mr. Shirkay. He has managed Elegant Furnitures all his life. It was in college that Kamini met Ravi. He was the college hero—extreme good looks but a perfect gentleman. Intelligent too. I remember we were all quite surprised that he'd chosen Kamini out of all the beautiful girls. Kamini could never boast good looks and she was honest and unconcerned about it. She had a heart of gold, but who bothers about that? Ravi did, though. They would act in college plays and they paired very well. Won many competitions together. I guess all those rehearsals made them realize that they were made for each other. Anyway, they didn't get married immediately. Ravi took up a job in Elegant Furnitures and slowly and steadily rose up the ladder, more due to his hard work than any pulls. When it was time, Mr. Shirkay was most happy to get his niece married to him and to hand over the reins of the business to Ravi. He now lives in their native village, in the Konkan area."

"I see." Sonia was thoughtful.

"The couple was quite happy but for one hitch. They couldn't have kids. They'd been married for five years and still there was no child. Until a few weeks ago, when Kamini discovered that she was pregnant. But considering that motherhood was the sole aim of her life, she hardly seems excited or happy."

"Who else is in the family?"

"Shirkay's son, Vivek—the astrologer I told you about. He

has always guided Kamini with his predictions. Apparently, he'd predicted this pregnancy. He works in the company too. They all live together. In fact Ravi and Kamini live in the Shirkay's old bungalow."

"Can we go over to her place right now?" Sonia asked.

Rita nodded. "Right away."

"Do you know the name of her doctor?"

"Dr. Panchwagh on Main Street."

Jatin looked at his boss. "Any instructions for me?"

"Yes, I want you to visit Doctor Panchwagh. Try to find out all you can about Kamini's physical condition. If he raises any objections, just say that the questions are in Kamini's best interest."

"Right, boss." Jatin readily stood up.

"May we leave now?" Sonia asked Rita.

The cheery, celebratory air was very much evident, as Sonia drove the van to Prabhat Road. Colorful paper and plastic lanterns hung from houses and balconies. Crowds, attired in crisp new and kaleidoscopic clothes, strolled on the streets. The festive season had taken a grip on the city.

The sprawling stone bungalow on Prabhat Road bespoke wealth and antiquity. As did the well-maintained garden, which seemed more like a small park than a private retreat. But the absence of even a single Diwali lantern, made the grandeur appear bleak and unattended.

They had just stepped out of the car, when a man strode out of the door. An athletic body fitted into a navy blue suit, a clean-shaven face, an aquiline nose which gave him just the right amount of arrogance. Jet black eyes rested on the two women, registering surprise.

"Hello Ravi, meet Sonia, my friend. She's come to see Kamini," Rita made the introductions.

"Hello! I'm glad my wife has friends to divert her mind. She's in such a sorry state that it pains me to see her like this."

Ravi's cultured voice was tinged with sadness.

"She'll be all right, now that Sonia's here," Rita said optimistically.

Ravi looked at them with so much grief in the depths of his eyes, that Sonia was startled. This man knew something, she sensed. The tragic expression on his face wasn't natural. It seemed as if it arose out of some secret knowledge. Did Ravi know what was troubling Kamini?

"What do the doctors say?" she asked casually.

"That some great tension's eating away at her heart. Something so stressful, that she's shrinking and sinking. And not only is it harmful to her but it's also harmful to our baby." Ravi almost choked on the words. "Excuse me…" He brushed an arm over his eyes and hastily stepped away.

Sonia felt sorry for him. It must be terrible to long for a child, then see both, mother and child, under the shadow of some grave, nameless threat.

They entered the long hall and Rita led her to a door on the left. She knocked lightly and without waiting for response, stepped inside. Rita's descriptions had warned Sonia of what she would find. But nothing had prepared her for the shock. Kamini lay in bed and she was crying softly. She glanced up startled, as the two entered. Her eyes and nose were red, her complexion sallow and she looked positively ill. Not an iota of her resembled the sweet, smiling Kamini Sonia had encountered on M. G. Road. What could have transpired to turn a normal healthy woman into a nervous wreck?

"Kamini! Why're you crying?" Rita hastened to her, her voice raised in panic.

"What's wrong, Kamini?" Sonia asked, in a more controlled tone.

"N..nothing!" the wretched woman sobbed.

Rita and Sonia exchanged concerned glances. Sonia moved ahead and sat down on the edge of Kamini's bed. She held

Kamini's hand, allowing the woman time to recompose herself. Then she said in a gentle voice, "Do you know why I'm here, Kamini? Because I heard that you were under some tremendous pressure which was destroying you. Do you want to die? To kill yourself and your baby? Because that's exactly what will happen if you don't pull yourself together."

Kamini looked taken aback. Her face went taut and white. "No..." she whispered. "I don't want to die but I *will die*...!"

"What do you mean?" Sonia asked, sharply.

"I will die... soon. I know it... I hear it every day... they don't want me to know, but I can't help hearing every word they speak..." she lamented softly.

"Who's 'they'? Kamini, please explain! Who's been telling you that you're going to die?"

"Ravi and Vivek. I overheard them talking in the study. Vivek has predicted it and he's always right..."

"Did they speak to you directly?"

"No, I overhear Ravi talking in the study, discussing me. He loves me so much that he keeps asking Vivek for a way out! Oh, I can't bear it! Why do I have to die when everything seemed to be so perfect?"

"Listen to me, Kamini. You're not going to die. I'm an astrologer too and I know that you cannot predict death! No one can. You can predict a bad health patch, but that does not mean death! Are you listening to me? Stop sobbing and stop feeling sorry for yourself. This way you will kill yourself and you'll be responsible for killing the baby too!" Sonia's scolding tone finally seeped through Kamini's weeping.

Her head jerked up, her eyes wet with tears. "What should I do?" she wailed.

"Forget about the prediction and start living at once. There's nothing wrong with you, so get dressed and go out with Rita. It's Diwali time, go out and buy yourself something really nice—for Ravi and the baby as well. Enjoy the beautiful Diwali atmosphere outside."

"Yes, let's go. We'll have some lunch first and then go shopping," Rita chipped in readily.

Kamini hesitated. Then fresh resolve made her sit up slowly. "I'll have to go upstairs to change," she murmured.

"Why, isn't this your room?" Sonia asked puzzled.

"No, Ravi asked me to move downstairs, so that he could keep an eye on me. That way, when he's in the study, I can call out to him, if I need him. He's so very loving and caring, I don't know what I would've done without him."

Rita put an arm around her and the two women made their way slowly out of the room. Sonia stared at Kamini's receding back in thoughtful silence. Her instincts were suddenly very finely tuned to the situation. Something was not right here, she sensed. She'd got the same impression, when she'd met Ravi in the garden. All was not well in this elegant home of the Ranes.

She stepped out of the sick room and glanced around. A door immediately on the right attracted her attention. This must be the study. She tried the handle and the polished wooden door swung open into a paneled study-cum-library. Sonia stepped in, shutting the door behind her. A large table with a glass top occupied maximum space in the center of the room. Windows lined one side of the wall and the other wall was paneled wood. Sonia strode casually to the table and ran her eye over the top. A phone, an appointment calendar diary, some papers, pen-stand, a lap-top, some law books. She flipped the pages of the appointment calendar. There weren't many appointments, so she assumed that this wasn't an official diary. Her hand riffled aimlessly through the pages and then slowed. A name seemed to leap regularly off the pages, at repeated intervals, in the beginning of the year. Meena Sajane. The time also seemed to vary. However, she observed that the entries got fewer. In the last month there had been only one. Sonia raised her head, her mind a warren of sudden ideas.

The door opened and Sonia stepped back guiltily. In reality, she wasn't supposed to be here.

A man in his late twenties looked equally startled to find her. Then his eyes narrowed, as he regarded her with suspicion.

"I… I'm Sonia Samarth. Kamini's friend," she hastily offered in explanation.

Immediately his stance changed. "I'm Vivek and I've heard about you! Aren't you the one who has combined astrology with investigation?"

Sonia couldn't help feeling flattered. "Yes."

"How wonderful to meet you! I'd a good mind to call you up one day and congratulate you on changing the whole outlook toward astrology which had so sadly been ruined by quacks. I'm really glad that you're doing wonders to straighten such a grossly misunderstood science. What a coincidence that we should meet like this," he enthused.

"And you're an astrologer too. A very precise one, I've heard."

Vivek shrugged. "Not a professional, though. I use my knowledge in guiding family and friends."

"Could you forecast Kamini's illness?"

Vivek looked startled. "Actually I did, to Ravi, but we didn't want Kamini to hear about it. That didn't help, though. Her health deteriorated very fast. But Ravi has been so wonderful. He's taking such good care of her. It surprised me. His devotion, his concern. We've been discussing her case every night, wondering what can be done. But it's no use. Sometimes fate is very cruel."

"Vivek, can I take a look at the horoscopes—all of them?"

"Of course. You'll see that I'm right," he agreed without hesitation. "They're in that drawer there on the left. I'll give them to you now."

He strode over to the table, slid open a drawer and from it extracted a small cotton bag. Opening the bag, he checked the contents. From the drawer, he withdrew another small plastic pouch, scribbled something on a paper and added them both to the bag. "They're all in there. Mine too." He smiled.

Sonia accepted the cotton bag. "Why did you say that you were surprised at Ravi's devotion to Kamini?"

"Did I say that? Oh it must've slipped out." Vivek avoided her eye. Then he glanced up and sighed. "Well, I may as well—I've seen Ravi with a woman several times. I'm not saying there's anything between them, because I don't know. But I couldn't help wondering..."

"Do you have this woman's name? Or her address?"

"Meena Sajane. Works as a social worker for 'Aajol', the Old Home for Women. And, in the passing, I've noticed some fat cheques in her name too. There are also one or two things I'd like to tell you, but not now. Perhaps we can meet later?"

"Sure, I'll give you a call."

Vivek lifted some books from the table and followed Sonia out of the room. "Let me know what you think of the horoscopes."

"I will," she promised, nodding.

Rita and Kamini were descending the stairs as he crossed them. The surprise on Vivek's face was evident.

"You look so much better, Kamini. Are you going out?" he asked.

Kamini smiled weakly and nodded.

"Good. Keep it up!" Vivek encouraged, and whistling, he made his exit.

Sonia sat in her office, listening to the melodious notes of the flute, floating through the office. Rita had dropped her at the office and then proceeded to Kamini's favorite restaurant, though Kamini had insisted that she wouldn't be able to eat. Rita would take good care of Kamini, Sonia thought. She was a good friend.

Nidhi lolled on her pillow on the windowsill, cleaning

herself with her tongue, granting her mistress the freedom to occupy herself as she pleased. Through the window, Sonia watched two green birds sitting on the electric wire. A pair of Vedha-Raghu, swinging on the electric cable, totally unaware of the peril it presented. Something seemed to stir within her. A nebulous hunch. The horoscopes lay on the table in front of her, neat little booklets with calculations and mathematics drawn out with a seasoned hand. Essentially neat and at first appearance, harmless. And yet, the horoscopes troubled her. Something about the star combinations—Sonia couldn't place a finger on her doubt, but she felt an acute sense of frustration. It was like trying to look into vast space, sensing that something was out there. Something which eluded capture but which was transmitting tiny warning pricks to her brain. At length, with a sigh of annoyance, she thrust the booklets back into their little cotton bag and wound the top with a knot. She'd refer to them later, with a fresh and open mind and when her instinct had cropped away unnecessary matter

Still, her mind flicked from question to question. Who was Meena Sajane and what relationship did this unknown woman have with Ravi? Why did he pay her large amounts of money? Was Kamini's state of mind curable or was she already over the edge? Did the presence of Meena in Ravi's life have anything to do with Kamini's illness? The bunch of horoscopes on the table were beckoning at her again. She touched them absently, then, on an impulse, untied the bag. There were the three booklets inside and a small white packet of powder. A paper rustled against it.

Jatin walked in with a tray in his hand.

"*Pav bhaji!*" he announced.

"Good. I am ravenous." Sonia smiled. "What did the doctor have to say about Kamini?"

"Not much." Jatin spoke between bites. "He says she was very ecstatic and excited when she came to get her report. Fit and in excellent health. He can't figure out what's gone wrong in the past few days. He's treating her, of course, for tension and pressure. But he hasn't been able to identify her illness at all."

"Hmm...I thought as much. There's nothing really wrong with her," Sonia remarked reflectively, spooning the bhaji.

"Then what exactly is the matter with her? Do you know, Boss?"

"This is a perfect example of what blind belief in astrology can do to you. Kamini believes that she's going to die very soon—that's what has been prophesied by her cousin Vivek. So foolish and immature of him to voice his doubts aloud and for her to believe them! Rationality and responsibility are the two necessary accessories of an astrologer. Like all sciences, astrology is neither complete nor precise. Used sensibly, it can do wonders. But used carelessly and blindly, it can prove to be a most deadly weapon. And that's what Kamini..." Sonia paused abruptly.

"Boss?"

She stared straight ahead, zoned out for a full minute. Then she shut her eyes.

"Boss!" Jatin was beginning to get worried.

"Of course! Why didn't I think of it before!" Sonia exclaimed.

"Think of what before?"

"Too half-baked to explain right now. Let's quickly get done with the meal. I've got to go somewhere."

"Go where? And you haven't even gone through the horoscopes yet," he reminded.

"I will. There's something that I simply must check out first. I have to pay someone a visit."

"But boss, what's the hurry? As far as I can see, there's really no case here. Just a frightened woman, who doesn't have enough sense—"

"No Jatin, that's where we're wrong. Have you ever lighted an *agarbatti*—a joss stick?"

"Of course! I do it every day before God."

"Then you must've noticed that the immediate impulse on lighting a joss stick is to extinguish the match. Very often, I feel the joss stick has caught fire and I puff the match stick out, only to realize that the joss stick hasn't lit yet!"

"Boss, what are you getting at?" Poor Jatin was bewildered.

"Simply that a case is like a joss stick. Our immediate impulse is to form opinions and reach conclusions, sometimes ignoring, or even deliberately extinguishing the other options, just as we extinguish the matchstick. But most often, it is advisable for the joss stick to light. A good investigator must wait, wait for the joss stick to light, wait for the case to ripen. Besides, it is always useful to remember that superficial appearances are as deadly as blind faith in astrology!" Sonia remarked, enigmatically.

To Jatin's amazement, she polished off the *pav bhaji* at super speed. Then, without further ado, she picked up her purse and the horoscope bag and zipped out of the office. Jatin shook his head in annoyance. Really, sometimes his boss simply failed to communicate. How in heavens was Jatin supposed to keep track of her multi-layered thinking? Joss sticks. Grumbling, he took his time, doing justice to the delicious *pav bhaji.*

The lab took just a few minutes of her time. Then Sonia headed for her next stop—The Home for Old Women. She parked her car outside the gate and slowly made her way inside. *Aajol*—a mother's home. How apt a name and place for all these homeless women, Sonia thought. Women in white, blue-bordered saris, strolled leisurely, alone or in groups, in a tree-shaded garden. Questions swarmed in Sonia's mind. Did they miss their families, were they happy, had they come here of their own volition, had this lonely life been thrust on them by their children so that they had no choice but to spend the rest of their lives in a home? She experienced a twinge of sadness at the growing trend in India. She couldn't imagine parting with any member of her family. But to deliberately subject old parents or grandparents to the horrors of a lonely, bondless, life of a home, was so humiliating. Sometimes it was the only course open to these old people, especially when their children preferred to squander wads of money instead of love.

A plastic lantern hung from the main door of the office. Even the single hint of Diwali, cheered the cause of the home. Sonia pushed the iron gate and approached the security guard in uniform, standing at the office door.

"I'd like to speak to Meena Sajane. Does she work here?"

"Of course! She's the most active worker we have." The guard beamed. "I'll fetch her in a jiffy."

He hastened away and Sonia leaned against the wall, waiting. A few minutes later, she could see the guard returning. A woman in a formal white sari was accompanying him. As they strode toward her, Sonia's pulse raced. The tall, slim woman with the aquiline nose was the splitting image of Ravi...

The dawn of Diwali was spectacular. Every house projected rows and rows of earthen lamps which glowed and twinkled in the dark. Lanterns adorned balconies and some enthusiastic houses had even put up strings of tiny, lighted bulbs. Fireworks lit the dark sky, in psychedelic patterns, as if a war was being waged in the sky. Firecrackers burst in every lane, the ceaseless ear-splitting sounds now like familiar background music. Rather unwelcome music, Sonia mused.

The Samarth bungalow was like a small illuminated palace. Sonia had awoken early, had helped her mother draw floral patterns with the flowing, white rangoli on the verandah. She had applied oil and *utana*—a paste of gram flour and scented powder—before the traditional bath. Then having worn the beautiful, flowing red sari, speckled with gold, which showed off her figure to perfection, she had enjoyed a *chakli* and *laadoo* breakfast with her parents. And then, as daylight settled on the world, relatives began arriving, one by one and the house became a lively park. But Sonia began to get restless.

Much to her parents' surprise, Sonia, ignoring her mom's frowns, excused herself, slipped out of the house, climbed into the van and drove to the office.

The beautiful day had suddenly turned cloudy and lifeless, she noticed. The sky was a dull ink-grey and heavy rain threatened to make an appearance any minute. As she stepped into the office, Nidhi meowed loudly, surprised to see her mistress this early. But after sloshing a generous amount of milk into Nidhi's bowl and dropping her pieces of the spicy *chakli*, her mistress switched on some music. Then she became quite busy pouring over some tiny booklets. Nidhi tackled the food leisurely, but the loud bangs of firecrackers in the distance, startled the cat. She rubbed against Sonia's legs for a while, not exactly liking the feel and smell of her new clothes. Then purring her protest, she stared up at Sonia's bent face, willing her to pay attention.

"I know sweetie-pie, I hate crackers too," Sonia murmured absently. "I'll turn the music on louder."

Sonia increased the volume and settled down to work again. Nidhi meowed her complains, but her attention seeking gimmicks did not seem to move her mistress. Finally, feeling totally neglected and indignant, Nidhi curled up on her cushion, trying to sleep amidst the jing-bang made by the firecrackers and her mistress's music.

Then, much to the cat's great surprise, Sonia suddenly stood up.

She tapped her feet with the latest Hindi song number and as the song picked up beat, she began dancing. Nidhi eyed her lazily, then closed her eyes. This was nothing new! She had seen her mistress behave this strangely several times!

Sonia swirled with the music, the pleats and the *pallu* of her sari, twirling prettily. Finally, the song ended and she halted, a glow of satisfaction on her face. She dropped into her chair and stared at the horoscopes before her, They were most intriguing. Ravi, Kamini and Vivek. Yes, Vivek had been absolutely right. Kamini was going through the worst phase of her life. But death? Certainly not, unless… she paused. Her heart began a familiar tattoo as her eye fell on the other two horoscopes. There was something worth exploring here, she thought, her breath quickening. She'd been right with her misgivings. Swiftly she lifted an almanac from the shelf, leafed through its pages, made notes, then nodded in satisfaction. There was more here than met the eye. She was dealing with an extremely clever person and she needed to keep all her wits around her. If she was right… She picked up the phone and dialed a number.

"Just a few days left, Vivek, just a few days! What can I do?"

"Pray to God. You've got to be prepared. Talk to her about—"

"Don't! Don't speak like that. Nothing must happen to Kamini, I wouldn't be able to bear it!" Ravi exclaimed. "How can I ask my own wife to make a will? A will is for old people, not for a young woman who's carrying my child!"

"I understand, but sometimes it pays to be practical. If anything happens to Kamini, her half of the property will come to me. Then there'll be nothing for you. All your hard work in the company will prove futile. You've got to talk to her!"

"I don't care if I don't get any share of the property! I just want my wife to live and be happy."

In the next room, Kamini listened with bated breath. The catch in Ravi's voice brought tears to her eyes. Oh Ravi, I love you so much, she thought. Her heart was racing and her pulse felt unnaturally fast. She fumbled for the glass of water and her tablet. Trembling, she managed to swallow the tablet. Then, with a hand on her heart, she rested against the pillows. Just two days left before… before Vivek's prediction came true. Ravi loved her too much, but he just wasn't practical. She had to do something about the will. Not that she knew anything about her inheritance. She'd never bothered to get matters clarified. She'd been so happy and content marrying a handsome guy like Ravi. It had never occurred to her to check out how her money was placed. But perhaps, now it was time to do it. Time to make a will and leave matters uncluttered and simple.

She stretched out her hand to the mobile phone and dialed her lawyer's number.

The phone rang shrilly and Sonia lifted the receiver.

"Hello?"

"She's had a relapse, Sonia!" Rita sounded frantic. "I don't know what to do; even the doctor feels that he's helpless if she herself makes no effort. Sonia, I'm so scared!"

"Calm down. I'll be there in half an hour," Sonia replied.

She scribbled a note for Jatin and left it on his table. Driving on a cloudy Diwali morning to Prabhat Road was not a pleasant experience. It certainly was an unusually depressing day. Never had the first day of Diwali looked so dull. Not that it had dampened the enthusiasm of people, which was obvious with the cluttering of spent firecrackers on the road. Sonia despised crackers, which according to her, were a source of menace to humans as well as animals, serving the sole purpose of adding to the air and noise pollution. But it would take a long time for the youth to realize that bursting of deafening crackers was not an act of valor but an abuse of money!

Besides, the traffic didn't help. The orange-and-cream public transport busses rumbled past, almost forcing her off the road. She slowed, allowing the next bus to overtake her. Sonia sighed. Really, it was true, that if you could drive in Pune, you could drive anywhere in the world!

A heavy shower, once and for all, would help lift the hazy veil that enveloped the city, she felt irritably. Then she wondered : Why was she suddenly highlighting the negative aspect of life?

Was it because it was Diwali and the festival meant everything good and pure? Was it subliminally instigating within her a burning desire to purge the negative—the evil? If so, did she have it in her power to do so, Sonia asked herself.

Minutes later, Sonia drew into the Rane drive. Still no lantern hung from their main door, she noticed idly and hastened to Kamini's room. She'd imagined a repeat performance, with Kamini full of tears. Instead, a very different sight met her eyes. Kamini lay quietly in her bed, with Rita at her side and Ravi standing silently in the background. The silence in the room was almost deafening. It was the silence of impending doom.

"What's happening here?" Sonia asked sharply.

"Thank God you're here!" Rita exclaimed. "She won't listen to me."

"I don't need to listen to anyone. I know when my time has come," Kamini whispered.

"I never heard such trash before!" Sonia told her. "You were getting better, Kamini, what happened to make you think like this?"

The sick girl glanced at her husband. Ravi instantly bent forward, trying to catch her words.

"Do you need anything, dear?" he asked anxiously.

"I wish to talk to my friends. I hate to ask you, but can you go out for a while?"

"Of course!" Surprise flickered over Ravi's face, but he left the room immediately.

Kamini's gaze followed him out, strong affection written all over her face.

"Okay, shoot! Tell me what's the matter," Sonia pressed.

In halting words, Kamini repeated the conversation she'd overheard the evening before. Her soft voice narrated her anguish.

"Did Ravi ask you directly to make a will?" Sonia asked.

"No. He loves me too much for that!"

"So, what did you do?" Sonia asked.

"I called my lawyer, Advocate Bhate, and asked him to make a will."

"A will!"

"Yes, but he refused."

"Refused?" Sonia's voice held sudden hope.

"He said I didn't need to make a will. Because it was already made by my grandparents and it was unchangeable."

"Oh I see… Which means that, if anything happened… your half of the property would go to Vivek. So Vivek was right!" Sonia remarked dryly.

Rita glanced at Sonia, with a sudden gleam of understanding in her eyes. But Kamini shook her head.

"Oh poor Ravi I can't even leave my property to him! Even though I know, that he's not interested and has never wanted my money. He's never bothered, never asked me anything about the way the Shirkay property is tied up or if he'll ever get a share of it. But I wish I could do something about it!"

"Relax, Kamini, I'm sure we'll never reach that stage," Sonia cut in smoothly. "Now just relax. I've gone through your horoscope and found out that there's nothing wrong with you and that nothing whatsoever's going to happen to you. You're just a little stressed out with all this emotional trauma that you've built around yourself. Take rest and you'll feel better. Everything's going to be quite fine. Trust me, can you do that?"

Kamini's eyes welled over with tears, but she nodded.

Sonia turned to her friend. "Rita, can you stay with her today?"

"Of course! I won't leave her alone for a minute." Rita answered promptly.

"Good. Kamini, I'd like to talk to your lawyer if you don't mind. You have his number, right?"

Mr. Bhate looked at Sonia, with narrow shrewd eyes,

surrounded by wrinkles. His snowy hair was thick and his eyebrows bushy.

"I've been most concerned about Kamini," he spoke in a gruff voice. "She called me with a very odd request last night. Some cock-and-bull story about her dying in the next forty-eight hours and needing to make a will! That too on the auspicious occasion of Diwali! I told her it was all trash. A young and healthy girl like her—she's going through motherhood jitters—that's what I told her. But she wouldn't agree, of course. Insisted that I make a will!"

"But there's a problem, right?" Sonia asked.

"Actually the Shirkay money is tied up quite indisputably. Kamini's mother was the elder daughter and Vivek's father the younger brother. Since it was the hard-earned money of Kamini's grandparents, they made a non-contestable will. All the property was equally divided between Kamini and Vivek. If anything happens to Kamini, then all the property reverts to Vivek. And in the event of Vivek's death, his share of the property, will automatically go to Kamini. And nothing can change this will."

Sonia nodded, her mind churning. It all added up. The three horoscopes and their star combinations stood like a clear picture before her eyes. And they perfectly matched her conclusions. She turned back to the lawyer.

"One last question. Are Ravi and Vivek aware of the contents of the Shirkay will?"

"As far as I know, Vivek is. But does Ravi know? I wouldn't be able to say. I've never had this kind of discussion with him, ever. He could have of course gleaned it out of Kamini, but she herself is pretty ignorant of these affairs."

"Thank you, Mr. Bhate. You've been of tremendous help to me." Sonia shook hands with the old man.

"I'm glad to be of help, my dear. I only hope that Kamini will be able to pull herself out of this emotional mess she's tumbled into!"

"Oh she will, I promise you that!" Sonia said grimly.

Jatin was footling around the office and watching television, when Sonia breezed into the room. He was about to hastily switch off the TV when he paused and stared at her.

"Wow, boss, you look splendid in a sari!" he exclaimed. "Why don't you wear it more often?"

"Thanks, but it's not the most practical attire when you have to hop in and out of vans and have work to do." Sonia grimaced.

"You've got another of those 'Secret Admirer' bouquets," he told her.

"Toss it in the bin," she ordered.

"But it says 'Happy Diwali.'"

"Okay, keep it."

"What's happening, boss?" Jatin followed her into the inner office. "You look excited."

"We're reaching the end of the tale, Jatin."

"You mean there is a tale here?"

"Yes. I told you, didn't I? Never go by appearances," she reminded.

"Oh, the joss sticks—I'm afraid I'm all at sea, boss."

"Never mind. We've got to go out."

"But you're just back and it's dark as night outside."

"Don't blame me if the weather's bad and it looks like eight in the evening at three in the afternoon—a *Diwali* afternoon!" Sonia grimaced.

"Okay." Jatin sighed. "Where are we going and what are we doing there?"

"We're going to try and save an innocent woman from being slowly forced to death!"

"You mean..."

"That's right. But first I must speak to Inspector Divekar."

"But your sari...."

"Will have to do!"

The thunder clapped with shattering certainty and then relapsed into silence. Sonia, femininely draped in a festive sari, studied the two men, seated across her. Ravi, dressed in casual kurta pajama, looked handsome and dignified. But the anxiety on his face and his restless hands belied his calm stance. Vivek rested his hand on the table, toying with a pen, his eyes on Sonia. Jatin sat beside his boss, unsure of how to proceed, but ready for any instructions.

"I guess you're aware why I've called this meeting this afternoon," Sonia began, clearing her throat. "I know that both of you are very concerned about Kamini. Vivek, you've predicted her bad physical phase quite accurately, though I, as a responsible astrologer would never ever predict death. But there are some who do it, and you did it. You told Ravi about it and both of you discussed it in this very room."

"What are you getting at?" Ravi asked, a little impatiently.

"What I'm getting at is this: that while you two have been dissecting Kamini's moods and voicing your concerns over her health, she's been an active audience to it all. Listening to your predictions and believing them to be consummately true!"

Ravi gasped. "But that's exactly what we didn't want—for her to ever know!"

"Unfortunately, your study is not as soundproof as you would like to believe," Sonia remarked dryly. "Or ought I to say, that the study *is* as sound proof as you would like it to be?"

"What do you mean?" Vivek asked sharply.

"What I mean is quite simple, but I will come to that later. Ravi, you claim that you love your wife a lot. And yet you lied to her. You allowed her to believe that she really would die?"

"I never lied to her. And I wasn't at all aware that she'd overheard us. I trusted the doctor to diagnose her illness and treat her!" Ravi exclaimed.

"But why haven't you told her about Meena?"

Ravi stared at her with wide eyes. An amused smile lit up

Vivek's face and he leaned forward to observe his brother-in-law.

"How do you know about Meena?" Ravi asked Sonia.

"I know a lot of things about all three of you—I have your horoscopes, remember?" Sonia shrugged. "But I repeat: why didn't you tell Kamini about Meena?"

"I couldn't—I was too ashamed!"

"What Meena did was not your fault," Sonia pointed out.

"No, but when we got married I hid the fact that I had… had a sister—a sister who'd been to prison for being caught in the red-light area!"

Vivek's expressions changed from amusement to disappointment. A sister?

"It was too humiliating and I didn't want to reveal my relationship with her."

"Even though she'd reformed and joined the home for the old, devoting all her life to the service of needy, lonely women?" Sonia asked gently. "I think that's unfair of you, don't you? Simply signing huge amounts of cheques to relieve your guilt won't help, though I'm sure the money was put to good use. But there's more to life than money, isn't there?"

Ravi blinked at Sonia. "I know what you mean. Maybe it's not too late to make amends?"

"I'm sure it's not." Sonia smiled. Then she turned to Vivek. "And you, Vivek, you believe in astrology and practice it. At first, I thought, you were an amateur, unaware of the powerful tool in your hands. But then I checked all your horoscopes and realized that you were a professional. Your predictions about Kamini were accurate, about her pregnancy, her bad patch. But no astrologer in his right mind would predict death—but you did, for a reason."

"I only wanted to warn Ravi," Vivek told her.

"Yes, warn him from time to time, in this room, so that Kamini would hear every word you spoke. Kamini, who would believe your predictions so blindly, that she would sink and die. And she would be generously helped, minute by minute, by your deliberate manipulations and discussions on her approaching demise—a sure-fire method of killing a woman who trusted in you. It was a unique plan—you poisoned her mind and then throttled the life out of her, little by little!"

"You're kidding! Why would I go to such lengths?" Vivek asked, almost jocularly.

"For the inheritance, of course. I'll grant you this much—you're not a professional criminal. You didn't really wish to go into a messy murder scene. But that didn't mean you didn't want your inheritance badly. So badly that you thought of a most subtle and clever plan, one which would use Kamini's trust to your advantage. You knew her better than she knows herself. You were aware of her faults, her good points, because you've known her all your life. You knew how much she relied on your word. How weak-willed she was. You were positive that if you kept brainwashing her into believing that she was going to die, you would play to her psychology and destroy her mentally and physically. If it worked, no one would ever know you'd played any role in the whole sordid affair. After all you hadn't done a thing, physically, to injure her. There was minimal chance of anyone ever discovering any foul play. If it didn't work, which according to you, was rather unlikely, you would've eventually thought of another bad astrological concoction to reach your goal.

"You even deliberately spoke of the will, cashing in on Ravi's ignorance, and knowing quite well that Kamini could not make a will. On her death, everything she owned, would go automatically to you. But you did talk about it, asking Ravi to get Kamini's half of the property transferred to his name. You needed to chip away at her confidence and make her psychologically weaker by discoloring her image of her husband."

"What crap!" Vivek exclaimed. "You're insane! Why would I do something like that to my cousin who is like a real sister to me?"

"Because you were simply not satisfied with your half of the bequest, you were greedy and lusted for the whole inheritance. What an insidious plan it was. Slow, mental torturing, until Kamini weakened, guttered out, and died!"

"I won't sit and listen to your accusations!" Vivek stood up, his face red with rage.

At that moment, the door of the study opened and Rita and Kamini stood at the entrance. Kamini's crumpled sari was trailing and tears were coursing down her cheeks. Vivek turned wildly to her.

"Kamini, let me explain. You've got to listen to me! These are all lies!"

"I did listen to you—every word, in the other room," the weeping woman replied. "I believed in you, I trusted you… Would you be happy if I were to really die?"

"That's it! I'm leaving," Vivek stated emphatically.

"Before you do, listen to this." Sonia's voice was ominously low. She held out two horoscopes. "You predicted Kamini's bad patch, didn't you, but you didn't notice one thing in it. Neither did you go through your own horoscope. Otherwise, you wouldn't be here today plotting someone else's death. You would be more concerned about *your life*! Uranus is in the eighth house afflicted by Saturn and a whole of negative influences. It's a similar combination to Kamini's horoscope. Don't you know what your horoscopes read? Kamini's horoscope says that her brother will soon go through the worst patch of his life. Anything could happen to him—*anything!* Her brother would die before her… And as for your horoscope—you've got to be careful… Just a few days left…"

Vivek froze, his face white. He snatched the horoscopes from Sonia's hands, rapidly scrutinizing them. "No… !" His voice was a low croak.

"Yes," she repeated.

Suddenly discarding the horoscopes, he dashed through the door, out into the night. Jatin made as if to go after him, but Sonia shook her head.

"Let him go," she said sadly.

Minutes later, they heard a car screeching out of the drive. The rain began its downpour just then, crashing down upon the earth in full fury. The roads would be flooded in no time—slippery and dangerous, especially in the inky blackness...

"Life has a strange way of doling out justice!" she reflected softly.

Kamini ran straight into Ravi's arms, sobbing uncontrollably. He flashed a grateful, weak smile at Sonia, then led his wife out, supporting her tenderly.

Rita hugged Sonia. "You're wonderful!" she remarked quietly. "You've saved Kamini's life!"

"I only hope she's learnt never to put blind faith in anything or anyone" Sonia said thoughtfully. Then she glanced at her sari and brightened. "Come on, let's get going! I'd like to get back home, change into something comfortable and sit with some nice romantic book! And Jatin, you can take rest of the day off! Go enjoy Diwali with your cousins from Mumbai and please don't burst crackers!"

The stormy afternoon continued its downpour, silver streaks of rain silhouetted against the street lamps. Kamini and Ravi poured drinks into their glasses, snuggling down on the sofa.

"Cheers!" Kamini laughed, clinking the glass with Ravi. "Happy Diwali to both of us! And to my lucky little one," she patted her stomach.

Her husband raised his glass and blew her a kiss. "That was some drama, sweetheart. The world's best plan! You're a brilliant actress! But you always were, weren't you?"

"Yes, I always won in inter-collegiate competitions. I never thought our acting skills would prove so useful in life."

"Vivek's gone. And even if he were to return, not a soul would trust him, let alone take his word seriously. We're safe!" Ravi laughed, giddy with success.

"For a while, I was really worried that Vivek would squeal to the police and put a stop to our well-established business. Poor fellow had no idea how he walked straight into our trap. Me and my bad patch! At least Sonia was right about *that* prediction—it has turned out to be *his* bad patch!" Kamini pealed into more laughter.

"Fool! He thought he could threaten us and slap drug-trafficking charges on us. He'd no idea what he was up against," laughed Ravi. "At least our next consignment will be a smooth affair."

"Yes, thanks to Vivek and Sonia and my best friend Rita," Kamini replied gaily. "Sonia—her astrology and all her goody-goody advises. So insufferable, so pompous. I felt so angry—I was so tempted to ask her to stop meddling and get lost! But that's not fair, is it? She was the one who really gave momentum and spirit to our plan. She turned out to be our biggest asset. Right, hubby dear?"

"You bet, sweetheart," a voice answered from the door. Both Ravi and Kamini jerked up, startled. Kamini screamed.

"Cut out those histrionics Kamini, I'm afraid you're quite an established flop." Sonia leaned against the door jamb, arms folded, smiling sweetly. Behind her stood Rita, Vivek, Jatin and Inspector Divekar.

"Inspector, please arrest Ravi and Kamini Rane for drug trafficking!" Sonia commanded calmly.

Two Constables hastened forward and snapped cuffs on the wrists of the bewildered couple.

"What's happening here? I'm an ill woman just out of bed..." Kamini began.

"The drama's over, Sis. Learn to exit gracefully," Vivek responded sarcastically.

"You! What're you doing here? Inspector, if you've been listening to this rat—" Ravi shouted.

"You can have your say in the court. Take them away, Constables," Inspector Divekar ordered.

The others watched as the couple struggled but were led away by firm hands.

Inspector Divekar turned to Sonia. "You've got to explain—I'm thoroughly confused."

"So am I," Jatin remarked.

Sonia glanced at Vivek and smiled. "Thanks to Vivek, it's been a most remarkable case."

"If you hadn't believed me, we wouldn't have been able to pull off our plan with such finesse," Vivek reminded her.

"I had your horoscope, remember? I know whom to trust and whom not to trust."

"You two just stop it and start right at the beginning," Rita ordered. "I can't believe what I just saw. Where did this drug-trafficking business pop up from? I thought we were helping Kamini out of her depression."

"I admit that I was taken in by her too, initially. But somehow, this niggling doubt seemed to lodge in my mind—not about either Vivek or Ravi, but about Kamini. I remembered meeting her on M. G. Road. She seemed quick-witted, generous and quite sensible. How could a level-headed person like her believe that she would die—and then begin dying? And she made it a point to inform us, quite categorically, about these conversations that she kept overhearing. She was very cautious not to point a finger at anyone, of course, couching her sentences in martyr-soft expressions. Then I met Vivek and he hinted at some goings-on at Elegant Furnitures. I didn't catch on then, of course. But when he slipped a little packet inside the astrology bag with a brief note, I began to think I needed to see the whole picture in a different light. I sent the packet to the lab and they confirmed that it was cocaine. Even then, I double-checked with the horoscopes and they indeed revealed startling features. Ravi and Kamini's horoscopes were unequivocal indicators of criminal tendencies. These two were cunning, shrewd, manipulative and vindictive. When Vivek innocently warned Ravi to take care of Kamini, they decided to trap Vivek in his own good-will. Weave a web for Vivek, *by Vivek* and then jettison him to be ensnared. They were manipulating him so smoothly that it took him several days to realize that he was being used, am I right?"

"Yes," Vivek agreed. "I began to think it very strange that Ravi would constantly discuss Kamini in the study, especially since I was aware that sound tended to travel to the room in which she was sleeping. It also seemed a great coincidence that Kamini should sink into a shadow at the same time as my predictions, which she was not supposed to be aware of. I found it all fishy. But I would've sounded like a cold, unfeeling, selfish person, had I said that Kamini was pretending to be unwell."

"You're right. No one would've believed you either," Sonia agreed. "And that was their plan—to deliberately malign you, by gradually revealing that you had as good as killed Kamini by your predictions—all for the inheritance."

"But why?" Jatin asked, still looking confused.

"The inheritance was just a façade. The truth was that, they really wanted Vivek out of the way, because he knew too much. He had discovered that they were using Elegant Furnitures to import and export cocaine, and they wanted to entangle him in an attempted murder case, discredit his name, so that nobody would believe him if he decided to expose them."

"They'd no idea that I'd retained a sample of the cocaine packet, which I had by chance discovered in Ravi's car," Vivek added. "It was the same packet, I passed on to you, rather instinctively. Somehow I had this feeling that you were the right person."

"Vivek, could you please how this whole thing started?" Sonia asked.

Vivek nodded. "When I first discovered that some shady business was going on under the cover of Elegant Furnitures, my impulsive reaction was to confront the two of them. I accused them of becoming a link in the chain of smuggling drugs into India. They put on an excellent act, demanding forgiveness, promising that they would immediately end all these activities. They were so genuine in their repentance that, like a gullible fool, I believed them and decided against going to the law. It was then that they began using my predictions to prove that I was deliberately weakening Kamini's will and slowly and surely killing her. By the time I realized what their plan was, I was in it too deep."

"Why didn't you go to the police?" Inspector Divekar asked Vivek.

"I did consider it, but it was my word against theirs."

"But you had the cocaine packet as proof," Rita pointed out.

"Which I could've obtained from any place—or which could be mine, for all they knew. Anyway, I was wondering how to disentangle myself from their clever trap, when Sonia arrived and I realized that this was my chance. With her belief in astrology, she was the right person to deal with my problem. So I slipped the cocaine packet into the astrology bag and wrote a note saying what I knew. I also mentioned Meena Sajane, though I had no idea what her connection to Ravi was. And I'm glad I trusted my instinct. But for Sonia, their plan would've worked!"

"It was a piece of luck that Rita asked me to get involved," Sonia remarked. "Kamini found me a great hindrance at first, but then she decided to use me too, expending all her histrionics on me! She was so engrossed in her role of the dying woman, so busy flaunting her acting skills that she never suspected, for an atom of a moment that I was playing along with her tricks, allowing her to think that I believed in her.

"It was when the lab confirmed that the white powder was indeed cocaine and after I'd confirmed that Meena, Ravi's sister was no way involved with the couple, that I confided in Vivek and we hatched our little plan. Ravi had been hinting to Vivek about the will, hoping that he would talk about it in the study, preferably in Rita's presence. Then it would appear as if Vivek really was after the inheritance. So we decided to help them along with their plan a bit. Vivek was to speak about the inheritance—but in Rita's absence. Then I decided we needed to accuse Vivek openly. Vivek would walk away, as if forever and Ravi and Kamini would relax feeling safe and protected. And then they'd show their true colors which they did immediately. Unfortunately for them, we were all here to witness the end of their nasty drama!"

"Excellent Sonia! You've handled this case brilliantly!" Inspector Divekar looked fondly at her.

"Not me alone. It would've been impossible to capsize Ravi and Kamini's plotting without your assistance, Uncle Jeevan and without Jatin and my never-failing maps of course." Sonia smiled at them.

"I must thank you, officially for helping me clear my name and my family's name from this mess," Vivek spoke quite formally.

"You don't have to thank me. I did my job." Sonia seemed a little embarrassed.

"You did more than that." Rita spoke up. "You saved an innocent man from being accused of a crime he had never committed."

"Not to mention the many lives you've saved by putting a stop to these drug-peddlers," Jatin added.

"Are you guys trying to erase all the horrible things Kamini said about me?" Sonia asked with mock harshness. "You know, *insufferable* and *pompous*—that really hurt you know!"

"It proved that she deserves the sentence she'll be facing

now," Jatin replied. "But boss, all those things you told Vivek, about her brother dying before her..."

"All a product of my highly fertile imagination. I told you, no one can predict death and if they can, they shouldn't. Astrology's not a game—it's serious business."

"Got the point!" Vivek grinned sheepishly.

"Do you think we can have some chai?" Sonia asked on a cheerful note.

"Of course!" Vivek stood up at once. "We all need it."

"And Vivek," she continued, "it's Diwali, could you please hang up a lantern at the entrance?"

Vivek nodded. "At once!"

"Hey, the rain's stopped and the sky's clearing." Rita glanced out of the window. A pink and yellow glow streaked the sky, as a weak sun slowly peeked out of the thinning clouds.

"A real Diwali atmosphere," Sonia sighed.

Understanding flickered in Jatin's eyes. "This is what Diwali, in its true spirit, means to you, isn't it, boss? Good over evil, cleaning of minds..."

Sonia nodded at him, sharing a special moment with her assistant.

He looked at her, awe and respect stamped on his face. "I don't know if I've said this before. But, boss, you're the greatest!"

"Thank you, Jatin," Sonia smiled. "Oh, by the way, do you have Mohnish's number on you?"

"Sure! Do you want me to call him up?"

"Yes, could you call him over to the office in half an hour?"

"Yes, I can, but boss, don't you want to go home and change?" Jatin eyed the sari, which was beginning to look a sorry sight.

"Actually Jatin, that's exactly why I wish to call him! I'd like to meet him before I go home and change!" she remarked naughtily, then laughed, as Jatin's eyes widened in shock and Rita eyed her with a suspicious twinkle.

CHAPTER X

The Stalker

The flickering disco lights illuminated the dancing crowd in iridescent flashes. Music pulsed through the room and into the frenzied dancers—mostly couples, partying groups and youngsters. Mohnish didn't particularly fancy going to discos, finding the whole scene too much below his adult taste. But Sonia had agreed to go out with him, only if he took her to Frenzy—the happening disco club of the town. And he'd decided that he'd rather take her to a childish disco than forego the chance of taking her out at all!

Now as he sipped the orange juice, standing by the DJ counter, he observed Sonia unwind on the dance floor. She was simply amazing! Clad in a turquoise blue Salwar Kameez, she seemed to charge the place with her magnetic presence. Her silky hair bounced and her body swayed and curved gracefully as the music seemed to touch and caress her. Oblivious to her surroundings, she danced unselfconsciously, as if her life depended on it, dedicating herself to the music, to the moment! Her body emanated a sizzling energy, singling her out from the others. She seemed to relish each note, committing herself totally to the melody, as if the beats that rocked the club were being played solely for her. The idlers on the sidelines stared at her with candid curiosity. Unaware of the interest she was attracting, she danced with complete abandon. *Like wild flowers dancing with the wind…* Mohnish thought.

With every passing minute, he could sense within him, the rising tide of liking for Sonia. He had never before witnessed a more attractive blend of intelligence and empathy. She was clear-sighted in her goals and yet sensitive, and her sporadic moments of eccentricity and psychedelic thought patterns were fascinating. And last but not the least, her formidable ally, "astrology," had turned her into a trailblazer on the crime investigation scene! With her unswerving belief and tenacity, she was managing to break through the blinkered opinions and conventional notions of hard-core critics, impressing on them the importance of her pioneering investigative methods. The slings and arrows were gradually and grudgingly turning to bouquets. Sonia truly had set a trend rolling.

The number ended and the strobe lights picked her out, as she made her way toward Mohnish. She looked flushed and exultant.

"That was simply great!" she gushed, in a slightly slurred tone.

"It was," Mohnish agreed.

"But you barely danced!"

"I told you that I have ten left feet and ten right feet when it comes to dancing." He chuckled.

"If you're young at heart, you could still dance with a hundred left feet," she drawled. "Do you know who—or to put it correctly—what drew me to dancing? Music—it just swept through my body and made it move of its own accord. Freeing me from thoughts, stress, and inhibitions and taking me on flights of fantasy, tranquility and meditation. Only dancing can elicit from within me the zest and zing for life."

"So I can see," Mohnish agreed, with a smile.

"But I shall relieve you from this torture now! I'm ready to leave."

"What? So early? I thought you liked to dance all night!"

"I do, but like some people can't hold their drink, I can't hold music! I'm already intoxicated with it—if I dance any more, I'll get tipsy and then I can't be responsible for any of my actions!"

"Hm... that sounds incredibly intriguing," Mohnish remarked, with a mischievous twinkle in his eyes.

"Come one, let's go before the music begins and I'm tempted to stay after all."

Mohnish placed his glass on the counter and they edged their way through the crowd to the entrance. He breathed a sigh of relief, as they stepped out into the cold winter night. A reddish glow tinged the sky, where a crescent moon nestled. A cool breeze rustled along the tree-lined road. Mercury street lamps on the dividers illuminated the road with a yellow sheen. The jazzy name of the disco Frenzy flashed behind them, as they strolled to Mohnish's Indica.

He glanced at Sonia, a little concerned. The cold did not seem to affect her an iota. She genuinely seemed intoxicated, without having touched a drop of alcohol!

"Are you alright?" he asked.

"Never better!" she acknowledged. "Thank you for taking me. I've wanted to visit this place for so long. Have you ever taken any girl to a disco before?"

"Once long ago. I'm too old now."

"An old flame? What was she like?" Sonia asked curiously. "I can imagine you with someone tall and beautiful and chic—" Her face was still flushed and her tone was carefree.

"I'm not going to gossip about any old flames right now!" Mohnish exclaimed. "And I don't want to be enlightened about any of your ex-boyfriends either!"

"Good, because once I get started, I won't know where to stop and I really have to go home!" she declared recklessly.

Mohnish looked so startled that she peeled into laughter.

"Just kidding! Come on lets go home," she flung her arm through his in a friendly manner.

"Fine—I have to run an errand, anyway. But let me warn you, the next time we go out, I choose the place and time," Mohnish remarked severely.

"Oh, is there going to be a next time?" she asked cheekily.

"You can bet on anything there is going to be one!"

Rani turned the ignition key of the car. The engine fired, spluttered, then died. She tried again, but to no avail. Banging her hand on the driving wheel, she uttered a curse. Of all nights! It was pitch dark and the streetlights were out. It was only a short distance to home. She'd leave the car by the road and walk home, she decided.

Locking up the car securely, she stepped out on the deserted street and glanced around cautiously. Not a soul was out on the cold winter night. An icy breeze rustled the dead leaves of the Nilgiri trees lining the street. Rani swung her warm shawl tightly round her, gripped her handbag and began walking. Her high heels clicked on the tar road, echoing into the night. If it only weren't so dark. But the electricity power cut in Pune was a regular activity and it didn't surprise her that the entire lane seemed to be plunged into darkness. The next time she had to stay out late, she must remember to carry a torch.

A figure on a cycle emerged out of the darkness, heading toward her. For a moment, Rani's spirits lifted. The presence of another human being was most welcome. But as the man drew closer, she changed her mind. Small mean eyes flicked curiously over her. A tuneless whistle blew out of his fat lips. The man swung towards her, overtook her, then turned around, passing very close to her. Rani could even smell his repulsive odour! She clutched her handbag tight, ready to swing it straight into his face if he tried any stunts. But he cycled past her, content with whistling an unrecognizable popular Hindi number. Rani sighed in relief.

They were living too far out of town, she thought for the hundredth time. Time and time again, she'd told Sanjay that they should move closer to town. But he'd flatly refused. He liked the peace and solitude of the outskirts of Pune. It was fine for him. He stayed out for days on end, on business and partying, she thought bitterly. It was she who had to find activities to keep herself busy and not dying from boredom. She had to settle this issue once and for all, she decided. It was really dangerous trudging home, late at night.

A twig creaked behind her and Rani wheeled around. But the lonely road stretched long and dark into infinity. She began walking again, her ears on alert. The crackling of dried leaves disturbed the silence and her mouth went dry. She stopped and, slowly, turned around. She searched the shadows. A movement on the right behind a tree caught her eye. Rani didn't wait to find out what it was. She pivoted and broke into a run. Her right ankle twisted and protested with an agonizing twinge, but she ignored the pain. Her pulse raced, as she ran for her life. Her chest felt as if it was squeezed tight. She could see the gate of her house a few paces away. She'd be safe once inside the gate, she thought wildly. All she had to do was reach the house, before he caught up. She was almost at the gate, when a hand touched her shoulder and she screamed, struggling to get away.

"Let go, let go!" she screamed, kicking.

"Rani, Rani, stop it! It's me!"

The familiar voice cut through her fear.

"Mohnish. *Mohnish!* Oh I'm so glad to see you!" And she burst into tears, falling into his arms.

Mohnish quietly supported her, allowing her to vent her clogged tears. Finally, she raised a frightened, wet face.

"What is it? Why were you running?" he asked.

"Someone… one… was stalking me," she sobbed.

Mohnish threw a quick look around them. Without warning, the streetlights flickered. The illuminated road, with its fancy street lamps, looked pretty and quaint, nothing like the cold dark night that had met his gaze moments before.

"I can see absolutely no one," he told her. "Are you sure you didn't imagine it?"

Rani raised soulful, moist eyes to his face. "No. Because it's not the first time that this has happened."

"What! You mean you've been stalked? Do you know by whom?" Mohnish asked, instantly worried.

Rani shook her head. "I... don't know. But I think it's a man...I'm not sure..."

"Have you told Sanjay?"

"No..."

"Why not?"

Rani sighed. "Let's go in."

"Right, we need to talk about this," Mohnish agreed, grimly.

As she made her way to the door, he shut the main gate behind them, but not before he'd thrown another searching scrutiny to the shadows.

Sonia was busy working on the computer as Jatin approached her, a little hesitantly.

"Boss, did you actually go to Frenzy last evening?" he asked.

"Yes." Sonia continued to concentrate on her work at the computer.

"I can't believe it! I've been there a couple of times with my friends—it's just the right place for youngsters. But don't you think you are a little too old to go there on a date with Mohnish? I could've easily suggested more appropriate places—"

Sonia turned from the computer and faced Jatin, incredulity written on her face. "To set the record straight, Jatin, firstly, it was not a date. And secondly, I'm just about four years older than you!"

Her assistant floundered. "That's all? Why did I get the impression that there's a big age gap, or rather a generation gap, between us?"

"Because I'm indisputably far more mature than you and I'm an intelligent boss, that's why! And I'd thank you not to forget that," Sonia remarked crossly.

Jatin looked a little flustered. "Sorry boss, I was just trying to save you some embarrassment."

Sonia threw him such a scalding look that he scrambled away, muttering about fetching some chai for the cold morning. A few minutes later, he returned with two steaming cups and placed one on the table. Mercifully, she seemed to have regained her composure.

"Chai!" he announced.

Sonia absently took the cup and warmed her hands on it. Jatin looked over her shoulder at the site she was surfing.

"Boss, you can't imagine how glad I am to know we can afford the internet facility *and* a cell phone."

"Yes, I know. No point scrimping over necessities. They were must assets for Stellar Investigations. I was just waiting for some extra cash to invest in the facilities," Sonia agreed.

"What are you surfing?"

"I'm looking up all the material available on the Owl."

"The Owl? Oh, the international crook! Are we going to be working on finding him?"

"Wish we could. It would certainly be a feather in our cap. But it's not so easy. He's a mysterious figure, with an aura around him. And he's almost invincible since not a soul knows how he looks, where he lives. For all we know, he could be the neighbor you greet every morning! It's almost an impossibility for us to recognize him or for us to ever cross roads." Sonia shrugged.

"Then what's the point of looking him up on the net?"

"Educating myself on the international scene," she replied. "It pays to be prepared."

"Absolutely," Mohnish endorsed, entering the office with a warm smile. "Good morning, everybody!"

"You seem quite cheerful for a cold winter morning," Sonia observed.

Donned in a sky blue cowl-neck sweater and jeans, he appeared as handsome as ever.

He grinned. "It warms my heart to see the two busiest souls in the world! While Pune city is either huddled around heaters or basking in the sun to avoid the chill of the cold wave, it's a pleasant difference to see you two indoors, using all the newest technology!"

"I'll take that as a compliment, back-handed though it is," Sonia remarked.

"No really; it feels good to see that rain, shine or cold doesn't hamper your determination to work."

"Hey, now that's going too far," Sonia laughed. "What's up? You don't sound normal!" she teased.

"Actually I'm not. I'm terribly worried." His pleasant smile vanished.

"Worried?" the other two echoed.

"Can I have some chai, Jatin?" Mohnish settled down on a chair, realizing too late, that Nidhi was curled up inside.

"Ouch!" he yelled. "Hey, what're you doing in this room?"

"She felt lonely sitting inside," Sonia told him.

"She displays more dog features than cat features. She follows boss everywhere." Jatin chuckled, as he placed the chai pot on the hotplate.

"Good, at least you won't miss not having a dog here!" Mohnish retorted.

"So are you going to tell us what's worrying you?" Sonia turned from the computer to face Mohnish.

He nodded, accepting the mug from Jatin. "It's about this friend of mine. Her name is Rani. Actually her husband Sanjay is a college friend of mine but over the years, Rani has also become a good friend. Last night, a very strange thing happened. Sanjay and Rani live on Mulshi road, rather out of town. We're planning to organize a students' reunion next week and it was my duty to drop some names and addresses at Sanjay's place. I'd spoken to Rani and knew that Sanjay wouldn't be home, but I expected her to be there. After dropping you at your place, when I reached their house, it was locked. Rani wasn't there, so I thought I'd wait for her, since I'd gone that far. And then out of the blue, I saw Rani running for her life toward her house. When I tried to stop her, she began screaming and kicking. Finally, I got her pacified. She told me, that her car had broken down, so she had to walk. But someone began following her and she got a fright of her life. It was then that she told me that lately she's being stalked. Even during broad daylight."

"Has she seen her stalker?" Sonia asked.

"No, but she senses him. And she's terrified. Because she doesn't know who he is, what he wants, and why he's stalking her."

"I see…" Sonia looked thoughtful.

"Do you think you can meet her?" Mohnish asked. "I think it would help her tremendously if another woman talks to her. She's quite a lonely woman actually; she doesn't have many friends."

"What about her husband?"

"She confided in me last night that she and Sanjay are having problems. Which is quite surprising, since theirs was a love marriage."

"Then of course I'll speak to her. Would you like to bring her here or…"

"I've been thinking about that. When I mentioned the police last night, she was most reluctant. Said she had no proof and that she didn't want to make a fool of herself. On the other hand, I don't think she should have a problem talking to you. Maybe I'll just give her a ring and ask her if you and I could drive over?"

"Do that," Sonia agreed.

The afternoon was pleasant as Mohnish, Jatin and Sonia drove along the winding Mulshi road. The sun wove golden trellis patterns on the pavements. The trees overhead formed kaleidoscopic figures, as the leaves danced with the breeze.

"Not a very convenient place to live," Sonia observed, as they left the main road, and drove into a tree-lined road.

"Well, Rani feels the same, but Sanjay always wanted a place amid nature. He refuses to budge from here. In fact, he went out of his way to build this bungalow."

"What exactly does Sanjay do?"

"He's into business. Production of organic fertilizers from different sources. He's got a factory further on down this road, so that he can commute to and fro easily. The rest of the time, he's moving around India, contacting customers and organizing sale deeds. But it's tough for Rani. She's a housewife and she's got a few close friends, but they're all married. And I drop in from time to time, but not very often."

"Sounds like a lonely life to me. Doesn't she have any special interests? Perhaps a hobby?" Sonia queried.

"Not that I know of. One tends to be cut off, so far away from the city. Though she drives herself everywhere and attends the occasional party."

"No children?"

"No, and maybe that's the real problem. If they had a kid or two, she wouldn't feel so alone."

"You're quite concerned about her, aren't you?" Sonia turned to face him.

"To be really honest, yes I am. I like Rani. She's a good girl. Always was. She came from a lower–class family, not very rich. But she was always so dignified. Quiet, but not self-effacing, if you know what I mean."

Sonia studied Mohnish's face. "Correct me if I'm wrong, but do your feelings run deeper than normal here?" she persisted. She found herself waiting anxiously for his answer.

"Well, okay, I admit that I did have a crush on her, when we were studying together in college."

"You mean *she's* the one you took to the disco?"

"Oh, you remember, I thought you were too intoxicated with music to remember a word that passed between us." Mohnish grinned.

"Don't embarrass me!" Sonia blushed, as the memory brought back a pleasant tingling sensation. She had thoroughly enjoyed herself last evening. So much so that she had let down her guard and rambled on unabashedly. It had been a relief to let go, but with Mohnish? Was that wise?

"Tell me about you and Rani," she insisted before her thoughts treaded in another direction. "Rani means a queen, does she still rule your heart?" she teased.

"Of course not! And there's nothing to tell about us. I dropped the idea the moment I realized that Sanjay and she were dating and were serious about each other. And that—before you allow your fertile brain to go any further—was ages ago! She's just a friend now and I don't have any special feeling for her any more."

"Good, because I don't believe in promoting extra-marital affairs," Sonia said primly. She secretly expelled a sigh of relief, then wondered promptly why Mohnish's private life should be any concern of hers!

"That makes two of us." Mohnish laughed. "Here we are."

"What a lovely garden!" Sonia exclaimed, as Mohnish pulled the car along side the bungalow. It was a sprawling cottage, surrounded by a huge garden. Mango and banana trees looped around the house, interspersed with guava and chikkoo trees.

"Yes, this garden is Sanjay's very own personal creation."

They went in through the big iron gate. Steps led up to the white, double front doors, which opened as they approached. A tall, slim woman in her late twenties stood at the entrance.

A pale pink sari was draped over an exquisite figure. Long, jet-black hair fell like a silky curtain to her waist. The word 'wow' triggered in Sonia's brain. Mohnish had forgotten to mention how beautiful his friend was.

"Hello!" the woman greeted them in a musical voice.

A beautiful voice to match the face, Sonia thought.

"Hi Rani! Meet Sonia and Jatin," Mohnish responded cheerfully.

They followed her into a cozy hall, furnished with plush sofas.

"I'm sorry Mohnish went to all this trouble," Rani spoke in a lilting apologetic tone.

"Why should you be sorry?" Sonia asked her.

"Because I didn't wish him to entangle himself in my affairs," Rani replied.

They sank into a sofa and she sat facing them.

"Don't be silly Rani. This is serious. Remember how frightened you were last night?" Mohnish reminded her.

Reluctantly, she nodded and sighed. "I guess you're right. Mohnish is a good friend." She told Sonia. "A very old friend. He's the only one I trust."

Sonia flashed a glance at Mohnish and raised an eyebrow. He flushed.

"Can you tell me exactly what you've been experiencing?" Sonia returned to Rani.

"For the last few weeks, I've had this strangest feeling that I'm being followed. Once in the market and then near the railway station. But they're usually crowded and safe, so I didn't think much of it. But one evening on this same road, I was taking a walk and I felt goose bumps on my arms. I turned around and saw someone duck into the bushes. I called out, but no one responded. It was then that I began getting tense. And then, last night, I was positive that someone is deliberately trying to scare me."

"Interesting…" Sonia remarked, a thoughtful expression on her face. "And where is your husband?"

"He's out of town at the moment."

"So you're all alone in this house when he's not here?"

"I ask the maid to stop overnight. It can get kind of scary—all alone on this road."

"Rani, do you suspect anyone?"

The other woman hesitated, then slowly shook her head.

"You don't know anyone who would like to play a prank on you?" Sonia persisted.

"I don't think anyone would even bother to put themselves to so much trouble for me!" The bitterness in Rani's voice was unmistakable.

Mohnish and Sonia exchanged glances.

Sonia asked, "How long is your husband scheduled to be away?"

"A couple of days."

"And your maid is staying with you until then."

"Yes, she agreed to."

"Is there no place in the city that you can stay for a few days? At least until your husband returns?"

"My in-laws live in the city. But I don't see eye to eye with them." Rani shrugged.

"In that case, all I can say is, be careful. Keep your door shut. And don't stay out late." Sonia admonished. "And Rani, do you and Sanjay have your horoscopes made?"

"Horoscopes?" the other woman flashed Mohnish a surprised look. "Yes, we do."

"Can you give them to me?"

"Sure, but why—" Rani glanced at Mohnish questioningly.

"I'll explain later," he interrupted hastily. "Just do as Sonia says."

"Fine!" Rani shrugged.

Sonia was silent on the drive back home. Mohnish flashed her questioning glances but she didn't seem to notice them. The evening sun brushed the brown-green countryside with gold. A cool breeze skimmed over the clumps of bushes and trees, making them sway gracefully.

"What're you thinking, boss?" Jatin could wait no longer.

"Rani… Didn't you find her too reluctant?"

"She seemed quite resigned to me—like she'd accepted what was happening to her as inevitable," Mohnish remarked.

"Exactly. And she was most reluctant to discuss it. If I were scared to death about someone stalking me, I would immediately go for police protection. I wouldn't dillydally over issues of proof like she told you."

"So what are you getting at?" Jatin asked.

"Nothing as yet. These are mere observations. I just thought that she was too calm and collected for a frightened woman. Mohnish's description of her had set a different picture before my eyes. I'd expected to find a terrified woman, ready to co-operate. Instead, I find a woman who doesn't want any help. Or should I say—a woman who shows that she doesn't need any help!"

"Maybe she knows more about her stalker than she's letting on," Jatin suggested.

"Or there's a possibility that someone or something has frightened her so much that she doesn't wish to speak?" Mohnish added.

"You could be right. Fear plays a major role in loosening tongues or shutting mouths!" Sonia agreed. "You did take the horoscopes from her, didn't you, Jatin?"

"Yes, though she thought it most funny. If she only knew what avenues lie open when you go through them!"

"Why Jatin! Spoken like a true friend!" Sonia smiled.

"I mean it. And I've decided that since I'm your assistant, it's also time to begin learning astrology from you. After all, in your absence I can apply my knowledge and try some deductions."

Sonia hid a smile. "Right," she said and winked at Mohnish.

An instrumental played in the background as Sonia shoved aside the clutter on her table and laid out the two horoscopes. She needed to see Mohnish's' horoscope too, she thought. After all, he was connected with Rani, one way or the other. The woman certainly was beautiful and it wasn't too difficult to fathom why Mohnish had fallen for her once upon a time. But, Sonia couldn't help wondering, did he still carry a torch for her? Unexpectedly, a shard of jealousy dug sharply into her and she was startled. Jealousy? What in heavens was happening to her? She and Mohnish were just friends! Okay, good friends. But that's all. What were a couple of outings for a guy who moved in high-power, ritzy media circles? Just that. A little bit of relaxation with a friend.

And that clinched the matter. She'd much rather work, than subject herself to the meanderings of a fanciful mind!

With determination, she bent closely over Rani and Sanjay's horoscopes. Immediately, the music beats seemed to drum a passage of clarity through her brain, turfing out unnecessary thought and helping her to concentrate on the star constellations. She ran her eye casually over the combinations. They certainly had a very strong attraction for each other but strong possibilities of divorce were also indicated. Or at least, separation of some kind. Too bad. Sonia focused her attention on Rani's horoscope. Zodiac Sign Gemini with Taurus as the ascendant. Good-looking, surely. It also revealed a childhood fraught with hardships. And... Suddenly Sonia paused. Venus, Sun and Mercury in the eighth house with Saturn and Mars aspecting them. What could it mean? What a strange horoscope, one of the rarest of its kind. Yes, it was absolutely clear. This wasn't just a childhood of hardships... it was something more... And if she was right... it could mean that Rani was in terrible danger… Sometimes the demons of the past overtook you and wreaked havoc with the present…

Sonia leaned against her chair, deep lines etched into her forehead. Could Mohnish do the needful for her? After all, Rani trusted him. Hadn't she said so herself? She must handle this with utmost care, she decided. There were many, many delicate factors to consider.

It was a cold night and a mist hung over the mercury-lamp lit incandescent street. The traffic had eased considerably. The myriad neon signs of the advertising hoardings, flashed luminously against tall buildings as Mohnish pulled the shutter of his flower shop. He shivered slightly in his warm woolen cardigan. The boy in-charge had left long ago, so he drew down the shutter, and padlocked it. It was past nine and he was hungry. He didn't fancy going home alone and preparing some snack. Invariably, his thoughts turned to Sonia. A vision of her carefree dancing rose in his mind and he smiled. What a mind-blowing combination she was! What would she be doing now? Chatting with her parents over a hot meal? She was beginning to feature regularly in his thoughts, he realized and shook his head reproachfully.

His mobile rang and Mohnish glanced at the number in surprise. Sanjay's number? Could he be home already?

"Mohnish! Thank God I caught you!"

"Rani! Are you alright?"

"Oh Mohnish, I'm so scared! Can you come over, please? I know it's late but my maid hasn't turned up yet and I've got this awful anonymous note… And it's not signed…"

The break in her voice was enough for Mohnish. "Hang on, I'll be there. And don't open the door to anyone. To anyone, understand?"

Mohnish ran to his car, his brow puckered in worry. Poor Rani! Who was stalking her and now sending her an anonymous letter? What a frightening experience for a lone woman. If only Sanjay was here to take care of her. But he wasn't even aware of the trauma his wife was experiencing. He would have to talk to him. Instill some sense into his head. Ask him to patch things up with Rani, settle their problems and relive the old magic of their marriage. He couldn't keep running to Rani at odd hours. Apart from the fact that it was not his place, it could also set tongues wagging. Which would do no good to a marriage that was already on the fire.

He navigated his way through the night traffic and headed towards the Mulshi road, wondering if he ought to call Sonia and inform her of the latest development. He decided against it. He would wait until he met Rani and read the note himself.

The drive was long and set his teeth on edge. Cold air brushed past his face and he shivered. He wouldn't have come out this far if it hadn't been for Rani. He simply could not refuse to meet her. Not when she was so spooked. Not when she needed him.

The house finally came in sight and he pulled in along the road. Throwing the gate open, he took the steps two at a time. But before he could ring the bell, the door opened. Rani stood there, her beautiful face white and strained.

Mohnish stared at her. Blood had clotted around a deep gash, on her forehead.

"Rani, what happened!" he exclaimed in alarm.

"I..." She could barely utter the words. "He...he...hit me!"

"Who hit you?"

But before she could answer, Rani swayed. Mohnish caught her, as she fell into a swoon.

Shaken to the core, he swiftly lifted her and carried her to a sofa. A groan escaped her lips. Quickly, he fetched a glass of water from a jug nearby.

"Drink this please, Rani, you're going to be fine. I'm right beside you," he entreated.

Her eyes opened slowly and recognition flickered in them. Immediately, she raised herself. "What happened…ouch…my head..!"

"Someone hit you on the head. Just point out the first-aid kit and I'll fix that wound."

Within minutes, he had done a neat job of bandaging the head.

"I'm so sorry, Mohnish," Rani spoke softly. "You've been so wonderful, but I'm such a pain in the neck, aren't I?"

"Nonsense! I think you've been very brave. Any other woman would have been a mass of nerves!" Mohnish replied, warmly. "But tell me exactly what happened. How did this intruder manage to get in?"

"After I phoned you, I realized that the front door was open, so I went to shut it and wham! Something hit me so hard, that I went sprawling!" Rani's voice shook as she relived the shock of the experience.

"You're lucky he didn't come in! Or did he?"

"I've no idea. I was too stunned and in pain to notice anything else."

"I can understand. On the phone you mentioned an anonymous note," he reminded her.

She nodded, extending her hand to the phone and recovering a slip of paper.

Mohnish took it and read the single line of the computer printout. I SHALL GET YOU.

"When did you get this and how did it reach you?" he asked grimly.

"It was pushed under the front door." Rani spoke in a dead voice.

Mohnish began pacing the floor, anger and worry pulling him apart. What a terrible thing to happen to Rani. And where was Sanjay? He was her husband. He was supposed to be here, lending support and love to his wife. Business couldn't be so all-consuming!

"I think it's time to drag Sanjay back home at once," he remarked savagely.

"I did try his mobile. But it says that he's out of reach."

"Damn! We've got to do something. I can't leave you alone in such circumstances. You need to be with people, not be in the middle of nowhere, alone, fighting off madmen!" he exclaimed hotly.

"Mohnish, it's really nice of you to be so concerned. But I'm fine now. And even feeling hungry." She smiled weakly.

"Haven't you had dinner?"

"No, I was about to when I saw the note. What about you? Have you had anything to eat?" she asked, solicitously.

Mohnish grinned, suddenly aware that hunger rumbled inside his stomach. "I'm starving."

"In that case, we're going to eat. No, I'm not listening to any protests. It's the least I can offer you, for calling you all the way here. Please, Mohnish, let me serve you some dinner." And with that, she rose and walked to the kitchen.

The doorbell rang and he froze. He hastened to the door and spied through the peephole.

"Who is it?"

"I'm the *bai*!"

Relief washed over him. He pulled open the door and Rani's maid walked in, flashing him an apologetic smile.

An hour later, well past midnight, Mohnish returned to the city. He halted at the traffic signal near Fountain Hotel, drumming his fingers impatiently on the driving wheel. A figure crossed the road and entered the hotel. It took Mohnish a full minute to recognize the man clad in a thick jacket, with his face almost obscured by the high collar. It was Sanjay!

"Can you describe this person who attacked you?" Sonia asked.

She and Jatin were once again seated in Rani's house. Her face was pale and drawn and Sonia sensed a growing concern for this friendless woman. A little blood had seeped out of the white bandage, revealing the viciousness of the attack.

Rani shook her head. "I'm afraid I can't. I hardly saw him. I was taken so much by surprise that all I saw was a blur of blue sweater—a huge blue sweater."

"Hmm..."

"Not very helpful, am I?" Rani grimaced.

"It would help if you could give some precise descriptions, of course, but don't worry too much about it. Inspector Divekar and his constables are checking your garden for any telltale signs that may give a clue to the identity of the attacker. But try to think, Rani: is there any one—any one at all—who may wish to hurt you?"

A look of concentration replaced the worried expression on Rani's face, as she dug into her memory for the slightest clue. But she shook her head, woebegonely. "I truly can't think of any one who'd wish me harm. You can't imagine how perplexed I am!"

"I don't mean just recent contacts." Sonia tried again. "It could be any person connected to your past. Often something that happened long ago can reflect on you today. Think, Rani, think back. Perhaps there's someone associated with your childhood, who may still want to get back at you? Who would want to get even for some old grudge?"

Rani shook her head in frustration. "I don't know! And my head feels as if it'll burst!" she exclaimed. Her eyes had an almost wild look.

Sonia glanced at her anxiously. The poor woman genuinely appeared worn out.

Inspector Divekar clattered up the steps, his face grim. He held a blue cardigan in his hands.

"We found this in the garden. It was flung over a guava tree."

Rani glanced up at once and her beautiful eyes widened in

recognition. "But that's Sanjay's sweater!"

"Are you sure?" Sonia asked, as she took the garment from the Inspector. It was wool of the softest kind.

"I'm positive! We'd bought it on our trip to Kashmir. It's his favorite sweater."

"I think it's time to track Sanjay down," Sonia said grimly. "Have you any idea where your husband might be? Perhaps at the factory?"

"I've been trying his mobile, but it's inaccessible."

"Don't worry, we'll track him down," Inspector Divekar remarked dryly.

It was when they were on their way back to the office that a question formed in Sonia's mind. She turned to Mohnish, who was beginning to carry a perpetual look of worry on his face.

"How good a friend are you of Rani's?" she asked.

Surprise flickered in his eyes. "As good a friend as any other." He shrugged.

"Then why does she insist on calling you when in need?"

"I don't know. She obviously feels safe around me. Perhaps, she feels that she can depend on me."

"Have you encouraged her to believe so?"

"Of course not! But why these questions? So what if she turned to me for help? It's natural isn't it?"

"Perhaps it is," Sonia commented but her tone was non-committal.

Sanjay drove toward the factory, his face dreamy and soft. Love was a wonderful thing! He loved being in love. But it was also time to set things rolling. He had deceived her for too long. It was only fair that he came out in the open and put all his cards on the table. He owed her that much. After all, they'd shared some great times together. And he wanted to cherish those memories and add new ones to them, not mess things up so much that all that remained were the charred remnants of a relationship. A brown envelope sat on the seat beside him and he patted it appreciatively. Jagdish had done an excellent job in no time. Which was good, because he wanted to get this over with, fast and quick.

He pulled into the drive of his factory, relishing the strong fertilizer smells seeping through the air. He double-parked beside a car. Mohnish?

"Hello!" Sanjay greeted him five minutes later, as he entered his office. "Long time no see!"

"Sure! Meet Sonia Samarth. An investigator," Mohnish introduced.

"An investigator? How interesting!" Sanjay nodded his acknowledgement and then returned to Mohnish with a curious look. "What's brought you here? Surely—"

"First be so kind as to answer my question," Mohnish cut abruptly. "Where have you been and why haven't you been going home?"

Sanjay relaxed into his swivel chair, dropping his mobile casually on the table. "I've been out of town. I just got back last night."

"But you didn't go home last night, did you?" his old friend insisted.

Sanjay dropped his eyes. "How did you know?"

Sonia leaned forward, with a hard glint in her eyes. "Mr. Sanjay Gosavi, I think you ought to know that you're very close to being arrested for attacking your wife."

Sanjay shot backward, as if he'd been punched in the stomach. His nonchalant attitude vanished. "What the hell are you talking about? I haven't seen or been near my wife for the whole of last week!"

"Can you prove that?" Sonia asked.

"Yes, I can! I was with—" Sanjay halted, mid-sentence.

"Who can provide you with an alibi, Sanjay? It's vital that you have one," Mohnish pressed.

"I don't understand this. Please explain. Why am I being accused of attacking Rani?" Frustration marred his handsome face.

Mohnish glanced at Sonia. She nodded.

"I'm assuming that you know nothing of this. You would have though, had you been considerate enough to keep in touch with your wife!" Mohnish couldn't keep the anger from his voice. He went on to explain everything that had happened to Rani in the last few days.

Consternation registered on Sanjay's face. "A stalker! My God, I had absolutely no idea. But why didn't she try to contact me on the mobile?"

"She did but you were out of reach. But that's not the point Sanjay. You should've been with her, should've been her anchor and support at a time like this," Mohnish spoke harshly.

"Unless you're the action man behind it!" Sonia said it coldly.

Sanjay took a deep breath. "Believe me, Miss Samarth, I have nothing to do with all this. I'm truly sorry that I wasn't with Rani when so much was happening, but I had absolutely no inkling."

"Unfortunately, we have only your word for that. And given the circumstances, I'm not sure of its validity. We found your blue sweater in the garden and Rani claims that her attacker was wearing a blue sweater. We have no reason to disbelieve her."

Sanjay thrust a restless hand through his ample hair. "The sweater that we'd bought on a holiday in Kashmir? I've stopped wearing that particular sweater long ago."

"That doesn't matter. You still have to prove that you were not at home, attacking Rani last night." Mohnish added, severely.

Sanjay stared at Mohnish, an imploring look in his eyes. Finally, he shrugged, resignedly. "Okay, I may as well tell you. I was with Anita, the girl I'm going to marry after I divorce Rani!"

A loaded silence ensued.

"Is that where you were last night? At Fountain Hotel with Anita?" Mohnish asked.

"Yes. We've been seeing each other for the last six months. She works as a manager at the hotel. We met at a party and fell in love. I've been wanting to tell Rani for some time now, but of late she's been getting more and more moody. It was impossible to communicate with her, since we always landed up having a roaring argument. Finally, I walked out of the house. I had some work in Goa. I returned to Pune last night, then went straight to Anita at the hotel. She's got a room there. And then, this morning I came here, with the full intention of handing my wife the divorce papers."

"Divorce papers!" Mohnish exclaimed. "Do you know what that will do to Rani? She's already suffering so much!"

"Do you have the papers with you, Mr. Gosavi?"

"They're in my car."

"Could you fetch them, please?"

"Right away." Sanjay rose readily.

The moment he was out of the room, Sonia bent forward and picked up his mobile. To Mohnish's surprise, she flicked it open and speedily ran through the numbers. The mobile was back in its place before Sanjay returned with the papers.

"Here they are." Sanjay handed Sonia a sheaf of official documents.

Sonia flipped through them, then passed them on to Mohnish.

"So you're serious about this relationship with Anita," she remarked. "Is there any particular reason why you don't wish to continue your marriage to Rani?"

"Actually when we got married, we were very much in love. But we like different things, our ideas and concepts varied. In fact, we have nothing in common. Rani turned out to be possessive and moody and she began throwing tantrums.

Actually, there are so many things that didn't work out. And finally it dawned on me that we were simply not suited," Sanjay explained.

"Mr. Gosavi, I want to ask you something very private. Something which you as a husband would know. Do you know if, as a child, Rani had any particularly unpleasant experience? I mean, I know that she came from a poor family, but was she in any way molested...." Sonia paused delicately.

"It's strange that you should ask, because not a soul under the sun is aware of this. Rani told me about it on our honeymoon. Yes, as a child she used to live in a lower middle class *chawl*—you know, a group of buildings with one-room flats—and there was an Uncle living next door. Once, when Rani was about fourteen, she was alone in the flat. And this guy tried to force herself on her. She raised a cry and was rescued in time, but it left her extremely paranoid about men."

A small silence followed as Sonia digested the bit of news. So she'd been on the right track. The scratches on a building were not formed in a day, she thought...The past demons did tend to catch up with the present....

"Do you know where I can find this man?" she asked.

"I know the place, since Rani once pointed out her old house to me. It's in Gokhalenagar. But his name....I think he's called Bhajimama."

"Bhajimama? What an odd name!"

"Apparently he would bring *bhajiyas* for all the children in the building to eat, so they nicknamed him Bhajimama."

"Right. Thank you, Mr. Gosavi, you've really passed a valuable piece of information to us." Sonia stood up.

"Are you going to Rani now?" Mohnish asked Sanjay.

"I can't. I promised Anita that I would break up with Rani and never enter the house as long as she's there!"

"I don't believe this! Rani is facing such grave danger—some one has attacked her, for God's sake! And instead of being with your wife and taking care of her, all you can think of is your lady love! You're despicable, Sanjay, and I'm glad that Rani's rid of you!" Mohnish threw his old friend a scalding look, unable to control his anger any more. He strode out of the office without a backward glance.

"I'm so glad you dropped by," Rani said. "Because I have another of these letters that I wanted to show you."

She held out another computer printout.

Seated on the sofa, Sonia and Mohnish read the bold, printed lines. TONIGHT. I'LL GET YOU!

Sonia glanced at Rani. There was fear in the other woman's eyes. She was looking at Mohnish, an unspoken appeal on her face. A wave of sympathy swamped Sonia. Fear can cripple the best of people and Rani was just a lonesome young woman. Poor Rani. She had a lot to face before she extracted herself from this mess.

"When did you get this?" she asked, gesturing at the printout.

"It was slipped under the door as usual, a while ago," Rani explained, despondently. "I'm getting quite used to it by now."

"Don't!" Mohnish exclaimed. "Don't talk as if this is going to continue all your life."

Rani looked at him resignedly. "I wish that were true," she whispered. "I wish I knew that I would get out of this situation without getting hurt."

"Of course you will!" Mohnish took her hand in his.

Sonia stood up abruptly. "Do you mind if I look around the house?"

"Not at all."

"Can you just tell what is where, so that I don't get lost?"

"The kitchen is on your right and there's a guest room on the left. On the first floor are three rooms. One is Sanjay's and my bedroom, one is my husband's study and the other is a spare room."

"Thanks. I'd just like to check them out, if you don't mind."

"Go ahead."

Sonia made her way upstairs. Her mind was in a whirl. Mohnish and Rani were so comfortable with each other. Rani was truly leaning on him for support and Mohnish was only too eager to lend it. They seemed to really hit it off well, like a mouse clicking on an icon. Now how did that analogy crop into her mind? She looked down at the anonymous note in her hand. A computer printout. Someone who had access to Sanjay's sweater and a computer. A sweater which he claimed he'd stopped wearing long ago. Had Rani given it away to someone and then overlooked the fact?

Sonia opened doors and peeped into rooms, feeling more like an intruder herself. Somehow, she felt uncharacteristically uncomfortable moving through Rani's house. As if she ought not to. But that was surely ridiculous. This was a question of Rani's life. Anything could happen if she did not get to the bottom of this affair and soon. She pushed open another door and surveyed the room. A computer set-up on a table caught her attention. Sonia slipped into the room and shut the door behind her.

"Poor Rani, I'm beginning to get really worried about her," Sonia commented, as they drove toward the city.

"I know, I am too," Mohnish agreed. "And to think that Sanjay is going to drop her like a hot potato just when she needs him!"

"Mohnish, these things happen. Marriages either work, or bust up. It's life," Sonia reminded. "And we don't really know who is to blame in their break-up. There's no point in you getting all worked up over it!"

"I can't help it. She's going through so much. It must be tough, learning that someone is trying to hunt you down for no rhyme or reason."

"Maybe there is a reason," Sonia murmured. "Perhaps this visit to Bhajimama would provide us with the motive."

"You mean you suspect Bhajimama of having something to do with the stalking? But that incident happened years ago!"

"It's an extremely likely answer, although I shall refrain from forming definite opinions right now."

They drove on in silence, both deep in thought. Sonia stole a look in Mohnish's direction. His firm jaw was set in a grim line and his brows were knitted in a reflective frown.

"Don't worry, she'll be fine." Sonia spoke softly, resting a hand on his shoulder.

"I hope so. Of course, the fact that Inspector Divekar's men are on guard outside her house, makes me feel a whole lot better. But I can't help feeling tremendously sorry for her, especially now that I know that Sanjay is going to drop his bombshell."

"I know what you mean. This is Gokhalenagar, right?"

Mohnish turned into a lane with narrow buildings on either side and stopped by a grocery store.

"Excuse me, can you tell me where Bhajimama lives?" he asked the storeowner in Marathi.

The storeowner looked at them in surprise. It was not every day that two sophisticated people asked for a drunkard like Bhajimama! "Oh he must be at home, drunk and asleep." The storeowner laughed, but readily pointed out the well-worn chawl building and floor.

Within minutes, Sonia and Mohnish were in a corridor, knocking on a dilapidated wooden door. The paint was peeling so badly through the rotten wood that there were gaps in the door. It was a while before it was opened by a very unsteady hand.

"Who's it?" a coarse voice demanded.

Mohnish thrust the door open and they stepped inside a room which reeked of country liquor. A single iron bed occupied the cubicle of a room.

A man in his fifties, with white stubble and a lean face, stared back at them.

"Who're you?" he demanded.

"Police!" Mohnish rasped.

The man gaped.

"What have I done, *saheb*?" he asked unsteadily, but fear rose in his eyes.

"Tried to rape a young girl and then tired to blackmail her," Sonia remarked.

"What…what are you talking about? I've done no wrong. I don't know any girl!"

"Of course you do. We're talking about Rani, the girl who lived next door!"

Bhajimama's face blanched. "I don't know what—"

"Stop it! Don't pretend you know nothing about this. You attacked her two nights ago, didn't you?" Mohnish added, stepping forward. There was a dangerous glint in his eyes.

The drunk cowered in fright. "Attack… no… I didn't! I haven't seen Rani in years, *saheb!* I don't even know where she lives now!"

Mohnish held him by the scruff of his torn collar. "Are you sure?"

"Yes *saheb,* I know nothing about this girl. Why should I attack her… please believe me, *saheb!*" Bhajimama begged.

Sonia tapped on Mohnish's arm. "Let him go," she commanded quietly.

Mohnish released the collar and the old man went staggering backwards. "If I ever discover that you went anywhere near Rani, you'll be in lock-up, remember that!" he warned.

"Never, *saheb*. Never, I swear!"

The moment they stepped out into the corridor, Bhajimama slammed the door on their back. Mohnish and Sonia ignored the sound and headed to the van.

"What happened? Why did you ask me to stop?" Mohnish

asked puzzled and still angry.

"Because he was speaking the truth. That man cannot be the stalker. A person who can barely stand on his two feet cannot be a stalker. And he's certainly not in a position to use a computer and send out threatening notes! I doubt if he's ever sober!"

"But I thought…"

"We just came here to confirm my doubt," Sonia explained.

"I don't understand—".

"You will, soon. Can we drive to my office?"

"Fine."

It was dusk by the time they reached F.C.Road. Sonia sat in silence, during the drive, a finger twirling a lock of hair. Mohnish thought it wise not to disturb her. By now, he knew when something was on her mind. The moment they'd parked, she jumped out of the van and ran inside.

"Jatin, don't disturb me for a while. Mohnish, do you mind?"

"Not at all, just go ahead and do what you have to."

He watched in fascination as Jatin switched on the music system and loud beats rocked the office. Sonia settled down at her table, laying out two horoscopes before her. She studied them with the concentration and intensity of a cat observing its prey. She seemed totally unaware that she made a very pretty picture. At length she glanced up, and the excitement in her face caught Mohnish by surprise. Without a word, she moved to the computer and connected to the internet. In a moment, she was surfing and gathering information. Suddenly, Mohnish's mobile rang.

Sonia swung around in her chair toward Mohnish. "Wait! Don't answer it yet!" she exclaimed.

Mohnish paused in his action. "Why?"

"Because that is Rani calling. Now listen carefully…" Sonia's voice was urgent as the mobile continued to ring insistently. "Be very careful what you say to her. She's going to ask you to come to her house. She's scared and panicky. Soothe her down. Tell her you'll be there any minute. That you're on your way. Tell her that you care for her well-being—which is not a lie—that you want her to be safe and sound. Will you remember all this?"

Mohnish nodded, astonishment written all over his face. "Hello?" he spoke into the mobile.

"Mohnish! Thank God, I caught you. I thought, with the phone ringing for so long…"

"Rani, what is it?"

"Mohnish, can you please come here? I'm so frightened!" Rani's voice was quavering.

"Of course I can, but what's the matter? Are you okay?"

"I will be, the moment you arrive. I… I can't stand this any more, this fear, this stalker…"

"Don't worry. I'll be right there!"

"I think he's at the door, Mohnish, I heard him… I don't know what I'll do…"

"Rani, keep the door locked and don't do anything rash!"

"Yes, Mohnish… I feel so alone… He's knocking… someone's at the door…"

"Don't open it! Call out to the constables standing outside, they'll help you! And I'm on my way! Rani, remember I care for you, you're a good friend of mine, so don't worry. I'll be there in a jiffy!" Mohnish switched off the mobile. "She's terrified!"

"I know." Sonia told him. "Jatin give Inspector Divekar a call and ask him to fetch a doctor, we may need him. Come on, let's go!"

"What's happening? How did you know it would be Rani on the line?" Mohnish asked as the three hastened to the van.

"I'll explain everything later. First, we have to reach her house and fast. She's in grave danger!" Sonia's serious tone brooked no further conversation.

They hopped into the van and Mohnish speeded out of town. Jatin made quick calls on the mobile. The cold winter night was dark and foggy but Mohnish maneuvered the vehicle skillfully through the traffic and mist. Silence reigned as the mounting tension of the moment seemed to grip all three of them.

"I hope she's okay!" Mohnish muttered under his breath. "If only she weren't living so far out!"

"I know. Just pray that she's safe," Sonia responded, her voice grim.

Time seemed to crawl and the road was endless, as the van threaded its way through the night. Jatin glanced repeatedly at his watch and then at his boss. She seemed remarkably collected and yet concern clouded her face. The mobile trilled melodiously into the silence, startling them. Mohnish snatched the handset.

"Rani?"

"I think… he's in the house… what do I do?" Her whisper was barely audible.

"Rani, I'm just round the corner, be brave! Did you call out to the constables on guard outside? Call them!" Mohnish spoke urgently into the phone. A sudden crashing met his ears. "Rani! What was that?"

"I don't know, I think he broke a window…"

The phone went dead.

"My God!"

"What's wrong?" Sonia asked, alarmed.

"He's in the house!" Mohnish put his foot on the accelerator.

The van turned into the Nilgiri-lined road and sped toward the Gosavi house. The cottage was enveloped in a veil of mist. The moon shone eerily over it, casting a hazy blue glow over it.

The van screeched to a halt by the pavement. Mohnish rushed out and was about to push the gate open, when Sonia pressed a restraining hand on his arm. "Wait, Mohnish."

She beckoned to the two constables on duty, who had moved ahead, on seeing them.

"Did she call out to you for help?" she asked them.

"No ma'am. Is there a problem?" The constable looked concerned.

Sonia nodded, then turned to the impatient Mohnish. "Listen Mohnish. Only you will go up to the front door and ask Rani to open that door. Don't let her know that all of us are with you. It's important!"

"But why?" Mohnish cried impatiently. "This is no time for games, Sonia!"

"I'm aware of that," Sonia retorted gravely. "Just do as I say if you care for her and want her unharmed."

Mohnish took one look at her flushed face, then nodded. He strode up to the front door and rang the bell. "Rani? It's me, Mohnish!"

Silence.

"Rani?" Mohnish's voice held an urgency. "*Rani!*"

"Is that you, Mohnish?" a faint voice asked from behind the door.

"Yes, I'm here! Open the door!"

"I… I can't ! He's here!"

"What! Open the door!"

A splintering of glass echoed through the night.

"Rani!" Mohnish yelled, panic coursing through his veins.

He banged on the door and suddenly it moved. He pushed it open and ran inside. Rani was standing with her back to the window, her hand holding a shard of glass.

"I've been waiting for you, Mohnish. Oh for so long! Why didn't you come earlier?"

"Drop that glass! You'll cut yourself!"

"Yes, I will, but only then will you come to me and take me in your arms, you'll care for me, you'll love me…" she whispered.

Mohnish froze at her words. *What was she talking about?*

"You will love me, won't you?" she asked, her eyes wild and her hair streaming behind her. She looked like a beautiful apparition in a white sari.

Mohnish stared at her, hesitation outstripping his panic. A voice spoke into his head. Sonia's voice. *Say yes! Say you care for her!*

"Yes… of course, I will. Rani, you're my friend and I… I care for you. Drop that glass and come to me." Mohnish struggled to keep his voice level.

Rani smiled, a chill ghostly smile. "I knew that this was the only way…"

A sudden sound from the broken window made Rani whirl around. In a flash, a figure had swept forward from the door and knocked the glass out of Rani's hand. Another figure rushed ahead and grasped her hands. Someone turned on the lights. Rani twisted around and stared at the faces surrounding her. Sonia, Jatin, Inspector Divekar, the Constables and a man in a white coat. And then Mohnish, standing stunned beside the door. Her sight dimmed and she crumbled in a faint into the arms of the Inspector.

"This is what is often called as the Munchausen Syndrome," Sonia explained.

"Boss, I'm so confused that I still can't make head nor tail of this affair," Jatin admitted, handing out the cups of chai to Mohnish and Inspector Divekar.

Mohnish accepted the cup absently, his expressions still incredulous. He shook his head, as if attempting to clear the muddle it was flooded with.

"I just don't understand. I mean what's the point?" he asked, bewildered.

"What is the Munchausen Syndrome?" Inspector Divekar asked, quite sensibly.

"It's a factitional disorder, wherein a person pretends or imagines being sick or ill so as to gain attention. Sometimes such people create stalkers and even inflict injuries upon themselves to gain sympathy. In this case, Rani was so much in love with Mohnish and wanted his attention, love and care so intensely that she created this whole affair of the stalker and the attacks. Because somewhere, at the back of her mind, she was convinced that he would love her only if she presented this sorry picture of herself. And it was working. Mohnish was getting more and more concerned and involved with her," Sonia explained, flashing him a quick look. "Often this kind of a condition—which is a rare condition—can be a result of neglect in childhood. Or if the person has undergone a childhood trauma. In Rani's case, her experience with Bhajimama left a big scar. Her need for love and care simply could not be satiated by Sanjay, so she turned to Mohnish."

"But if this factitional disorder is such a rare occurrence in people, how did you guess that Rani was suffering from it?" Mohnish demanded.

"First Rani's horoscope. Mars and Uranus in the fifth house with Virgo clearly indicated that something terrible had happened in Rani's childhood. If that was not all, Venus, Sun and Mercury in the eighth house were aspected by Saturn and Mars. It was a very strange combination of planets. Such a person is eccentric and a liar and can do anything to herself—it is usually interpreted as a suicidal tendency, but I read it as a self-traumatizing, self-destructive behavior. Besides, the Lord of Virgo of the fifth house was in the eighth house, which meant that her mental health was also questionable. Initially I was puzzled, uncertain whether to work along my theory. After all, it's not every day that you find people who inflict wounds on themselves, to create sympathy. But I was also unwilling to forego the idea without testing it. I was in a dilemma. I couldn't just get up and voice my suspicions. It had to be illustrated with proof. To say that someone was suffering from the Munchausen's Syndrome and was inflicting wounds on herself could destroy a person for life. I realized that I had to be careful and sensitive with the whole issue!

"I also found it extremely odd that not once did Rani of her own volition come to me. Neither did she go to the police, which, given her claim, would've been the obvious solution.

"Anyway, I decided to check out Sanjay and then Bhajimama. It was when I searched Sanjay's mobile for Rani's number that I realized that there was no sign of the number of calls she claimed she'd been making to him. Also, I made a printout on Rani's computer at her house and discovered that the two notes she'd got were printed on the same printer. Which set me thinking. If Rani deliberately wished to fool us all—for example if she wished to frame Sanjay or was angling for the property—she would certainly use more cunning. She wouldn't use the computer in the house or fling Sanjay's sweater out in the garden. Which meant that she had a shortsighted goal—Mohnish. And that she wasn't really equipped mentally to chalk out an elaborate plan. Which set me right back on my original conclusions, that Rani was dicing with death. It didn't take me long to figure out what really was happening, after that, or to recognize, my Munchausen theory as a fact."

"It's unbelievable, isn't it?" Inspector Divekar sounded amazed. "Such a beautiful and sane woman, deliberately hurting herself…"

"A victim of loneliness and a desperate craving for love."

"But is she going to get well?" Mohnish asked.

"She's at the right place, in the hospital. But whether she shall ever be totally cured of this disorder, is something only the doctors can tell," Sonia replied gravely.

"But why didn't you tell me? A hint or something?" he asked, frowning deeply.

"For the simple reason that you would've found it hard to believe me. You were completely taken in by her and had I said this whole business is made up, you would've thought me crazy. And secondly, it was paramount that you sound absolutely genuine and concerned every time she called you. Even the slightest suspicion on her part of your doubt would have most definitely resulted in something terrible happening to Rani. To reconvince you, she would've gone to any length, even damaging herself permanently. It was a risk I couldn't take. I had to leave you in the dark regarding her real condition."

Mohnish nodded. "And here I was, wondering what kind of games you were playing! When the games were actually being played by Rani! She really had me utterly fooled."

"Sometimes pain is the only secret you want to share, but it's the one thing you cannot pass on. You can neither live nor experience the pain of others, nor can you share it," Sonia reflected.

Mohnish sighed. "Sonia, I'm sorry..."

"Oh please!" Sonia brushed off the apology. "You were going crazy with anxiety, I could see that."

"But I ought to have trusted you."

"You will the next time, when your emotions are not as clouded as they were in this case," she assured, with a faint smile.

"Hey, hold it, Rani is a friend and only a friend. Please don't overtax your brain with romantic notions," Mohnish warned, the dimple on his cheek showing up.

"Well let's hope that she gets well and starts over again," Inspector Divekar finished off his chai and stood up. "Sonia, good work."

"I wish I could say so too. I can't help feeling kind of incomplete about it all. And I'm truly sorry that I can't help Rani, in the real sense," Sonia said wistfully. She did not add that she was grateful to Vedic astrology for providing different dimensions to a study, even the complex workings of the human mind. It was her one solace in the entire case.

"It's now the doctor's job to help her, not yours, *beti*. Anyway, call me if you need anything!" Inspector Divekar strode out of the office.

Sonia gazed after his receding back. Jatin discreetly exited. Mohnish regarded Sonia with a compassionate smile.

"Thank you Sonia," he said quietly, his gaze pinioning her.

"Thank you? For what?" She felt foolish. Her momentary jealousy over the sick Rani seemed like a crime now. How petty and stupid of her to grudge the lonely woman her treasured meetings with Mohnish! She tired to force back the unexpected wave of conflicting emotions

"For finding the right place for her—the hospital. At least she'll get the treatment she deserves and not be thrown into jail for hatching a plot of her own death."

Sonia's throat constricted with sudden unshed tears. "Poor Rani."

Mohnish swiftly moved ahead and held Sonia's hand comfortingly.

CHAPTER XI

The Proposal

Nidhi put out a paw and played with the tiny silver bell hanging on the Christmas tree. As the bell swung, the cat cocked her head and stared at it. Sonia stroked her furry body and laughed.

"Don't you dare contemplate pulling off my decorations," she warned the cat, as she placed a star on top of the tree.

"You really meant it!" Mohnish exclaimed, observing the activity in the inner room of the office.

"Meant what?" Sonia asked over her shoulder.

"That you celebrate Christmas although you are a Hindu. I remember you specifically added that to your long list of likes in our second meeting!" Mohnish settled into a chair.

"Doesn't the tree look beautiful? Nidhi loves it too!" Sonia stepped back and admired her work. "I've asked Jatin to fetch some thermacol for snow."

The three-foot tree in a medium-sized earthen pot was placed beside the window. Laden with silver and gold paper frills and curls, the fir tree looked charming. Gifts, wrapped in glossy paper, nestled at the foot of the tree and some tiny ones even hung from the branches.

"It's amazing! You take this as seriously as a true Christian." Mohnish couldn't hide the surprise he felt. "How did this come about—I mean you celebrating X'mas?"

"Oh, it's a long story. You wouldn't be interested." Sonia turned from the tree and lifted the curious Nidhi from the window, before she was tempted to fiddle with any more bells .

"Try me," he offered.

"Ok!" Sonia seated herself in her chair and Nidhi immediately curled up in the warmth of the lap. "I studied in a convent school, where nuns taught us. I was in the first standard when my teacher explained how Santa Claus comes home on Christmas Eve and brings presents for good children, stuffing it into their stockings. I was curious. I went home and asked my parents if that was true. My mom confirmed it and suggested that I try putting up my stocking on Christmas Eve and that Santa would definitely bring me presents. I was a little anxious because I was not a Christian, but my mom assured me that made no difference to Santa. A good child is a good child! So that Christmas Eve, I brought a tree and decorated it and put up my socks. At the stroke of twelve, I cut a cake for Jesus and prayed. Then I tried to sleep, but I was so excited, that I lay awake for hours hoping to meet Santa. But of course, I didn't. Then on Christmas morning, I saw these gifts around the tree and I was so happy! After that, I celebrated Christmas every year and Santa never failed me. I really and truly believed in him. As I grew up, I went to church on Christmas Eve and prayed—I still do sometimes." Sonia's eyes held a look of reverence.

Mohnish gazed at the serenity that had stolen over her face. "But that wasn't really Santa, was he?" he prompted.

"No, of course not. It was my mom. She was so good at making me believe in Santa. She would hang up strings of sweets with Dad's help and later I could even write letters to Santa. I tried to be especially good the whole year, just so that Santa could visit a Hindu household." An amused smile lit up Sonia's face. "I was in the eighth standard, when a friend declared that Santa did not exist. I challenged her, insisting that he did and that he visited my house every year. She laughed at me and called me a baby. It was then that I realized the truth. I cried and cried! I was heartbroken! It was not just the gifts. It was my total belief in a father figure, in magic, in the rewards of being good… My Mom had to work hard at consoling me. She explained to me how Santa and the concept behind him could live on. We could give each other gifts and continue our very own Christmas. This would be the time of the year when we would think of others, give them what they need in the form of gifts and spread peace and harmony. And till date, we are practicing it! I love the month of December. It heralds the arrival of Christmas, the season of peace and harmony. I truly love it."

"Wow! What a fascinating story." Mohnish expelled a slow sigh.

"I've never told this to anyone," Sonia added, a little abashedly.

"Thank you for sharing it with me." Mohnish held Sonia's gaze.

"This year my parents are out of town, so I thought I'd celebrate the festival in the office the day after. It would also be Stellar Investigations' first Christmas. I have a present for the office too!"

"Boss, does that mean we have to buy presents for you too?" Jatin entered, with a box of thermacol.

"No compulsions," Sonia assured him, although she'd noticed that her assistant had already hung up a colored parcel on the tree. "And anyway it's the thought that counts."

Mohnish's mobile trilled. He took one look at it and rose. "Well, I've got to get going."

"Be here on Christmas morning to open your present," Sonia reminded him lightly.

"I will. Bye."

Sonia glanced out of her bedroom window. The man was still on the same spot. Reading a newspaper and leaning casually against a banyan tree. She frowned. She felt positive now that he was keeping a watch on their bungalow. Attired in casual blue jeans and a gray shirt, he'd been standing under that tree for the last hour. She didn't like it one bit. Who was he and what did he want?

She stepped resolutely out of the house and reversed the van out of the garage. At the gate, however, she paused, deliberately looking in the direction of the tree. The man had vanished. Thank God. Perhaps she'd been wrong after all. The overtime work of her skeptical, detective mind, she realized.

Jatin was already in the office, intently reading a book on astrology. He greeted her with a bright smile.

"Good morning, boss!"

"Good morning," she greeted.

"Firstly, Mohnish was here. He waited for you for quite a while in your office but finally left. I think he's added a gift to your tree! And secondly, your active admirer has sent you another bouquet of fresh, sweet-scented roses!" he reported with a grin. "I've left it on your table."

"Thanks," Sonia nodded.

The bouquet looked inviting and pretty as it sat, waiting to be appreciated. Sonia hung up her handbag and glanced at the card.

There's so much I want to say,
So much I must tell you.
For me, it's a year—a day
When I don't see you!
How long will this go on?
When will the sun shine?
Will I never see dawn?
Will you never be mine...

Sonia stared at the lines of the poem, printed in a beautiful hand. It was signed 'Your Secret Admirer.' She frowned.

She'd received roses before, of course, each with a card signed 'Secret Admirer'. Despite his denials, she'd assumed that the sender was Mohnish. But for the first time, the poetic lines seemed to disturb her. They were poignant words and if meant seriously, could mean trouble. She shook her head, smiling. Now she was taking this a bit too seriously. It was meant to be just a joke and she ought to treat it as one. She picked up the bouquet, so as to move it near the window and as she did so, her eye fell on a white envelope and a leather wallet beside it. She flicked the wallet open and realized at once, that it belonged to Mohnish. He seemed to have forgotten it on the table. She shut it immediately. For a moment, she was tempted to riffle through its contents but tamped the thought. She laughed. Her curiosity was certainly playing dangerous games. Her personal interests were infringing on her investigative ethics. She took up the envelope instead and extracted a single sheet of paper. Surprise speared through her as she read the scrawled, handwritten words. *Midnight. The Owl.*

The Owl? In Mohnish's handwriting? What did it mean? Apparently he'd forgotten both his wallet and the envelope, while waiting for her. Sonia sat down at the table, her mind chugging and churning out a combination of ideas and answers. What did she know about Mohnish? Nothing really, except that he was a journalist; he appeared on and off on television and owned a flower shop, a garage and a photo studio. But he hardly ever seemed to be working. And he hardly ever appeared to write! He materialized at her office when his heart pleased and vanished just as mysteriously. And she still had not forgotten how he had appeared in Panchgani—almost as if he was following her. *Mysterious.* The word lingered in her mind. It was time to take a good long look at Mohnish's horoscope. She'd taken it from him weeks before, with a view to studying it but had never got down to it. Now was as good a time as any.

She opened the drawer and extracted a cream booklet. Moon sign Sagittarius with Scorpio in the ascendant. Sun in the first house in conjunction with Jupiter, Mercury, Neptune and Venus. That's where his good looks came from. Not to mention a highly imaginative brain, courage and dynamism. It also indicated a great deal of success and fame. But on the flip side, Saturn also aspected the first house. It certainly revealed a streak—a cunning streak. Uranus in the eleventh house. Strange array of friends—eccentric, whimsical, dubious? Sonia paused. Mohnish's horoscope had told her more than she'd have ever discovered from him. One thing was for sure. There was more to this man than he let on. Which provided her with the perfect motive to try to strip away the hidden layers of Mohnish Rai.

A little distraught Sonia fondled Nidhi, who was basking in the winter sun. The cat was more interested in pawing the silver bells on the Christmas tree, to see them swing, than pay attention to her mistress. Sonia moved her hand over the little cat's leather, steel studded collar and wondered for the nth time who she belonged to.

Jatin bustled in, looking positively excited.

"Boss, there's a guy outside who looks like a film star! In fact, I'm quite sure he *is* a film star. He's too handsome not to be one!" Jatin gushed.

Sonia was amused. "Doesn't sound like a client to me."

"Client or not, it's worth meeting him," her assistant proclaimed.

"And what happened to all those fancy ideas of postponing appointments for a week, creating an image..." Sonia teased.

"Exceptions to every rule, boss. This is one, mark my words. This guy spells business," Jatin prophesied.

"Fine, send him in."

Sonia automatically adjusted her lemon yellow kameez and *duppatta*. The upsurge of her inherent curiosity amused her.

Knowing how finicky Jatin was, she was all the more keen to meet this definition of film-star looks.

The door swung open and she glanced up. A pair of sea-green eyes set in a lean, fair-complexioned face studied her. A strong chin and thick brown hair, swept backwards to reveal a shapely forehead. Veering on mid-thirties, more than six feet tall with a perfect body that emanated dynamism, a presence. The stranger almost took Sonia's breath away.

"Hello!" his voice was deep and cultured and laced with the faintest accent. "Sonia Samarth?"

"That's me!"

"Varun Thakur." He proffered his hand.

She took it. It was an unimpeachable and flawless handshake. Firm, friendly and warm.

"Please sit down and tell me what I can do for you," she offered.

Varun drew a chair. "Thank you. I must admit that I've come here on an impulse." He had a pearly set of teeth. And a dazzling smile. Jatin couldn't have been more right. He really was a specimen of good looks.

"Impulse?" Sonia raised an eyebrow.

"Let me explain. I'm heading the Orphan Children's Centre in the South Asia region and we were planning a big function, with plenty of competitions for children. I wanted you to be the Chief Guest."

"Chief Guest!" Sonia remarked, astonished. No one had ever invited her to be one before.

"And that's not all. I was wondering if you could design a game for the children—you know the treasure hunt kind?" His smile widened disarmingly.

"A game? I'm afraid, I'm not good at such things," Sonia admitted.

"Oh, don't worry, I'll help you. And there's another thing," he added almost apologetically. "Two of the teenagers from the

Orphan Centre have fallen in love and are so determined to get married. I've kept them on hold, saying that we should at least match their horoscopes. But unfortunately, we don't have their horoscopes. I was wondering if there's any way of finding out if the two are compatible?"

"Yes, there is. But unfortunately, I don't do matchmaking. I use my astrology knowledge exclusively for resolving crime-related issues," Sonia explained.

"Oh, I'm aware of that. I just felt that, since these are orphans you would make an exception…" His green eyes were on her.

Sonia hesitated. It wasn't an odd request. People often came to her asking her to match horoscopes. And she had always refused. But just this time, an unbending of strict rules for a good cause…

"Well, okay, but this truly would be a special case," she warned, her smile softening her words.

"Good! I knew you would see the point." He sounded relieved. "The function is scheduled for the end of this month and I was going to suggest that we meet once before that, if it's convenient for you, of course. At my office preferably, then we can discuss the game and the horoscopes."

Judging by the drift of the conversation, Sonia had the distinct feeling that she was being relieved of major decisions. Very smoothly and quite intelligently. But, amazingly, she didn't mind.

"And lastly…"

She sat back, smiling. "I should've guessed that wasn't the end of it."

"It's not, because now I've come to the most important part of my visit. I need you to find something for me."

Sonia leaned forward, her interest quickened. At last, some real business?

"Some months ago a friend of mine left some valuables for safekeeping, in my custody. He was going abroad and since he lived alone, he did not wish to risk leaving them in his house."

"Why didn't he opt for the bank?"

Varun flashed another smile. "He...didn't want to... for obvious reasons like tax hassles, I guess. Anyway, a while ago, my house was broken into and his valuables were stolen from my safe."

"What else was stolen?"

"Surprisingly, nothing else."

"Were there other... valuables in your safe?"

Varun nodded. "That's what really struck me as odd, but I was too panicky to think about my stuff when his was stolen."

"Did you go to the police?"

"No, of course not. No one was supposed to know that the valuables were with me—how could I call in the police and expose... my friend? It would've been a breach of trust."

Sonia stared contemplatively at Varun. What a strange story. And one with conspicuous and glaring gaps. She had an uncanny feeling that he was intentionally leaving out the details. What had he edited out?

"What do you want me to do?" she asked.

Varun leaned forward and his green eyes held an anticipatory glint. "I've heard that you can solve almost anything with the help of horoscopes. Perhaps you can help me? Help me locate these valuables. I'm quite desperate because my friend is scheduled to return in a couple of days and I'm at a loss how to face him!"

His earnestness was charming. But the gaps in his story continued to trouble her. Should she or shouldn't she?

"What exactly were these valuables?" she asked finally.

Varun hesitated, then looked at her candidly. "Diamonds."

Sonia just about managed not to gasp. Diamonds? "I think you ought to go to the police," she stated flatly.

Varun was silent for a minute. Then he said in a quiet, dignified voice, "Miss Samarth, would you believe me if I said that I have more faith in you than the police? Somehow I have this gut feeling that you're just the right person for me!"

His words startled Sonia, and involuntarily she blushed. Hastily bending to slap away an imaginary mosquito, she steadied herself. What was wrong with her? Here was a client—a handsome one no doubt—and she was reading all the wrong meanings into his sentences! Was it time for her to find a good decent boy and settle down?

"Mr. Thakur, I'm not so sure I wish to take up your case. I honestly feel that the police would be better equipped to handle it, than me. But even so, I wouldn't be able to really assist you with accurate directions to the diamonds. And there's a huge possibility that I wouldn't be able to help you at all!"

"Now you're being modest." He flashed his teeth. "I trust you explicitly to handle this problem and let me assure you that even if you take all week to make up your mind, you shall still remain my first and last choice. I refuse to go to anyone else." His voice was dispassionate and implicit but the sharp edge to his words brooked no further argument.

He stood up abruptly. "I'll give you a call on your mobile, around four. And please remember—you being a Chief Guest has no bearing, whatsoever, on your decision."

It was only after he'd left that Sonia realized that she had neither his contact number nor address. And that no one, except Jatin and Mohnish, had her mobile number. She sat rooted to her seat, nonplussed.

"But boss, a case is a case," Jatin argued.

"I know, but it's my moral duty to check out if he's genuine and that I'm not supporting some shady activity."

"He sounds like an influential guy, working for a good cause. Could prove to be useful in providing us with more clients later," Jatin reasoned.

Sonia had to accept his logic.

A vision of a person playing a card game known as *rammi* rose before her eyes. She was the observer, watching a player with thirteen cards in his hand. From her side, it appeared as if the player was selecting random cards from the lot in hand and replacing them randomly with the other cards in his hand. But from his side, the player was actually arranging the thirteen cards in sequential orders of color and number. Different view points? Different motives?

Now why had that thought crossed her mind? Who was the player? As usual, the workings of her mind stumped her. Her brain spoke a language of its own, dredging out answers from the unfathomable subconscious and unveiling the answers for her to read. But regrettably, they were often unintelligible truths to her, since she was almost always incapable of deciphering the code.

Sonia sighed.

What an unpredictable day, it was. First, the man she thought was spying on her house, then Mohnish's cryptic written words, then the bouquet with its enigmatic message. And now Varun, with his peculiar requests. Were these incidents an overture to something? She grimaced. She ought to take a look at her own horoscope. Why not, she thought. With a laugh, she flicked open her handbag and extracted her horoscope. Their family astrologer had marked out her horoscope in full detail. She enjoyed studying it, from time to time and analyzing the way her life was progressing. Zodiac sign Sagittarius with Pisces on the ascendant. Progress on the career front was indicated. Some fantastic opportunities were about to fall straight into her lap, she realized. Lots of money. Oh good, she needed that. Some more dimensions to her career. Her eyes flew over the twelve houses and suddenly halted. How had she missed this? Jupiter was favorably aspecting her seventh house along with Venus. A time to fall in love? Now in the midst of her burgeoning business? Her eyes narrowed. It was a strange period on the personal front. Uranus was going to provide some startling interactions with the opposite sex—on a personal level as well in her professional life. Sonia shut the booklet. Excitement spiraled through her. She couldn't wait to see what was going to happen!

Varun sat across the table, looking quite handsome in a navy blue shirt and cream trousers. His sea-green eyes reflected the color of the shirt and a gleam of triumph shone in their depths. Sonia ignored his gaze. She was already too finely tuned to his presence to appreciate the color of his eyes and his overwhelming physical appearance.

"Mr. Thakur…"

"Please, I insist on being called Varun," he cut in.

"Okay, Varun. You've made some remarkable requests, all of which are totally at odds with my regular schedule. I don't quite know why, but I've accepted most of them."

"Thank you," he replied gravely.

"I'm also not very certain that you've been completely honest with me, regarding the diamond business. Have you?" She searched his face.

He dropped his eyes. "Unfortunately, I can't be expressly clear about it," he admitted.

"Which is most irregular. Precisely the reason why I need to state that it's mandatory that no shady business be involved in it. If there is, I refuse to help." She stated bluntly.

"Sonia, rest assured. My problem is personal and entirely overboard. I promise to explain it all to you, once the diamonds are found."

"I would appreciate it."

Jatin popped his head in through the door. "Boss, do you need me?"

"No, thanks, Jatin. And we'd like some chai."

Jatin's eyes gleamed. Chai as usual meant business.

"Have you brought your horoscope?" she asked her new client.

Varun slipped a sheet of paper across the table. Sonia ran her eye over it. Zodiac sign Leo with Sagittarius as the ascendant. The star combinations indicated a dynamic, successful, powerful person. Cultured, talented and disciplined. Stubborn, famous and...and—yes—shrewd and cunning. Saturn in the fourth house aspected the Sun in the first house.

Varun's gaze was glued on her, intent and concentrated. And yet, in a flash, a bland expression replaced the intense one and Sonia almost wondered if she'd imagined it.

"Are you very famous?" she asked him. "Your horoscope indicates world fame after the age of thirty." She cast about in her brain hoping his name would ring a bell but no memory seemed to tinkle.

"In my own field and in my own small way," he replied.

"Are you a person who would go to any lengths to achieve his goal, however negative? There are some cruel shades to your character—"

"Why are you asking me these questions?" he interrupted harshly. "You're supposed to help pinpoint the location of those diamonds!"

"You're obviously sensitive to some issues," Sonia answered evenly. "But it's my policy to confirm that the horoscope is correct. Often the birth date and time are wrong. It is always wise to double check with the character of the person or the incidents in his life."

"Well, this *is* my horoscope and I can vouch for its accuracy. Now can we get on with it?"

Sonia bristled. "Look Varun, either we do it my way or we don't do it at all!"

Immediately his stance changed and he smiled woebegonely. "I'm sorry. It's just that I'm so tense. Half the time I'd been worrying whether you'd say yes...and now somehow all this dissection of my horoscope, I'm worried that ..."

"That I might disclose some skeletons in your cupboard?"

"Right." He shrugged.

Sonia opened a file and withdrew a blank sheet of paper. On the sheet, she drew the twelve empty squares of a horoscope on the sheet. Varun observed her with a great deal of interest.

"What are you doing?"

"I'm making a horoscope, which I call 'questionoscope'. It's a horoscope based on your query. Now rephrase your question exactly the way you want to."

"Will I find the diamonds and where will they be?" Varun replied, curiosity stamped all over his face.

She opened the current almanac and filled the squares with the star signs and planets. Pisces as the Moon Sign with Cancer on the ascendant. Sun, Mars and Jupiter in the first house with Cancer. She plotted out all the planetary positions in Revati Nakshatra—Revati star constellation.

"Based on your question I've formed a horoscope which shall give us some, if not all, the answers," she explained.

Jatin arrived with the chai. He placed two cups on the table, threw a glance at the horoscope and immediately switched on the music system. The husky, euphonious notes of a *ghazal* singer flowed in the background. Very quietly, he receded from the room.

Varun watched the entire action with frank interest. Sonia's head was bent, a finger twirling a lock of hair. Totally engrossed in the squares before her and the planetary positions which were speaking to her in a different language. At length she glanced up. There was a puzzled expression on her face.

"I don't understand," she said, finally.

"What is it? Am I going to find the diamonds or not?" Varun asked nervously.

"Yes. Moon is a planet of the mind and Jupiter aspects it favorably. So your desire will be fulfilled. You are going to find the valuables, within twenty-four hours."

"Thank God! Where are they?" Relief washed over Varun's anxious face.

"I can't tell you the exact location, of course. But I can say this much. Since the horoscope was charted in the Rewati star constellation and the Lord of the sixth house is in the first house, we can safely assume that the valuables are to your east. And—this is what I don't understand—the four planets in your first house indicate that the gems are very close to where you are at the moment!"

Varun looked startled. "Are you sure?"

"Positive. It's amazing and as far as I know, quite impossible, but that's what this horoscope indicates. Your diamonds are very close to where you're sitting."

"Do you mean in this office?"

"In the office, maybe in the street to your east, I don't know. You'll have to look."

They stared at each other, incomprehension on their faces.

"That's all I can tell you. But in twenty-four hours, you'll be back here to inform me that you found them," Sonia concluded.

Varun smiled. "I like your confidence. And you've most certainly relieved my mind. Thank you so much." He rose to leave.

Nidhi meowed loudly at that moment, stretching herself lazily, and Varun turned in surprise.

"A cat!" he exclaimed.

"Yes, she lives here." Sonia moved to the cat and fondled her lovingly.

"I love cats," Varun added.

"Oh really? You can touch her, she's quite gentle."

Varun stroked the cat who instantly arched, rubbing herself against him and allowing herself to be petted.

"She's healthy and well-cared for. The collar suits her. Did you put it on her?"

"No, she came with it. Someone evidently cared for her once upon a time. She simply arrived one evening and stayed. I call her Nidhi."

"It's obvious that you love her a lot." Varun turned appreciative eyes on her and Sonia blushed.

"I like animals," she told him.

"Good, I like animals too. By the way, do you think you can drop by my office tomorrow, to discuss the rest of the requests I made?" he asked, with a twinkle in his eyes.

Sonia laughed. "You mean the Chief Guest, game and matchmaking affair!"

"That's right. We can talk over lunch."

Sonia hesitated for a fraction before she accepted.

He scribbled an address on a sheet of paper. "Half past noon?"

"I'll be there," she promised. "And I hope you have some good news for me by then."

"I'm sure of that. And oh, I almost forgot to give you this!" He extracted a cheque from his pocket and handed it to her.

Sonia glanced at the amount and her jaw dropped. "But this is ridiculous… !"

"It's not. It means I value what you did for me, by going against your principles and your gut instinct. The least I can do is pay for what I think it's worth."

"But…"

"Until tomorrow then?" He pressed her hand in a warm clasp and was gone.

Sonia stood beside Nidhi, patting her absently. Her gaze dropped once more to the cheque in hand. What an enigmatic man! Intriguing! There seemed to be two strong forces working at odds in him. Positive and negative. It was these same alternating forces which seemed to simultaneously attract and repel her. He'd effortlessly managed to work around her arguments and cajole her into dealing with his problem. Had she tread on her own toes, in overriding her misgivings and reservations? Only time would tell.

M.G.Road was alive on Christmas Eve. Huge windows displayed elaborate decorations of Christmas trees, flowing with crepe paper, stars and angels. The whole street was lit like daylight and the crowds jostled merrily. With every passing moment, the holiday mood seemed to spike, in the beautiful winter night.

Sonia pushed her way through the people and out of the store. She had just finished buying her last gift and was pleased with herself. For a few minutes, she strolled on the pavement watching the activity around her, a little wistfully. The rippling enjoyment of the crowds was a sure sign that religion was never a bar for Indians to enjoy festivities. In fact, they needed the slightest excuse for merry-making with friends and family. Alone in the midst of hundreds of people, Sonia couldn't help feeling slightly lonely. If only her parents didn't have to attend a business emergency out of town. But she was being silly. They would be back the next afternoon.

A huge Santa arrived in a cart with wooden reindeers and the youngsters screamed. He jangled a large bell and threw sweats from his big red bag. The children jumped around in glee trying to collect the sweets. Sonia thrust through the shouting youngsters and caught a few toffees in her hand. She waved to the smiling Santa, who waved back. It cheered her enormously, the wave of loneliness waning as she threaded her way to the van.

Sonia was just about to climb into the van when her cell phone rang.

"Boss!" Jatin sounded breathless. "I'm afraid someone's broken into our office."

"What!" Sonia could barely hear over the din. "How do you know?"

"I was passing by and saw the light on. At first, I thought you were working on something. But I found the door forced open and the lights on!"

"I'll be there right away," Sonia informed him.

Her mind was racing as the van slowly edged out of the busy M.G. Road. What would anyone want in her office? She carried no case papers, nothing that was so secretive that it merited a theft. Perhaps it was a minor thief looking for petty cash. But she hardly kept more than a few hundred rupees in the office safe. Once out of the street, her vehicle roared into action and she was zipping past the night vehicles at record speed.

Jatin was in the outer office, going through papers and files.

"Anything missing?" she demanded as she strode into the office.

"Absolutely nothing!" Jatin sounded bewildered.

"The cash?"

"All intact."

Sonia sighed. "Thank God. The office seems in pretty good shape. For a minute, I imagined it in its worst possible state." Then she walked into the inner office and stopped short. "Where's Nidhi?"

Jatin shrugged. "May have gone out for a walk."

"Nidhi!" Sonia called out. "Spss….."

"Boss, she'll return," Jatin said patiently.

"I don't think so," Sonia's voice trembled. "Look!"

Some of the balls from the Christmas tree were crushed. And there were drops of blood on the tiled floor.

"My God, what's happened!" Jatin exclaimed.

What exactly had transpired here? Had Nidhi attacked the intruder and had he injured her? Was the poor creature hurt? And most importantly, where was she? Sonia sunk into a chair, her legs giving way. *Let Nidhi be okay, God, let her be safe,* she prayed. Jatin thrust a glass under her nose and she accepted it gratefully, drinking gulpfuls of water.

"I'm sure she's fine, boss. Even if she's a little hurt, she'll nurse herself. She'll be back here in no time to demand her share of the milk."

"I hope to God that you're right. We wait until tomorrow. If she doesn't turn up, I'm going to launch a massive hunt for her."

"Right," he agreed. "Though I still fail to understand what the thief wanted in this office."

"Maybe he thought he'd find some meaty documents. Anyway I'm glad nothing's gone and I hope Nidhi returns during the night and that she's safe and sound."

"She'll be all right, don't you worry."

"We should report the break-in. Do you think you could handle that?"

"I'll file a report at the police station on my way back home. Don't worry, I'll handle everything. Should I lock up now?"

Sonia nodded. She felt confused, worried and disoriented. Suddenly life seemed to be playing tricks with her. And she didn't like the way matters seemed to be slipping out of her hand and out of her control.

Jatin had his bike, so Sonia bid him goodnight and slowly drove homewards. She felt disturbed and uneasy. Where was Nidhi? If only she knew for sure that the cat was safe. The Church loomed on her left and instinctively she braked. A glance at her watch revealed that there was still time before people arrived for the midnight service.

She parked the van by the road and headed into the church. Her steps echoed inside the monument which was lit up with hundreds of candles. Sonia made her way to the first row of the pew and knelt down on the bench. For a moment, she stared up at the illuminated statue of Jesus Christ, a tear gathering in the corner of her eye. Then clasping her hands together, she bent her head. And prayed, with her whole heart and soul for Nidhi—for the wonderful, special cat, who was now an inseparable part of her life. The red-yellow glow of the candles;

the deep tranquilizing silence; the aura of reverence emanating from every nook and cranny of the graceful stone structure; and the magic of Christmas eve filled Sonia with peace. She raised her head and her eyes were shining, her faith restored. Nothing could happen to Nidhi!

With a lighter step and a more relaxed frame of mind, she climbed into her van. The moon shone in a crescent as she drove past the shopping complex which held Mohnish's flower shop. And then she spotted him. Just outside his shop, in deep conversation with another man. Mohnish, at this hour? Astonished, Sonia drove on. She parked the vehicle along the pavement, under a tree. Twisting in her seat, she observed the two men intently. They talked for a while, then went inside the shop. Sonia glanced at her watch. It was a quarter past eleven. Suddenly she recalled Mohnish's envelope. What had it said? Midnight. The Owl. A grim determination swept over her. Something was very wrong here. Mohnish was up to something and she needed to know what it was. The Owl. What did he have to do with the Owl? She remembered the times he'd passed on tidbits on the international crook. He'd been most curious as to her operative methods and had asked more than once if she could hunt down the Owl with the aid of a horoscope. Now, in hindsight, she found his questions too demanding and inquisitive. How was Mohnish connected with the crook? Well, it was time to zero in on the answers.

Half an hour passed. The traffic had thinned and Sonia grew cold. How long could she sit waiting for them to come out? With sudden resolve, she stepped out of the car and locked it up.

Darkness hung over the flower shop, shrouding any hint of activity or life. She approached the door cautiously and peeped through the glass. Silence. Not a mouse stirred inside the shop. But she had distinctly seen the two men go inside, she thought. Was there another exit to the shop? Had Mohnish left by another door?

There was no point hanging around here in the middle of the night. It would be wiser to confront him tomorrow, she decided.

That night, Sonia found it extremely difficult to fall asleep. The recent happenings were rife in her mind. So much had happened in a day that it felt like a week. Sleep seemed to evade her. Finally around dawn, she dozed fitfully, only to be disturbed by the cell phone again. She awoke startled and lifted the phone, straining her eyes to figure out the number.

"Hello?" she asked in a groggy voice.

"Sonia, sorry to wake you up this early, but I need to meet with you," a familiar deep voice said.

"Varun!" She was wide awake at once.

"Glad you recognized me. Look, I'm going jogging up Hanuman Tekdi—the hill behind your office—and then I'm flying to Mumbai to catch a flight to New York. But I must meet with you before I leave. Do you think you can join me on the hill?"

"Now?" Sonia asked incredulously. "It's five-thirty in the morning!"

"I know. You can make it, right?" His tone was almost a command.

"Really Varun, you're an odd man! Imagine asking someone out at this ungodly hour! What's so urgent?"

"I'll explain, at the top of the hill, in half an hour." The phone went dead.

Sonia muttered under her breath. This was the strangest rendezvous she'd ever had. She felt sleepy, groggy and totally unfit for any adventure. But, nevertheless, she slipped out of bed and splashed cold water on her face. She dragged on jeans and a warm white sweater. Serve Varun right if she looked messy and tired.

It was a beautiful dawn. A pink glow was staining the sky and the breeze was nippy and fresh. Sonia breathed in deeply as she parked her van at the foot of the hill and began her ascent. All she needed after a sleepless night was rigorous morning exercise. Thanks to Varun. What in heavens could the guy want at this hour?

It took her twenty minutes to climb up the hill. She passed early walkers, mostly senior citizens, appropriately dressed to keep the morning chill at bay. Youngsters in their tracksuits, jogging for fitness and children along with their grandparents. Pune city sprawled as far as the eye could see all around her, the lights winking like tiny stars in the fast dawning light. She reached the top and stopped for breath. She felt alive and tingling with good health.

A figure in a cream tracksuit approached her. Even if the orange of dawn hadn't revealed those classic features to her, Sonia would have reconized that tall athletic figure and spring of energy in his step anytime.

"Good morning!" she greeted.

"Merry Christmas! Glad you could make it," Varun's face lit up with a charming smile. "Should we sit on that rock there?"

She followed him to a rocky ledge which overlooked the whole of Pune and squatted down beside him. The saffron ball of sun was slowly creeping up along the horizon. Cool breeze riffled through her hair, caressing her perspiring cheeks. She couldn't really believe that she was having this early morning date with Varun, a guy whose existence, until yesterday, was as foreign to her as an unknown planet.

"Okay, I'm all ears,' she prompted.

Varun turned to her and smiled. "Impatient, I can understand. It's rather unusual to call someone to Hanuman Tekdi, right? But since I had to cancel this afternoon's appointment due to some urgent work, and there was no way I could depart without one last meeting, I had no option but to invite you here."

"Does that mean that you've found your diamonds?"

"Yes, I've found them. And exactly in the direction you mentioned. Sonia, perhaps you're not aware, but you have an art, a rare gift. I've known astrologers who make unforgivable predictions, gross mistakes, with not even the remotest chance of the predictions ever coming true. But you're different. Not only do you know your work, but you also possess a strong instinct which you pay heed to. And that is a good combination. Instinct is the genesis of any true feeling. And you *feel* for people, you feel for your profession, you feel for astrology. That is what makes you so unique and so precious. Like an oracle, you encourage the annulment of apathy in mankind. I marvel at your resourcefulness and your steadfast singular devotion to your cause. Frankly, it kind of kindles a similar reciprocating glow in my heart and weaves a spell around me. You can make a difference to the world, Sonia."

"Thank you Varun, I'm flattered. I just don't know what to say." Sonia felt a pale blush stealing over her hot cheeks.

"Sonia, I'm aware that you hardly know me, but I'd still like to say this. Will you marry me?" Green eyes fastened on to Sonia's honey ones.

She stared at him, stunned. Was this some kind of a joke? But the intensity of his blue-green gaze had set her heart racing.

"You're kidding, right?"

"No, I'm not kidding. And I don't want you to answer me immediately. Take your time. I'll call you when I return to Pune next."

"But you don't know me at all! I mean…"

"I feel as if I've known you all my life. And poetry apart, I know more about you than you can imagine."

She studied his profile, as he looked out at the beautiful landscape. A marriage proposal from a guy she met less than twenty-four hours before? Sure, he was the most handsome man she'd ever met. Successful, intelligent and wealthy. But she had to consider the negative and positive forces that she'd glimpsed in his horoscope. She knew nothing about them. Common sense buffeted against emotion, willing her to ignore her increased heartbeats.

He suddenly rose. "I've got to go. Think about it, Sonia, and don't be hasty in refusing my proposal. Take as long as you wish, I'll be waiting for you. And don't ever feel lonely. The sun will shine and we will see dawn..."

Sonia's head shot up sharply. He stood for a moment, smiling enigmatically and then he was gone. She watched him descend with nimble, easy strides and then turn into a cream blur to merge into the hillside. She felt cold and frozen, as if all the warmth in the world had suddenly deserted her. *"The sun will shine and we will see dawn..."* and would his next words have been *"you will be mine?"* Those lines from the bouquet... had he sent those flowers or had he simply repeated the lines he'd read by chance in her office? She ought to have asked him, but she'd been too shocked to hear him utter parts of the poem. She shook her head nonplussed.

Sudden hasty footsteps made her turn around. To her great surprise, she saw Inspector Divekar and Mohnish running towards her.

"Hi! What're you doing here?" she asked, astonished.

"Are you okay? We were worried about you!" Mohnish gasped for breath.

"Why shouldn't I be okay?"

"You're lucky no harm's come to you. And I've been the world's worst fool! Why didn't I suspect, why didn't I keep a watch on you?" Inspector Divekar muttered.

"What are you two talking about?" Sonia cried impatiently. "What's happening?"

"You've been interacting with the world's most dreaded criminal. Remember I told you about him? No one knows his real name or how he looks. He's smart, extremely intelligent, speaks several languages fluently and has successfully given wide berth to the police for the last five years! His specialty is diamonds," Inspector Divekar said.

Sonia gasped. "You mean…"

"Some months ago, the famous royal diamonds were stolen from the Kerkar Palace. There was only one person who could dare attempt that theft. The Owl. The diamonds just seemed to vanish into thin air. The police have been gunning for him for a long time and were on the look-out for the valuables. They were bound to come out some time for sale. But they never did and were never heard of again."

"No, they were stolen from him, too. And now he's found them, thanks to me and my astrology!" Sonia remarked glumly.

"Oh come on, how were you to know that Varun Thakur is The Owl?" Mohnish said. "I spoke to Jatin yesterday and he told me about this handsome hunk of a man who was your new client."

"And I didn't suspect a thing at that time. I didn't think, though I had the tip-off the night before last, that he's…" Inspector Divekar halted abruptly.

"He's what?" Sonia turned to him.

"He's taken a great fancy to you. Reliable sources wised us up that he's been collecting information about you for a while now. So we secretly kept a watch on your house, quite positive that he wouldn't dare show up at your office in broad day-light. But I was wrong. However, one of my men, Suresh, continued to keep watch on your house and this morning, saw you leave. He immediately contacted me and I sensed that something was wrong. So, we followed you here. I met Mohnish at the foot of the hill and he accompanied me. Suresh is, at the moment, keeping an eye on your van. I even called you on the cell phone, to warn you, but there was no reply."

"I left it in the van when I climbed up."

"We saw you sitting on the ledge and we realized at once

that it was Varun Thakur who had called you here!" Mohnish told her.

"Can we go home? I haven't slept all night and this morning… I'm worried about Nidhi." Sonia interrupted, a wave of fatigue swamping her.

"Of course," Mohnish agreed readily, but he threw a quick glance toward the Inspector. His brow puckered with worry. "Are you sure you're feeling okay, Sonia?"

"Just tired. I think I need my bed," Sonia assured him. She didn't tell him that she felt like a duffer. She choked down the sudden tears that threatened to reveal her weakness. Conflicting emotions surged inside her. Anger bubbled like molten lava along with a crazy desire to burst into laughter. She was gradually coming to grips with the fact that she'd just been proposed to by the Owl! Ought she to feel flattered, honored or plain ashamed? If only she could answer that. Sonia Samarth—the level-headed Investigator who prided herself on always being at the helm of affairs, on finding her way out of every dilemma, had been neatly tricked by Varun. He'd chatted her up, dropped a few wonderful–sounding praises and, like a gullible novice, she'd fallen for his trap. So much for cool-headedness.

Out of the blue, the funny side of the situation surfaced and laughter finally rose inside her. She'd thought that Mohnish was involved in some shady activity, that he was perhaps the Owl himself, when all along she was being taken for a lovely long ride by Varun Thakur! She almost laughed at her buffoonery. She ought to feel flattered, she decided with a grin as she drove back home. No girl on the right side of the law had ever been proposed to by a dynamic diamond thief on the wrong side of the law. What remained to be seen was if she would accept his proposal. The diamonds. Suddenly an idea began forming in her head. Where had he found them? And why had her office been broken into? It had to be Varun of course, or one of his men. Since she had so categorically hinted at the office being a prospective hiding place for his diamonds, it was as good as an official invitation to ransack the place. And he'd certainly jumped at the opportunity, without losing precious time. Wherever he had found the diamonds, she'd led him straight to them. She sighed. Regretfully, astrology could also work for criminals. No law stated that it only worked for the good of mankind. She'd have to live with the stigma of having assisted the Owl until she had a chance to settle the score.

Her cell phone rang and she parked the van on the side of the street. The number seemed unfamiliar.

"Hello?"

"Sonia, by now you're well-versed with my true identity, right?" a deep voice asked.

"Varun! Or should I call you the Owl?" Sonia replied sweetly, dispensing with formalities.

"The Owl? Now, why should you call me that?"

"You are the famous international crook—the Owl and don't waste your breath denying the fact!"

"Okay I won't, even if I'm not the Owl. Call me whatever you wish—the Owl or the Lark, it's all the same to me. But be rational, how could I reveal my real intentions to you? Admit it; you would've never helped me find the diamonds. Instead you would've laid a trap to catch me and haul me over to the welcoming arms of the police," he drawled into her ear.

"You're absolutely right. I have no relish for ever associating with a criminal," she stated emphatically.

"I know, you're a good soul. But we have some unfinished business to finish, you and I."

"Where are you calling from?"

He laughed. "I'm half way to New York. But don't worry, I shall never be too far away from you. And I'll keep in touch. Remember what I told you. Don't be hasty in refusing my proposal, even though now you know what I do for a living.

We'll make a formidable combination—with my brain and your gift... Think about it."

"You really have some cheek! How can you even dream of such a match!" Sonia flared up. "You and I have nothing in common."

"Oh yes we do. We resonate with each other perfectly. We're both fiery, stung by commitment, spurred on by our love and feeling for people, hurtling toward a goal..."

"In opposite directions," she chipped in.

"Sure, for the moment. But one never knows when the borders will be crossed," he drawled enigmatically.

"I, for one, don't wish to be enlightened on that, either."

"Not yet, perhaps, but one day, you will. You're like a glow-worm, Sonia. You glow best and shine best in the dark. With me," he said significantly.

Sonia paused, unable to react. *Glow-worm...*

"I really don't care an atom for your opinion of me." She finally found her voice. "What I'd like to know is why you broke into my office? I don't care a damn about your trinkets. I just want to know where Nidhi, my cat, is!"

"Nidhi's a nice name." The smile in his voice was obvious. "But actually her name is Chinky. And she's *my* cat. But since I've been away on and off, I think she preferred to find a permanent home of her own."

"Your cat!" Sonia exclaimed in disbelief. "You're lying!"

"Credit me with some honesty, Sonia. Just because I have a criminal record, it doesn't mean that every word I utter should be treated with the utmost suspicion." Varun sounded hurt. "I love Chinky, but professional obligations made me neglect her. And I was truly amazed when I found her in your office. That's when I became convinced that we're destined to be together. Because my cat had already chosen you!"

"But you didn't come to me looking for your cat, you were searching for the jewels," Sonia pointed out.

"Yes, the diamonds, which were in Chinky's collar. I'd kept them there for safe-keeping. Unfortunately, before I could remove them from their hiding place, she took matters in to her own hand. She didn't like my continued absence, so one day, she just vanished."

"And now you've taken her! Where is she? Is she hurt? There was blood on my office floor." Sonia couldn't keep the anxiety from her voice.

"She's fine, don't worry about her. She just didn't like being woken from her cozy sleep and so she clawed my man quite badly. Well, Sonia, I've got to go. Thank you for everything. I'll be in touch."

"Wait…!" But the line was dead.

Varun Thakur or whatever your name is, you're going to pay for this, Sonia thundered. If anything happened to Nidhi, he'd pay for it. She turned the ignition key and drove off home, her thoughts racing at supersonic speed.

Sonia paced restlessly. She'd taken a brief nap, but hating to sleep in on Christmas day, she had returned to the office.

Jatin and Mohnish observed her silently. Past experience had taught them both that she took her mistakes very seriously. They impinged upon her sense of justice. Anger, along with a sense of helplessness seemed to be on the rampage. She wouldn't be at peace until she had divested herself of her fury and frustration.

"Boss, does that mean you're not going to be a Chief Guest anymore?" Jatin asked innocently.

Sonia stopped pacing and glared at him. Then she burst into laughter. "I'd forgotten that! My chance of being a Chief Guest! The best part is that he seemed like such a gentleman. He was sweet-talking me and I *allowed* him to sweet-talk me."

"Then you're lucky. Because he's known to be a man of few words and more action," Mohnish remarked, drily. "I'm just glad that you came to no harm."

"I don't think I was in any kind of danger, Mohnish. In his own way, he was quite genuine," Sonia admitted.

"Genuine!"

"Yes, he didn't lie out-and-out. He did tell me about the diamonds. And I could read the negative traits in his horoscope."

"Great!"

"And he paid a very fat check for the lead on the diamonds," Jatin reminded them. "Not to forget the fact that he's so handsome."

"I can't believe this. You two are actually defending the Owl!" Mohnish couldn't hide his disgust.

"He wasn't the Owl for us. He was Varun Thakur—attractive, charming and intelligent and as honest as he could be. And you know what's strange, he sounded quite surprised at being called the Owl!" Sonia recalled.

"He would be, of course," Mohnish retaliated. "You don't expect him to come out in the open with his true identity, not after weaving an aura of secrecy around himself for years?"

Sonia frowned in contemplation. "It wasn't that kind of a denial—not the hot, defensive kind. It was more a casual brush—off, almost as if it wasn't important, as if he really had no inkling of what I was talking about."

"There he goes fooling you again," Mohnish commented grimly. "Varun Thakur is the Owl and there's not the least doubt about it!"

"I hope you're right. Anyway, enough about him. I've learnt my lesson. No falling under the spell of charmers. My main concern now is Nidhi and how to find her."

"But he's taken his cat back, he told you so," Jatin said. "We always knew she belonged to someone. She was too well-trained and well-fed to be a stray. But to think that she belonged to the Owl…!"

"Stolen Nidhi and deposited her God knows where, while

he jet-sets to all ends of the world!" Sonia began pacing the floor again. "I'm going to find her."

"In the meanwhile, boss, can we open our gifts? I thought you wanted to celebrate Christmas today," Jatin complained.

"Oh, I'm sorry. Yes, of course, let's go ahead and open our gifts."

"And I took the liberty of ordering us some steaming hot *idli-sambar* for breakfast, from the hotel next door. It should arrive any minute now," Jatin informed her.

They gathered round the fir tree, which seemed to be patiently awaiting attention with its boughs draped in gold and silver. Sonia handed Mohnish and Jatin their gifts.

"You first," she told her assistant.

The childlike excitement on Jatin's face made Sonia smile. He impatiently tore open the gift paper and extracted a box. Then whistled loud and slow.

"A cell phone!" he cried in amazement. "Why, boss, thank you! But… but do I deserve it?"

"Come on, Jatin, this is no time for a belated display of conscience! Of course, you deserve it! You are the best assistant anyone could ever want!" Sonia said, warmly.

"Thank you, boss." Jatin's voice betrayed the deep emotion he felt. "Now let's see Mohnish's gift."

With a sheepish grin, Mohnish unwrapped the slim, gold speckled glossy parcel. The transparent box inside revealed a silver-coated pen. "What a wonderful gift for a journalist to remind him of his duties!" Mohnish laughed, his dimple deepening prominently. "Thank you, I really appreciate the gesture."

"Now boss, open my gifts." Jatin insisted, then waited anxiously for Sonia's reaction as she removed the paper from the package.

"An appointment dairy!" Sonia exclaimed, pleased.

"I want the diary to be full of appointments in the coming

year!" he declared.

"For once, I agree whole-heartedly and indisputably with you! Thanks a lot Jatin." She flashed him a disarming smile.

"Is it finally my turn? My gift is waiting on the tree," Mohnish chipped in.

Sonia grinned and unhooked the small colored package from the top of the tree. She unstuck the cello tape and a plastic, elongated box slipped out of the paper. A beautiful studded bracelet nestled on purple velvet. Jatin whistled in appreciation.

"It's beautiful!" Sonia gasped. "I hope it's not—"

"Real?" Mohnish completed with a grin. "Don't worry, it's not. Do you like it?"

Sonia placed it around her wrist and the stones shone like real diamonds. "I love it, thank you!"

The glint in Mohnish's eyes revealed his pleasure at her acceptance.

"Now I have three more gifts," Sonia announced. "One for the office, one for my astrology and one for Nidhi."

She extracted a big bronze OM—the sacred Hindu syllable—from a cardboard box. "This is for the outer room. We shall hang it up on the wall for good luck. And this new yellow shelf is for my almanacs—for astrology—my magic elixir in problem solving! As for Nidhi's gift, I shall wait for her to return before I open it."

"And here comes the *idli-sambar*. I was starving!" Jatin announced.

The South Indian dish made of steamed cake of rice with a curry of dal, vegetables and spices to go with it, was served in deep dishes by the hotel boy. It was while they were tucking into the hot breakfast when the doorbell sounded.

"I'll get it." Jatin slipped outside.

Mohnish glanced at Sonia, his gaze contemplative. "You liked him—the Owl—didn't you?"

"He was different." she admitted.

Mohnish pursed his lips. "And you'd like to meet him again?"

"Of course! But at the moment, I'm not thinking of him. Neither am I thinking about what you were doing at midnight in your flower shop."

"Flower shop!" Mohnish appeared startled. "You mean last night? Oh, that was a friend—"

"We'll talk about that later," Sonia interposed. "My top priority is to find Nidhi."

"Boss, there's another Christmas present for you!" Jatin's excited voice called out.

Sonia and Mohnish hastened out. Jatin stood with the office door open. A small cage stood on the threshold. Protesting meows emerged from the cage.

"Nidhi!" Sonia cried out in joy.

She ran to the cage and swung open its door. Immediately, the cat rushed out and bounced up to the table, purring and complaining. Jatin placed milk before her and within seconds, the bowl was empty and sparkling.

"Thank God, she's back home." Sonia sighed happily, dropping a kiss on the cat's silky forehead. Her collar was missing. She turned to Jatin. "Who brought her here?"

"That's a mystery, since there wasn't a soul around. But I found this note tucked into the handle of the cage."

Sonia accepted the piece of paper, her heart suddenly beating faster. She recognized the handwriting at once. Scrawled in a beautiful hand was a message.

Merry Christmas! The best gift I can think for you is my love—Chinky. You may call her Nidhi. I know that you will take good care of her. Until the sun shines and we see dawn together... Your Secret Admirer.

Sonia stared at the words and couldn't help experiencing a ripple of pleasure. She handed the note to Mohnish who read it with a frown.

"That solves another mystery. Now for Nidhi's present,

which I specially went and bought this morning!"

Jatin sped to the inner room and produced a colorful parcel. Sonia unwrapped it. A blue velvet, beaded, fancy collar! She wound it lovingly round the neck of her cat, who meowed in appreciation. Then she lifted Nidhi and hugged her.

"Yes," Sonia murmured, "we shall meet again Varun Thakur. Whether you are the Owl or not, we shall most certainly meet again."

She looked at Mohnish and Jatin and flashed a scintillating smile.

Dr.(Ms.) Manjiri Prabhu
1145/2, F.C.Road,
Shivajinagar,
Pune – 411016. INDIA
Tel: +91 20 25654902/ 25813034
Email: contact@manjiriprabhu.com

JAICO PUBLISHING HOUSE

Elevate Your Life. Transform Your World.

ESTABLISHED IN 1946, Jaico Publishing House is home to world-transforming authors such as Sri Sri Paramahansa Yogananda, Osho, The Dalai Lama, Sri Sri Ravi Shankar, Robin Sharma, Deepak Chopra, Jack Canfield, Eknath Easwaran, Devdutt Pattanaik, Khushwant Singh, John Maxwell, Brian Tracy and Stephen Hawking.

Our late founder Mr. Jaman Shah first established Jaico as a book distribution company. Sensing that independence was around the corner, he aptly named his company Jaico ('Jai' means victory in Hindi). In order to service the significant demand for affordable books in a developing nation, Mr. Shah initiated Jaico's own publications. Jaico was India's first publisher of paperback books in the English language.

While self-help, religion and philosophy, mind/body/spirit, and business titles form the cornerstone of our non-fiction list, we publish an exciting range of travel, current affairs, biography, and popular science books as well. Our renewed focus on popular fiction is evident in our new titles by a host of fresh young talent from India and abroad. Jaico's recently established Translations Division translates selected English content into nine regional languages.

Jaico's Higher Education Division (HED) is recognized for its student-friendly textbooks in Business Management and Engineering which are in use countrywide.

In addition to being a publisher and distributor of its own titles, Jaico is a major national distributor of books of leading international and Indian publishers. With its headquarters in Mumbai, Jaico has branches and sales offices in Ahmedabad, Bangalore, Bhopal, Bhubaneswar, Chennai, Delhi, Hyderabad, Kolkata and Lucknow.

SINCE 1946